THE CRITICS RAVE ABOUT *ROMANTIC TIMES* AWARD WINNER COLLEEN SHANNON!

THE STEADFAST HEART

"Colleen Shannon mixes a heady tale of suspense and passion in *The Steadfast Heart,* teaching us that love and trust are intricately entwined."

—*Romantic Times*

PRINCE OF KISSES

Colleen Shannon "has brilliantly mastered the technique of creating a fairy tale fantasy that delights and enchants readers seeking adult entertainment while remembering a cherished childhood story."

—*Romantic Times*

THE GENTLE BEAST

"Colleen Shannon has infused her tale with all the drama, excitement and mystery of the classic [fairy tale] and added her own magical style, turning this into a wondrous tale to be cherished."

—*Romantic Times*

"Colleen Shannon's *The Gentle Beast* will make you believe in happily ever after. It's a wonderful story told with all the magic of a fairy tale."

—Jill Barnett, bestselling author of *Carried Away*

COME TO LIFE ...

Tears streaming down her face, Honor knelt before her marble David and wrapped her arms about his strong calves. Even losing her job was not as wrenching as this parting. She'd known it would come eventually, but not like this. In disgrace, the statue possibly even slated for destruction if it was proved to be a cheap trick. Instinctively, she recognized in this graceful creature the soul mate she'd always pined for and the champion she sorely needed. But she was to lose him, too, as she'd lost all she'd ever loved.

Honor's tears flowed faster, dripping down her nose and cheeks, staining those perfect feet and ankles. "Oh God, why can't you be real?" Honor's grief echoed down the years past and the years yet to come.

A hush fell on the room, blocking out the distant, quiet chaos of a bustling museum. There was only the girl, the statue, and the magic of dreams . . . .

A faint tinkling sound came, so slight that it didn't impinge on Honor's consciousness. A slight wisp of air stirred above Honor's head, as if an angel hovered over her with protective, beating wings. A mist of white flakes fluttered down.

Then a hand fell gently on the back of her head, stroking down over the hair she'd loosened in her grief. "You saved me with your tears, sweet little virgin. But why do you cry?"

Her dazed mind resisted, but slowly, she tilted her head back and looked up.

David still towered above her.

But he was no longer white, and he was no longer cold.

"Come now, bellissima," the voice spoke again. "Tell me who has hurt you and I will kill him."

HEAVEN'S ROGUE

COLLEEN SHANNON

LOVE SPELL BOOKS ◆ NEW YORK CITY

LOVE SPELL®

September 1999

Published by

Dorchester Publishing Co., Inc.
276 Fifth Avenue
New York, NY 10001

ISBN 0-505-52340-X

The name "Love Spell" and its logo are trademarks of Dorchester Publishing Co., Inc.

Printed in the United States of America.

HEAVEN'S
ROGUE

Part One

"They wove bright fables in the days of old,
When reason borrowed fancy's painted wings;
When truth's clear river flowed o'er sands of
  gold,
And told in song its high and mystic things!
And such the sweet and solemn tale of her
The pilgrim-heart, to whom a dream was given,
That led her through the world—love's
  worshipper—
To seek on earth for him whose home was
  heaven!"

        —T. K. Harvey

Chapter One

He was man as God intended, strong legs braced to stride to a destiny of his own making. His head was turned to look into the distance for his foe, smooth brow frowning with fierce resolve. His arms were poetry in motion, sharply defined with strength, but not bulging. Broad, muscular shoulders tapered to a slim, flat waist. His firm hips cradled a manhood as perfect as the rest of him. Even in the shadows, he glowed with health and virility.

Honoria Psyche Fitzhugh walked around her subject admiringly. The buttocks were pleasing to her eye, not too round, not too flat. Circling again, Honoria touched his chest tentatively. She looked over her shoulder, but she was alone. She finally gave in to temptation, running her hand over the smooth angles down to the hips, to the . . . The marble warmed, seeming to stir at her touch.

Gasping, Honoria jerked her hand away. She stumbled back, fumbling for the switch on the side of the stage. Brilliant light reflected off the pure whiteness of the life-size statue. Her hand over her pounding heart, Honor stared, reassuring herself. The statue was so full of life and movement, it was hardly any wonder she'd imagined living flesh instead of cool stone. After the months of preparation and research, an hour before the unveiling, her nerves were on edge. That was all.

Snapping the light off, Honor resolutely turned away from the most perfect specimen of manhood she'd ever beheld and went into the wings to review her notes again. Still, she couldn't quell a wistful sigh. How often over the months of living with him had she wished he'd step down off his pedestal and walk straight into her arms.

As he'd already walked into her heart. . . .

"Dr. Fitzhugh!" The breathless voice preceded her assistant. "We just got confirmation of an acceptance from the Metropolis director of Renaissance art." Ernie Escavido climbed the side steps, his long, lithe legs and swiveling hips no less striking because he was gay. Still, there was something in the graceful way he moved, the tilt of his head, the way he talked, that served as a red flag to heterosexual males.

Poor Ernie was still in mourning over his broken romance with a handsome young construction laborer who'd left him for a musician. Honor was glad to see him so excited for a change.

"So congrats, Doc!" Ernie hugged her. "Even the art world's heavyweights are giving us the benefit of the doubt. Maybe all those months of on-line chat helped, after all."

Without the usual cool reserve she showed most males, Honor hugged him back. Ernie was her best friend. Maybe even, sometimes, her only friend. He didn't threaten her, flirt with her or push too hard. He was the kindest, most intuitive male she'd ever met, and she valued him both as a coworker and as a decent human being.

She replied, "Aided by those months of press releases and preparation for tonight. I couldn't have done it without you, Ernie. I'll just freshen up and then I'll be ready." Honor kissed his cheek and went back to get her purse. As she passed the statue, out of the corner of her eye, she caught movement.

Her skin crawling, she froze. Slowly she turned her head.

The large almond-shaped eyes still scowled into the distance. The perfect male form still stood firmly on its pedestal. She took a deep breath, wishing, for the first time in her life, for a Valium. Books had always been both companion and sedative enough, but she'd never started seeing things before, either. She swung her purse over her shoulder, turning to leave, but another slight movement stopped her again. She whipped her head to the side, blinking in disbelief, but the eyes were still, graven images in stone.

She stalked off, wiping her clammy forehead

with her hand. For a minute there, she'd imagined . . . a wink? A statue winking at her? *Nonsense.*

Get a grip, Honor. This is your chance to be taken seriously, maybe even get offered your first curatorship. After tonight, she was taking a couple of weeks off. She obviously needed some rest.

Thirty minutes later, she put her lipstick back in her purse and blotted her lips on a tissue. She cocked her head and appraised herself critically. She hated the artificiality of makeup, and in fact usually wore only lipstick and light mascara. But this time she'd added a bit of blush so she wouldn't be washed out in the lights. Her long blond hair was neatly smoothed back in a tortoiseshell barrette that matched her tortoiseshell glasses. She brushed down her conservative navy suit and straightened her little lace collar so that it flared over her lapels, but her small breasts didn't offer much flare. Sighing, she stared at her depressing image, her father's comments ringing in her ears as if spoken yesterday instead of years before.

Skinny as a rail, that girl is. Keeps her silly head filled with fancy stories instead of doin' proper women's work. Pity her ma, God rest her soul, filled her head with all them tales o' heroes and flyin' horses and such. I never shoulda agreed to give her them strange names, neither. Her father, a tall, bluff man with the red hair of his Irish roots, shook his head mournfully at his listening friend. *Poor little gal won't never amount to nothin', and won't no boy never want to marry a pale little slip like her.*

Honor swallowed hard, remembering how, at

the tender age of fourteen, after overhearing her father's opinion of his only daughter, she'd slipped away to her crying tree. There, yet again, she'd grieved over her lovely, kind mother, who'd died in childbirth the year before while bearing her husband a fourth strong son. They were too poor to afford more than a midwife. . . . Honor blinked back to the present, gripping the counter-top hard.

This was no time for her old inferiority complex to rear its ugly head. Her pa, who'd died of coal miner's black lung disease before she graduated from Wellesley, had been right about one thing, though.

" 'T won't never turn a sparrow into a bluebird, Honnie. Don't do no good wishin' for what can't be."

Slipping her purse strap over her shoulder, Honor stuck her tongue out at her image. All her life, she'd wished to be a fiery redhead to match the secret passions she kept so fiercely in check. Instead, she was a washed-out blond with an almost washed-up career but for a lucky fall on a hiking trip. The few men who tried to melt her icy veneer usually retreated quickly with frostbite. Which suited her just fine. She'd come too far, on too hard a road, to be waylaid now.

Lifting her chin, she said softly, with the measured, careful diction that was perhaps her best legacy from Wellesley, "I hope you're watching, Pa. Because you're wrong about me. I will amount to somethin.' Some*thing*." Pivoting, she swept through the bathroom doors and returned to the auditorium of the Portland Arts and Sciences Museum. Portland was as far as she could get from the coal mines of West Virginia and still stay in the United States, but sometimes she felt as though she carried coal dust with her, depositing residue and losing a bit more of herself with every step she took.

To her relief, Ernie was already circulating through the room, greeting the early arrivals. Plastering the Wellesley smile to her face, she held out her hand to the Life and Arts editor of the Portland paper. "Delighted you could come. Won't you have some punch and cookies?" She saw him to the refreshment table and then held out her hand to one of the museum's most important benefactors.

As the hour she'd awaited all her life drew near, the auditorium became so packed that new arrivals had to stand. Some of the art world's most powerful people sat in the front row in the reserved seating. Finally, five minutes before show time, Honor shook her last hand, smiled her last smile, and made the long, lonely walk to the stage. She studied her notes for a few more moments. Then, to remind herself why she was doing this, she touched the statue again. She closed her eyes. Inexplicably, she felt the strength and resolve the image personified flow through her. Slipping through the curtain precisely at the hour of eight, she took center stage.

The coughs, chair squeakings and whispers died as she walked gracefully to the podium. She stacked her notes neatly before her. She wouldn't have to refer to them because she knew her talk— and her subject—literally by heart.

After testing the mike, she smiled out at the multitude of faces turned toward her. Some of these people were tourists who'd happened into town during this much-discussed debut; others were art students; others were Portland benefactors. But the people she had to impress were the ones sitting in the first two rows. If she couldn't convince the art historians, the curators and the media that her find was genuine, then she might as well give up her aspirations, give in to her brothers' pleas and retreat back to the hills of West Virginia to raise a passel of rowdy kids, like so many of her ancestors before her.

The thought stiffened her spine and steadied her knocking knees. "Thank you all for coming. I am Dr. Honoria Fitzhugh, assistant curator of the Portland Arts and Sciences Museum, and I welcome you to our lovely city. I know many of you had to fly long hours to get here, and I'm grateful for your time and am certain you will be glad you came." She glanced down at her notes more for style than substance and began, feeling as if she'd just rowed across the Rubicon.

"As many of you know, one of Michelangelo's most famous works of art is his *David,* now displayed at the Galleria dell'Accademia in Florence." The Italian words tripped easily off her tongue, for two years in Italy as a foreign exchange student had helped her college Italian become fluent.

Emboldened, she continued more easily. "As historians are also aware, Michelangelo did extensive preparations for many of his statues, sometimes spending years sketching and working

17

Colleen Shannon

with smaller models before beginning the final sculpture. He was still in his twenties when he completed *David*, arguably one of the greatest sculptures of all time." She nodded at Ernie, who lowered a huge screen from the ceiling and turned on the overhead projector. A picture of *David* was beamed onto the screen.

The few in the audience unfamiliar with the statue gaped. Even in the flat portrayal, the beauty of the sculpted muscles and tilted head was striking. Sling relaxed over his shoulder, a naked David looked as if he saw Goliath in the distance and was about to stalk off the screen in pursuit.

Using a laser pointer, Honor indicated the height of the statue. "The accepted original work of art is over fourteen feet tall. It is still considered the high achievement of Michelangelo's early style, and was carved out of a block of Carrara marble intended for a work by Agostino di Duccio that was begun and abandoned. Historians have speculated that the *operai*, or cathedral committee members, gave the young Michelangelo the important commission both because of his impressive *Pietà*, and because his proposal used this single historic 'badly blocked out' piece of marble rather than adding new marble to the old, as his competitor Jacopo Sansovino planned. His progress was closely monitored, and he worked on the piece between 1501 and 1504, when it was placed in the Piazza Della Signoria in front of the Florentine town hall. Furthermore, of all of Michelangelo's works, *David* is most symbolic of the new Florentine Republic, in its emblematic defeat of the tyranny of the Medicis. It also solidified Michelangelo's growing prominence as an artist and garnered him an additional thirty-three commissions, though he is *known*"— she emphasized the word slightly— "to have completed only four of these, possibly because of his inability to delegate work." A few of the art historians in the front row nodded their agreement.

So far, so good. Now that she'd proved she knew her subject, Honor paused for a deep breath, then used the pointer again to outline the face. "Observe the fierce determination of the expression, which art historians term *terribilita*. This fiery personality is characteristic of many of Michelangelo's figures, and, most say, of himself. And yet if you look closely, you can see a certain wistful longing behind the determination, for what or whom, well, I guess those answers lie in the heart of each of us."

The silence in the auditorium was so complete now that Honor's soft voice seemed to reverberate with the power of her convictions. "In short, it is my belief as both an art historian and an art lover, that Michelangelo imparted so much of himself into *David* that I am skeptical that any other artist could ever copy this vitality. Furthermore, Michelangelo was so meticulous, and no doubt keenly aware of what was at stake in this commission, that it is highly possible, in my opinion, that he could well have sculpted a smaller model prior to the final work."

She turned off the pointer. Ernie lifted the screen and went to the side of the stage, where he stood waiting to tug open the curtain. Honor took an even deeper breath. "When I returned to Italy a year ago to see friends from my foreign exchange days, I had no intention of working, or of starting such a controversy. But the moment I saw this work of art, I knew it came from the hand of Michelangelo himself. No one else could achieve his astounding mastery of the male nude." She nodded at Ernie.

The red curtains swept aside. Soft lighting fell on the statue from all sides. People in the back craned their necks to see, and those closer gasped. Whispers flitted about the room.

Honor waited to let the admiration die down before she spoke again. "As you can see, this version is slightly less than half the size of the original. But look closely at the curvature of the muscles, the vitality of the figure. Even the chisel marks in the base have the same strokes. And observe carefully the facial features, wearing the same fierce expression. No artist save one, no matter how talented, could so exactly capture the wonderful life of the original. I believe that, although my months of attempting to get written authentication in Italy have yielded little, this statue was actually the original *David*, a smaller model Michelangelo completed before attempting the accepted work."

Honor paused to let the murmurs and excited speculation quiet before she concluded. "However, as Michelangelo signed only one of his works, verification will be, to put it mildly, challenging. I have several more months to complete my research before the statue must be returned to Michelangelo's birthplace of Caprese, where I found it. Any help I can get with the documentation from my learned colleagues would be greatly appreciated." Honor bowed slightly toward the front rows. "I now open the podium for questions."

A hand immediately went up in the first row. Bruno Trotterman, the director, of the Metropolis Museum in New York was a portly little man Honor recognized from pictures. "How did you get the statue out of the country? How do we even know it originated in Italy, and this isn't some publicity stunt you've devised for your museum? It wouldn't be the first time—"

Honor interrupted. "I have permission from the Italian government to keep him here for six months while I try to authenticate him. I did find him, after all."

"Him? Come now, Doctor, your bias is showing. The statue is surely an *it*, not some divine creation," chided Trotterman. With his upstanding coif, his bow tie and scruffy suit, he himself looked more like an *it* than a *him*, Honor decided. No wonder he was jealous of her statue's male beauty.

He seemed to read the hostility in her cool gray eyes, for he blustered, "And a pretty sterile copy at that, I'll warrant, when the truth is known. Why have you not published your authentication tests in any of the accepted journals?"

"Patination and other molecular tests are still being performed. I expect the results any day. I am confident that, though this stone seems to come from a different stratum, it will prove to come from the same quarry in Italy Michelangelo used for the larger statue. When our tests are final, I assure you I will publish my findings."

"I won't hold my breath," he said in a huff, sitting down again.

Honor gripped the podium, quelling her urge to retort. "Any other questions?"

The reporter she'd spoken to earlier stood. "Could you tell us exactly how you found the statue?"

"I was on a hiking tour of the Italian countryside when I fell into an abandoned cistern. It was dry, and so primitive that it looked like it had been dug in Roman times. Along with the statue, we found several weapons, since dated as being from the mid-Renaissance period, and a trunk of clothes from the same era. Plus various other toiletry items such as an old mirror, a silver brush set and so on."

The reporter frowned. "Are you telling me someone lived in this cistern?"

"I have no idea. I do know, and tests since conducted verify, that it looks as though this cache remained hidden from the time of its burial until I found it last year." Honor glanced at the director again. "I would ask, since the weapons and clothing were authenticated, and the cache appeared undisturbed, how the statue itself could be a modern copy? From a purely scientific viewpoint, the facts support my conclusion. As to how it got there and who put it there, I haven't an explanation. I doubt we shall ever know, but I will go to my grave believing that this statue is a creation of Michelangelo himself."

More hands went up, but Honor was exhausted.

"Thank you again for your interest. And please return for our upcoming exhibit of Egyptian art, with priceless antiquities from the old, new and Coptic kingdoms of Egyptian history." Honor walked offstage.

A few days later, Honor returned to the site of her recent victory, the taste of ashes in her mouth. In her limp hand, she carried the Portland paper. She still couldn't believe the headline that had glared at her that morning as she drank her coffee.

ASSISTANT CURATOR FAKES STATUE! The story went on to report that an anonymous source had pre-released the test results on the tiny stone flakes they'd taken from the base of the statue. The flakes not only didn't originate from the Carrara marble quarry in Tuscany; they weren't even stone! They were some type of new hybrid material, obviously man-made, as yet unidentified.

Honor's coffee cup had slipped from her hand to shatter on the floor. When she'd collected her scattered wits, she'd reached out to call the lab director at Cal Tech, who'd promised to release the test results to her before anyone else. The phone rang. The curator ordered her to come in immediately.

Hours later, here she stood, darkness lapping at the windows outside, threatening to consume her. She'd been summarily fired, and with the scandal, she was informed, she'd never work in the museum or art worlds again.

Honor cleared her throat, but the ache only grew worse. Since this morning, she'd stifled tears. The past year, so exciting, so revelatory, was all she'd take away of the only life she'd ever wanted. Since her earliest memory, when her mother used to read mythology to her and show her tattered art books of the world's treasures, Honor had wanted to spend her life among beautiful things.

Honor gnawed the back of her hand to stifle a sob, but once tapped, her grief was a bottomless well. Most of her things were boxed and in her battered Toyota. She'd failed to renew the lease on her apartment, intending to move to a larger one with the raise she'd counted on, so she had nothing to keep her in Portland. Where she'd go, or what she'd do, she had no idea, but she had to get far away.

Tomorrow, the curator had informed her, a representative of the Italian government would arrive to take the statue back to Italy and conduct his own tests. Both the museum's board and the Italian government would decide, depending upon their conclusions, whether to prosecute Honor for fraud. She'd promised to give them a forwarding address. When she had one.

Her vision blurring, she staggered up the stage steps behind the curtain and snapped on the light. There he stood, as perfect and unattainable as all he represented. Strength. Honor. Nobility. Masculine passion. Someone to believe in. Someone to finally believe in her. Someone who needed her.

How could I have been so wrong?

Tears streaming down her face, Honor knelt before her *David* and wrapped her arms about his strong calves. Even losing her job was not as wrenching as this parting. She'd known it would come eventually, but not like this. In disgrace, the statue possibly even slated for destruction if it was proved to be a cheap trick. Instinctively, she recognized in this graceful creature the soul mate she'd always pined for and the champion she sorely needed. But she was to lose him, too, as she'd lost all she'd ever loved.

Honor's tears flowed faster, dripping down her nose and cheeks, staining those perfect feet and ankles. "Oh, God, why can't you be real?" Honor's grief echoed down the years past and the years yet to come.

A hush fell on the room, blocking out the distant, quiet chaos of a bustling museum. There was only the girl, the statue, and the magic of dreams. . . .

A faint tinkling sound came, so soft that it didn't impinge on Honor's consciousness. A slight wisp of air stirred above Honor's head, as if an angel hovered over her with protective, beating wings. A mist of white flakes fluttered down.

Then a hand fell gently on the back of her head, stroking down over the hair she'd loosened in her grief. "You save me with your tears, sweet little virgin. But why do you cry?"

A breath caught in Honor's throat. For a moment she thought Ernie must have heard the news and come to comfort her. But Ernie didn't speak with that deep-timbred Italian accent. And why did the legs she still clutched suddenly feel warm?

"Come now, *bellissima*." The voice spoke again. "Tell me who has hurt you and I will kill him."

Her dazed mind resisted, but slowly, she tilted her head back and looked up.

David still towered above her.

But he was no longer white, and he was no longer cold.

His skin was a glorious golden color, dusted lightly with gilded hair. His thick, wavy hair absorbed every available ray of light, casting it back in luminous shades of brown, red and gold. And his eyes, those fearless, almond-shaped eyes, were the most piercing blue she'd ever seen. They glowed down at her, as if lit from within by an unearthly light she could neither explain nor capture.

Weak, Honor closed her eyes, swaying on her knees. Dear God, she was losing her mind. Somehow she found the strength to scramble back.

Wishing don't make it so, Honoria Psyche. Her father's voice echoed in her ears.

Biting her lip until she drew blood just to assure herself of her own place in reality, Honor opened her eyes. The statue was gone!

Her pounding heart almost choked her. She staggered to her feet, one hand at her throat, turning her head wildly. Then she saw him, pulling a janitor's dirty coveralls over his lean hips. Living, breathing proof of her own madness. She stared stupidly at the bare pedestal, then back at·him.

He'd paused in closing the overalls, staring at the David poster on the wall behind the stage as if he barely recognized himself. He blinked owlishly at the name Michelangelo scattered on innumerable museum flyers on the floor and walls.

Even as part of her comprehended his own shock, joy fluttered inside her like the beating wings she'd felt earlier.

Could he be real?

Could she keep him?

Could miracles really happen?

But fear stilled the fragile wings, shoving them, dewy and weak, back in the hard shell of reality. No, she wasn't crazy. Somehow, there had to be a rational explanation for this. Dumbfounded, she stared at him.

He seemed to have some trouble with the zipper, twisting the end oddly as if he'd never seen one before, but finally he got it pulled up and walked toward her again. The confident grace of his strides, the arrogant tilt of his head as he eyed her as if he owned her, rather than the reverse, mocked her sane discourse with herself.

Sent by heaven or hell, creation of the Divine Angel or not, somehow her find was made flesh. Honor backed away as he advanced, sensing that if he touched her, this dream of her heart and mind would own her, as she'd longed to own him. "S-stop!"

He paused, but his determined expression did not change. "Something has frightened you. Surely it is not me you fear? I am but your humble servant, saved by your tears and your prayer. This is the dawn of a new millennium, is it not?"

She couldn't believe it; she just couldn't believe she was talking to a statue. Honor kept backing away, getting dangerously close to the stage steps. "Y-yes. How did you know?"

He whistled softly to himself. "Five hundred years. Odd. I remember Caprese as if it were yesterday. . . ."

Honor kept shaking her head in denial, but he'd begun to approach her again. "Careful, *signorina*. You come too close to—" He grabbed, but he was two steps too far away.

Honor's foot slipped, missing the top step. She fell backward, hitting her head. The horror-wonder went black. Her last conscious thought flitted through an overloaded brain before it short-circuited.

Wishing does make it so, sometimes.

Reality was a hard taskmaster. Honor had spent her life trying to twist it, shape it, escape it, if only briefly, in beautiful stories and objects. Thus, when she came to, her head aching, she groaned, keeping her eyes closed so she wouldn't have to face the ugly truth again.

It had been such a lovely dream. A perfect end to a nightmare. When she opened her eyes, all would be as it had been before. Odd, though, that her bed felt so uncommonly hard and lumpy. Still, it was warm. Wake up, she told herself. When she did, she'd be waiting to hear the test results, hard at work on the Net and phone, trying to track down support for her theory.

Experimentally, she slitted open one eye. An ugly, blank brick wall loomed across from her. She opened her other eye. A flashing light in her peripheral vision drew her attention. She turned her head, noticing a garish neon restaurant sign down what appeared to be an alley—an alley that looked vaguely familiar.

Honor frowned, disoriented even more when, as she turned her head, her cheek scraped against something strangely soft yet slightly prickly. Pain stabbed behind her eyelids as she tilted her head back to look up. Her eyes widened as she stared up at the unforgettable face above her. Reality and imagination warred within her cloudy mind, leaving her to face a victory that both ennobled and immobilized her.

For the first time in her life, dreams *were* truth.

She wasn't mad.

But lord, was she in trouble.

Delectable trouble.

The lumpy bed was his lap. The prickles were his chest hair, where the zipper to his coveralls had slipped as he held her. And the warm firmness, well, he was warm, firm and delicious all over. She wanted to melt into him and forget everything but the miracle of his presence.

Adriatic blue eyes as warm as the sun that gave him life glowed down at her. Long lashes brushed his bronzed, beautiful cheekbones as he bent his head to kiss her temple. "Ah, do not look at me so, *bellissima*. It has been so long. . . . " His tousled head lowered. Those perfectly sculpted male lips loomed over hers.

She stared at them, trying to remember the last time she'd been kissed. Never, by such a beautiful man . . . statue. Did it really matter who, or what, he was? All that mattered was that he made her feel things she'd never felt, and dream things she'd never dreamed. Honor's head swam as she lifted her head slightly to span that tiny gap, to know flesh and blood humanity.

She felt the warmth of his breath. His heartbeat quickened, inciting a staccato cadence from her own. Their lips almost brushed together, but a siren blasted them apart. Honor jerked back, groaning as her head felt as if it would topple off her shoulders. Red and white lights flashed past the alley as two police cars zipped up the street.

"The watchmen seek us, *sì?* They think you stole me."

"*Sì,*" Honor whispered.

Still holding her, he rose, the ease of his movements under her weight astonishing her. He began to lope up the alley in the opposite direction, carrying her.

"Honor! Over here!"

Honor had closed her eyes again as the jostling made her head feel like it would split in two, but she opened them in time to see Ernie waiting at the safe end of the alley. He held the door to his old Pinto open for them. His mellow brown eyes widened when her rescuer came under the lights. He appraised Honor's find appreciatively. "Who's this, Honnie?"

"Uh, I'll explain later," she said as she was deposited gently in the backseat. "Get us out of here, Ernie." She pulled her Renaissance man inside beside her, reaching past him to close the door as he fumbled with it. When the old car lurched into motion, puttering up the street, he braced himself, teeth showing in an alarmed grimace.

It must feel like they were flying to him, Honor realized, but it felt like they were crawling to her. She saw Ernie staring at his odd passenger and said quickly, to distract him, "Are they looking for me, Ernie?"

"Yeah. What'd you do with the statue? How on earth did you get it out of there so quickly?"

"Well, it's sort of a long story. I didn't actually steal it, but . . . " Honor looked at said statue, sitting wide-eyed beside her staring out the window at Portland zipping past. "I'm afraid no one would believe the truth."

"I'd believe you, Honnie," Ernie said, turning the corner toward her apartment.

Dear, sweet Ernie. Honor longed to tell him the truth, but one art historian in the loony bin was enough. Ernie slowed as they saw a police car parked in front of her apartment.

Honor clutched the back of his seat. "Drive on past."

Ernie gunned the old motor.

"No, slow, normal."

Ernie slowed. "Where to?"

Honor cradled her aching head in her hands and tried to think. How on earth would she clear her name without admitting the truth? She contemplated and discarded several notions. There were replicas of David available for purchase, but she'd never seen one of the right size, and even if she could find one, a mere copy would never have the life and vitality of the genuine article sitting next to her.

"I need time to regroup, Ernie. Just drop us at some nondescript motel for the night."

"Us? Who is this guy? I don't remember a janitor who looks like him."

"I'll be fine, Ernie. I . . . need his help for the moment. Don't worry about me. He's harmless."

The subject of their conversation turned his head to look at her. Now that he seemed reassured that this strange contraption carrying him was reasonably safe, he turned the full force of his formidable persona back on her. His gaze wandered over her, touching the vulnerable hollow of her throat, her lips, her small bosom, her slim hips. Adriatic blue darkened to midnight as his eyes consumed her long, slim legs and dainty ankles. Her legs were her best feature, Honor had always thought. Apparently he agreed. Equally apparent, his curiosity was as boundless about her as hers was about him.

Torn between flattery and alarm, Honor jerked her skirt down over her knees. She was in enough trouble without committing a sin with a five-hundred-year-old man. The car entered a rough parking lot on the outskirts of town and stopped in front of a dingy lobby, drawing her away from the fascination with the unknown that had always been her *raison d'être*.

Or, as her new friend would say, *la dolce vita*. Except, based on his expression, he had something else in mind for their mutual "sweet life."

"This nondescript enough, Honnie?" Ernie drew the car to a stop.

Honor barely glanced at the lobby with its one dim light, glad that she'd stuck her wallet in her jacket pocket when she'd left her apartment that morning, too busy to finish changing her purse.

"It's fine, Ernie. I'll call you in the morning when I figure out what to do." Honor moved carefully as she opened the door and got out.

The Renaissance man watched analytically. Imitating her movements, he tentatively pulled the lever on his own side and got out.

They stared at one another over the fading roof of Ernie's car as Honor said, "And Ernie? Please don't tell anyone about my . . . friend. OK?"

"OK. Just . . . be safe. If I can get into your apartment later, I'll bring you the rest of your things. I still have my key." Ernie glared a warning out the window at Honor's companion and slowly drove away.

Honor's knees sagged, but when the Renaissance man reached out to help her, she drew a deep breath, straightened and waved him away. "Stay here. I'll be right back." And she marched into the lobby.

A couple of hours later, Honor came out of the bathroom, toweling her long hair. The Renaissance man sat where she'd left him, glued to the TV. The long, hot soak had relaxed her, and she was beginning to come alive to possibility instead of calamity. How many women were so fortunate as to bring to life their own perfect mate?

She stifled a smile as she saw how quickly he'd learned to use the remote. He wasn't so different from the modern male, after all. Next he'd ask for a beer.

Honor thought about sitting next to him on the bed, but instead chose the straight-backed chair at the tiny table. She draped the towel over her shoulders. She'd buttoned her blouse over her slip and felt awkward, but she'd dirtied her suit in the alley and couldn't bear to put it back on over her clean skin. With luck, Ernie would be able to rescue her bags before he came back in the morning. "So what do you think of this dawn of a new millennium?"

The Renaissance man glanced at her once, eyes widening with interest, then looked quickly away when she shifted uneasily. "How much things stay the same, even as they change."

"What do you mean?"

He switched to an all-news channel, where the newscaster was doing in-depth coverage on the latest atrocities in Kosovo. "Religious intolerance follows humankind like the waste we leave behind."

How strange it felt sitting there justifying her place and time to a man far past his. Still, it wouldn't do for him to think them savages. Glancing at the channel list beside her, Honor told him to switch to a science channel.

He did so, watching with amazement as the latest space shuttle launch filled the airwaves with a clamor of noise and glory. "*Magnifico!* So Leonardo was right. Manned flight is possible."

It was Honor's turn for amazement. The casual way he said the name . . . could he possibly mean . . . ? She cleared her throat. "Leonardo . . . da Vinci?"

He didn't seem to share her reverence for the name. "Hmmm. Interesting man, if rather arrogant. But this . . . vessel. Where does it go?"

"Space. To conduct experiments."

Digesting this, he stared at the screen for a moment. "Do you think mankind's destiny lies in the stars?"

"Yes, I do. Someday far in the future."

"How I envy the man who will see that future."

"Same here. It would be great to come back in, say, the year three thousand and see how far we've gone."

Nodding his head, he still didn't look at her, but the tentative bond already formed between them strengthened. How odd that, being from two different times and two different places, they thought so much alike.

Restlessly, he stood and jiggled the knobs on the TV.

Honor briefly covered her ears with her hands as the volume screamed and then quieted. The picture went bright, then dim, and the vertical and horizontal jiggled crazily. Carefully, when he'd satisfied himself as to the working of each knob, he adjusted everything to the way it had been.

He knelt and peered at the bottom of the TV, behind it, tapping the screen as if to verify that people didn't actually live there behind a glass wall. Finally he stood and went back to the bed, satisfied. "A moving picture, somehow sent by that long rope sticking into the wall."

Honor was impressed with his deductive reasoning. "Close. Inside the TV is something called a picture tube. It has three receptors that each broadcast colors when their electrons are excited by a beam that is sent through the air, making tiny dots called pixels on the screen light up and create a picture. The box is powered by the same electrical current that makes the lights work."

He nodded at the complicated explanation, not in the least intimidated. In the same conversational tone, as if they still discussed science, he said carefully, "Might I request that you clothe yourself a bit more? It has been a very long time since I was alone with a beautiful woman."

Honor's blush started at her hairline and spread to her toes. She glanced down, unable to stop herself, and the bulge straining the coarse fabric between his legs proved his attraction to her. Proved beyond all doubt that he really was a man now, with a man's urges. She was torn between pleasure at the thrill of hearing every woman's favorite compliment and embarrassment that he apparently found her attire seductive.

Wait until he went to his first beach!

Honor draped the towel over her legs. "I . . . don't have anything else but my dirty suit. We'll both have to go shopping in the morning."

Still refusing to look at her, he stood, ripped the bedspread off the bed and offered it to her with a slight bow. Honor wrapped it around herself like a chrysalis. The symbolism of the moment made her vaguely realize that this day that had begun so badly was perhaps the beginning of a profound change in her. Would she emerge from this blanket and this trial a lovely creature of flight or the same old earthbound worm?

She was so involved in thought that it took her a moment to realize he'd turned off the TV to pace the room. Now it was her turn to stare in admiration. Goose bumps skittered up her spine. A delicious sense of danger enveloped her as warmly as the spread. This man was from an earlier time, when women kept to their place. A time when a man took what he wanted. And, miracle of miracles, this man obviously wanted her. Her heart tapped nervously at her ribs, but liquid warmth flowed through her, seeming concentrated between her legs. The by-product of physical desire surprised her, for she'd never felt it for a living male before.

Only in her dreams . . . The same dream that strode about her motel room like a tiger unleashed.

Would it be so bad to lose her viginity? For once not count the cost, or worry about what would follow? She was already half in love with this stranger, and even their brief time together made her sense that he was more than a pretty face and form. Honor longed to toss off the spread and her inhibitions with equal ease, to give this dream of her heart and mind a tiny measure of the wonder he'd already given her. She was struggling between her usual twin demons of impulse and practicality when he turned on her.

"Why have you not asked me how I came to be imprisoned in stone?"

The liquid warmth dried up, leaving her feeling as old and wrinkled as before. Still, she owed him the truth. "Perhaps because I'm afraid to find out."

He froze at the soft response, staring at her in surprise. With one leg cocked to the side, an arm up as he rubbed the back of his neck, scowling slightly, he reminded her all too vividly of his former incarnation. All she had to do was squint a little, and the bright light in the room pouring down on him made him white as marble, pure, untouched . . . and lost to her forever. A chill chased away the last of the delicious warmth. This was only their first day together, and already she feared losing him. But the same magic that had brought him to life could take him back. Every minute with her amazing creation was a gift she wanted to cherish.

He seemed disarmed by her honesty. "Honor," he said solemnly, "you are well named. What is the rest of your name?"

"Honoria Psyche Fitzhugh."

A melancholy smile stretched his full lips. "It sounds like a name from my time. Whatever comes of this day, *bellissima*, this I know: we were fated to meet."

And love.

He didn't say the words, but they hovered in the air between them like the charged particles she'd earlier explained so analytically.

"Do you know the story of Psyche?"

Honor blushed and hung her head.

"Venus herself was jealous of her, but Psyche knew not, and cared not, for her own beauty. She was a dreamer, curious about all things. Even when she wed, she could not distinguish between ugliness or beauty in her lover. And when she found out that her monstrous lover was none other than Cupid himself, she still had to go through many self-imposed trials to win him. Her curiosity almost killed her on numerous occasions. Only Cupid's plea to the gods to unite them saved her and brought them together."

The allegory didn't escape her, but she wasn't beautiful, and he wasn't Cupid. Was he trying to warn her that he was a monster in a beautiful shell and she couldn't see the difference?

Sighing, he swooped down on her. She shrank back, wondering if her newest wish was about to come true, but he only picked her up and plopped her on the bed beside him. Her cocoon settled about her, safe and secure.

But his voice began to weave a spell as he began simply, "I have a story to tell you, *bellissima*. You are mine. I want to keep you. But my task will be difficult. What month is it?"

"Ah, September first, 1999."

"Four months. I have four months to complete my quest."

"And what happens if you don't?"

"I return again to stone, where I will forever remain imprisoned."

Chapter Two

Despite the warm covering, Honor's bone deep chill grew worse. Her knees and lips quivered as she whispered, "But why?"

"That I do not fully understand myself, except that the angel told me I must pay penance for my sins."

"Angel?" Honor pulled the cover closer about her shoulders. She believed in God, not the grim and righteous judge of her childhood, but a loving deity who forgave and offered guidance. But as for all the talk about guardian angels, well, she'd dismissed that as New Age mysticism. "Perhaps you'd better start from the beginning. What is your name?"

"Dominico Paolo Constantine Castiglione. But

you"—he inclined his head graciously—"may call me Dom."

Dom. She tested the name silently on her tongue. It suited him, somehow.

"I am . . . was the son of a nobleman and a peasant. I was a bastard, but my father adored my mother so much that he defied his family and wed her. They cast him out. He was an artist who assisted Leonardo at times. I myself was an apprentice under Michelangelo. We both grew up in Florence, attending the same school. I was a few years older, but we were good friends."

Both names were virtually synonymous with gods to her. The casual way he uttered them still made her blink. "Ah, sculpting or painting?"

"Sculpting. It was when I traveled to Tuscany with him, as a matter of fact, to help him select the marble for the *Pietà*, that I met my Marta."

His voice softened reverently on the name.

Honor's chill moved lower, to the pit of her belly.

"She was the daughter of an English merchant who was in Tuscany setting up trade partnerships. She taught me English, and I taught her Italian. Ah, those were the happiest days of my life. Even Michelangelo's arrogance and perfectionism bothered me less while I had Marta." His soft basso took on a staccato beat, as if he wanted to get through the rest of his tale quickly.

Indeed, quickly, please. By now, Honor had to force herself to listen. Only she could defy physical laws, bringing her perfect mate to life, and then lose him to another woman before she had a chance to win him.

"We were to be married in 1499 on the eve of my thirtieth birthday. But the plague descended that year, brought by travelers from the east. Marta contracted it while I was in Rome with Michelangelo. By the time I found out she was sick and hurried home, she was very ill."

Tears dewed Honor's eyes at the pain in his voice. She tentatively covered his hand with her own, but he pulled away, making a fist, as if he couldn't bear to be touched. Honor retreated, physically and emotionally, back inside her cocoon.

He didn't notice. Dully, he continued, "Michelangelo and I had been fighting even before Marta died. My skills had much improved under his tutelage, but still he gave me only the most menial tasks. He did not delegate well."

At another time, Honor might have been happy at hearing her theory confirmed.

"We fought for the last time in the summer of 1499, a few months after Marta died. I left him and returned to carousing with new friends I'd made in Rome. They were soldiers in a Condottiere's army, and they convinced me to go with them to make my fortune. Do you know what a Condottiere is?"

"Yes." Honor had to clear her husky voice. "A mercenary soldier captain for hire."

"In those days, I was drunk more often than I was sober, yet that is little excuse for the things I saw and the things I didn't try to stop. Even the things I did. I was paid to defend if possible, attack if necessary. And while I tried to stop my fellow soldiers from the worst of their viciousness, all too often I could only turn away. I was in his army barely a month before I tried to desert, but he caught me and had me beaten. I would probably have died with a sword in my hand, a fitting end to what I'd become, if I hadn't accidentally killed a rich young nobleman in a tavern brawl, setting in motion the events that brought me here."

He paused for a long time, staring blankly into space. Honor longed to ease his pain and draw him to her bosom, but she didn't dare. Only he could get through the bleak memories.

"I have killed with these hands." He thrust his unusually large hands out and stared at them, then stuck them back in his pockets. "I have enjoyed many women, yet I have only truly loved one. I have been drunk more times than I can count. And yet, God, in his mercy, has given me a chance to right the wrongs I've done." With a combination of wonder and foreboding, he shook his head. "If I am strong enough this time to take it.

"When I awoke in an alley the next morning, my friends told me the young man's titled relatives, the Landuccis, were already looking for me to kill me. I ran, ran to the only safe place I knew—back home to Caprese. There I found my parents both dead of a bandit attack, my only brother missing. I stopped only to gather a few belongings and purchase more brandy, and hid in my and Michelangelo's favorite hiding place as children."

Honor's heart lurched in her breast. "The Roman cistern."

He turned his head to look at her, his Adriatic eyes storm-cloud navy. "Of course. You are the one who found me. My things? Where are they?"

"The Italian government let me bring them with you so I could try to verify their authenticity. They're in an office in New York at the port. I hoped dating them would lead to proof that you were . . ."

A wry smiled eased the torment in his eyes. "Genuine? Indeed, I am genuine. A genuine rogue, perhaps even a coward." He held up his hand when she protested. "No, hear me out, Honoria Psyche. Do not weave dreams about me, little virgin, for I would not have your illusions spoiled as mine were."

"How do you know I'm a virgin?"

"The prophecy. You see, that time alone in the dark was the worst of my life. In a few months, I'd lost my only love, my parents, my best friend, and I didn't know if I'd ever see my brother again. Scant excuse, but the only one I have for what I did next."

Honor braced herself, her mouth dry with fear.

"Drink only blunted my pain, but at the bottom of the bottle, I took the easy path. I should have blamed myself for not staying with Marta, for letting my own ambitions take me to Rome. But no, like the selfish rogue I'd become, I blamed God. To my everlasting shame, that dark night I cursed God and all the angels."

Honor gasped. Even in her time, such defiance was frowned upon; in his time, it was rank sacrilege. "What happened?"

"A light shone where there was none. Air

44

stirred the hairs on my body, for I had stripped myself to wash away the poisons of the drink. To my amazement, an angel appeared. I cannot describe how beautiful she was, but what remains most in my mind is the severe look on her perfect face. She hovered above me, her wings snowy white as if to reproach me for the blackness of my deeds. She told me to look into my mirror."

Honor recalled the large mirror, trimmed in an elaborate gilt frame. It must have cost a king's ransom in a time when glass was precious. She'd wondered why it was there, pristine and unbroken.

He briefly covered his eyes with his hand, as if he couldn't bear the memory of his own image. "I was revolted at the ugliness of my own hatred. It was like a weapon I'd turned upon myself. She bade me stand, pick up the slingshot I'd used so often as a boy, and hold it over my shoulder. Stunned, I did as ordered, uncertain why she seemed to be posing me. Then she informed me that I was to be imprisoned for five hundred years for my sins. On the dawn of a new millennium, God would give me one chance to right the wrongs I'd done. A virgin's tears and prayers would bring me to life again. I had until the year 2000 to find my last living descendant, a far future grandson of my brother named Raphael. I must bring him back to the straight and narrow path lest he end alone and drunkard as I did. The angel told me that he is to be vital to the fate of humankind, and even if I had to risk my life to save him, I must."

Honor's awe was no less great because of her fear. He had only four months to accomplish what sounded like a monumental task. "And if you don't?"

"If I don't find him and save him from my own fate, on December thirty-first, this year, I return to stone and stay thus forever." He slumped a little, running a weary hand through his tousled hair, as if glad the recounting was over. "And that's all I remember before I awoke to find you kneeling at my feet, healing me with your tears."

Honor's teeth chattered. Her instincts had been right. She'd been present at the wonder of his rebirth only to hear how fragile was the life she'd helped wrest from the ages. Dear Lord, she was a sparrow, not an eagle. A dreamer, not a doer. How could she help him? But how could she bear to lose him, either? Her voice was husky when she finally managed, "And what happens if you succeed?"

"The angel told me I could return to my own time, or stay here, whatever I wished. She did not explain how, but I shall be able to figure it out in the ensuing months, no doubt."

Dizzy as she was at his revelations, Honor still knew one question remained to be answered. The most puzzling question of all. "But . . . why are you an exact match to *David?*"

He smiled sadly, luminous eyes fixed on a wondrous past she could only dream of. Then he looked at her, his smile deepening. "I admire your logical brain, *bellissima*. Most unusual for a woman."

Even in her exhaustion, his chauvinism grated

on her, but now was not the time to argue women's rights with a five-hundred-year-old man.

"But for the first time, you are wrong. It is not I who resemble *David*. Quite the reverse. You see, I believe that Michelangelo must have been as upset at our quarrel as I. It is *David* that resembles me, for I must have been the model for his design."

Honor tapped her forehead with her hand, distressed at her own obtuseness. "Of course." She slumped back on her elbows, but roused herself to ask, "What now? How do we begin?"

"We?" His eyes dropped to her ankles, visible under the edge of the coverlet.

Hastily she sat up, tucking the cover back under her knees. Ludicrous that a glimpse of ankle could light that fire in his eyes. He had so much to learn. Strong as he was, he'd be a babe in the woods in the ruthless twentieth century. Her career was already in ruins, so she had nothing to lose by helping him. She said more firmly, "Yes. We."

His eyes wandered to the slight curve of her bosom.

Even through three layers of fabric, she felt the power of his gaze as something tangible. They'd better get back to the subject at hand. Hands . . . Her own gaze wandered to his huge, capable hands, and a delicious shiver coursed through her as she wondered what it would be like to be touched by them. "Ah, I don't suppose you have any idea when, or where, your ancestors came to America?"

Still gazing fixedly at her bosom, he shook his head. His breathing had quickened.

Her own heart pounding, Honor forced herself to look away and stand. She tottered over to the second bed like a mummy, barely able to walk. In truth, given the day she'd had, she felt half-dead. The worst of it was, she had a distinct feeling her troubles were only beginning. She flopped down, wriggling under the covers.

He watched with interest as she became an amorphous mound, making interesting shapes beneath the covers as she twisted and turned. A slim arm came out and offered him the spread. Lips twitching, he accepted it and smoothed it neatly back on his bed.

While his back was turned, she removed her blouse and bra, dropping them unobtrusively beside the bed and leaving her slip on. Odd how she wasn't afraid. Here she was, an innocent awkward around men, who felt safe sleeping in the same room with a virtual stranger from an earlier, savage age. A self-confessed rogue. Honor covered a huge yawn with her hand, too tired to contemplate the puzzle of her own feelings, much less his.

Yawning again, she managed a slurred, "There's only one place to start, really. The same place most immigrants entered this country in years past. Ellis Island. New York City. Ernie's from New York. I'll pick his brain when he returns in the morning. One good thing: there can't be that many Castigliones." Her eyes drifted shut. "Good night, Dom."

Did she imagine the tenderness in his voice? His basso sounded as sonorous as a lullaby when he replied, *"Buona notte, bambina."*

Her last conscious thought drifted away on a cloud as sleep claimed her.

Baby. Virgin. Lady.

Would she ever be a woman to him?

Beatific morning light roused Honor, and a gentle touch. She brushed at the side of her face, thinking her own hair tickled her. The feeling went away, only to move down to the warm, tender hollow of her throat. Honor blinked awake. A luminous head of red, gold and tawny brown hovered over her, the sun behind casting a halo about an impossibly beautiful face. The fingertip he'd used to rouse her rested now at her throat, testing the acceleration of her heart rate.

In the dawn of a bright day, a new millennium hovering just over the horizon, a Renaissance man and a twentieth-century woman stared at one another. Her dreams of the night past were far surpassed by Dom's reality, and Honor knew that no matter what came, she was honored at being chosen to assist in his rebirth. Her career was perhaps a high price to pay for this moment, but she still had no regrets.

For once, instinct won over practicality. In that misty haze between light and dark, a sparrow could pretend to be an eagle. Who would know? For that matter, who would care? Least of all the brothers who'd given her up for lost.

Catching his hand, Honor kissed his palm and boldly drew it down to cradle the heart that was his for the taking.

His white teeth showed in his gasp. For an instant stolen out of time, his huge hand enveloped her small breast, pressing gently as if he, too, found it hard to grasp the glory of her reality. His handsome, exquisitely proportioned face lowered. His full lips parted. At the last moment, he made a tormented sound in his throat, half snarl, half plea, and surged to his feet, stumbling away.

Apparently, rather than sleep in the coarse, dirty coveralls, he'd wrapped the much-abused spread about his lower body. When he stumbled, his foot caught the fabric. It fell in a heap at his feet.

Honor squelched a gasp with her hand, but he still heard. He froze as he began to bend to pick up the cover, his back to her. The sun peeked through the half-drawn curtains, as if even it were curious at his astounding male beauty.

Honor drank him in with her eyes. He was stunning in stone, but in the glory of sunlight he was resplendent, as if the Divine Angel had bestowed some of his own grace upon him. The firm buttocks, the strong thighs and calves, the straight spine and broad shoulders . . . Dear Lord, had any woman in human history ever faced such a dilemma? Here she was, a virgin, chafing at her own chastity, drooling over a shape she knew more intimately than any married woman ever could. In her months of living with him, she'd sketched him, touched him, photographed him from every imaginable angle.

But she'd known him long before then.

From the time of her childhood, Honor had admired every supple curve, every strong plane of this form that expressed all that was noble about the male body. Her college mates could post pin-ups from *Playgirl* and sneak off to view overmuscular male strippers, but Honor had interest in neither.

She had her David—and her dreams. Despite unmerciful teasing from her peers, he was the only poster on her dorm wall. Perhaps he was why she was still a virgin. What man could live up to such an ideal?

And yet, when he slowly turned to face her, his expression arrested as if he were fascinated at her fascination, she felt as if she'd never seen him before. This living, breathing symbol of male beauty was no longer a dream that had sustained her through too many lonely years.

Now he had a name.

Dominico Paolo Constantine Castiglione. A rogue? Perhaps, but most of all a man. Her man. Foolish or wise, Honor knew that this sense of belonging she'd never felt with any living being was something to be cherished, not shunned. He met her tender gaze, holding one hand before his eyes as if she, not the sun, blinded him.

"Do not look at me so, Honoria Psyche. I am not fit to kiss your feet, much less . . . " He trailed off, but the stirring at his loins was far more eloquent than words.

Awed, Honor watched the part that proclaimed him so boldly male begin to change. His shaft expanded, standing out from the nest of hair with titanic proportions even Michelangelo could not have visualized. Honor blushed, going hot and cold all at once, but still she stared. The delicious shivers returned, part fear, part fascination.

Again, the imaginings of a lonely coed were far surpassed by reality.

Growling deep in his throat, he turned away from her and grabbed up the coveralls.

This time Honor let instinct guide her, ceding her last remaining reserve to its tutelage. Whether God had given him to her or humanity, she was meant to love this man, and they had only four months together. Tossing the covers aside, she hurried to him, grabbing him about the waist and resting her cheek on his broad back. His heart thrummed against her ear. Shyly, she moved closer until her bare breasts pressed against him.

His heart lurched, then pounded faster. She felt the rumble of his protest reverberate through them both, like a tremor forecasting an earthquake. "Do not begin what you cannot finish."

"Dom," she whispered against his smooth skin, "you're not the only anomaly in my time. Do you know how rare a virgin my age is?"

"Yesss . . . " His breath ended on a hiss as she rubbed slightly against him. "And how precious. Move, *bambina. Now.*"

The gritty agony in the last word moved her, literally, as nothing else could have. Swallowing her hurt, she stepped back. He whirled to face her, holding the coveralls to his loins. The flush on his high cheekbones accented his beauty . . . and her ugliness. Biting her lip at her own foolishness, she began to turn away. He must have seen the pain on her face, for he caught her shoulder with his free hand.

"You do not know how lovely you are, do you?"

"Don't mock me." She kept her face averted.

He turned her face with a gentle fingertip. When she was looking at him, her eyes charcoal gray, burning with resentment, he let his finger drift down her cheek, tracing the outline of her mouth. "Such a lovely mouth. Such passion it yearns for, such wonder it promises."

While she was still gasping, the finger drifted lower still, touching the pounding hollow of her throat, then wandering from one delicate collarbone to the other. "You are so tiny. And I am so large. I could not bear to hurt you, *bellissima*."

Everywhere he touched, heat drifted lazily through her veins. And when his fingertip finally traced the outline of one small, firm breast, the heat became a current, sweeping all inhibitions before it. Vaguely she heard his muttered, "Perfect. Not too large, not too small. You are slim and shapely, unlike the fat women so admired in my own time."

The current became a torrent. She saw his tongue hungrily lick his lips, as if he, too, yearned to kiss her. But then she heard no more of his muttered endearments. Her blood rushed too loud, demanding one thing. . . .

Standing on her tiptoes, she threw her arms about his neck and pulled his head down to hers. The union of lips was both completion and beginning. For, despite his hesitation, finally, she could believe he was real. He was so warm, so male, so . . . hers.

What she lacked in experience, she made up in enthusiasm. She turned her head to slant her lips more closely against his. His unresponsive mouth trembled to life. At first he merely kissed her back, his lips gently nuzzling, as if he still feared hurting her, but when she arched her aching breasts into his chest, he made a strangled groan. He dropped the coveralls, sank his fingers into her hair to tilt her head at an even better angle, and kissed her as she longed to be kissed.

As if she truly were beautiful.

As if he could not resist this wondrous need any more than she could.

Warm, firm lips urged her own apart, nibbling and teasing until he could get his tongue inside. The intimacy that foretold a greater one had never appealed much to Honor, but it was only fitting that Dom, a work of art himself, was also master of this ancient art. The tip of his tongue played in its new playground, darting in and out, sallying along the perimeter until she missed him and called him back in. For long moments they dallied, dancing tongues becoming bolder as she learned how to answer his thrust and retreat.

She felt the proof of his desire thrust urgently into her abdomen. The torrent of heat moved lower, centering in her loins. She squirmed against him, resenting the twin barriers of nylon, her mouth open now to the sweet invasion. Closer. She needed to get closer.

Panting, he lifted his mouth only to trace the side of her neck, nipping as he went. Shivers racked her even as heat curled around her like sunbeams. His large, tough sculptor's hands touched her breasts, cupping them with a tenderness that should have surprised her, but didn't.

Dear heavenly rogue, Honor thought vaguely as

she arched into his touch, show me how to be a woman. As he swept her up in his arms to carry her to the bed, it felt so right, so true, as if he really had been sent by divine prophecy not just for the world, but for Honor's sake. Dom was lowering his tender burden when a knock sounded at the door.

The luminous fire in his eyes was banked. He blinked, staring down at her bare breasts. His hands moved quickly away. She felt the emotional withdrawal more keenly than the physical one, for the look on his face could only be described as shame. He spied her blouse next to the bed and handed it to her. Numbly, she took it, feeling colder than ever as the ennobling heat faded away. Honor fumbled into her bra and blouse, wondering if, despite his smooth flattery, he found her appeal limited next to that if his beloved Marta. He stepped into the coveralls.

The knock sounded again. Ernie said, "Honnie, you in there?"

Blanking her feelings, Honor quickly stepped into her dirty, wrinkled skirt and threw her jacket over her blouse. She opened the door, peering past Ernie, but saw no one else in the lot. He hurried inside. He looked between Dom's rigid features and Honor's empty ones. Honor didn't give him time to comment on the stifled emotions he obviously sensed.

"Were you able to get my things?" she asked.

"Most of them, except the furniture." Ernie stared at Dom. His gaze wandered from the exposed skin at Dom's chest, down to his flat belly and strong legs. He licked his lips.

Uh-oh. Honor said politely, "Dom, would you mind bringing in my bags?"

Dom gave Ernie a wide berth as he went to the door.

"Doors are open," Ernie said. "Need any help?"

"I shall contrive quite capably."

Ernie waited until the door was closed before he turned on Honor. "Where did you *find* that guy? He looks like something out of a Renaissance painting. Talks like one, too. But man, I've never seen such purity of face and form—"

"He's straight, Ernie." Whatever Dom's true feelings about her beauty or lack thereof, he couldn't pretend the rampant lust he'd shown a few minutes earlier. And she didn't want Ernie to be hurt again.

Ernie sighed heavily. "Figures." He looked at her speculatively. "So what's going on here? It's not like you to spend the night with a stranger. In fact, in the two years I've known you, you've gone on exactly two dates that I'm aware of."

How on earth could she put this? She had to satisfy enough of his curiosity, but not too much. "Well, let's just say my interest in him is professional." *Liar.*

Ernie obviously thought so, too. He didn't quite laugh, but he stifled a smile as he said, "Honor, you're one of the most driven, honest people I've ever known, with the possible exception of my big brother Nick, but even you're not blind. The guy's a hunk. And he wants you. That's obvious."

Was it? Honor longed to believe him, but now wasn't the time to debate him. "Anyway, you see, Dom is going to help me—"

"Dom? That's his name?"

"Yeah. Dominico Castiglione."

"Whewww." Ernie whistled. "A name like that, I'd be kind of edgy too. He Italian?"

"Yes." That, at least, was the truth. "And the woman who taught him English used sort of an old style of speaking."

Ernie nodded. "So? What now? How's he help clear you?"

"Well, we have a lead that we need to follow to New York. I was wondering . . . would you mind terribly if we borrowed your car? Mine's been impounded by now, probably. I'll pay you back as soon as I can."

"That's fine. You know I'd rather bicycle to work, anyway. Old heap's not worth more than a grand. I hope it gets you there."

The door opened. Dom entered, a towering pile of suitcases and bags in his arms, but he still walked in that erect, effortless way, as if he carried sacks of feathers. He set his burdens carefully down on the bed.

Ernie stepped up to the pile and pulled out a sack marked *Nordstrom's*. He dumped out a heap of clothing: jeans, a soft lavender pullover and button-down pink shirt, plus a sack of underwear and socks. "Thought you might need these, since you didn't seem to have any bags."

Dom poked at the garments, his expression showing surprise at the soft texture of the sweater. He opened the underwear and shook out a pair. He held them up to the light, one suspicious eye peering through the slit at Honor and Ernie. "What use is this *bagatelle*? It already has a hole in it."

57

Colleen Shannon

Ernie blinked, his mellow brown eyes darkening for the first time. He glanced suspiciously at Honor.

Honor cleared her throat. "Dom comes from a very small Italian town, and he's used to the old style of longer underwear. Right, Dom?" Honor willed him to cooperate.

Shrugging, Dom tossed the underwear down. "I'm going to clean myself. When I come out, we will go to this new place, yes?"

Honor stifled a groan, for she could see Ernie growing more suspicious by the minute. "Yes."

The bathroom door had barely closed before Ernie turned on Honor. "The guy may be gorgeous, but what a bumpkin! I can't believe anywhere in Europe is as backward as he seems to be. You telling me he's never heard of New York?"

No, because the New World was barely discovered during his time. But of course Honor couldn't tell Ernie that. "I don't know him that well, Ernie. It's just . . . he has a lead on the statue."

"Why?"

"He was there when it, ah, disappeared, and he's going to help me recover it." Well, that was sort of true. Honor checked the receipt from the Nordstrom's bag. She paled. Ernie had good taste, even if his choice of color was a bit too feminine, but Dom was so masculine he'd look deliciously male in lace. She went to her wallet and gamely handed Ernie most of her remaining cash. She'd just have to risk using her bank card on the trip, but her account would be dry by the time they made it to the city.

Ernie waved the money away and snatched the receipt. "Consider it a gift. The car, too. You know big brother sends me money every month. He makes a pile with his own security firm."

The mysterious brother again. Ernie mentioned him in passing every so often, but he never really talked about Nick. Honor sensed there was some sort of reserve between the two brothers, but since she wasn't exactly first on the priority list with her own siblings, she'd never pried.

"Honnie"— Ernie scribbled something on the back of the receipt he'd taken from her— "this is Nick's phone number and address. I'm going to call him and ask him to give you the loft rent-free for a couple of months until you have time to get settled. He evicted his last tenants, so right now he's just rattling around by himself in our old brownstone."

"Oh, I couldn't—"

"You must. I'll worry about you so much that I won't be able to work, and then I'll get fired, too. You want that?"

Tears misted Honor's vision. She caught Ernie's handsome face in her hands and kissed his cheek. "You're a doll, Ernie. I'll miss you."

The bathroom door opened. A wave of steam came out of the bathroom, followed by something even more elemental: six feet plus of warm, muscular male wrapped only in a towel. Dom's hands had been raking back his hair, but when he saw Honor kissing Ernie, he froze. His *terribilita* scowl returned.

Ernie and Honor turned to face him. Ernie's mouth twitched at the look on Dom's face. He dropped a casual arm about Honor's shoulders. Honor didn't try to pull away. She didn't owe Dom any explanations, especially since he seemed determined not to touch her. They were both going to New York, that was all. Dom to find his ancestor, she to clear her name. And if the thought occurred to her that only recovering the statue would clear her name, and recovering the statue would be possible only if Dom failed in his quest and returned to stone, well, she shoved the thought violently away. She had enough painful issues to deal with. For once in her life, she'd take everything one day at a time.

Dom glared at her, but then his dark blue eyes went opaque. He went to the bed, let the towel drop and began to wriggle into the underwear. Two pairs of eyes widened, one brown, one gray, both flaring with equal interest. Dom kept his back to them as he shimmied the tight cotton over his loins.

His muscles flexed gracefully. Whimsically, Honor decided that if all else failed, Dom could make a fortune as an erotic dancer. He didn't seem to have much modesty, and since the entire world knew what he looked like naked, that was just as well. Ernie all but salivated. Let him drool all over his Polo oxford shirt if he wanted to, but Honoria Psyche had better things to do.

Honor eased out from under his arm to go through her own bags. She pulled out a comfortable pair of jeans, a suede blazer and a white cotton turtleneck and went into the bathroom to dress. She only hoped that Ernie could control himself while she was gone. Dom had already shown that he didn't take kindly to unwanted advances.

Honor took her time, brushing her hair until it shone, then holding it back from her face with a black suede headband that matched her jacket. Everything was quiet in the next room. Too quiet. She opened the door and peeked out.

Dom stood on one side of the room, arms folded over a broad chest still indomitable even covered in a pink shirt and lilac sweater. The pastels threw his masculine features into sharp relief. And the jeans . . . Honor would have loved to have seen Ernie's expression as Dom wriggled into them. Either Ernie had misjudged Dom's proportions, or, with his usual impish sense of humor, he had picked the jeans a size too tight.

When she exited, Dom switched his grim stare from Ernie's innocent expression and turned it on Honor. Something fired in his eyes as they wandered over her, something that harked back to their earlier embrace, but then he took a deep breath and said quietly, "People here must like torturing themselves. I see you, too, wear this stiff fabric." He tried to pull a pinch of denim away from his poured-in thigh, couldn't, and continued, "I feel like I'm wearing one of Leonardo's canvases."

"You look like one, too," Ernie said softly. He blushed, and Honor knew the thought had just slipped out. Dom had been human less than a day, and already he had a way of drawing people out, forcing them into behavior and feelings they normally stifled.

That grim stare lowered on him again. "If that

is meant as a compliment, young man, try it on some young lady who cares."

"You do look very nice, Dom," Honor inserted at Ernie's hurt expression. "The jeans will stretch. In time you'll grow to like them."

"Time, *bellissima*, is a luxury I do not have. May we leave now and start for this new place?"

"I'm ready when you are." Honor picked up a couple of her bags, but Dom snatched them away.

"Ladies do not carry such heavy things." He piled the bags in his arms, kicked the door open and went outside.

"Bit old-fashioned, isn't he?" Ernie said, picking up the last bag. "You sure you're OK with this caveman, Honnie?"

She stifled a hysterical laugh. In his sweet way, Ernie was worrying about her virtue. He knew she was still a virgin. If Ernie only knew that she'd served her virtue up on a platter just this morning, only to be refused. . . .

Honor swallowed the fresh hurt away. "Yes, Ernie. He'd never hurt me. And I . . . need him." The lump returned, too big for her to swallow this time.

When they reached his car, Ernie tossed his bag in the backseat and then kissed her cheek. "Be well and safe and happy, dear friend. Call me when you get settled." He pulled his expensive racing bike down from the rack on the car roof. "If I'm asked, I'll just tell them you haven't called me. It's true, as far as it goes."

Ernie got astride his bike, but he paused for an

unwontedly harsh stare at Dom. "Take good care of her, Dominico, if that's even your real name."

Honor held her breath, but amusement, not anger, curled Dom's full mouth.

"You truly love Honoria Psyche, do you not, young man?"

"I do."

Dom nodded approvingly. "I will take care of her. You have my promise." Dom got into the passenger side of the car.

In other circumstances, Honor might have been amused at their typically male exchange, but at the moment, she wanted to scream her frustration at them both. Still, touched at Ernie's concern, she stifled her ire, waved and then took the driver's seat. As she turned the key, she said, "You could have been a little nicer to Ernie. He's the only friend I have, and he's already dumped a bundle to help us."

"Dumped a bundle? You mean the bags he brought?"

"Ah, no, it's an expression that means he's spent much money to help us." Honor turned onto the street, keeping an eye on her rearview mirror. "And for the record, buster, I don't need protecting. I've supported myself since college and done just fine, thank you very much."

Dom blinked his shock. "You have actually attended a place of learning?"

Silently, Honor counted to ten. She kept her tone quiet despite the urge to scream. "Women in this day and age often do everything men do, from fighting fires to flying jets."

"Jets?"

"Flying machines. Dom, lots of things change in five hundred years, thank God, and if you question everything, everyone will question us."

As she turned onto the expressway east, he lapsed into a hurt silence.

Finally he said quietly, "I am merely as curious about your time as you seem to be about mine."

Guiltily, Honor bit her lip. "At our next stop, I'll buy you some news magazines so you can bone up, OK?" Before he could ask, she clarified, "Learn quickly. You do read, don't you?"

"Of course. Though few women in my time could." He shot her a sideways, provoking glance.

She ignored it. This was going to be a long trip.

Arduous, tiring, maybe even scary . . . Honor gave in and, for an instant stamped forever in her memory, she drank in the purity of his profile silhouetted against the clear blue sky. He stared, fascinated, out the window at the lush mountains they were navigating on hairpin turns. She looked quickly back at the road, certain he would read the wistfulness in her expression if he looked at her.

The journey would also be exciting, fun and unforgettable.

She might as well enjoy it, because four months would probably be all she would ever have of this amazing Renaissance man. With his successful quest went her career.

And all chance of happiness.

Chapter Three

Time, Honor had always found, was a fluid medium. When one was bored, it oozed like molasses in January; when one was happy, it raged like rapids. And yet now that she saw her own "modern" world through a Renaissance man's eyes, time had become both more real and more frightening: to Dom, yesterday was 1499. He had gone to sleep in the Renaissance and awakened on the dawn of a new millennium.

In the final analysis, five hundred years was only a tick on the celestial clock. Their own petty trials and tribulations meant nothing in the larger scheme of things. In truth, as Dom helped her realize, time was but a man-made monument, a futile effort to stop and mark the infinite.

Yet . . . if she and Dom were so infinitesimal to history, why had God sent him to her?

The first day of the journey literally flew past along with the grandeur of the West. Dom's eyes remained glued to the changing panorama of spacious skies segueing into "amber waves of grain and purple mountains majesty." After she answered his innumerable questions, Honor was so tickled by his total fascination with her country that she broke into song and taught him the lyrics of "America the Beautiful." He had a robust baritone mellow to the ear, and he seemed to enjoy singing. But when they'd finished a rollicking chorus of the last verse, and night was shimmying up the Idaho branch of the Rockies, Dom grew pensive.

"America," he repeated softly. "So is your country named after Amerigo Vespucci? I remember him. He was from Florence, too, and made several voyages right before I . . . left."

"Yes. Actually, he and a few of his influential friends gave him the honor, and the name stuck. Vespucci claimed to be the true discoverer of the New World, since Columbus thought he'd discovered the Indies."

Melancholy shaded his expression. "Yet I still haven't met anyone who even speaks Italian. If my country discovered your world, why do we not own it?"

"The Italians are quite influential in many ways. Many of their goods are coveted worldwide. Their fashions, their leathers, their cars, their shoes."

"*Shoes?*" Dom looked appalled.

Honor's mouth quivered, but she said seriously, "The Vatican's still in Rome. And of course the Sistine Chapel is still there, with its gorgeous frescoes. They were recently refurbished."

"What frescoes?"

Honor rolled her eyes at her own stupidity. Michelangelo didn't paint the chapel until the early 1500s. "Michelangelo spent over thirty years there painting some of the most gorgeous images the world has ever seen."

Dom cocked his head, puzzled. "But Michelangelo was a sculptor, not a painter."

"True enough, but he was a gifted painter, too. Dom, do you have any idea how revered Michelangelo and da Vinci are in my world?"

He shrugged, and a note of cynicism entered his voice. "Doubtless no more than they thought they deserved. Michelangelo, in particular, was a very volatile personality with a rather flexible notion of reality. His solution to many problems was just to walk away."

Amazing. He was still mad after five hundred years. Honor had to struggle to remember that 1499 was yesterday to him. As disoriented as she felt at the rapid changes life had brought during the last two days, she could multiply her feelings by one hundred and still not approach his own sense of displacement.

But he seemed more troubled by Italy's lack of prominence than by his own situation, at least for the moment. "I cannot believe that Italians do not rule Europe, at the very least."

How could Honor explain to him that five hundred years of global politics, and choosing the wrong side in a world war, had kept Italy from achieving the world dominance that might have seemed likely in Dom's time? She chose her words carefully. "Italy is a rich, important country today, Dom. But people of my time have found strength in alliances. There are fifty separate states in America, but for over two hundred years we've had one federal government. Italy was ruled by a fascist dictator only fifty years ago, and even today Italians change their governing officials frequently."

Dom gave a short bark of laughter. "Now this I believe. This sounds like my country."

"Still, Italy has changed a great deal since your time. Cities there don't have their own armies anymore, or create their own states. Nowadays cities allow themselves to be ruled by one central government for the good of all."

That *terribilita* frown turned on her. "But how do you settle your differences? How does law survive if no one fights for what's right? Do people in your time have no spirit?"

After that, the conversation did indeed become a bit spirited. Honor tried to convince him that subjecting all to the same rule of law was a more advanced way of living; Dom remained adamant that in some cases, only force could achieve justice.

Neither of them realized that circumstances would soon put philosophy to the test.

In Wyoming, they picked up Interstate 80, which would take them all the way to New York, and Honor relaxed a bit. They'd passed innumerable highway patrolmen, none of whom paid them the least attention. Either the museum hadn't yet pressed charges, or they didn't know she'd taken Ernie's car. Or, best of all, they were such tadpoles in the cesspool of crime that they could swim to a bigger pond unnoticed.

She noted that Dom, even in the midst of their good-natured arguments, paid close attention to her driving. She had to smile ruefully as she waited to hear him criticize her. Primitive man or not, he showed many of the same predilections of his contemporaries. The next thing she knew, he'd refuse to let her drive.

And something else became harder to ignore with every mile on the odometer: they were each acutely aware of one another. Out of the corner of her eye, Honor admired the purity of his profile, silhouetted against a vivid scarlet and purple sunset. His lean hips and powerful thighs were beautifully defined by the tight denim. Many times she had to curl her hands tightly about the wheel to avoid the urge to touch his thigh to see if it felt as strong as it looked.

While she might be an innocent about the full intimacy of men and women, she knew when a man was attracted to her. When he thought she wasn't looking, he'd tilt his head slightly to the side with that distinctively macho Italian sensuality and appraise her under half-lowered eyelashes. He, too, seemed to enjoy the sight of her long legs in the tight denim. Sometimes, in the midst of her rational arguments that her way of life was better than the one he'd known, his blue gaze would fix on the curve of her breasts, or the slender arch of her throat. Reason would suddenly fly out of the window.

There was nothing reasonable about this situation. Or about her feelings for Dom.

Dom was so full of questions that Honor finally laughed, pulled over at a rest stop and bought an atlas. Dom read about Mount Rushmore, the Grand Canyon, the Badlands and other monuments, getting her help occasionally with a word he didn't recognize, but he was growing increasingly restless.

When they began to hit traffic congestion, he clutched his door rest, tension stiffening his tall frame. He responded to her occasional comments in monosyllables. By the time night fell and they stopped again, she'd grown quiet. The second night in a shabby motel passed as the first had: Dom stayed outside until she was finished with her shower and safe in bed. He undressed in the dark and was up before she awoke. That day, as she had from the beginning, Honor swallowed her hurt and pretended not to care.

But she did care. Far too much. What manner of man was he, that he found her attractive on the one hand, but not good enough for him on the other? If she was willing to lose her cursed virginity, why did he refuse her when he obviously needed a woman? Surely it was her choice to make.

They grabbed a fast-food breakfast, with Dom almost gagging on the precooked, prepackaged bacon, egg and cheese biscuit. With his usual innate courtesy, Dom put the waste from their meal in the trash. He bumped into a huge man turning away from the counter with a loaded tray. Hot coffee tipped over, splattering the man's alligator-skin boots.

"*Scusi,*" Dom said. He grabbed a handful of napkins and offered them. "I did not see you."

The man, who wore a trucking company logo on his cap, glared at Dom. "Look closer next time, pretty boy." The trucker cast a disparaging look at Dom's lavender sweater and pink shirt.

Dom's eyes narrowed slightly, but he only shrugged. "I will get you more coffee." And he got back in line.

"Damn tootin'," the trucker said. He looked around the crowded restaurant, eyed the seat next to Honor and smiled at her. A gold tooth gleamed in the light coming through the windows. "Pretty little thing like you shouldn't be alone." He plopped his huge bulk so close to her that she had to sidle away.

"Uh, I'm not," she said.

Her nose wrinkled as he ignored her rebuff and began to consume the pile of artery-clogging food on his loaded tray. He winked at her as he told a story about a stranded family he'd helped, edging closer to her as he spoke.

His table manners were no better than his social skills, and Honor looked away from his open mouth full of masticated eggs and sausage. Dom finally made his way to the front of the line, but he hadn't turned and didn't realize she had a visitor.

That was fine with Honor. She'd handled this type before. It constantly amazed her that so many unattached males assumed a woman alone was fair game, regardless of her looks or even, sometimes, her age. Honor's mouth barely moved in the chilly smile she reserved for unruly children, thoughtless museum visitors and unwanted admirers. "It was nice meeting you, but I'll have to get back on the road now."

A meaty hand pulled her back down. "What's your hurry? Where you headed? Maybe we can convoy together." That tooth gleamed at her again.

The convoy he had in mind made her stomach churn. She tried to pry his hand loose, still keeping her smile in place. "No, I know where I'm going. But thanks for the offer."

The grip tightened, pulling her under his arm. "Baby doll, you got no idea how *much* I got to offer." His hip bumped against hers.

Honor was about to elbow him in the ribs when a shadow fell over the small table. A large cup of coffee was set down before the trucker, sloshing slightly over the sides.

The trucker's muddy brown eyes, the exact color of the coffee, looked up into glowing blue.

"You will release her. Now." Dom's voice was soft. Too soft.

The arm tightened.

Uh-oh. Honor saw the glow flare into incandescent blue. Before Honor could bring her elbow up into the trucker's ribs, Dom picked up the coffee and lifted her with one arm to pull her out of range. He neatly dumped the hot coffee onto the trucker's bulging denims.

The man yowled and leaped up, sending the small table flying. Paper, cardboard and food bits flew, landing on other patrons. Several women screeched and began to yell for the manager.

The trucker was dancing in place, hands cupped at his groin, oblivious to everything but his own pain. A policeman in the back looked up from his meal and paper.

Grabbing Dom's arm, Honor hauled him out the door. For a minute he resisted, but when the cop rose and began to make his way forward, Dom let Honor lead him away. Honor took note of the enormous black eighteen-wheeler parked behind the restaurant as they screeched out of the parking lot. The side bore the same logo as the trucker's cap.

When they were safely on the freeway, Honor finally stopped shaking. "What possessed you to do that? That guy could have prosecuted you for assault."

"And what of his inappropriate behavior toward you?"

"There's nothing illegal about flirting."

"Flirting?"

"Letting a woman know you like her."

Dom nibbled his lip. "So you want me to put my arm around you, leer at you and make obscene comments to show my interest?"

"Uh, well, not exactly." He didn't have to do anything but smile at her and she melted.

Honor's heart began to race. Had she misread him after all? She couldn't imagine him being intimidated by anything, but maybe he was still uncomfortable with the transition in time and mores he was having to make. Maybe, wonder of wonders, this man who had no modesty was embarrassed. His next question seemed to substantiate her theory.

"This is what women expect from suitors in your time?"

"No. We still like flowers and jewelry and poetry. But few men offer that much these days. And those who do often expect a lot in return."

"What?"

"A night in bed."

He cocked his head. "But women who have sex for gain are whores."

Irritated, Honor flipped her visor down. "Can we change the subject?"

He sighed deeply, but buried himself in the atlas.

They didn't speak much for the rest of the morning, until they reached Chicago. As they passed through the maze of freeways, Dom stared out the window at the skyscrapers. "But how do they build them so tall and keep them from leaning? The only tall building I knew was in Pisa."

"They use steel beams, which are much stronger than wood. As for the Pisa tower . . . It's still leaning; in fact some say it's about to fall down."

Dom sighed. "Pity. It seems so much of my time has failed to survive. Tell me, is the pope still powerful?"

"Oh, yes. Very. But he doesn't conduct wars anymore. He tries to stop them."

Dom gave a little disbelieving grunt at this. To Honor's amusement, he seemed disappointed. As innately kind and courteous as he was to women, he still had a wild streak that had, after all, landed him in this predicament.

After lunch, when they approached the car, his big hand caught her arm. Fire singed a hungry trail up Honor's sleeve. He'd been so careful not to touch her on this interminable trip.

She managed a hushed, "Yes?"

"I wish to drive, Honoria Psyche. I have been watching you for two days. I know what to do."

"I don't think that's a good idea, Dom. The freeways are going to be crowded from now on, and—"

"I am tired of your treating me like a child."

She snapped her mouth shut.

"Just because I ask questions, that does not mean I am simple, or stupid."

"Of course not. I didn't mean to imply—"

"In fact, I need to learn all I can of this place God has sent me to. How else can I accomplish my mission and get home safely?"

Honor couldn't bear that earnest gaze that spoke to her worst fears. Of course he didn't like it here. He'd leave the first chance he got. Wordlessly, Honor handed him the keys. She felt too depressed and tired to drive anyway.

He started the car easily enough, shifted into reverse and made his way smoothly into the flow of traffic. He oversteered at first, and the car had a tendency to crowd too close to the line, but he soon realized his mistake and brought it back to the center of his lane.

Honor was tense for the first hour, but he caught on so quickly that she began to relax. She hadn't slept well the entire trip, and when she saw him carefully checking his mirrors, maintaining proper speed and competently keeping to his lane, she relaxed. She yawned. He was a Renaissance man, after all. Was there anything he wasn't good at?

Yes. Making love to virgins. Too tired to be miserable anymore, she flipped her seat back and went to sleep.

A jolt brought her rudely awake.

It was dark. The lights of a large city gleamed brightly, but where had the waterfall come from? Had they reached Niagara? Honor turned to ask Dom, but his door was open and he was gone. The car was still idling.

Honor realized four things at once: the roaring sound was the huge black eighteen-wheeler parked so close behind them that it must have run them off the road; the bright lights were its headlights trained on them; they were in the middle of nowhere, between cities; and Dom was arguing with the trucker who'd clumsily made a pass at her.

Wide-awake, Honor bolted out of the car in time to get the gist of the confrontation.

" . . . dangerous driving that way. If you wished me to stop, you could have asked." Dom's voice had a quiet rumble that reminded Honor of a tremor before an earthquake.

"Ask? I'd not ask a dirty foreigner like you the time a' day. No one treats me that way and gets away with it! And when I'm done with you, your snooty girlfriend gets it next. But first that pansy face needs a few more lumps!"

Dom stood impassively, his arms crossed over his chest, and said evenly, "Why? I think yours has enough for both of us."

The trucker took a swing at him. Dom dodged so quickly that Honor blinked in disbelief. One minute Dom's chin was in the path of the missile-like fist; the next Dom was a foot away, legs spread for balance in the classic fighter's stance, fists up.

The trucker blinked in shock, but he only lowered his head on his ox-yoke shoulders and charged.

"Stop it!" Honor yelled.

Neither of them even looked at her.

This time, as he sidestepped, Dom hooked his foot around the trucker's ankle. The man went sprawling, an elbow and knee catching his great bulk.

Honor winced at the *whump*ing sound he made as he fell.

Dom waited, watching analytically as the trucker heaved himself to his feet. "Please, I do not wish to hurt you. Let us go on our way and—" His pretty reconciliation speech was cut brutally short by a fist in the mouth. He didn't dodge in time, but he followed quickly with an uppercut that cracked the trucker's head to the side.

The trucker shook his shaggy mane, slapping the side of his head with his hand.

His ears must be ringing, Honor decided. This had gone quite far enough. She stepped forward, intending to get between the combatants. "Please, we're drawing a crowd."

Indeed, passing cars had begun to slow as people stared at them. Any time, some enterprising citizen would use a cell phone to call the police. Honor put out one hand toward Dom, and the other toward the trucker. "We'd better go or we'll end up in j—" She gasped as the trucker caught her by the neck and began to drag her backward toward his open door.

"You wanna leave in peace, do ya, fella? Fine by me, long as she's my consolation prize."

Dom's calm facade dissipated. His negligent stance had exuded the measured strength of deterrence, not violence. But between one breath and the next, his frame stiffened into pure, unsheathed steel. The trucker had only dragged Honor two steps before Dom was on him.

Using two fingers, Dom poked the trucker in the eyes. Grunting in combined pain and shock, the trucker released Honor to shield his tearing eyes.

Gently, Dom lifted Honor and moved her out of harm's way. He whirled, one fist landing a punch in the paunch overhanging the trucker's belt, the other following up with a brutal sock to the jaw.

The trucker tried to jerk aside, blinking moisture from his eyes, and return his own blow, but Dom ducked. He crouched, surging up on his iron-thewed thighs almost from the ground, and tackled the heavier man. Both of them fell to the pavement, Dom on top.

And Dom came from a time that had never heard of the Marquis of Queensberry. . . .

The trucker tried to knee him in the groin, but Dom was too close. His expression the fiercest Honor had ever seen it, Dom began a systematic pummeling of the trucker's face, as if he truly thought the man needed more lumps. He managed a lecture with each jab.

"Only rabid dogs attack women." *Bop!* The trucker's lip began to bleed.

"Size is not always an advantage." *Wham!* The trucker yowled as his nose made a cracking sound.

Several cars had slowed to a crawl now. Honor rubbed her sore neck and tentatively put her hand on Dom's shoulder. He was rigid as oak and didn't seem to feel her touch.

"And next time someone says *scusi*, you oaf . . ." *Jab!* This time, the trucker managed to block the blow aimed at his eye. His hands went for Dom's throat, but Dom brought his forearms up and slammed them outward. Honor, too, went flying sideways, but Dom didn't notice.

"Next time, get out of the way!" Dom stood and rammed the heel of his foot into the trucker's solar plexus. The big man's eyes crossed. He gasped and then went limp. Staring at Dom as if she'd never seen him before, Honor knelt and gingerly felt the trucker's pulse. It beat strongly against her fingers. She rose slowly, almost unaware of the gawkers who'd stopped on the roadside but stayed safely in their cars.

Dom still stood over his felled opponent, his huge hands flexing and unflexing. Blood oozed from his knuckles—his own or the trucker's?— and his sweater was dirty, his lip slightly puffy, but he bore no other marks from the vicious fight. And the trucker must outweigh him by thirty pounds at least and was several inches taller.

A car door slammed. Honor blinked and looked away from the curiously blank violence in her Renaissance man's eyes. Was this how gladiators looked as they fought to the death? Or the de' Medicis as they led their minions into battle?

Chilled at the reminder that this man was, after all, from a more primitive time, Honor caught his sleeve and dragged him toward the car. She shoved him into the passenger side. She felt the fury leave him as his muscles relaxed. He slumped into the seat. Honor paused to look at the trucker. A man holding a cell phone to his ear warily came into the circle of light.

Shaking his head, the trucker sat up. In the brilliant headlights, his wounds were clear—and damning. One eye was swollen shut. His lip was split and bleeding, and his breathing rattled through his bleeding nose, but at least he was coherent. "Bastard! I'll get ya for this"

Honor's sympathy hardened. She looked at the businessman eyeing her askance. "He ran us off the road and tried to kidnap me. It was self-defense. Tell the police that when they arrive."

She got into the driver's seat and stayed on the median to bypass the rubberneckers, weaving in and out until she was back in the flow of traffic. But she was well aware that the businessman had written down their license plate number. They wouldn't need the car much once they were in New York, anyway.

Dom stared out his window.

Honor sensed his despair, but the image in her head of the huge man bleeding and almost

80

unconscious would not leave her. "Did you have to hit him so hard?"

No answer. Dom kept his head turned.

Honor felt in her pocket and offered him a clean handkerchief. "Here. There's a bottle of water in the back."

He didn't take the handkerchief. Honor put it back in her pocket.

The miles passed very slowly for the rest of the night.

By unspoken agreement, they decided to drive the rest of the way through. Dom didn't ask any more questions; Honor didn't offer any more explanations. Each kept to his own side of the car and to his own thoughts. However, when Dom insisted on taking the wheel, Honor paused to verify there were no black eighteen-wheelers in her mirror before she stopped on the roadside.

At dawn they took a breakfast break at a small coffee shop. The pretty waitress smiled at Dom, leaning too close as she set his coffee before him. But when his big hand reached out to pick it up, she saw the blood on his knuckles and hurried off to turn in their order.

Dom put his cup down with a clatter and stared at his hand. He'd obviously forgotten about the blood.

Honor hadn't. "Are you wearing it as a badge of honor or a hair shirt?"

Absently, Dom flexed his knuckles. His jaw tightened. Suddenly he thrust his hands over the table under her nose. Very slowly, he opened and closed them. "Neither. As a reminder to you of what and who I am."

Indeed, Honor saw the strength in those hands. They had the calluses of a sculptor, and a soldier, and a brawler. But she had also felt their tenderness, and their kindness. Acting on instinct, Honor caught his huge hands, turned them over and kissed the palms, one by one. She felt the tremor run through him as she whispered into his skin, "A man, Dominico. Just a man."

A man I want. A man I need. The words reverberated between them all the more loudly because they were suppressed. But they both heard them and they both understood.

He snatched his hands away. A flush high on his cheekbones, he hurried to the bathroom.

Resting her chin in her palms, Honor stared blindly out the window. It was true. They'd been together now for days, and Honor was beginning to forget the miracle of his rebirth in the sheer wonder of his masculinity. He was all she'd ever wanted in a man—strong, kind, intelligent, passionate and wild. And yes, maybe he had a streak of violence when provoked, but that only said much about the depth of his feelings.

Honor watched the second hand go around on her watch. Less than four months now. Four months to last her a lifetime. How could she convince him that she knew what she was doing? That she'd rather have all of him now and be left with regrets, than a haunting wish for what might have been . . . ?

Dom was subdued when he came back out, his hands clean, his sweater wet where he'd dabbed water on the stains. "How much farther?"

Honor mentally calculated. "About three hours."

After breakfast, she started to get in the driver's seat, but he pointedly opened the passenger door.

"You've led long enough, Honoria Psyche. It is not in my nature to follow." Across the car roof, they stared at one another.

Did he intend a double meaning? Those Adriatic eyes had darkened to North Sea blue. But he only held out his hand for the keys.

Reluctantly, Honor handed them over, feeling, oddly, as if she'd surrendered far more than her right to drive.

Hours later, Honor awoke to a glorious view: the famous New York skyline looming outside the windshield. Thank God the trip was over.

Dom had long since lost his awe of the tall buildings they'd passed, but he still had to whistle appreciatively at the twin towers of the World Trade Center. "But why are they so plain? Are buildings not considered works of art anymore?"

Honor was about to explain that contemporary architecture valued function over style when the road angled and gave them a view of the Empire State Building. Dom nodded approvingly. "I like that much better."

"You and King Kong. Appropriate." Honor bit back more caustic words at his suspicious glance, but he didn't ask for clarification. She was still stung at his insistence that she'd led long enough. She'd gotten them safely here, hadn't she? She'd always realized he was, literally, an old-fashioned

83

macho man. But, if truth were told, she knew it was his puritanical rejection of her that bothered her most. Besides, his determination to keep her chaste seemed ludicrous given his propensity for physical violence. Honor would never forget the image of the huge truck driver coldcocked on the pavement, blood oozing from his various cuts and bruises.

Dom had never seemed more appropriately named as he stood indomitable over his foe, having vanquished his own Goliath like the David he'd once represented. Honor shivered, for the first time doubting her wisdom in beginning this quest that could well end in her own imprisonment.

Warily, Dom glanced at her, his long, thick lashes shadowing his usually warm eyes into glacier blue. "Where do I go now, Honoria Psyche?"

The formality was symptomatic of the growing distance between them, despite the close quarters of the car. Honor gritted her teeth. "Would you quit calling me that? My name is Honnie, or Honor."

He lapsed into hurt silence.

"Pull over. I'll drive from here."

Honor pulled Ernie's directions from her pocket and read them yet again as she rounded the car. She'd once studied for a summer in the city, and knew the subway and bus routes, but she'd never owned a car until she moved to Portland. Still, the address shouldn't be difficult to find.

Two frustrating hours, many turns and innumerable traffic jams later, Honor pulled up before Ernie's brother's brownstone. It matched the others on the block, three stories of discreet elegance fronted by lacy ironwork. Honor looked around, but typically, there was nowhere to park. So she left the car in front of the building.

When Dom reached for his own door latch, she said, "I should handle this. I've never met Ernie's brother, and I feel a bit awkward."

Dom shoved open his door. "All the more reason for me to be with you. He could be like that other man." Faint satisfaction colored his tone.

He really was a rogue. He'd used the blood on his hands to keep her at bay, but his guilt certainly hadn't lasted long. Honor took a deep breath and counted to ten. "Dom, I appreciate your concern, but I've been taking care of myself for years now, and—"

The forest green door, the only color on the plain exterior, swung open. A cool, deep voice said, "May I help you?"

Dismayed at being caught arguing on his steps, Honor swung around to face Ernie's brother. This man, dressed in expensive jogging clothes, could be none other than Nick. He was an older, taller, more muscular, and much harder version of Ernie. The thick, curly dark hair and large dark eyes fringed with sooty lashes reminded Honor of Ernie. However, where Ernie's eyes were a soft, mellow brown, Nick's reminded Honor of charcoal. Charcoal slowly compressing to diamonds. Nick's eyes had the same hard-edged clarity. They were both glittering things of beauty and possessed of the inherent ability to cut any living thing into shreds.

Unnerved, Honor stammered, "Ah, w-we just got here. I mean, Ernie sent me. I mean—"

A firm, courteous hand on Honor's elbow moved her aside. "I am Dominico Castiglione, at your service." Dom bowed slightly.

That hard gaze swung onto him. Nick didn't reply, though his thick eyebrow arched quizzically at Dom's old-fashioned courtesy.

"We have traveled days, and we are weary. We were told by your brother that we would be welcome here. . . . " Dom gave Nick an opportunity to reply, but when he remained silent, Dom concluded with dignity, "But he was apparently in error. Come along, Honoria Psyche." Dom caught Honor's elbow again.

She was about to jerk away when Nick drawled, "Ernie owns half of this building, so if he wants to have guests, that's his business. But don't expect me to hold your hand or make you feel welcome. I've met too many of his low-life friends to even care why you've come." Nick rummaged around in his jacket pocket and tossed a set of keys at Dom. "Top floor's yours as long as you need it, provided you follow the rules. What rent you pay's up to Ernie."

Honor felt Dom bristling beside her like a cock confronted by a banty rooster crowing for a fight. But Nick's rudeness irked her, too. Instead of jerking away, she latched on to Dom's tense arm, afraid he'd lunge first and think later. "What rules?"

"No wild parties, no drugs, no overnight guests or pets. No trespassing on my floors unless invited. And you won't be."

Well, really! If she'd had the money for a hotel, Honor would have spit his grudging offer back in his face. But since her account was frozen, as she'd discovered when she'd tried to withdraw money on the trip, she had exactly ten dollars left for them to live on until they could find jobs. "What did Ernie tell you about us?"

"Usual sob story. Hey, don't look so hurt. I got nothing against you personally, but I've had too many of Ernie's friends steal from me and drag him into trouble to rely on his judgment of character."

At least he apparently didn't know that she and Ernie had worked together. That was just as well. And since she didn't disagree about Ernie's assessment of character, she could understand why Nick was less than delighted with his unwanted new guests.

Nick glanced at the curb. "That looks like Ernie's car."

Honor swallowed.

Dom glared. "We did not steal it."

Nick made a noncommittal grunt in his throat. "Probably gave you the shirt on your back, too."

Dom pinkened to match said shirt.

Nick rolled his eyes and said something that sounded like *"Pendejo."*

Honor remembered that Ernie had a Spanish father and an Italian mother. A fiery combination, but she still didn't like hearing Ernie's own brother call him an idiot.

Zipping his jacket up with spare, decisive movements, Nick brusquely pointed up the street at a garage. "We own three spots. You can have thirty-three, but thirty-one and-two are mine.

You keep to your space and I'll keep to mine, and we'll get along just fine."

Dom muttered beside her in a spate of Italian Nick ignored and Honor pretended not to hear.

Nick brushed past them to begin jogging up the street. He jogged backward in place for a few steps so he could keep his voice low as he added ominously, "Oh, and one more thing. You break any laws and I'll haul you down to the precinct myself." White teeth flashed in his swarthy face, but the smile sent a chill down Honor's spine as he added, "I used to be a cop, and I can scent scum a mile away." He turned around and loped up the street with a rangy, effortless stride, disappearing around a building.

Blinking, Dom stared after him. "The people in your time make no sense to me. Even Michelangelo was not so rude to guests, whether he knew them or not. And where does he go? He doesn't seem like he's in a hurry, yet he runs."

Too tired to explain the concept of jogging, Honor rubbed her aching temples. Ernie had deliberately withheld the information that Nick used to be a cop. Still, Nick's apparent hostility could be a blessing in disguise.

At least they wouldn't have to see him much.

Chapter Four

The moment she had walked in, Honor realized
the top-floor apartment must have been Ernie's.
Ernie's taste was evident in the elegant furnish-
ings and the warm decor mixing cranberry, forest
green and navy. The Tiffany-style wall sconces
and Art Deco posters accented the genteel shabbi-
ness of the antique furniture. However, the artful
ambience was overlaid by an equal layer of dust
and neglect. Honor stuck her finger in a cigarette
burn on the couch. And the spindly Sheraton-
style coffee table had a frosty ring where someone had carelessly set a glass. Honor could see
that the previous tenants had not kept the place
in proper repair, and she began to understand
Nick's hostility.

"Dom, we need to give the place a thorough cleaning before we start looking for jobs." Honor took off her jacket and rolled up her sleeves. "You can have the larger bedroom. I like the smaller one better any . . . " She trailed off. Dom was nowhere to be found.

Honor went into the larger bedroom. Her bags sat there. She peeked into the smaller room, but Dom's toiletry case, which she'd bought him on the trip, wasn't there, nor was his slingshot, which he seldom let out of his sight.

Honor was about to go look for him when she heard a slight thumping above her head. Following the sound, she found a spiral staircase that led upward. She climbed, emerging at the top into a huge studio flooded with light.

Dom was in the process of wrestling a mattress to the floor. He must have brought up a small table and a couple of chairs while she was freshening up in the bathroom.

Honor swallowed, forcing her voice to an even tempo despite the thumping of her heart. "Ah, what are you doing?"

Walking to the huge wall of windows flanking one wall, Dom stood there, his body silhouetted by blue sky and green trees. His response was so low she had to strain to hear him. "It is best that we sleep far apart, Honoria Psyche."

For whom? For him? "But there are two bedrooms—"

"Next to each other. Please do not argue. I wish it this way. I assure you I have known far worse quarters." He finally turned, but she couldn't read his face against the bright background.

Perhaps she'd never been able to read him, as she'd so blithely thought. Perhaps he really was a rogue who wielded his power over women as easily as his slingshot. Now she'd brought him to his goal, he didn't need her anymore and was deliberately putting distance between them since he obviously found her so unappetizing. She'd counted on the close quarters to give them a chance to get to know one another, maybe even to—Honor closed her eyes on her own foolish thoughts.

Dreamer. How could she even hope that one of the most beautiful men the world had ever produced could love her?

Can't turn a sparrow into a bluebird, Honnie. Her father shook his shaggy head at her.

Opening her eyes, Honor said brightly, "Well, that's fine, then. I'll unpack, and then I'm out for a while. See you later." She hesitated, but added quietly, "Until I get a chance to show you around, it's probably best that you not leave the apartment. We have plenty of dangers in New York, too, you know."

"Honor." Ignoring her concern as she'd known he would Dom took a step toward her, one large, gentle hand held out.

Her eyes blurred by tears, Honor hurried away. She stumbled once on the spiral stairs, caught herself and ran out of the apartment, not even taking time to get her jacket.

Inside the studio, Dominico Castiglione gripped the window ledge, gritting his teeth to avoid the urge to run after Honor, to toss her down on the mattress and spend a week making love to her. But he could not. He smiled bitterly.

In truth, his situation gave new meaning to the phrase *honor bound*. He was honor bound not to sully the virginity that had given him rebirth. Honor bound not to desecrate the fragile dreams of a girl who saw him not as Dominico Castiglione, rogue, mediocre artist and failed soldier, but as some impossible ideal graven in stone. Forever out of reach of them both, for that David existed only in Michelangelo's mind.

Dom closed his eyes, but he knew he'd never forget his first sight of her: kneeling at his feet, luminous silver eyes glowing with tears, creamy skin flushed with emotion, thick blond hair tumbling about her fragile shoulders and long, slim neck. A woman as perfect for him as if God had removed his own rib and offered it to him. More perfect for him in every way even than Marta had been, for a woman such as Honoria Psyche was a jewel formed only by the weight of five centuries. She appealed to him, body and soul: her sylphlike looks so appropriate to her name, her logical mind, her kindness. . . .

Her loving, jealously guarded heart.

It was the supreme irony that he'd found his perfect mate five hundred years too late.

Or, more likely, God's plan. Punishment for his sins. Penitence beyond any a priest could imagine.

Opening his eyes, Dom stared at his own shadowy reflection in the window glass. The slanted light gave him a too-long nose, a bulbous forehead and a twisted mouth that formed a truer image than the perfect face and body Honor had idealized. She was not the first woman to gauge him by looks alone. He'd seldom met a woman who wouldn't warm his bed the second he crooked a finger at her. During those last grim months, he'd almost worn himself out clutching a warm bottle in one hand and a warm body in the other.

In a time devoted to the depiction of angels and man's nobility, he had been considered unusually handsome. Even Michelangelo had been envious of the looks Dom considered more curse than blessing. From childhood to the night of the punishment, Dom had fought to prove he was more than a pretty face. By the time he reached sixteen he was already arrogant, eager to fight, not flee; his soldiering duties had come easily to him.

Too easily. Dom stared down at his scraped knuckles. He'd left a trail of black eyes and broken noses behind him as he moved about Italy. Now he'd come five hundred years and half a world away, and still couldn't stifle his rage at being called pretty.

In this new reality, he must learn the control that had always eluded him back home. From what he'd already seen on that box of moving pictures and of the suggestive way modern women dressed, he had a shrewd suspicion that Honor was right. She was even more of an anomaly here than she would have been in his own time. Virginity in 1999 was cast aside as easily as a tight garment, cheapening both the giver and the recipient. But Dominico Castiglione was not a product of this "modern" age.

Precisely because he'd lived so wickedly, he knew the true value of virtue.

He honored this amazing young woman with every particle of his being, and he could not follow his baser instincts and tarnish those foolish dreams that seemed so important to her.

Saddened beyond measure, Dom muttered a quick paternoster, his head bowed. Even as he prayed, he knew he had no one but himself to blame for this predicament.

To want, not touch.

To love, not stay.

In less than four months, he'd either be gone from this wondrous, troubling place, or lost to himself and humanity forever. Should he succeed in his quest, he'd have no choice but to leave Honor behind. Already he missed the dirt roads, the daily fruit market, the quarrelsome nobles, the stench and bustle of his own time. Though he could marvel at the technological wonders Leonardo and other visionaries had dreamed of, he could also see that the nature of man had changed little.

And not for the better, if that oaf in the enormous vehicle was an example.

He could no more adjust to this time than Honor could adjust to his, even if he followed his heart's desire and tried, somehow, to take her with him. She would never fit in the Renaissance. She was too smart, too logical, too stubborn to pretend to be a woman of the Middle Ages. She was so tiny, and he would never forgive himself if she died having a baby, as so many women did.

Dom raised his head from his prayer and

stared blindly out the window. An enormous jet roared across the sky, leaving a blistering trail to mark its path like a fire-breathing creature of legend. Dom laid his hand flat against the glass, smiling wistfully as he visualized Michelangelo's expression were he here to see the sight.

The jet disappeared behind a cloud. Sighing, Dom turned away from the bright possibilities. He had been given a great gift that many of his contemporaries would have killed for, but Dominico Castiglione felt the weight of five centuries pressing down on him. The angel had warned him this would be the most critical trial of his life, and that the choices he made here would affect the future of humanity itself. He had failed at so many things. This time he had to be strong. For Honor's sake, though she did not know it.

Far better that he hurt her now than leave her, possibly carrying his child, in a few months. Her heart was too pure, her morals too fine, for him to sully her without a second thought as he had so many others. The fact that she would gladly fall into his arms made his task all the harder. He grimaced, rubbing the ridge in his pants that rose urgently in response to his thoughts. He'd have to find a woman soon if he were to master this guttearing desire for his sweet little sylph. Surely there were still prostitutes in this century.

But that required money.

Tired of his grim thoughts, Dom hurried down the stairs. This maudlin regret accomplished nothing. If he were to find his descendant, he'd best get started. As to Honor's fear for his safety, well, that was ridiculous. He knew exactly what he was doing and how to avoid any unpleasantness.

As if his thoughts had conjured him, their unpleasant landlord ascended the joint stairs as Dom went down to the ground floor. Automatically polite, Dom stood aside to give Nick more room.

Nick rubbed a towel over his wet head, his broad shoulders heaving as he panted, and stared at his new tenant. "Settled in yet?"

"Tolerably. The apartment is quite lovely."

"See it stays that way." Nick brushed past him and went up to the second-story level.

Dom continued out, shaking his head. Everyone in this century seemed to be unpleasant, with the exception of Honor and her friend Ernie.

At street level, Dom paused to look both ways. More buildings that looked exactly alike, more of the four-wheeled contraptions called cars. Far down the street, Dom saw a broader avenue crowded with yet more cars, honking, jockeying for position in the cramped roadway.

In some ways this city reminded him more of home than the other place Honor had lived in. Instead of horses and carts there were cars, but people still meandered along crowded streets. They still carried bags full of food or clothing. The streets were packed with pedestrians. At the end of the block that opened onto a broader avenue, he even saw a bearded troubador singing and strumming a strange type of mandolin.

Feeling at ease for the first time since his rebirth, Dom wended his way into the flow of humanity and disappeared.

* * *

Honor had always been amazed that a great city was the best place in the world to be alone. Surrounded by people, all busy with their own agendas, Honor might have been faceless for all the heed they paid her tearstained cheeks and red eyes. But slowly, anonymity began to make her feel strong, as it had the first time she came here. People who learned to navigate New York safely and swiftly could find their way virtually anywhere in the world.

First Honor wandered Fifth Avenue, window-shopping as she had so often that lonely summer years ago. She watched Chanel-suited women and Armani-attired men rush in and out of Saks, but this time she felt no envy. Even if she someday became rich, she'd not spend outrageous sums on clothes or jewels or cars. She'd rather have one cashmere jacket she could mix and match with than a closet full of St. John. What Honor Fitzhugh wanted and needed most could not be purchased. She was tired of feeling like an outcast.

She wanted a home. Children. A man who loved her as much as she loved him. A career among the art objects she adored. Then she could be content, no matter if she lived in a hovel or a mansion. And yet, at this moment, those things had never seemed so out of reach, in view of her obsession with an impossible relationship. Honor swallowed harshly and swung about to hurry against the throng.

Impulsively, she counted the change in her pocket and took the subway. Where, it didn't really matter. No one at the apartment would miss her. She sat next to a tiny woman holding a huge shopping bag. The woman returned her smile readily enough, easing sideways to allow Honor to sit next to the window. Long after the older woman got off, Honor stayed put, listening to the clickety-clack, seeing the light-dark patches leading from tunnels to way stations as she traveled in and out of the bowels of New York City. Slowly, Honor put her despair into proper perspective.

Dom didn't want her. So? It wasn't the first time, and wouldn't be the last, that she'd wanted something she couldn't have. Perhaps his rejection was a blessing in disguise. Just as her isolation and alienation as a child had given her the strength to claw her way to a success few in her family had attained, maybe Dom's distaste of her would lead to better things.

He'd be gone, one way or another, in a few months, and he obviously had no desire to take her with him, even if such an unlikely thing were possible. She wasn't too sure she wanted to live in the Renaissance, anyway. As an art historian, Honor knew far more about the period than most. And while it had yielded some of the finest art and greatest minds the world had ever known, it was still a brutish time of disease, famine, prejudice, and warfare.

But oh, how she would miss him. At this moment she wished passionately that she'd never gone back for that last good-bye. The thought had scarcely escaped her before she smiled sadly. *Liar.* Even if she would never be brave enough to

love again, she was still glad that God had sent
him to her.

Honor swallowed her tears, her eyes blurring
on the name of the upcoming stop. The bold
block letters seemed to blink at her. The thought
leaped full-blown into her head: perhaps Dom
wasn't the only one sent on a mission. Maybe her
role in all this had been preordained, too. Why
else had all the labyrinthine tracks in New York's
subway system led her here?

She followed the escalator up to street level and
stared at the massive building. The creamy stone
seemed to glow like a beacon in the mellow fall
light, and the massive pillars had never been
more lordly. Colorful banners flapped in the
breeze. A steady stream of patrons dashed up and
down the steps.

In a rush that made her ears roar, hope surged
in Honor's heart again.

Answers lie within, the enormous windows
seemed to say with sly winks. Somehow, there
had to be a way to save Dom and preserve her
career.

Honor joined the stream of traffic entering the
Metropolis Museum.

Dom listened attentively to the strange drummers
set up on the edge of a vast parkland. The men
were of African blood, and many wore their hair
in a manner Dom had never seen, but he found
their braids quite attractive. The sounds they
made with their barrels and kettles were nothing
short of amazing. They soon had the admiring

crowd stomping their feet and clapping their hands. Dom noted that some in the crowd tossed coins and even a few bills into a bucket, and he realized that the talented musicians likely lived on these meager earnings. Remembering the many times he would not have eaten without the kindness of patrons, Dom searched his pockets. He had only what Honor had called a quarter, change from a cup of coffee.

He waited until the crowd had dissipated, and then went to the bucket. He tossed the quarter in. One of the drummers paused in the task of collecting his sticks and music. He glared. "Keep your money, if that's all you got, man. I hate chickenshit PC hypocrites like you."

Too proud to admit that was all he had, Dom returned the big fellow's glare. He wasn't exactly sure what the man had said, but the insult rang loud and clear. The man bent, retrieved Dom's quarter and tossed it back. Dom caught it deftly. He weighed the heavy silver coin in his hand, considering throwing it at the man's face. Instead he clasped it tightly and stalked away.

Why were people so hostile here, especially to those different from themselves? In Florence, though the nobility seldom mingled with peasants, the streets were great levelers. Mud spattered blue-and red-blooded folk alike, and it wasn't unusual to see a lord converse with and even patronize traders far below his station.

Here, the rich folk seemed to stay on the broader avenues and cleaner streets, totally ignoring those poor souls who slumbered beneath park benches or huddled on street grates for warmth. Strange. Dom shook his head.

Charity had apparently not advanced as much as science.

Dom wandered the outskirts of the vast greensward that seemed central to the huge, bustling city. He was glad to see boys flying kites and young families feasting on suppers partaken on the grass. Simple joys, at least, had not changed that much. Dom was across the street from a huge building of creamy stone with bright banners-advertising strange names when he heard a distinctive *svttt!* sound he recognized. From the corner of his eye, he saw a small man cross the street, staring at him pointedly.

Ignoring the man's curiosity, Dom loped into a run, following the sound behind a copse of trees to an open area that had been roped off. To his delight, he found an archery contest in progress. A huge poster listed a series of cash prizes, while two men jotted down scores in a tally book, as solemn as if a knighthood hung in the balance. Another man passed out leaflets touting membership in an archery club.

Dom watched for a while. Half the archers were boys, a few were women, but only two men lifted, aimed and fired with the fluid grace of true marksmen. Dom went to get in line where the bows and arrows were passed out, but then he noted that each person offered a bill for the entry fee. His heart sank. He turned away, coming face-to-face with the man who had followed him.

He was a small, rotund individual with a coif of silvery hair and an odd tie in the shape of a bow.

"Do I know you?" the little man asked. "You look very familiar."

"I do not believe so. Now, if you will excuse me—"

"Italian, huh?" The man switched to Italian. "What brings you to the Big Apple?"

Big Apple? Dom had seen no apple carts since arriving, large or otherwise. "Ah, I am seeking a relative of mine. Now, please, I must—"

The man blocked the path as Dom tried to walk around him. "Tell you what, if you'll model for my art class, I'll see what I can do to help."

"Model?"

"Yes. Pose nude."

Blood rushed to Dom's head. Before he paused to think, he picked the officious little fellow up under the arms and set him down, none too gently, off the path and out of his way.

The man's pudgy little mouth worked, and his plump breast puffed out like a pouter pigeon's. He said with a squawk; "An 'excuse me, please' would do."

"*Scusi,*" Dom barked, veering toward the street. He heard another *svttt!* and spared a last, longing look over his shoulder, but he had a flyer in his pocket. Perhaps after he earned the entry fee, he could try another day.

The little man's eyes narrowed on Dom's torn, dirty sweater. "I'll spot you the fee."

Dom froze. Did he mean what he seemed to imply?

"If you'll agree to model for my class, one night only, that is."

Fists clenched, Dom swung on him again. He had no idea how many people over the centuries had viewed Michelangelo's statue. However, he had a shrewd notion how many gawkers had been in the audience when Honor literally unveiled him. He had no desire to put his privates on display again.

But then the little man pulled a bill from his pocket and waved it under Dom's nose. Dom glanced over his head to see the two best archers apparently tied in score, preening before an admiring crowd.

Feeling alive and himself for the first time since his rebirth, Dom recklessly snatched the bill. "Very well. But if I win, I'll double your sum, and I don't have to model."

The pudgy mouth smirked. "Done." Blatant skepticism oozed from the little fellow as he trotted behind Dom.

Dom smiled grimly to himself. *Good.* It wouldn't be the first time his looks had caught an opponent off guard.

Dom plunked the entry fee down and selected a bow. He almost fell over when he felt how light it was. He reverently smoothed the feathers and sighted down the arrow, which was likewise both very hard, yet very smooth. This arrow was not made of wood, but it wasn't heavy enough to be any metal he knew. Dom was sent to the edge of the barrier for a couple of practice shots.

He was astounded at how light the apparatus

was, and he used too much force the first two times. Both shots went wide. He glanced over his shoulder. The rotund little man stared back innocently, but he couldn't hide his gleeful anticipation.

Scowling, Dom took a deep breath. He hefted the bow, learning its weight and resiliency. This would be his last practice shot. Notching the arrow in place, Dom lifted the bow in one smooth motion, sighted along it, and slowly, evenly, pulled the arrow back. The bowstring grew taut, quivering with a life and vibrancy Dom enjoyed feeling almost as much as a woman's skin. Dom released the arrow, watching as it embedded itself with a solid thunk. The arrow quivered dead center in the bull's-eye.

Dom smiled over his shoulder at his now glum patron and waited for his cue to shoot again. He glanced at the prize board. He had no idea how much money five hundred dollars was. He hoped it was a lot.

More optimistic, Honor hurried down the steps. She had several sources of David statues scribbled on a piece of paper, courtesy of the museum's art shop. If she could find one the right size, and earn the fortune it would require to pay for it, she might get out of this yet without going to jail. Even better, she'd landed a job as a waitress in the museum café. Actually working here, she could keep her ear to the ground for gossip. The world's art community was paradoxically both vast and tiny. Since the advent of the Internet, news traveled in seconds, not days. Maybe she'd get some warning if the New York police started looking for them.

She wrinkled her nose as a less welcome thought tugged at her. There was always the chance she could run into Trotterman, but she doubted the great man would fraternize with the huddled masses. Even if he did venture in, he probably wouldn't recognize her. With her hair scraped back, wearing an apron and uniform, she'd look appropriately dowdy.

The sun was lowering in the sky, and she still had to find a pawnshop so she could scrounge up enough cash for them to eat until her first pay-check. She'd turned toward the subway when a loud burst of applause and cheers from the park caught her attention.

Ever curious, she decided she had a moment to see what was going on in Central Park. Dom wouldn't miss her anyway. Gloom hovered over her again. To distract herself, she hurried toward a copse of trees. People were crowded around a roped-off area in a clearing. She jumped up and down, but couldn't see much except that it was an archery contest. She moved to a different angle to get a better view.

And then the slanting sun lovingly caressed an unusual head of hair that wasn't quite auburn or gold or brown, but a luxurious combination of the three. A head that towered over most of the gawkers. Honor's hand crept to her throat. She wasn't quite ready to see him again, especially so unexpectedly.

Dom? What was he doing here? She began inching through the curious throng. "Pardon me. . . .

Excuse me." One foot closer, two. Finally she could see that Dom stood at the center of the barrier, aiming for the farthest target. It was so far behind the other two targets that it looked as though it had recently been moved specifically for Dom. A rise and a large pond stretched behind the targets.

"No way will he hit it," said one young man to another. They each loosely held bows in their hands, so Honor assumed they must be Dom's competition. They watched tensely as Dom released the arrow.

It hurtled through space like a guided missile, *thwonk*ing loudly. Honor squinted. She could barely make the arrow out, but she thought it had landed just off center of the bull's-eyes.

Two men at a table adjacent to the barricade huddled over a tally sheet. One looked up. "That puts Mr. Castiglione ahead, guys, unless you can hit the bull's-eye."

One young man moved up to the barricade, took a deep breath, aimed and fired. His arrow went wide, missing the target. The second man's arrow fell to the ground before reaching the target.

The scorekeeper stood and lifted Dom's hand. "And the winner is Mr. Castiglione from Italy!"

Applause and cheers sounded. Dom bowed graciously. Several young women in the crowd smiled at him flirtatiously, but he seemed oblivious. The needling smile Honor was familiar with zoomed in on someone facing him—a pudgy little man with upstanding gray hair. Honor's breath caught. As Dom moved to accept his prize, the little man turned in profile to her.

Honor gasped and ducked behind a tall hedge. Of all the people in New York, why did Dom have to run across Bruno Trotterman? If anyone would recognize Dom, it would be an art expert like Bruno. She cursed the impulse that had led them each to the section of Central Park behind the museum.

From a scraggly patch in the thick hedge, Honor watched as Dom pocketed his prize. Honor wonded if it was just a certificate or cold, hard cash. She stayed put as the two men walked closer and stopped, apparently to conclude some kind of transaction. Dom pulled a few bills out of his pocket and looked at them uncertainly. Bruno's hand was held out. Abruptly, light dawned. Bruno must have given Dom the entry fee, and now Dom was paying him back.

Honor closed her eyes, unable to watch. He didn't understand their money system, coming from a time when only coins were used. If Bruno wasn't suspicious of Dom already, he would be in a few seconds. . . .

Dom fumbled with the wad of bills. The one the patron gave him was marked with a two and a zero, but he couldn't find one marked with a four and a zero, so he offered one marked with a five and a zero instead. The little man grumpily pocketed the bill. One hand went behind his butt to a back pocket, but when Dom didn't speak, he paused.

The man's calculating blue eyes narrowed again. "Now how much would that be that I owe you?"

Colleen Shannon

"Ahh, a bill with a one and a zero," Dom answered slowly.

"A one and a zero, eh? What part of Italy are you from, anyway, never to have seen American money?" The man pulled a small black leather case from his pocket and offered Dom a bill.

Eager to get back and show Honor his winnings, Dom didn't glance at it, sticking all the money inside his shirt pocket beneath the sweater. He shrugged. *"Grazie. Ciao."* *Except I hope I don't see you later.* Dom heard a slight rustling in the bushes as he walked off. He paused and stared, the hair rising on his neck. He felt as though someone was watching him, but he saw nothing behind the thick hedge.

The little man stopped, too. He offered a card. "If you ever decide you need the money, I'll pay a thousand dollars for one day's worth of modeling even though it's far more than the usual rate. You'd make a great subject."

Dom longed to refuse, but he'd been poor too many times in his former life. Necessity might come calling. He stuck the card in his pants pocket and walked faster, reaching the path that led to the street. He turned toward the lower-numbered streets. To his great relief, the nosy little man finally walked in the opposite direction. Uptown, Dom had heard some describe it.

Dom had barely started walking before a soft hand caught his arm. He jerked away, turning with a fist raised. Honor took two quick steps back.

His hand dropped. He flushed a dull red.

108

"*Santa Maria,* Honoria Psyche! Do not sneak up on me like that."

She bit her lip. "Dom, where did you come across that man?"

"He came across me. In that grassland over there."

"Did he follow you?"

"*Sì.*"

Honor closed her eyes. "Great. Just great."

"It is? Why?"

"That's sarcasm. Dom, that man is an expert on Renaissance art."

"Ah, I see." Dom nodded. "That explains his offer then."

"Offer?"

Both of them were obtuse today. "To model for him."

Honor took another step back. "You can't. He'll recognize you for sure."

Dom smiled whimsically. "So? Do you think anyone will believe him if he claims a statue came to life?"

"No, but they might believe him if he says you and I are part of an art theft ring."

Dom's smile faded. *Stupido.* He had almost forgotten that the authorities believed she'd stolen him. He'd best give the fellow a wide berth, even though the sum he'd offered had sounded high. High enough to pay for an expensive prostitute and also buy the item he needed to begin his surprise for Honor.

They began to walk to what the people here called downtown, toward the brownstone. Even though she kept up a running commentary on the interesting sights they passed, Honor was . . . different. Where before she'd tried to cling to him, now she started away like a nervous rabbit if his elbow came too close. The euphoria at his win began to fade. The problems surrounding him seemed insurmountable. He had no idea how to begin looking for his descendant, and this walking, talking piece of temptation had no idea what she did to him. He couldn't touch her, much less take her.

As they passed yet another tavern, Dom swallowed. He was parched, and not for water. He was tempted, mightily tempted, to spend some of his winnings, but he only got in fights when he drank. He pulled the money from his pocket and offered it to Honor.

She shook her head. "You won it. You keep it. You need to buy more clothes, anyway." She'd been watching the shops they passed, and when they came to one that said PAWNSHOP, she stopped at the door. "I need to stop here for a minute."

"Pawnshop? What is that?"

She held her hand out palm down, and stared at the pretty gold ring he'd admired before. "They'll lend me money on my ring. I have a job, but it will be a week before I get paid."

She spoke evenly to hide her regret, but she was too honest. He pulled her back when she tried to walk through the door. "No, Honoria Psyche. You've already lost enough on my account."

"We have to eat, Dom. And you need clothes—"

Dom scanned the street for inspiration. Down an alley he saw a tiny shop with a sign that said,

RETREADS. GENTLY USED. A suit of strange clothes was in the window.

He dragged her along with him. "Come along. You will help me select something."

When she saw their destination, Honor dug in her heels. "Used clothes? *You?*"

She spoke as if the mere thought were sacrilege. Dom gritted his teeth and stopped short, turning on her. "Tell me, Honoria Psyche, if I looked like that Bruno fellow, would you care?"

Honor looked down.

"I thought not." Dom gently lifted her chin. Even that slight contact tingled through him, down his arm to his gut. He mastered the stirring in his loins and released her hastily, saying more harshly than he intended, "You do not like to be judged on your looks, *signorina*. Offer me the same courtesy." He banged into the shop, making the bell on the door ring wildly, at that moment not caring if she came along or not.

Part Two

"There are more things in heaven and earth
. . . than are dreamt of . . . "
　　　　　　　　—William Shakespeare, *Hamlet*

Chapter Five

Outside on the pavement, Honor stared mournfully at the closed door. Why was he so touchy about his looks? Honor had found that everything came easily to the beautiful. She'd had a few gorgeous friends in college, and boys had swarmed around them. Even some of their professors had tried to date them, giving them easy, undeserved A's. But for people who looked like her, well, everything was difficult. She waited, dreading what clothes he'd select without guidance.

Honor cupped her hands over her eyes and peeked in the window, and was almost knocked down when Dom barreled out. She bolted sideways, out of the way. He had a woefully small sack in his hand and looked anything but thrilled with his shopping expedition.

He paused only to grab her arm. "*Muoviti!* We go."

They went.

She sneaked a peek at his tight mouth and flexing jaw. "What's wrong?"

"Has no one any modesty here? That *cane* actually came into the disrobing area with me." He stopped begrudgingly at a corner, waiting for the light to turn green.

Honor was amazed at how quickly he'd learned to navigate the modern world's version of a jungle, but he still seemed dubious of the customs. "To offer help, maybe?"

He made a scornful, distinctively Italian sound. "Help? He wanted to help me right out of my attire, this is true."

Honor coughed to muffle the sound of her nervous laugh. "Don't you have gay men in the Ren— where you come from?" She longed to ask him about Michelangelo, as art historians had debated the subject for years, but she knew Dom would consider the question an insult.

As they crossed the street, he replied, "Of course. But they are not so shameless."

They started walking past a tourist kiosk that displayed museum wares. A bored attendant looked up from a magazine, saw Dom's profile silhouetted against the sunset, and did a double take. Apparently Dom caught the movement out of the corner of his eye, for he glanced in his direction—and froze in the middle of the sidewalk.

116

Behind, a pedestrian bumped into him. "Move it, buddy. It's a public sidewalk."

Dom didn't budge.

Grumbling, the harried businessman walked around them.

Honor looked closer at the kiosk. She closed her eyes and groaned soundlessly. She'd known this would happen eventually, but now, when he was already mad, was not a good time. Dom dragged her willy-nilly over to the kiosk, still staring at the unfurled poster taped behind the attendant.

David stood there in all his glory.

All his naked glory.

"How many of those do you have?" Dom barked.

The attendant cowered back at his tone, but he quickly counted his inventory. "Uh, five."

"I'll take them all—including the one behind you."

"Don't you wanna know how much?"

"No." Dom fumbled in his pocket, and since he seemed preoccupied in holding the sack of clothes to his lower body at the same time, his movements were, for the first time in Honor's memory, awkward.

Honor's lips twitched. She'd always believed in the alleviating effects of humor, and this predicament was living proof. This gorgeous, chauvinistic, chivalrous mercenary from the past could accept their technological wonders with equanimity, fell ruthless modern thugs with ease, and navigate one of the world's largest cities like a

117

tour guide, but face him with the reality of his own flesh on display for generations to admire, and his composure was torn to shreds.

Grabbing the posters from the attendant, not even bothering to take his change, Dom began to tear them open. Then, systematically, his face set in determination, he proceeded to tear the thick, glossy paper into shreds.

Trash accumulated at his feet and began to blow around. Honor bent to retrieve it as Dom tossed it, but it was a losing battle.

A strolling beat cop stopped to stare at them.

Honor tugged the remnants of a poster out of Dom's hands. She said in a hiss, "Stop it, Dom! Littering is illegal."

He was heedless, ripping into the next poster with brutal hands. She had to chase several scraps down the street when the wind took them. As she bent to snag a scrap, another jagged piece was plastered about a blue-garbed leg. Honor looked up, way up, into the cop's suspicious face.

She popped up, feeling like a jack-in-the-box. "We're not littering, Officer." She dropped the trash into a nearby receptacle.

He kicked his leg. The scrap came loose. Honor caught it as it cartwheeled down the street. The cop ignored her, stalking over to the small crowd gathering about Dom.

"Hey, what's going on here? This guy off his rocker or what?" The cop stopped at the kiosk and rested his elbows on the window ledge. "He steal those?"

The attendant pushed his cap back. "Nope. Paid for every one. Y'know, I've seen a lotta screwy things in this job, but this takes the cake. Fifty bucks he just gave me. Guess he gets his jollies tearing up pictures."

The cop scratched his head under his cap, watching Dom unroll the last poster and tear it neatly in half, fold it, and tear it again. Honor's arms were full of trash now, but she grimly persisted, tossing and collecting, collecting and tossing, keeping a sharp ear out as she did so.

"Well, can't arrest him for that." The cop started to walk away.

Honor's frantic heart rate slowed, but picked up again at the attendant's next words.

"Funny thing is, he looks kinda like *David*."

The cop stopped. "David?"

"Y'know, the statue on the poster."

The cop stared at him blankly.

Looking impatient, the attendant flipped through a glossy art book.

Honor caught Dom's arm and tried to pull him up the street.

He wadded the remnants of the poster into a tight ball, tossed it over his shoulder into the trash can and followed her away. As they hurried off, Honor glanced back.

The cop was staring at an open art book while the attendant pointed.

Honor walked faster. They soon melted into the crowd, and to her relief, the cop didn't follow.

Honor gritted her teeth and said evenly, "We need to be discreet if we're to succeed without getting caught. Inconspicuous."

"I am tired of feeling like a playtoy."

"Aside from the waste of the fifty we sorely

need, you caused a ruckus. I can tell you right now, Bill Gates doesn't have enough money to buy up every image of you scattered about the world."

He stopped dead in the middle of the street. "What do you mean? Surely only art experts such as yourself are familiar, uh, know so much about me, uh—"

Honor bit back a reply as a car honked. Honor dragged Dom across Broadway. Darkness was falling like a velvet curtain about to unveil neon lights—and a very broad stage. Two hookers in miniskirts and spike-heeled boots lounged against a garish doorway, eyeing Dom seductively.

His steps dragged as he stared at them.

Honor jerked on his arm a bit harder than necessary. When they'd finally turned up the residential street that led to the brownstone, Honor released him and said through her teeth, "I'm going to say this once. Your image is plastered on everything imaginable, Dom. Cups, plates, postcards, books, playing cards. You might as well accept it, because we don't have time or money to waste on these foolish temper tantrums."

They'd reached the brownstone now. They stopped on the steps, staring at one another in the dim street lighting. The darkness both softened the masculine planes of his face and paradoxically made him more dangerous. He looked alert, edgy, intense, as he must have looked when he prowled the alehouses of Florence.

He replied softly, "No, it is you who must accept. I am not that image, Honoria Psyche. That statue is the creation of a genius. Some impossible ideal too pure to hate, or envy, or lust. I am but a man. I feel all those things."

Honor shivered at the way his gaze raked over her. Heat scoured her skin. Instinct warned her to flee, but Honoria Psyche had her limits, too. Sometimes another side of her personality pushed and clawed her way out. The same girl who'd once believed she could accomplish anything.

Like winning the world's most beautiful man. She opened her mouth to reply.

But then Dom took a deep breath, and the dangerous look faded away into the darkness. He replied, "As you wish, *signorina*. I will accept that my body is merely entertainment for the masses." He opened the brownstone door with his key and held it wide, arching an eyebrow at her.

Honor swept inside, confused yet again at the difference between what his eyes expressed and what his lips said. He was quiet for the rest of the night, even when he sampled the Chinese take-out food, his expression showing surprise and then enchantment as he ate heartily. She showed him how to open the fortune cookie.

Her fortune read, *Love today, for there may be no tomorrow*. She crumpled it in her hand, the sweet, crispy cookie turning to glue in her throat.

Gingerly Dom opened his own. He read it and barked a harsh laugh.

Honor held out her hand. "May I?"

He crumpled his, too. "No. A little homily I do not need."

After a moment she ventured, "We need to go to Ellis Island tomorrow and start looking for your descendant."

He nodded.

"If we draw a blank there, there's a huge genealogy center in Salt Lake City we can probably access on the Net. I just have a feeling that your relatives probably came through New York. Most Italian immigrants did."

He shrugged, shoving himself back from the table to prop an ankle on his thigh. "As you wish. But I, too, have something I must do tomorrow."

The movement displayed his powerful thighs—and the bulge above them—to advantage. Irritably, Honor rose from the table to clear the containers. To whose advantage? Certainly not hers. Sometimes she almost wished. . . . No, she was still glad he'd come to life, though it was growing increasingly difficult to look, not touch. At least in his former incarnation she'd been able to do both.

She stacked the dishes in the sink, aware of Dom's eyes on her legs. As she poured in dish soap, she said lightly over her shoulder, "I could use some help cleaning up." She extended a dish towel toward him.

He stayed put. "That's women's work."

Honor stiffened. With slow, definitive movements, she turned off the taps, methodically dried her hands and turned to face him. "I've left a comfortable apartment because of you, lost a job because of you, and may never work in a museum again because of you. And you balk at drying the dishes?"

He shrugged. "We will get a scullery wench." He rose and took the towel out of her hands.

122

"You look tired, *bambina*. Go on to bed. The dishes will wait."

If he called her a baby one more time. . . . They were in a decidedly adult situation, and the feelings he incited went past mature to X-rated. Honor took several deep breaths and finally managed, "Servants are very expensive in New York. We'll have to do our own dishes. You can either help me now or you're on your own. I spent enough time cooking and cleaning for my brothers and my father when I was a girl. I refuse to do it again."

Dom tossed the towel aside. "I did not ask you to. I will find a maidservant for us when we can pay for one. You have done enough, Honoria Psyche. I will take care of you." He patted her shoulder.

Honor's bridled passions had grown increasingly restive, and that condescending pat was like a lash to a haltered horse. Her tenuous calm bolted. Honor jabbed a forefinger into his broad chest with each sentence. "I don't need anyone to take care of me. I'm not a child, a madonna, or even a sheltered lady. I'm a woman, do you hear? I choose whom I see, where I go, and how I get there. And for your information, I'm beginning to wonder what the hell I'm doing here!"

He listened intently, his gaze fixed upon her mouth. When she was finished, his shoulders lifted in a deep sigh and his eyes, fathoms deep and dark blue, dragged reluctantly to her flushed face. "And so I have been trying to tell you. I have done many things I'm ashamed of, but never has

123

anyone else had to pay for my mistakes." He gave her a little push. "Go now. To the authorities. Tell them you were kidnapped by the man who stole the statue. It is not so far from the truth. Maybe they will believe you. Go back to the life I took from you and pretend I never stepped down from that pedestal." He stared over her shoulder into a distance she could not comprehend, much less see. "As things are going, in a few months it will be true."

That face, that face. Staring off into destiny, wearing that *terribilita* frown.

Honor closed her eyes to block out the flesh-and-blood humanity of her dream, but that didn't help. It was too late to walk away. Easier to whistle to stop the wind than to turn her back on him. She opened her eyes.

Staring at the linoleum, she said grimly, "I'm not leaving. Not yet. You're not the only one sent here for a reason, Dom. I just haven't figured out what mine is yet. Tomorrow afternoon, after I get off work, we go to Ellis Island. Be there."

"Or be square?"

Honor's gaze leaped to his face.

The frown had eased. He had the temerity to wink.

Her lips twitched. Just like that, he could charm her out of her snit. "Where did you hear that?"

"On the street. Along with, 'You're cruisin' for a bruisin',' which I believe is typically answered with, 'You're truckin' for a fu—"

Honor slapped a finger against his lips. "I get the picture."

He kissed her finger, mumbling against it, "Alas, I do not think you do. I am glad you are not leaving, Honoria Psyche. Though it would be best if you did."

Her fingertip caught fire at the feel of those soft, mobile lips. Heat traveled up her hand to her arm. She jerked her hand away, stuffing it in her pants pocket. "For me or for you?"

"For you." He was staring at her mouth again as if he wanted nothing more in life than to ravish it.

Too tired to chance being hurt again, Honor backed off, her heart thrumming at her ribs. "Well, I'm going to hit the sack." She answered the question in his eyes before it was voiced. "A colloquialism for going to bed."

"*Buona notte.*" He climbed the spiral stairs.

Her room was under the studio. She struggled between gladness and despair as she heard his pacing footsteps, up and down, over her head.

Apparently she wasn't the only one who felt like a cat on hot bricks. In the time it took her to prepare for bed, she heard him traverse the studio's confines over and over. His restlessness fed her own.

After tossing and turning for an hour, she got up and went to the kitchen to heat some milk. As she turned from the stove to pour it in a cup, she glimpsed a crumpled scrap of paper. She picked it up and spread it out. It was Dom's fortune.

A chill ran up her spine as she read it. *Chastity is a pearl beyond price.* She flung it across the room and hurried back to her room, forgetting the milk.

She tried to ignore the steps above her head by reading. Still, he paced. And then, as she tossed her paperback aside and turned the light off, trying to get some rest for her first day of work, she heard the steps stop.

Somehow the quiet was worse than the pacing.

Honor kept switching sides, but Ernie's comfortable mattress felt like a bed of nails. Honor punched up her pillow for the umpteenth time and grumpily pulled the covers under her chin. He must already be asleep, obviously undisturbed by the tension between them.

She glanced at the empty pillow beside her and tried not to think about how much better it would look crushed by a lordly face and a luxuriant head of reddish brown hair. It was not to be. For some reason God had sent him here with goals far loftier than deflowering an impatient virgin. He was determined to accomplish them with or without her help.

She turned on her side, away from the other pillow. After another hour of tossing and turning, she finally drifted into fitful sleep. On the fringes of awareness, she heard foot-steps descend, heard the outer door open, close, and lock, but she never fully awoke.

Until . . . She stirred when weight depressed the bed at her side. A gentle finger traced the contours of her face on a quest that had no beginning and no end. Still wrapped in the swaddling clothes of sleep, like a baby seeking mother's milk, Honor turned to the source of warmth and life and joy.

"Dom," she whispered.

A harsh groan sounded above her. Two rough but exquisitely gentle palms tilted her head back. In the dawn half light, she saw that thick head of hair bending closer, closer. Luxuriant silk brushed her cheeks as his curly locks fell forward, a seductive precursor to the softer, warmer touch of his lips.

He caught her gasp of surprise in his mouth and gave it back to her magnified into a deep murmur of pleasure. At the ineffably masculine sound, Honor's sleepy confusion fled. Dom was here. The idealized companion of her childhood was no longer a dream.

He was a man, showing her with hands and lips his exquisite reality of flesh and form. Proving yet again the simple but incredibly complex certainty that had brought them to this place and time: this was meant to be. Fated whether by the stars or heaven itself, Dom had been sent to end her loneliness.

Tossing her arms about his neck and her fate to destiny, Honor kissed him back. He had a strong taste of expensive brandy about him. A subtler scent clung to his clothes, but she was too enraptured to care.

He had come to her! He wanted her!

The tender caress of his lips barely brushing back and forth upon hers hardened at her eager response. When her tongue shyly darted out to learn the texture and taste of him, he pulled her free of the bedclothes, propped his back against the headboard and tucked her over his lap. His hands now had free rein to plunder her body as his lips plundered her mouth.

Dear heaven, this rogue can kiss.

The fleeting thought was all he allowed Honor before rational thought was beyond her. How did he know exactly when to dip his tongue into her mouth, or retreat to rake it along the rim of her teeth, or to tug her lower lip into his own mouth, nip it and then suckle it after he'd made it incredibly sensitive? His hands were equally dexterous, slipping her plain nightshirt off one arm to trace the exquisite curve of slim shoulder into graceful neck. All the while his lips tormented, tugging, pulling, slanting fully over hers. He stabbed his tongue deep into her mouth in a symbolism every woman instinctively understood.

Even reluctant virgins.

Especially reluctant virgins.

Honor felt the urgency of his need stabbing into her hip. She'd seen him. She knew the size and power of him. But oh, how she wanted that flagrant maleness to make her into a woman at last. Honor tried to turn to open his pants, but he held her still. *"Fermi, bellissima."*

Stop? Why stop? "No, *presto!"* *Not fast enough.*

Honor unbuttoned his shirt, vaguely aware that it was already half-unbuttoned. She buried her nose in his chest. That strange scent grew stronger. Reality came knocking again, but Honor told it to go away. She licked his nipple, delighted when it grew hard against her tongue.

He bolted rigid against the headboard, his hands tangled in her hair. Pleased at his reaction, Honor wriggled her hips over the hardness stabbing into her. He gave a strangled groan, hauled her up by a hank of hair and kissed her, deeply, thoroughly, as though he could kiss her forever and never get it exactly right—but he'd be glad to try, now and ever after. Their myriad feelings were too complex for either of them to accept at this charged moment, so they didn't attempt to.

For a heady instant, sheer sensation was enough. The sensation of skin against skin as he inched up her nightshirt until he could get his hands on her bare back and pull her naked, aching breasts against his chest. The sensation of his rough sculptor's hands, as exquisitely skillful as she'd known they'd be, rubbing a circular pattern over the sensitive nape of her neck, down her shivering spine, to the gentle curve of her buttocks. And the sensation of his damp, warm tongue, tickling the hollow of her throat, trailing a burning path down her collarbone to the tender flesh that fit so comfortably into his palm. He hefted her small breast, murmuring words in his native tongue against the sweet curve, words so explicit or so old that they were beyond even her fluent Italian to understand.

But her body understood.

And her heart . . . On some dim level she'd refused to acknowledge, Honor knew that she did not want Dom because of his beauty. Not even because of the primitive sense that she was meant to be his.

She'd been a truth seeker, a lover of beauty, all her life. And she had never known a truer, more beautiful certainty than this: she wanted Dom because she loved him. In these few short days, he'd proved that he was more complex, and far more fascinating, than the pure, noble man

Michelangelo had so poignantly captured. Dom wasn't perfect, as he'd often told her. He had a short temper, a chauvinistic bent, and a sensualist's enjoyment of tactile pleasures.

And he was chivalrous and intelligent and noble. . . . Honor buried her fingers in his thick hair and dragged his head back up to kiss him, deeply, passionately, with all the joy and vitality he took and gave in equal measure. When she nipped his full lower lip with her teeth, he gasped into her mouth.

Her world tilted, righting as it should have been all along: that face above her, flushed with the pleasure she gave him. On her back, Dom hovering over her, she traced the beautiful contours she knew so well, thrilling yet again at the warm touch of skin instead of stone.

He stared back, his hands caught in the hem of her nightshirt. His voice was so harsh with need that she scarcely recognized it. "You are sure, *bellissima?* It will hurt."

In answer, Honor raised her shoulders, covered his hands with hers and urged him to tug the garment off. Sure? She was pulsing in every secret cavity, vibrating with certainty that she would die if he didn't take her.

Dom swept the nightshirt up and over her head so fast that he ripped it. Honor pulled his shirt off his shoulders, sighing with pleasure when his powerful muscles contracted at her touch. Thrilled that she could make him tremble, Honor traced every plane and angle. Her eyes closed as she memorized his living, breathing flesh by touch as she already had by sight. She felt his breathing quicken, heard it rattle harshly through his lips.

And then her hands were slammed against the bed, her palms open, trusting, as he manacled her wrists beside her head with his hands. "Do not tease me. I already want you so badly that I—" He choked off the words, brought one of her hands down to the hard bulge in his jeans.

Instinctively, Honor jerked away at the power pulsing into her hand, but he forced her back, rocking his hips gently into her palm. With his free hand, he caught the nape of her neck, and his fiery blue eyes burned into her own. "Know that if we continue, this flesh you touch will join with you and make you mine. Neither heaven nor hell can stop it once we begin. Is this truly what you want, Honoria Psyche?"

Why did he persist in calling her that? It was as though he used her full name as a last barrier between them, a reminder to himself that he was not worthy of this woman heaven had sent him. Briefly, Honor was overwhelmed: the feel of him overflowing her palm, the sight of his blue eyes burning into her thoughts, as if he wanted to own more than her body, and the touch of his heavy weight pinning her to the bed. Honor's heart pounded an answer so frantically that her empty stomach began to feel queasy. Despite her instinctive fear, she knew she had no choice.

And no time.

If she didn't take advantage of this moment, she'd regret it for the rest of her life.

She struggled to free her other hand. He released her immediately, leaning back as if he was determined to make her choose, sanely, freely, with no inducement from him. Honor was reaching up to touch him when the rising sun winked through the gauzy curtains. There, low on his flat, hard belly was the clear outline of a lip print.

A red lip print.

Honor's hands fell back. She lifted her head and peered closer. She'd had her eyes closed earlier when she caressed his torso, so she'd not noticed it. Lipstick?

Her gaze flew to his face. He'd glanced down to see what she looked at. He went a dull red, but his proud head tossed back as he dared her to say something.

Honor sniffed. That strange scent she'd taken for the smell of the clean bedclothes was perfume. A woman's perfume.

The passion unfurling in her like a flower wilted on the vine. He came to her from another woman? He knew she wanted him so much she could scarcely sleep, and he went to waste himself on a prostitute? Honor used all the strength in her hips and legs to buck him off.

He went flying to the floor.

Honor leaped out of bed, so furious that she forgot she was naked, and stood over him, her hands on her hips. "You son of a bitch! You come to my bed from another woman's? I'm surprised you can muster up the interest."

He sat up slowly, his gaze unreadable where he sat shadowed by the bed.

She nudged him with her toe. But it was true. He was still hard. "Maybe it's not such a surprise after all. You're the original stud muffin, aren't you? Well, take that gorgeous bod somewhere else. I don't want it anymore. I'm tired of being second best, do you hear? Not this time. I'm first choice or nothing!" She tried to move, but he caught her ankle, holding her foot to his warm, hard groin.

Letting her see that he still pulsed with need of her. "Nothing happened, *bellissima*. I . . . would have, but she was cheap. I could not. Not with her."

Honor swayed where she stood, longing to believe him.

He circled her foot upon himself, saying so softly she had to strain to hear, "You are both my curse and my deliverance. Can you not see how you torment me? I feel with every beat of my heart that you belong to me, but I have no right to take you when I have such a short time here upon your earth. Ah, *Dios mio*, I would gladly pay a lifetime of penitence if only I could have one night with you."

Anguished at the raw pain vibrating in his deep baritone, Honor tugged at her foot so hard she almost lost her balance. At last he let her go, scrambling up. Now she could see his face, twisted in an agony that seemed sacrilege upon features that gave such joy. She turned away, stopping short as she faced their reflections in the bureau mirror. She bit her lip at her own naked vulnerability, grabbing for her nightshirt.

A big hand snatched it away. He stood before the mirror and pulled her in front of him. He forced her to look at their images. That huge, masculine hand splayed flat on her stomach, so large it almost reached from one of her hipbones to the other. "You are lovely, Honor. So lovely you make me ache. An angel sent to punish me for my sins."

Why did he lie to her? She shut her eyes tightly, unable to bear the contrast between them.

"*Bellissima*, why can you not see it? I want you as I've never wanted another woman. But I cannot take you. Not because you are not good enough for me. Because *I* am not good enough for *you*."

Shocked, Honor opened her eyes and stared at him in disbelief.

"Open your eyes wide and see. As I see you. As others see you." When she turned her head away, he gently caught her chin and tilted it up, insisting, "You are beautiful, Honoria Psyche. Not a full-blown rose about to crumble to dust, but a morning glory, sweet, sturdy, who blooms by dawn to give me strength for the day."

When she mutely shook her head, hating her small breasts and delicate rib cage, he lowered his head until his breath made her ear tingle. "I will not leave you until you know this. Walk tall, and be proud, for your body is as beautiful as your heart."

How she wanted to believe him. Mesmerized, Honor stared at his tender expression. As if he couldn't bear the doubt in her eyes, he lowered his thick lashes and scattered kisses on her shoulders and down the sweet curvature of her spine, saying between them, "Dear heaven . . . give me strength . . . to keep you pure . . . For once . . . in my life . . . I must be honorable."

Honor shivered, goose bumps making her nipples go hard, but he'd ripped away the last of her defenses as easily as he'd removed her clothes. She whispered, "And what of *my* honor? Would you keep me lonely for the rest of my life, saving myself for a man who exists only in my dreams?"

His hands tightened about her waist, squeezing reflexively. Slowly he straightened. "What are you saying?"

"I am a virgin by choice, Dom. But surely I have the right to bestow that gift as I see fit."

He released her quickly and turned away, his jaw flexing. "You are merely infatuated with me. You still see me as the *David* in that picture." He paced several steps away and then whirled back to face her, his hands clenching and unclenching. "If I could stay, if I could offer you an honorable choice, I would pin you to that bed and not let you up for days. But . . . I do not know where I shall be in four months. Do not know if I can return home, much less take you with me, even if I dared wrest you away from your own time. There would be no turning back—"

Honor covered her ears with her palms. "Enough! All my life I've been told I should be practical. Not to wish for what can't be." Honor's hands fell to her sides. "Well, wishing brought you to me. For once in my life I'm going to dream of what might be. Let tomorrow take care of itself." Taking a deep breath, Honor held out her hands.

His jeans still bulged, so Dom obviously wanted her. His hands trembled when he slowly reached out as if he couldn't stop himself. He inched nearer, one step, another, but Honor didn't move. He had to make choices, too.

A whispering hope away, Dom stopped. Their fingertips grazed each other's, and then her hands were swallowed in his warm, protective clasp. For a long instant they stood quietly, only their hands touching, while they stared at one another.

Suddenly Honor wasn't ashamed anymore. She pleased him, skinny or not, and that was all that mattered. Her breathing quickened. She tugged her hands away and traced the gilded hairs upon his chest, around his nipples, down his belly to where they disappeared into his jeans.

His abdomen clenched under her light touch. A groan escaped him. Then she was in his arms, her head cradled in one huge hand while he bent her backward like a bow to ravish her mouth with his. Honor quivered in his clasp, longing to fly free. Her mouth opened hotly under his, taking the urgent thrust of his hunger and answering with her own. She wrapped one long leg about his hips, thrusting upward toward the power that would end her aloneness forever.

His teeth nibbling her full lower lip, he swung her into his arms and began to walk back to the bed.

A knock sounded at the door. Both of them pretended not to hear it.

Honor's shoulder blades brushed the covers. Dom followed her down, pressing her into the mattress with his welcome weight while he learned her shape and softness with his hands and mouth.

A scraping sound came as a key was inserted in the lock. The front door swung open.

Snarling a rich Italian curse, Dom sat up and glared at the open bedroom door, his hands still roaming Honor's curves as if they had a will of their own.

Honor arched up toward him, clinging to him. "Tell him to go away," she begged, her voice hoarse with passion.

"Who is it?" Dom said in a growl.

"Hey, Honor, it's Ernie!" came the cheerful reply.

Honor's breath caught in her throat. Ernie always had bad timing. She took several deep breaths, trying to collect herself, and managed to push Dom off and roll under the covers just as Ernie poked his head in the doorway.

His broad grin faded. He went scarlet, his head disappearing as he flinched back and slammed the door. "Sorry. Guess I should've called." His steps retreated.

Honor's teeth clattered with reaction. Her emotions had been on a roller-coaster ride for too many days, and the ride didn't look as if it would end anytime soon. Slowly she raised her eyes to look at Dom. He had his back turned to her, so she couldn't see his expression, but his spine was stiff, and he oozed frustration. Hesitantly Honor reached out to touch his shoulder. He shrugged her off and stood.

"Get dressed. I will fix us some tea and speak with your friend." His deep voice was curt, cold.

The contrast to his earlier passion bit into her like a north wind.

He slipped into his shirt, buttoned it hastily and then stalked out. The door closed with a definitive thunk, as if he rejected both her and the reluctant passions she aroused.

Honor heard the murmur of his voice as he talked to Ernie.

Drawing the covers closer about her shivering shoulders, she sat upright, rocking back and forth in the big bed. Still a virgin, still alone. Still lost in a destiny that seemed increasingly unlikely to include Dom. . . .

Chapter Six

Outside in the small living area, Dom smiled woodenly at Ernie. The effete young man didn't look much like an angel, but God had sent him nonetheless. To give a sinner one last chance at honor.

Honor. Dom closed his eyes briefly, but his hands still felt the softness of her skin; his nose smelled the fresh scent of her soap. She was such a bundle of contradictions: so smart, but so naive, so kind, but so stubborn. Dom forced his thoughts away from what he'd left in that big, warm bed and listened to Ernie.

" . . . told them it was stolen. Didn't know what else to do. And since my job was a drag without

Honor anyway, I decided to come home to warn the two of you in person. Where is she?"

"Still asleep—"

"Wide-awake and glad to see you, Ernie," came the crisp contradiction from the doorway. Honor walked into the room, dressed only in a velvet robe.

Dom glanced at her and quickly away, finding the blank wall less tormenting. Her indifference to him was so studied it was almost comical. But Dom didn't feel like laughing. She was going to drive him stark raving mad—assuming he wasn't already. Sometimes he felt so alienated that he wondered if this strange reality wasn't the result of too much bad ale.

"Uh, hi, Honor," Ernie said. "Didn't mean to get you out of bed, but I figured I'd better warn you ASAP. And since I quit the museum—"

"Oh, Ernie, why? You would have stood a good chance of promotion now that . . . "

Even from where he stood, Dom heard her swallow harshly. Guilt ate at him like acid. Why did the price of his deliverance have to be her ruin? He dragged his attention back to Ernie's explanation.

"I didn't like working there anymore. Not without you. The new assistant curator acted like he had prunes for breakfast and cheese for dinner. Every day." Ernie rolled his eyes drolly. "And I was his first sight after his morning paper."

Honor laughed. She hugged him. "I'm glad to see you, I have to admit. I just caught the tail end of what you were saying—what were you warning us about?"

Ernie's reciprocal smile faded. "The police contacted me. Did y'all lose my car to a drug dealer or something? Some trucker said the driver of my car assaulted him."

Honor and Dom exchanged a charged glance. Dom clenched his fists. *Accidente!* He wished that *cretino* were here now, to be gifted with a few more lumps.

"Great. Just great." Honor sagged into a chair. "Thank God we haven't driven the car since we got here. Guess we can't now. Dom sort of, uh, had a run-in with this dimwit on the way in. He came on to me and, well, things just kind of escalated."

Ernie glanced doubtfully in Dom's direction. However, Dom was pleased that, unlike his brother, Ernie was not one to pass judgment.

"Anyway," Ernie concluded, "I was homesick, so I decided to give you the news in person, see if I could help you guys out. Any luck finding the guy you're looking for?"

"Not yet. We're supposed to start looking at Ellis Island tomorrow. But I have a job as a waitress, so we can't start until I'm off."

"I'll do it for you, if you want. You know how good I am at research."

"*Permesso*," Dom interrupted. "That is very kind of you, but—"

"Aw, come on. I didn't come all this way for nothing."

"Dom," Honor said, "I thought you had something to do tomorrow? Ernie's better at using the Net than I am."

What was this net they talked about all the time? Dom wondered irritably. Dom hesitated, torn between pride and concern for Honor. Indeed, his self-appointed task was very important. He had to get a price on what he needed and then figure out a way to earn the money for it. Doubtless it would be very dear.

Ernie apparently sensed his weakening, for he beamed a smile that, in other circumstances, Dom would have found charming. "That's settled, then! What's the name I'm looking for?"

While Dom gave him the particulars, Honor turned the kettle on and popped bread in the toaster. They were both occupied, but the back of Dom's neck prickled as he sensed a new arrival. The front door had opened and closed quietly, and measured footsteps approached. Footsteps that automatically stepped softly, as if stealth came second nature.

Ready for anything, Dom spun in a half crouch. He relaxed only slightly when he saw his landlord.

Nick scowled at his brother. "Ernie, don't tell me you quit again?"

Ernie jumped up and hugged his brother. "Hey, bro, good to see you, too!"

To Dom's amusement, dull red colored Nick's high cheekbones as he awkwardly patted his brother's shoulder. But Dom saw genuine affection in Nick's large dark eyes as Nick said gruffly, "Yeah, little brother. It would have been nice to be notified."

Ernie stepped back. "It all happened too suddenly. So, you been nice to my guests?"

Nick arched a challenging eyebrow at Dom. Dom covered his grunt by slurping his tea.

142

Honor smiled brightly. "We just got here and haven't seen him much."

"Oh, I see." Ernie glanced between Nick and Dom, apparently sensing the tension, but he only said, "Can I crash at your place, Nicky?"

Nicky? This time Dom couldn't control his laugh.

Nick scowled at him. "Sure."

Dom grinned. Any minute now, Ernie would sprout wings and a halo. "*Scusi*, but that is not necessary. I am sleeping in the loft above, so you can have a bedroom below, Ernie. I would not be comfortable depriving you of your own place."

Her cup halfway to her mouth, Honor stiffened. The brothers peered curiously between Dom's expressionless face and Honor's flushed one.

"Honor?" Ernie asked. "Will I be in the way?"

Her cup landed with more force than necessary on the table. "Of course not. Please excuse me, but I have to get ready for work." She hurried into her bedroom and eased the door closed.

The snick sounded like a thunderclap to Dom. He winced before he could stop himself. He didn't like hurting Honor by using Ernie as a wedge between them, but after this morning, drastic measures were needed. He wasn't strong enough to keep turning Honor away.

Nick's long mouth turned down in a cynical smile. "Trouble in paradise?"

Yes, and we don't need any assistance from snakes like you. But Dom was too polite to insult the detestable man in front of his brother. Abruptly he rose. "I, too, must clean myself for my work today." He stalked toward the loft, but his acute hearing still caught Nick's exasperated question.

"Ernie, who the hell are these people and what are they running from?"

As Dom climbed the spiral stairs, he reflected that he was very glad Ernie didn't know the real answers. He had a feeling Ernie kept few secrets from his astute older brother.

A few nights later, the three cohabitants of Unit B in the old brownstone sat down in uneasy comity. Over dinner, Honor and Dom listened as Ernie discussed his findings.

"A dozen or so Castiglicnes have come through since Ellis Island began keeping records about a century ago. Who knows where they moved to, but I've already called all the Castigliones in the New York database. None of their ancestors came from Caprese, though I did find one young woman who said her great-great-great-grandfather came from Florence. None of them knew a young man by the name of Raphael."

Honor chased her canned peas and carrots around her plate, but she had little appetite. Her feet ached, and she was exhausted. She hadn't stood for such an extended period of time since her college days. She'd also had to duck into the kitchen on three separate occasions to avoid Trotterman when he came into the café.

But most of all, she was hurt at Dom's continual rejection of their mutual desire. "Well, I guess he could have left the area after all," she suggested. She tried not to think of the consequences if they couldn't track this Raphael down.

Dom ate doggedly, but it was obvious he didn't like the frozen TV dinner.

Honor wondered what he'd done with the money he'd won. For the last three days he'd returned late. He was sweaty, tired, dusty—and broke.

Squelching a surge of pain as she wondered if maybe this time he'd let lust overtake his fastidiousness, she added, "Maybe we should try the Salt Lake City database now."

"I don't know, Honor. If Dom's ancestor immigrated a long time ago, that won't be any good, either."

"What of the book?" Dom asked, shoving his half-eaten dinner aside.

Honor and Ernie stared at him. Honor wondered if Dom could be referring to the Bible. Surely not. He thought his quest was foreordained, but this was ridiculous.

Dom wagged his fingers. "This place where you can look up anyone and any business."

Ernie walked his fingers across the table. "The phone book? How quaint. Does anyone still use it in this day and age when you can find anyone easier, and faster, electronically?"

"Sometimes quaint is better," Dom retorted. "Do you have one of these books?"

"No, but my brother does. It's worth a try. I'll be right back." Ernie hurried out.

Tension started with Ernie's exit, growing between Honor and Dom until it pervaded the apartment. "How do you know about the phone book?" Honor asked.

"Someone told me." Dom studied his plate as if

the answer to his quest lay just under his pre-processed beef and limp broccoli.

Honor studied him. "Are you working now, Dom?"

"*Sì.*"

Nothing else was forthcoming, and Honor was too proud to press him further. She sipped her hot tea quietly, trying to ignore the fact that the short gap between them seemed like a mile, growing wider every day.

But the words slipped out. "Are you angry with me about something?"

His startled gaze leaped to her face. Those Adriatic eyes darkened to storm-cloud blue as he growled, "I could never be angry with you, Honoria Psyche."

She was about to tell him he gave a good imitation of it when Ernie hurried back in and slapped the residential pages on the table between them. He fumbled with the thin pages in his excitement, and Dom finally brushed his hands aside to turn to the *C* listings.

Ernie stuck his hands in his pockets, flushing.

Unable to bear the longing in Ernie's eyes, Honor looked away, her heart lurching in sympathy for him. They exchanged a chagrined glance, and Honor could see that Ernie was no more thankful for his reluctant attraction than she.

Luckily, Dom was too busy turning pages to notice their reactions. He ran his finger down a column, reading off names.

Ernie shook his head at each one. "Nope, already tried that . . . Nope, disconnected . . . No."

When the list of Castigliones was exhausted,

Dom shook his head, blowing an exasperated breath through his teeth. "I should have known it could not be that easy." He closed the thick book with a definitive thump.

Honor started. Something tickled at the back of her mind. When he began to shove the book off the table in disgust, Honor grabbed it and flung it back open.

Dumbfounded, Dom and Ernie stared at her.

She paged through frantically, and finally started at *C*'s running her finger down each listing.

"But Honnie . . . " Ernie trailed off, obviously unwilling to insult her spelling.

"Don't you know, Ernie? How often immigrants changed the spelling of their names?"

Ernie slapped the table. "Sure!"

While Honor carefully read each name, Ernie explained to Dom. "The officials at Ellis Island often had trouble pronouncing foreign names, so sometimes the immigrant willingly changed it to blend in with the new society, and sometimes the authorities changed it for him by writing it down wrong."

Honor stared blindly at the tiny rows of names. She was getting awfully close to the Castigliones. . . . She stiffened. The name leaped out at her. "Castigi, Rafe. Maybe that's it!" She stood to shove the book over the table to Dom.

Dom read it and leaped up, poised to go to the door.

Ernie peered over her shoulder at the address. "It's on the edge of Spanish Harlem." He and Honor exchanged a glance. Honor sank back into her chair.

Colleen Shannon

"So?" Dom pressed.

"It's late, Dom. Why don't we just call?" Honor suggested tactfully.

"A call cannot tell me what he looks like, or how old he is." Dom jerked his head toward the door. "Come along."

"It's not a good idea," Ernie said, staying put.

Gripping the back of a chair, Dom stared at them. "You are afraid?"

"Yes," Ernie retorted. "I used to run with a kid from that part of town. He was Spanish, and he still stayed indoors after dark."

"I do not understand. Why do you people not mingle together more? Do you not attend the same cathedral, shop at the same market, walk the same streets?"

"No, no and only sometimes." Ernie's head cocked to the side as he stared curiously at Dom. City dwellers the world over understood the need for caution, but Dom was genuinely disgusted at a concern virtually every modern citizen felt.

Honor saw the questions hovering on the tip of Ernie's tongue. Hastily she intervened. "Let's try phoning to set up an appointment." A minute later she hung up the phone. "No answer, and no answering machine. So it wouldn't do any good to rush over."

Dom's white knuckles took on color again as he released the chair back. "Stay if you like. Me, I go." He read the address one last time, grabbed his slingshot and stalked out.

Forcing herself to stay put, Honor bit her lip. She'd seen what he could do with his fists. But

148

even that indomitable strength wouldn't stand before a bullet. Or a knife. Horrific visions made her head swim.

"What's his deal?" Ernie asked. "Why's it so important that he find this guy?"

"He . . . needs his help." Honor's teeth began to chatter as fear and anger battled with concern and love. *Damn him, why must he be so stubborn?* On the other hand, surely a visit uptown wouldn't hurt anything. Maybe she was being too cautious. It was not like gangs attacked any stranger on sight. In fact, Harlem had undergone a renaissance of its own in recent years. In many ways Dom would fit right in.

Smiling wryly, Ernie watched her try—and fail—to reassure herself. He was up and walking to the door by the time she'd collected her purse. "I'll get Nick."

Honor settled her purse strap firmly about her shoulder. "That's not necessary, Ernie. I'm sure everything will be fine. I just can't let him go alone."

"He does sort of seem like a stranger in a strange land sometimes. No, don't argue. Nick's Spanish is more fluent than mine, and he used to be a cop." Ernie disappeared out the door.

Honor winced as she visualized Dom's expression when he caught sight of Nick. The two alpha males were like sparks and kindling around one another. Maybe, Honor thought hopefully, Nick would refuse to go. She counted her tips from the last three days, praying it would be enough for cab fare there and back. She walked out, locking the door behind herself.

* * *

Dom clutched the seat in front of him with both hands. Necessity had forced him to learn to navigate the bus system, but he didn't like it. The site in Flushing where he'd finally found the marble was too far away to take a cab, and he didn't feel comfortable using Ernie's car, which had actually turned out to be a stroke of good fortune because of the police report. The bus jolted to a stop, wheezing like some beast about to go extinct.

Give him a good strong horse over these foul-smelling, jolting-wheeled carrion carriers, Dom decided. He disliked any mode of transport he couldn't control. Even in the car, the driver had only the illusion of control. One glance away, a slip of the wheel, and a driver traveling at an incredible rate of speed could force you off the road, as that trucker had, or even crash into you. Every evening news picture Dom had seen of car crash victims battled in his mind as the bus turned sharply around a corner, wheels screeching.

The plump lady next to him gave him a flirtatious look through thick, dark lashes and said in strongly accented English, "Thees driver, he is *bueno, señor.* He take me home every day for tree years."

Taking a deep breath, Dom released the seat back only to clench his hands on his knees. "It is kind of you to reassure me. I confess I have not gotten used to buses yet. Do you live nearby?"

To his delight, she gave him an address on the same street as the one he sought. Dom's fingers tightened about his knees. "Tell me, madam, do you know a Rafe Castigi?"

Her friendly expression went frosty. "*Sí.* He is . . . *amigo* of yours?"

"*Sí.*"

Crowding her plump hips to the seat edge, she whisked her skirt aside from him. "He dangerous man, *señor.* You not have good friends."

Despite more questioning, she had nothing else to say. She pulled sewing from her voluminous bag and began to stitch delicate embroidery on a blouse, ignoring him.

Dom swallowed, trying to contain his impatience as the scenery changed. They passed several colorful murals, and some of the buildings were painted in bright hues instead of the drab grays and browns Dom had grown used to in Nick's neighborhood. He leaned so close to the window that his breath frosted the glass.

TACQUERIA read one bold sign. Whatever that meant. And despite the late hour, light blazed from most of the shops, merry music blasting into the streets. On a street corner, a handsome young couple began gyrating to the music in a dance Dom had never seen before, but it was certainly a sensual one. As soon as the bus stopped and the lady beside him got off, Dom bolted after her. He watched where she turned, and then paused in the middle of the sidewalk, inhaling spicy aromas.

Now this he liked. Dom sighed deeply. This part of the great city had life and character. If he was forced to stay in this strange place much longer, perhaps he would move here. He'd barely finished the thought before someone jostled him from behind.

Dom turned, smiling automatically, to be met by three pairs of hostile dark eyes. Three youths, two dark-skinned, one light, glared at him. "Move, *puto!*" said the one who was obviously the leader. Each boy wore strange ink marks on their strong arms.

"Run away to Park Avenue, yuppie man," jeered the light-skinned one. "This is our turf."

Cursing the impulse that had made him shower and shave before dinner, dressing in the second-hand pants Honor called Dockers and a nice shirt with a horse on it, Dom replied evenly, "I will leave when I am ready." Dom wheeled away from them and turned down the residential street. It was narrower, and more dimly lit than the other. He heard footsteps behind him. His instincts went on full alert, but he couldn't believe the youths would attack him so foolishly.

The blow came between his shoulder blades.

As they obviously intended, he stumbled into a narrow alley devoid of lights, people or safety. He almost fell, but, with a quick sidestep, Dom caught his balance and whirled. Darkness lapped at his backside, wolves at his front, but it was a situation Dom had faced many times before. The lead youth, a menacing silhouette against the bright lights behind him, pulled a knife.

The tip gleamed, point downward as it was raised. The other two boys hovered next to him, ready to back him up.

Dom leaped backward, and the knife stabbed air. Still backing up, uncurling the slingshot as he went, Dom peered at the ground, looking for a rock. But the boys followed, obviously scenting blood. An iron staircase brushed him in the side. Dom grasped the railing and vaulted over it just as the knife stabbed again. From his higher vantage, using the slingshot as a whip, Dom lashed out at the lead youth's cheekbone. The hard leather end struck true.

Cradling his cheek, the boy yelped and dropped the knife, blood seeping through his fingers. Growling like the pack of dogs they resembled, the other two boys lunged for the staircase. Dom kicked one aside, but the other kept coming, joined now by the leader, who'd picked up his knife.

A very deep, very calm voice slurred out of the darkness, "Julio, your *mamasita* will cry if you don't stop robbing people. And that will make me angry."

With one step on the bottom rung of the stairs, Julio froze. He gritted his teeth in frustration. "Rafe, you're *loco* again. Butt out. I promise not to hurt him." He smiled up at Dom. "Too bad."

Dom was about to retort that he didn't need help to the tall shadow propped against the alley wall when the name clicked. Rafe? Could it be? Dom peered closely into the darkness, but he couldn't make out any features. And then he was too busy to wonder.

The knife struck closer this time. If Dom hadn't sucked in his stomach it would have grazed him. He knew better than to climb higher, because he had a feeling the grimy window above hadn't been opened in twenty years.

He had to make a stand now.

Dom looped the slingshot over the boy's knife

hand and tugged, hard. He heard a cracking sound and a scream and realized he'd dislocated the boy's wrist. The knife clattered below into the alley. The boy shrank against the rail, cradling his wounded hand, but he still tried to trip Dom when Dom brushed past him. Resigned, Dom rammed a vicious knee into Julio's solar plexus and caught him as he fell. Dragging him down the stairs, Dom dropped him in the alley, fists clenched as he prepared to face the other two. However, he was left with little to do but watch as his unknown ally engaged both youths in hand-to-hand combat.

Their older opponent made short work of them. He used moves Dom had never seen before, kicking with his legs in sharp sideways jabs at one, who dropped a short black weapon with a funny barrel on one end and crumpled against the wall.

The other boy had his arms about the man's throat, choking him from behind. Rafe didn't take time to gasp for air. He backed up and slammed all his weight into the wall, once, twice, three times. Groaning, the boy went limp, falling to the filthy pavement.

Rafe brushed his hair back and enunciated with great care, "I guess I'd better take Julio home so his mama can doctor him again. And you'd better get the hell outta here, mister, and get back to your own side of town." He lifted a still-unconscious Julio over one broad shoulder, staggering into the light.

Dom was surprised to see the large fellow stagger under the boy's slight weight, but when Rafe passed him, he realized why. A strong whiff of spirits emanated from him. Dom followed him out of the alley into the light, but Rafe had his back turned, so Dom still couldn't see his face. Whether he was related or not, Dom had to admire the strength and cunning that made Rafe such a formidable opponent even when drunk.

Rafe apparently realized he was being tailed, for he turned and said in a growl, "I don't need any help."

Under the bright streetlights, Rafe's face blazed into Dom's consciousness like a revelation. It was a strong face, a rough face with irregular features. A bold nose had been broken in one too many fights, but the wide mouth had a full, passionate lower lip. Rafe's bloodshot eyes were the same unusual blue as Dom's.

Eyes Dom recognized.

They were his brother's.

"You got any sense, mister, you'll get the hell away from here. From me. I'm not too popular in some quarters." Lightly, surefooted as a goat despite his condition, Rafe climbed the apartment stairs before him, apparently expecting he'd seen the last of Dom.

It would be only the first misconception he'd have to settle, Dom decided, plopping down on the steps to wait.

For the first time since arriving, he felt hopeful. Castigi was obviously a drunkard, as many of the Castiglione men had been, but Dom was living proof that that failing could be overcome.

Something else Rafe would have to learn: united, the Castigliones were a formidable force.

Rafe needed help, as the angel had said. And family obligation was just as important to Dom as his own salvation. . . .

Honor bit her lip on the urge to beg Nick to drive faster. The souped-up Firebird certainly had the capability, but Nick drove it like an old maid. Even Ernie, who was a conservative driver, grew impatient. Sitting beside Nick, he glanced at his watch.

"Dammit, bro, it's more than an hour since Dom left. We'd better hurry."

"I've already had three speeding tickets this year. I get another one and my license is revoked," Nick said in a growl.

Ernie sighed heavily. "They still giving you heat?"

"Yeah."

The single disgusted word spoke volumes, but Honor was mystified as to its message. Why would the police pick on Nick when he was a former cop? Had he left the department under a cloud? Honor couldn't believe that. Nick was too moralistic and judgmental to do anything illegal. In fact, Honor was growing increasingly nervous that Nick was suspicious they were running from the law.

Sometimes, during her comings and goings, she caught him watching out his lower-story window. If they passed on the stairs, those diamond-hard dark eyes would glitter at her sardonically, and his reply to her pleasantries would be monosyllabic.

When he sedately turned the corner, Honor

gritted her teeth in frustration, wishing she'd taken a cab. But Ernie had insisted that Nick take them, and since Honor didn't speak Spanish, she'd decided to wait. At least they knew where Dom was going.

When the outskirts of Spanish Harlem finally came into view, Honor leaned against her side window. Hoping, praying they weren't too late. But she had a feeling that if there was trouble to be found, Dom would find it.

Rafe exited so quietly that Dom felt his presence before he heard him. Rafe crossed his arms over his broad chest and scowled. "You deaf, mister?"

"No. Perhaps I'm more like you than you realize," Dom responded, crossing his arms over his chest, too.

A snort of disbelief released a cloud of alcohol-scented air in Dom's face. "Yeah, like how?"

It was too soon for the truth, so Dom contented himself with, "I don't take advice well. Not unless it is something I already wish to do."

Rafe brushed past him. "This is piss-poor thanks for saving your life. Can't you tell I just want to be left alone?"

Dom fell into step beside him. "First, you did not save my life. Second, I have a feeling you've been left alone too much. For too long."

Stopping short, Rafe clenched his fists and stuck his flushed face into Dom's. Dom wasn't used to being looked down upon, but he was at least three inches shorter than Rafe. *Odd*. His brother had been shorter than Dom by a good half a head, but Dom had observed that even the women here were taller than most of the men of his own time. He barely had time to complete the reflection before Rafe grabbed his shirt collar.

"The only feeling you're gonna have in about five seconds is a stinging nose if you don't leave me the hell alone!" Rafe released him abruptly and stalked up the street. He turned sharply into a dimly lit building, slamming the door behind him.

Dom hesitated outside, but the whiff of combined smoke, ale and cheap perfume told him all he needed to know. Rafe decidedly didn't need any more to drink, but then he also decidedly didn't know what was good for him. Another Castiglione failing. Dom grimaced. One he shared, alas.

Dom tried to peer in the window, but it was tinted glass. He hesitated a moment longer, and finally shoved open the door. He had to win Rafe's acceptance, if not liking, if he were to accomplish his task. Alienating his relative on first meeting was not exactly the way he'd choose to crack the shell of Rafe's stubborn isolation.

Then again, sometimes a crack on a thick skull was the best way to get attention.

Rafe was easy to spot. He lolled alone at a table in a corner, the other patrons, most of them obviously Spanish, glaring at him. Still, tough-looking as many of the fellows were, they didn't approach Rafe. Rafe slapped a bill on the table and grabbed a bottle from the waitress's hands, not bothering to use a glass as he slurped at the liquid forgetfulness.

Other unfriendly gazes turned in his direction, but Dom ignored them. However, the most unfriendly gaze of all—one very similar to his own—stared up at him as he hovered over Rafe. After another long swig, Rafe set the bottle down, capped it carefully, rose from the table, and tackled Dom about the waist. Both men went sprawling, punching as they fell.

Hoots and catcalls spattered them along with shattered glass as the bottle fell and broke. Dom felt the quick sting of the alcohol in his cuts, but he was too busy dodging brutal fists to pay it much attention. After several blows that made his ears ring, he managed to leverage a knee into Rafe's abdomen and pin Rafe's arms to the floor. Still, he had a feeling that if Rafe hadn't been drunk, the fight would have gone differently.

What manner of man was this? As many vicious fights as he'd survived, he'd never come across a man who used such underhanded, no-holds-barred tactics.

Using all his strength, he managed to subdue his relative long enough to say, panting, "Ten minutes, you listen to me. If you still want me to leave, I will."

Rafe's answer was succinct and brutal. He lifted his head off the ground and, like the stubborn mule he resembled, butted Dom in the chin.

Dom's head jerked back, feeling as if it would fly off his shoulders. His grip slackened. The next thing he knew, he *was* flying.

And unlike the angel who'd sent him on this cursed quest, he didn't have any wings. . . .

Leaning forward, Honor gripped the seat back tightly while they cruised the streets. They'd already tried the address, and the tiny apartment was quiet and dark. Now they were driving aimlessly, looking for Dom's distinctive profile.

A commotion down a street full of bars drew Nick's head around. He turned sharply and went down the side street. They passed a nondescript tavern just as a familiar figure came flying out the window, sprinkling glass and curses as he landed in an untidy heap on the crowded sidewalk. Several cuts on his face and hands trickled with blood. Pedestrians had to dart sideways. One man lost his balance, arms cartwheeling, and fell on his butt.

Nick screeched to a stop. "I should have known." Leaving the car idling, telling Ernie to stay put, he got out and warily approached the crowd around Dom.

There was nothing wary about Honor's approach. She shoved her way through Dom's reluctant audience, fell to her knees beside him, not even feeling the glass cutting into her jeans, and used the tail of her blouse to dab at his bleeding lip. "Dom, are you all right?"

He blinked, sitting up, brushing glass off his broad shoulders. His Polo shirt was ripped in several places and dotted with blood, dirt, sweat and . . . Honor sniffed. She sat back on her knees.

Well, really! His penitence certainly hadn't lasted long. And then that cocky smile blazed at her, squelching the last of her sympathy.

"Never better, *cara mio. Scusi.*"

He helped her up, dusted off the shards of safety glass, lowered his head on his shoulders and charged. A huge, scary-looking man stood there, arms akimbo, obviously waiting to resume their fight.

Gently Ernie drew her aside. "Well, I certainly hope that's not Castigi. You can kiss his help good-bye if it is."

Honor had glimpsed the unusual color of the man's eyes. The sinking feeling in her gut told her Dom had found his man.

Nick tried to haul them both back to the car. "Let's go, kiddies. Doesn't look like your friend needs our help."

The words were barely out of his mouth before a siren howled in the distance.

Nick's sardonic amusement faded. He mouthed something that was certainly a curse in Spanish. "Get in the car!"

Honor jerked away from him. She was angry with Dom, but she still couldn't leave him alone with a man trying to beat him up and police barreling down the street.

Nick hesitated, glancing between the car and the cruiser screeching to a stop. When Ernie arched an eyebrow at him, Nick's face lost all expression. He rested his buttocks against a shop front, propped a leg behind him, and waited, analytically watching the fight.

Chapter Seven

Wryly, Nick watched the two Italians fight. They were egged on by cheering, jeering bystanders. Pretty Boy's face flashed to the side as his handsome nose wrinkled under a forceful fist. But this other Italian was obviously no stranger to down-and-dirty fighting. Dominico leaned back from the blow to keep his nose from being broken and quickly returned an uppercut. The larger man's chin popped back.

All the while, Dominico spoke in a rapid spate of Italian that Nick would have given his cheap gold watch to understand. But then, the meritorious service watch was currently collecting dust in a drawer. The only time Nick pulled it out was on the rare occasion when he needed reminding that ideals belonged with his other outdated junk.

Perhaps that was why Dominico irritated him so. The strange Italian had the passion for courtesy and "honor" of a reformed sinner.

It takes one to know one. The thought crept slyly across Nick's consciousness, but he suppressed it. The only reformation in Nick Escavido's life was his recent vow, so far followed, to quit smoking. He was a hard, cynical, rude man, as his brother so often reminded him—which was the way he wanted it. Twice in his lifetime he'd tried to be noble. The first event led to a divorce, the second to quitting the only job he'd ever loved. So he stayed put, letting nature take its course.

Hell, to be honest, he was kinda curious to see who'd win.

Flashing lights drew Nick's attention away from the fight. Following procedure, the arriving beat cops had called for backup before getting out, obviously fearing a full-scale riot. The first two looked young, cocky, but Nick recognized the rookie bravado. They were both scared, but too proud to show it.

Glancing around at various tough-looking characters, Nick couldn't blame them. They hitched up their belts, one lifting a megaphone to his lips.

"All right, that's enough. Break it up, you guys!" the older one said. "Or we'll all march downtown to settle this."

That was enough for most of the bystanders. They scattered.

The two combatants barely glanced in their direction. Dominico whispered something else to the taller man. Again Nick had no idea what it was, but Honor, who watched tensely, winced. Dom's opponent gave a muted roar, charging. He caught Dom about the waist and shoved him against the brick wall, one forearm at Dom's throat. Dom tried to pry him away, but that forearm, bulging with muscles, was the size of a small tree trunk.

More car doors slammed. Four officers approached, hands warily at their nightsticks. The fighters were about to be pulled apart whether they were ready or not. As the cops came into the bright streetlights, Nick groaned inwardly. Dammit, just his luck. What the hell was Frankie Stanislav doing way up here? When had he changed precincts?

Nick stayed put, wishing he'd followed his instincts and left, with or without Ernie and his friends. If Frankie caught one look at him and realized he knew one of the combatants, Dom would definitely spend a night, or more, in lockup.

Dom was apparently too busy choking, pulling ineffectually at the tree-trunk arm, to realize the cops were closing in. Finally, twisting sideways with his hips for leverage, Dom made his move. He brought up his elbow, clasped his fingers about his other wrist and rammed the point of one elbow into his opponent's ribs. With an *oof* of surprise, the taller man gasped and stumbled back. Dom hooked his foot behind his opponent's ankle.

The bigger man fell to the ground, landing hard on his rump. Before he could scramble up, he was surrounded by police.

The first two young cops grabbed Dom's arms. One wrinkled his nose, rolling his eyes knowingly at his partner. "All right, buddy, party time's over. Time to sleep it off." Dom didn't struggle as they manhandled him toward a squad car. He even had the gall to wink at Honor and Ernie, who watched worriedly.

"But Officer, they didn't hurt anyone else," Honor protested, stepping in front of the trio.

The older cop nodded at the broken window. "They didn't do that either, right?"

"I'll pay for the damages," Ernie said, clasping Honor's arm.

"That's up to the proprietor, but they've been drunk and disorderly, that's for sure," said the younger cop. "Now move, please, miss. You can post his bail later if you want."

Nick listened to the conversation with half an ear because he was more concerned with the fate of Dom's opponent. Frankie liked to shove his weight around, show what a big man he was.

Wearily, as if he were used to being arrested, Dom's opponent rose, jerking away from the cops who tried to take his arms.

Frankie drew his nightstick, meeting that mean, blue-eyed stare head-on. "I know this one. Former navy SEAL, thinks he's still a badass."

SEAL? Nick slowly lowered his foot to the ground. No wonder this huge guy knew how to fight. But what did Dom want with him?

Even worse, Frankie obviously already had a

grudge against the guy. He poked the SEAL in the stomach with the nightstick. "This is Rafe Castigi, guys. Don't ya know him? He's a regular in the drunk tank. Third time in for disturbing the peace. Could be . . . " He poked again.

Even from where he stood, Nick saw that flat abdomen tighten with rage under a stained, tattered T-shirt. Huge fists clenched at Castigi's sides.

" . . . for more than a misdemeanor this time. How 'bout an assault charge?" All four cops glanced at Dom, who was more bruised and battered than Castigi.

Castigi remained quiescent as they cuffed him, hands in front, but Nick recognized that curiously blank look. One more poke, cuffs or no cuffs, and Frankie would be sorry.

The two more inexperienced cops eased Dom into a cruiser. His mouth was bleeding and puffy, but he watched Castigi with more concern than rancor as one cop pressed a hand on the top of his head to gently lower him into the backseat.

Ernie tried to hustle Honor to Nick's car, but she jerked away and came over to whisper fiercely, "Do something! Dom can't spend any time in jail."

Nick shushed her with a fierce look.

Honor went back to argue with the last young cop, who was getting into his car to drive Dom to jail. The cop curtly sent Honor away. Still angry, she let Ernie drag her back to the car.

The cops arresting Dom drove away.

Nick still stayed put, hidden in the shadows. Instinctively, he realized Dom wasn't the one in danger. He wanted to watch and see what happened with the other prisoner before Frankie noticed him. He wasn't sure why, but for some reason he felt sorry for this scraggly, broken warrior. Besides, this guy was important to Dom, and thus Ernie. Nick didn't give a damn about his tenants, but he'd spent too many years pulling Ernie out of scrapes to stop now.

Besides, it would sure feel good to finally nail Frankie.

Nick looked around. The street was deserted except for Frankie and his friends. The other cop car turned a corner, lights flashing, and disappeared. The bar's owner had already filled out his damage report and sent all his patrons home so he could clean up. Only Honor and Ernie hovered half a block away, peering toward Nick, wondering what was keeping him.

When the nightstick poked again, Castigi slapped the tip aside. The cuffs looked like dainty silver bracelets on those huge hands, accenting Castigi's raw power.

"Yeah, I remember you, too, Frankie," Castigi rumbled softly.

A prickle of alertness coasted up Nick's spine. He'd been a cop for over ten years before he quit, and he knew when a collar was dangerous.

And when a cop was dirty.

The two combined were an explosive combination.

Stay out of it, stay out of it, he told himself over and over. *You don't even know the man, don't owe him squat.*

"And I remember the queer you beat up last

time when your buddies weren't looking. And I heard about the bribe you took from a dealer in Harlem to leave his territory alone—" He stopped with a gasp as the stick rammed him in the gut.

"Shut up, ya piece a' turd!" Frankie rapped Castigi's kneecap next, hard enough for Nick to hear the impact.

The stoic way Castigi took the blow only infuriated Nick more. But even from where he stood, Nick saw Castigi's eyes catch the streetlight, flashing to a blue so brilliant it hurt to look at them. The SEAL raised his bulk slightly on his toes and lowered his head, preparing to charge.

Just what Frankie hoped for . . .

Aw, the hell with it. Jingling the keys in his pocket, Nick stepped out of the shadows. These guys already hated him anyway, did everything they could to make his life miserable. It was time he returned the favor. "Long time no see, Frankie. Good to know some things never change."

Startled, Frankie caught himself before the stick could land again and turned around.

That supernova brilliance in Castigi's eyes dimmed to solar blue. He blinked curiously at Nick.

"Butt out, Nick," Frankie said with a snarl. "Scabs don't got no right to bitch at how we do our collars." Roughly, Frankie shoved Castigi toward the squad car. Castigi stumbled and almost fell. He caught himself against a car door, wincing as his sore knee took the brunt of the impact.

The keys quit jingling as Nick responded softly,

"How about a complaint against police brutality instead? You know, just doing my civic duty."

Frankie slapped his nightstick against his palm, holding Nick's gaze all the while. "Go ahead. See if they believe you. Hell, way they look at you in the commissioner's office, I might even be promoted." Frankie jabbed an elbow into the small of Castigi's back as two cops shoved him into the backseat. He went sprawling.

Castigi's shaggy head turned like a wounded bear's, but they slammed the door on his snarl, locking him in.

Frankie grinned widely, his broad Slavic face gleeful under the streetlights. "But you're right about one thing, Nicky. Some things never change. Your word against mine and about a dozen others." He slapped his nightstick into its holder.

"Oh, yeah?" Nick beckoned to Ernie and Honor, who still hovered down the block next to the car. They came forward, frowning at the tension between the two men.

When Frankie jerked his head, two officers shot a warning glare at Nick, and then got in the front seat of their squad car to take Castigi to jail. The last cop, however, moved up to stand next to Frankie, his hand casually on his gun belt.

Ernie swallowed, but bravely stepped closer to his brother. "What's up, bro? They hassling you again?"

"Nothing I can't handle. Ernie, Honor—did you see the way they roughed up Castigi?"

"Sure," Ernie said. Honor nodded vehemently,

but Nick noted that she'd gone pale and tried to keep her face out of direct light.

Frankie covered his unease with a mean bark of laughter. "Go ahead. A fairy, a girl and a traitor against six decorated veterans—"

As if he hadn't spoken, Nick said steadily, "Guess we'll see how he looks tomorrow. If Castigi wants to press charges, I'm sure the DA will listen, with interest, to our version of the story."

Frankie's mouth snapped shut at the veiled threat. His eyes met Nick's as they both remembered the same thing.

The DA had shown great interest in Nick's version of events before. Until the hard evidence mysteriously disappeared.

Politely, Nick caught Honor's elbow. "But it probably won't be necessary. I'm sure Castigi will be treated well. Right, Frankie?" He turned on his heel and stalked away, Honor keeping pace with his long strides in half skips.

Bringing up the rear, Ernie walked more slowly, glancing over his shoulder from time to time. But the two cops only climbed into their car and skidded away.

Honor slumped into the backseat, Ernie into the front. "Man, oh, man, I thought we'd had it. Isn't that the dirty cop you testified against?"

"One of them." Nick drove sedately as he turned the car around to head home.

Sure enough, Frankie's squad car tailed him. The fact that Frankie didn't even bother to hide his presence ate at Nick, but there was little he could do about it, short of scrupulously obeying all traffic laws or filing a complaint as he'd threatened. He tried to ignore the car behind him while he contemplated his next move.

Problem was, as Frankie had pointed out with such relish, it would be the word of a discredited cop, his brother, and . . . Nick glanced in his rearview mirror. And . . . who? He had a feeling Honor would go to great lengths to avoid filling out any statements or complaints. She didn't want her name known, or her face recognized.

Question was . . . why?

Rafael Benito Castigi awoke as he had virtually every day for the past two years: head pounding, mouth foul, with little sense—and less interest—of where he was. His mattress was even harder than usual, and his pillow . . . He took a whiff and almost gagged.

A vaguely familiar voice above him said cheerfully, *"Ciao! Come stai?"*

"Like shit warmed over, thanks to you," Castigi answered with a growl. Slowly, carefully, he sat up, cradling his pounding head. He squinted at a too-handsome face decorated with a too-cheerful grin and considered lengthening his time in lockup with a too-tempting punch.

That grin only widened. "But your—how you say—hangover? would be much worse if I hadn't, ah, invited you to a more invigorating diversion."

Castigi blinked. He'd met his share of arrogant mavericks, especially in the SEALs, where testosterone level seemed to indicate level of advancement. But this blockhead from the old country took the cake for sheer gall.

"If this is your idea of therapy, AA won't recruit

you anytime soon." Rafe rubbed his still-sore jaw. He respected a man who could throw such a deft blow, especially when the jerk was being used as a punching bag at the time. "What did you say your name is?"

A smoky look clouded those sunny blue eyes. "I didn't, but it is Dominico Castiglione."

Rafe stiffened. At his grandfather's knee, he'd heard tales of his relatives back in Italy, how his great-great-grandpa changed his name when he came through Ellis Island because the immigration personnel couldn't pronounce it. But before his father was hit by a car while in a drunken stupor, he'd told Rafe all their old country relatives had died out or scattered to the four corners of the earth. Rafe, Pops had informed him, was the last of a proud line, and he was going to amount to something more than a lousy merchant seaman. Castigi closed his eyes again, but this time the memories flooded back.

For a while, he'd almost lived up to Pops's prediction. He didn't remember his mama much, because he'd been only seven when she died of pneumonia. Pops had sent him to stay with Mama's maiden aunt in an old neighborhood because it was respectable, and had good schools. The fact that he was lonely for his father, who was usually away at sea, and got little attention from his aunt, who had no idea how to deal with a rambunctious boy, carried little weight with Pops. He was going to be somebody someday, finally do the Castigi name proud.

Proud. Smiling sardonically to hide his anguish, Rafe looked around at his peers. One old geezer snored on an adjacent cot. Other degenerates had that glazed, hopeless look of half the people Rafe knew, slumped on cots or against the wall.

Illustrious line, all right. Aside from an old family myth that one of their uncles centuries ago had actually worked with Michelangelo, Rafe knew of not a single Castigi whose name would ever be recorded in *Who's Who*.

Least of all himself . . . The need for a drink grew stronger. Through the haze, that damnably melodious voice spoke again.

"Come, Rafael. Drink."

A gentle hand supported the back of Rafe's head as a cup was held to his lips. He sipped, realized it was lukewarm coffee of high quality, and drank greedily. He couldn't afford Starbucks coffee very often, living as he did on his disability pension, but right now it was the second-best thing in his life.

When the cup was empty, Rafe looked around, his head clearing slowly. Several of the drunk tank's other occupants eyed them greedily, but Dominico didn't seem concerned. He sipped leisurely from his own cup.

"Where'd the coffee come from?" Rafe asked.

"An angel of mercy." Sighing, Dominico set his cup aside, ratted through a sack and offered Rafe a clean shirt.

Rafe was in no mood for mysteries, but he smelled bad enough to turn his own stomach. Rafe hauled the tattered T-shirt over his head, tossed it in the trash, and went to the communal sink on the wall to use the institutional-grade soap. As he gave himself a spit bath, he was aware of the dropped jaws and wide-eyed stares, but he was used to that.

Funny how two years of living hand-to-mouth, occasionally working as a laborer, but mostly stumbling from tavern to bar to nightclub, hadn't ruined his physique. Oh, he still did calisthenics on the rare occasion when he didn't awaken hungover. And no doubt about it, he was in no shape to go back into the SEALs. Even if he'd wanted to.

The pounding in his head grew worse. Memories came knocking again, but, fortified with the coffee and the spit bath, he was strong enough to send them packing. And if the vague thought came to him that he wouldn't keep his strength for much longer unless he changed his lifestyle, well, that didn't seem important, either.

Nothing seemed important, except maybe helping the kids in his neighborhood when he could.

Dominico watched him, his blue eyes sympathetic. "How did you get the scars?"

Rafe glanced down. One on his knee came from a knife fight; another was the result of a bullet graze on a covert op. The one on his side was a shrapnel calling card. The others, well, they were so much a part of him that he no longer remembered where they'd come from.

He shrugged, his chest muscles rippling not quite as impressively as they used to, but still prominent. "You can sure dole 'em out, but can you take 'em?"

"*Scusi?*"

"Questions. For instance—what's that leather strap you never let out of your sight?"

The Italian glanced down at the piece of leather he'd laced in his belt loops to make it look like a belt so the cops wouldn't confiscate it. He answered slowly, "A slingshot."

Rafe frowned. It sure as hell didn't look like any slingshot he'd ever seen. And then a dim memory, a legacy of his Catholic heritage, flickered in his mind. In Rafe's lessons, the biblical hero David had been depicted carrying a slingshot like that.

Another glancing image made Rafe's headache worse. He'd been to Florence once, returning from the Mideast. He'd seen Michelangelo's version of the biblical hero, and the slingshot Dom carried looked exactly the same. "Where'd you find such an antique in such good shape?"

Dom turned away, saying softly out of the side of his mouth, "It was . . . a gift. Why do you do this to yourself?"

The image splintered along with Rafe's head as he turned hastily back to his own ugly face. "You can take your slingshot, your questions and your pretty face and stick 'em where the sun don't shine."

Dominico looked at him sadly. "To hate oneself is to make the worst enemy a man can know. Believe me, this I understand."

A retort rose to Rafe's lips, but then he looked, really looked, into Dominco's face. He glanced from those serious blue eyes to his own.

Identical color. Strange. Rafe had never met anyone else but his grandfather who had the bright blue Castigi eyes. Not aquamarine, not even turquoise. More a brilliant peacock blue when emotional, and dark blue when somber.

"Who the hell are you?" Rafe burst out.

Dominico nibbled at his lip and answered carefully, "A friend."

Rafe snorted. *Right.* He hadn't had one of those in more years than he cared to remember. Hadn't even wanted one. Friends meant ties, ties meant emotion, and emotion meant pain. He'd had enough of all of them for one lifetime.

He slapped under his arms with a disposable towel and hauled the *I Love New York* shirt over his head. His lip curled as he looked at the red heart strategically placed where his own used to be. "Well, you can take your bleeding heart elsewhere and offer it to someone who needs it. Now leave me the hell alone and quit following me. *Capisce?*"

"But what if I need you—*mi amico?*"

The words were spoken so softly that Rafe wasn't sure he heard right. Before he could retort, the door swung open. "Castigi, Castiglione, your bail's been paid."

Dominico collected the bag and walked to the open cell door, but he paused, sweeping a hand before him.

Rafe stalked out, wondering who the hell had paid his bail.

As they signed the release papers, Rafe saw the same strange trio he'd glimpsed last night in the midst of the fight. He listened with half an ear to the drill about not leaving town, his arraignment date, and so on, while he stared at the girl.

She was a dainty little thing, and she clung to Dominico's arm as if she feared letting him out of her sight.

Thrill to the most sensual, adventure-filled Romances on the market today...

FROM  LOVE SPELL BOOKS

As a home subscriber to the Love Spell Romance Book Club, you'll enjoy the best in today's BRAND-NEW Time Travel, Futuristic, Legendary Lovers, Perfect Heroes and other genre romance fiction. For five years, Love Spell has brought you the award-winning, high-quality authors you know and love to read. Each Love Spell romance will sweep you away to a world of high adventure...and intimate romance. Discover for yourself all the passion and excitement millions of readers thrill to each and every month.

Save $5.00 Each Time You Buy!

Every other month, the Love Spell Romance Book Club brings you four brand-new titles from Love Spell Books. EACH PACKAGE WILL SAVE YOU AT LEAST $5.00 FROM THE BOOK-STORE PRICE! And you'll never miss a new title with our convenient home delivery service.

Here's how we do it: Each package will carry a FREE 10-DAY EXAMINATION privilege. At the end of that time, if you decide to keep your books, simply pay the low invoice price of $17.96, no shipping or handling charges added. HOME DELIVERY IS ALWAYS FREE. With today's top romance novels selling for $5.99 and higher, our price SAVES YOU AT LEAST $5.00 with each shipment.

AND YOUR FIRST TWO-BOOK SHIP-MENT IS TOTALLY FREE!

IT'S A BARGAIN YOU CAN'T BEAT! A SUPER $11.48 Value!

Love Spell ⊕ A Division of Dorchester Publishing Co., Inc.

GET YOUR 2 FREE BOOKS NOW—AN $11.48 VALUE!

Mail the Free Book Certificate Today!

TWO FREE BOOKS

Free Books Certificate

YES! I want to subscribe to the Love Spell Romance Book Club. Please send me my 2 FREE BOOKS. Then every other month I'll receive the four newest Love Spell selections to Preview FREE for 10 days. If I decide to keep them, I will pay the Special Member's Only discounted price of just $4.49 each, a total of $17.96. This is a SAVINGS of at least $5.00 off the bookstore price. There are no shipping, handling, or other charges. There is no minimum number of books I must buy and I may cancel the program at any time. In any case, the 2 FREE BOOKS are mine to keep—A BIG $11.48 Value!

Offer valid only in the U.S.A.

Name _____

Address _____

City _____

State _____ *Zip* _____

Telephone _____

Signature _____

If under 18, Parent or Guardian must sign. Terms, prices and conditions subject to change. Subscription subject to acceptance. Leisure Books reserves the right to reject any order or cancel any subscription.

A $11.48 VALUE

Get Two Books Totally
FREE—
An $11.48 Value!

▼ Tear Here and Mail Your FREE Book Card Today! ▼

PLEASE RUSH
MY TWO FREE
BOOKS TO ME
RIGHT AWAY!

Love Spell Romance Book Club
P.O. Box 6613
Edison, NJ 08818-6613

AFFIX
STAMP
HERE

The kid next to her had the mannerisms of a queer, and Rafe didn't much care for the way the men looked at him. He glanced at the taller man next to the kid. Oh, yeah, this guy had intervened last night when the cops were roughing him up. He wasn't too drunk to notice that. But why? He'd never seen him before.

A large, well-groomed hand thrust out toward him. "Nick Escavido."

This guy had both money and the taste to spend it well. Feeling grimy and debased, Rafe shook it brusquely. "Rafe Castigi. You pay my bail?"

"Yeah."

"Why?"

"That's a bit complicated. Let's just say I want to spoil Frankie's fun."

That surprised a laugh out of Rafe. Even to his own ears, it sounded rusty.

"You won't run off, will you? I can get you a good lawyer. Pro bono. And I'll do what I can to see the charges are dismissed."

Rafe's eyes narrowed. These people were killing him with a bit too much kindness. What was their angle?

The kid intervened. "I paid the tavern manager's bills, so he's agreed not to press charges. And since Dom won't prosecute for assault . . . "

Rafe glared at Dom, who'd started the fight by pestering him. Dom smiled blandly.

"All they have on you is drunk and disorderly and disturbing the peace."

"Third conviction, it's enough for some judges." Rafe collected his wallet, keys and comb, shoving them into his pockets.

They walked out together. Dom swung the girl's hand. "Why don't you stay with us awhile? You don't mind, do you, Ernie?"

"Of course not."

"No, thanks." Outside, Rafe lifted his face to the weak sunshine. It was late September, and the wind was already brisk. "I have my own place."

For about three more days. If he didn't come up with two months' back rent, he'd be evicted, but they didn't need to know that. Time to look for a job again.

"We need strong men at my place of employment," Dom said as Rafe started to walk away.

"Which is?"

"Allied Marble and Granite, Flushing."

The girl next to him peered closely at Dom's face, but he didn't glance at her.

"Doing what?"

"Cutting and moving stone. Good for the body." Dom flexed his own impressive biceps.

How the hell had this Italian picked up on Rafe's concern for his own physique? "I'll think about it. See ya." *Hope not.* But fairness made Rafe pause at the bottom of the steps. "Thanks for the help."

The girl took a small pad from her purse and scribbled something on it, then thrust the leaf of paper in his hand. "Our address and phone number. Call if you can make it to dinner tomorrow night. I'm making fried chicken."

Rafe's mouth watered. He'd dated a girl from the South while he was in the SEALS, before the nightmare began. Eating her old-fashioned comfort food and enjoying her for dessert afterward was one of his few happy memories. Smiling stiffly, he stuffed the paper in his pocket and turned toward his place.

The walk would do him good. He felt the usual longing for a drink, but something, maybe just guilt at the trouble these people had gone to for a stranger, made him walk past one of his favorite bars. Besides, he was down to a few dollars.

Could be he'd look up that crazy Italian. Just to pester him. And at that moment, Rafe Castigi did something he hadn't done for two years.

He smiled twice in one day. . . .

Nick watched the tall, powerful loner disappear in the crowd. Even on the busy streets, however, Rafe's head towered above most of the pedestrians. He turned the corner and was gone. Nick had a shrewd suspicion they'd never see him again, and he regretted that. From what he'd learned from an old buddy in Records, Rafe needed all the friends he could get.

Ernie apparently read the contemplative look on his face, for he said as they walked down the block to where Nick had parked, "I saw you go into Records. Find out anything about Rafe?"

Nick hesitated. He was sure Rafe wouldn't want the details of his life known, but he was equally sure that Dom, at least, would persist in trying to make friends with the SEAL. Ernie had explained that Dom seemed to think his fate was somehow linked with this ex-seaman's.

As they got in the car, Nick glimpsed Dom's face in the rearview mirror. Dom watched closely, obviously hoping for any tidbit of information.

Ernie urged, "Come on, bro, fess up. He's a wounded warrior if I ever saw one, but he seems like a fairly decent guy. Why'd he leave the SEALS?"

They got caught in a traffic jam, so Nick began, "When he was arrested the first time, they checked him out. Someone on the force who used to be in the navy tracked down his service record, planning to help him get off. Apparently he was dishonorably discharged from the SEALS about two years ago."

Dom frowned. Honor covered her gasp with her hand.

And Ernie's big, mellow brown eyes took on that hangdog look that irritated the hell out of Nick. If there was a scruffy mutt, a three-legged cat, or a wounded veteran in the vicinity, Ernie would find a way to help. Didn't matter if he got himself into trouble in the process. Nick tapped the steering wheel, beeping on his own horn like everyone else just to vent his frustration.

"I don't believe it," Dom said flatly. "He is an honorable man."

"How can you be so sure?" Nick asked. "You cozy up to him in the drunk tank?"

Dom stiffened.

Ernie cleared his throat. "I agree with Dom. I heard a coupla women talking during the fight. They said he'd broken up a gang fight between their boys, sent everyone home before it got violent. Seems the gang kids in the neighborhood fear him. That's not the act of a coward."

"Never said he was dismissed for cowardice. But I had a buddy in the SEALS once. Minute you desert the pack, they turn on you. I'm sure his mates called him yellow, true or not."

Grimly, Nick reflected that cops and SEALS were a lot alike in some ways. Each member was part of a select brotherhood; if one was threatened, all were threatened. And they were merciless to any member so foolish as to put conscience above duty.

Scab. Traitor. Renegade. Oh, yeah. Nick knew exactly how Castigi felt. The bottle had almost pulled him in once, too.

Dom burst out, "But what did he do to be discharged?"

"Records don't specify, except to say that he accepted the discharge and disability pension in lieu of a trial." Nick's friend had heard rumors, but Nick intuitively knew that Castigi wouldn't want his dirty linen aired even to people who cared.

The traffic finally cleared. As Nick drew into the parking garage, he wondered if Castigi would show up tomorrow for dinner.

Somehow he doubted it.

Three mornings later, Rafe packed his few belongings in his duffel bag, wincing as his head pounded in syncopation with his landlady's screech. "You stinking *cabrón! Vaya!* I should never lease to you. All American GIs are arrogant pigs."

Colleen Shannon

"Yeah, yeah, lady," Rafe muttered. "I'm going. I'll send you the back rent when I can."

A snort expressed what she thought of that. She slammed the door behind him, still cursing him in rapid Spanish.

Out on the street, Rafe turned his collar up in the biting wind. It sure as hell didn't feel like October. Rafe blinked at the trees in the small park he passed. Where had the time gone?

The city was dressed in the full regalia of fall, those reds and golds that always drew him back east whenever he felt like wandering. Sighing, he watched leaves flutter on the breeze, feeling as if he, too, drifted on the wind.

The day he got out of jail, he'd worked unloading heavy bolts of cloth for a dressmaker in the garment district, but he'd sucked that money dry in two nights. Now, with winter coming on, he had no apartment, no job, and no more pension due for almost a week.

Rafe stuffed his hands in his pockets. Paper crackled. He drew out a scrap and squinted at it through aching, bleary eyes. The neat handwriting brought a vivid memory of that strange quartet, three men and one woman, who'd seemed genuinely concerned for him.

Hell with 'em. Systematically, Rafe tore the scrap of paper into tiny pieces and tossed it in a garbage can. He didn't need their pity or their help. If he wanted to wallow in a gutter, it was no one's business but his own. He stalked off. It didn't matter what direction. Having no destination and no goals was a goal in itself.

One he excelled at.

His sardonic grin faded as a destination flashed above the blunt nose of a bus as it drew to a stop at the curb. He jingled the change in his other pocket. Slowly, something beyond himself, something he'd long ago quit believing in, compelled him to count his change. Just enough. The sights and sounds of Spanish Harlem were a dreamlike haze about him as Rafe got on the bus.

He didn't want the pity of that pretty little blonde or her rich friends. But it would be a hoot to go bug that crazy Italian. Maybe they could even get in another fight, clear his head. Rafe cracked his knuckles in anticipation.

Despite the biting chill, Dom swiped sweat away from his brow, leaving a black streak on his forehead. They had him cutting black galaxy granite today, which he hated, but he hadn't complained. The massive cutting tool had fascinated Dom from the beginning, and he'd pestered the foreman until the man showed him how to use it. It had an enormous diamond rotary blade that cut through one of the hardest rocks in the world like butter.

When he went home—if he went home—he'd miss the wondrous tools of this era. Many of them worked on something they called compressed air, and they were more powerful than anything even Leonardo had imagined.

He already had the huge hunk of marble roughly formed. In his head, anyway. Of course they wouldn't let him touch it until he finished paying for it. Which, at his rate of pay, would be in another month. Too long. He'd never have time to finish his gift to Honor then.

Actually, Dom knew of only one way to raise a thousand dollars fast enough. He'd resisted the notion for weeks, but time was running out. Regardless of his own fate, he'd see to it that Honor could return, with the honor he'd almost stolen from her, to the life she'd enjoyed before he stepped down into her world.

He only hoped that Castigi came to his senses in time for Dom to have his own world to go back to. Dom had deliberately given his relative several days to recuperate before descending on him again.

Tonight he would return to that area of the great city that smelled so good and sounded so alive. To try yet again to make friends with a man who needed one badly. And, better still, he would avoid having to talk to Honor. He wanted her so badly now that it caused him physical pain to see her and not touch her as he longed to.

Sighing, Dom drew the helmet down and set the intricate dials that positioned the blade. The high-pitched whine of the circular blade cutting through granite blocked out every sound, even the beating of his own heart.

Dom carefully guided the granite slab. When it was cut through, he let up on the controls, and water no longer splattered as the great blade hummed down.

He started when a rough voice said, "Now you look natural. Covered in dirt and sweat—"

Joyfully, Dom flipped his faceplate up. "Rafe!"

"—and mean as hell."

Dom slapped Rafe on the shoulder. "*Amico,* it is good to see you! You come for a job, yes?"

Rafe eyed Dom's blackened arms and chest. "Well . . ."

Dom set his helmet aside, turned off the machine and dragged Rafe to the foreman's office.

Chapter Eight

Days had a way of marching into weeks. It was October and everywhere Honor looked signs celebrated the new millennium. Store turnstiles rotated continuously. That sound dearest to the heart of any merchant—the *ka-ching* of cash registers—added a subtle beat to the rhythm of musicians, singers and storytellers touting their talents on street corners.

New York was like an aging beauty primping to look her best for the biggest party the world had ever seen. Potholes were filled, vacant lots cleaned and building fronts painted. Even the famous tower in Times Square got the ultimate makeover: a glittering new crystal top made by Waterford.

Anticipation was almost palpable. All the hotels in the city had been booked for months. As Honor walked to work, she saw the occasional prophet warning of doom, but the lonely naysayers were far outnumbered by optimists. Local talk shows were full of debates that, once upon a time, Honor would not only have welcomed, but joined. Where had humanity been? Where were we going? What did we, as individuals, bring to the twenty-first century? Were we to be our own salvation—or our own ruin? As a historian, Honor had asked herself the same questions, finding the topic fascinating long before it became fashionable.

But in the midst of gaiety, she felt only despair.

In the middle of the philosophical discourse she'd once reveled in, she longed for certainties.

Quite simply, with humanity's new chance came her own loss. It was hard for her to exult with the masses when she felt so alone. Even Ernie was gone most of the time, either helping his brother in Nick's security business, or haunting the museum.

But Honor knew the true source of her disquiet. It stood six feet plus, was five hundred years old and living proof that God gave second chances.

Dom had changed everything. She'd lost her career because of him, her heart to him, and sometimes, it seemed, her very sanity would be forfeit when January 1 dawned. These hours that should be precious were being squandered. While she wanted to hoard every moment, he worked late nightly. When he finally came home, he was withdrawn, quiet. Every time she tried to get him alone to quiz him about Castigi, he avoided her. He seemed driven by some purpose beyond his own quest for redemption. He saved each spare dime. Even more frustrating, what was he saving himself for? Why couldn't she make him understand she'd rather have all of him now than always regret that he'd left her as he'd found her?

Chaste. Lonely. Unhappy.

She'd brooded and worried until she could barely sleep or eat. But one thing she knew: somehow she had to find a way to make Dom see her as a woman instead of as only his deliverance. A woman he wanted as much as she wanted him.

When she entered the café, Honor told herself that, just for today, she'd try to join the merriment by osmosis if possible—and sheer willpower if necessary. She pinned on her brightest smile, tied on her apron and began taking orders. She was rounding the salad bar when she came face-to-face with Bruno Trotterman. His eyes widened. The loaded salad bowl in his hand tipped.

Automatically, she reached out to catch it. Smiling vaguely, hoping he'd think she only looked familiar, she handed back the bowl and inched around him.

"Miss Fitzhugh?" he squeaked. "What are you doing here?"

She pretended deafness, continuing past him, but he caught her elbow and turned her to face him. She cursed her fair complexion, but she knew the flush gave her away. "Working," she answered shortly.

"But . . . the statue. What did you do with it?"

"Nothing. I didn't take it."

"Then who did?"

Honor pulled her arm out of his grasp. "Look, if you want to turn me in, go ahead. If not, leave me alone and let me do my job."

His pug nose wrinkling, he looked around at the crowded café, then back at her. "How can you bear to work as a waitress after being a curator?"

"We do what we must. Who'd hire me now, anyway?" She bit her lip, but the damage was done.

Suspicion replaced surprise. "Odd how you took a waitress job here, out of all the places in the city . . ."

Under the circumstances, Honor could scarcely blame him for his brooding suspicions. For Dom's sake, she mastered her surging resentment and said coolly, "I may not be a curator anymore, but I still love art. Where's the crime in that?"

He peered at her closely for a long moment. He shrugged. "None, I guess. Sorry I troubled you."

Thankfully, Honor hurried past him to her first table, but she suspected he'd go straight to the personnel office to check her out. The day was long, the café crowded, so Honor didn't have a lot of time to worry, but when she was finally able to take off her apron, she decided to beard the lion in his den. Or the surly little pug, anyway. She wasn't a good liar, but she had come up with a story to explain the statue's disappearance. She would tell him the lab had picked up the statue for further testing and that it must have been stolen in transit. He wasn't likely to trouble himself to check out her story.

Colleen Shannon

The executive office wing of the building was at one end of the museum. As she went through the displays, Honor felt the usual tug of regret that, in her new reality, she could look but not touch. She smiled bitterly. That seemed to be the pattern of her life now.

She stepped gingerly once she entered the office area, feeling like an intruder in her waitress uniform. She was reading the names on the plaques, looking for Trotterman's, mentally rehearsing her story, when she came to half-open double doors. She was about to walk past when she heard Trotterman's voice.

" . . . observe the fluidity of the musculature. As an architect cannot build without a blueprint, you cannot sculpt well without sketching. To capture the life and grace of the subject in stone, you must do so first on paper."

He must be teaching an art class, Honor realized. She'd heard the museum had studios and conference rooms for that purpose, but she'd never been down here before. She slipped between the double doors, automatically looking toward Trotterman. He sat below the raised platform, easel facing out, sketching furiously. A nude male form took slow shape under his skillful charcoal.

Half a dozen art students likewise sketched rapidly. Studiously, Honor avoided looking directly at the subject. In her peripheral vision she could see a tall man posed on the platform, but he was quite obviously nude. She felt her cheeks turning warm, and cursed her own awkwardness. She was an adult, for heaven's sake, not some naive schoolgirl. Still, it was obvious that now was not the proper time to confront Trotterman. Backing out as quietly as she'd entered, Honor allowed herself one quick peek at the model.

Blood left her head in a great gush. She felt herself go pale. She had to catch a chair back to steady her shaky knees. Even the width of the large room couldn't dim those warm, glowing Adriatic eyes. That earth-toned head of hair caught the bright lights, casting back gold, red and sienna. Oh, yes, she knew intimately what a perfect subject their model made. He stood there with obvious discomfort as men and women alike drew his private parts, but he stood there nonetheless.

"Dom," she whispered.

Betrayal, dark and deep, opened like a chasm at her feet. She could go around it, step over it or fall into it. Instead she backed away, still staring. She was unable to believe he allowed others to so casually admire him, learn every intimate curve and angle of that perfect form, all the while holding her aloof. His modesty was as false as his claims of gratitude.

The truth was, he didn't want her. Why else would he allow strangers the intimacy he denied her? Dear Lord, he avoided even touching her lately, much less letting her see him naked.

"No, *bambina*," Dom whispered. "Do not look at me like that."

Trotterman glanced up. He saw Honor, frowned, and rose. "Now see here, Miss Fitzhugh, you can't barge in like this and disturb my session." He glanced at Dom, apparently realized his subject's concentration was shattered, and tossed Dom his T-shirt.

It landed on Dom's shoulder. Reaching up with one hand to catch it, he turned his head to peer at Honor, wearing that *terribilita* frown, one foot braced before him. Even in the midst of her pain, Honor saw shock grow on the historian's face. Trotterman glanced from her to Dom and back. His mouth working like a fish gasping its last, Trotterman stared at the large poster of Michelangelo's *David* on the wall behind the platform. One pudgy hand rose to his bobbing Adam's apple. His eyes darted rapidly between Dom and *David*.

The two images were, but for skin color, a perfect match.

In that split second, Honor realized she was not the only one privy to the fact that miracles still happened. She felt vague surprise that Trotterman believed the evidence of his eyes rather than the discipline of his science. There must be more to the officious little man than she'd thought. But then, she of all people should know better than to judge people by their looks.

Honor turned again toward the door, but Trotterman called, "Wait!"

She kept walking.

"No, Honor, please, let me explain," Dom pleaded.

She stopped. For the first time, Dom had called her Honor. Even as she reveled in the sound of her name on his lips, she resented his timing and his stubbornness. "What?" She turned to him.

"You don't need to explain anything. We're both adults." She sensed the curiosity of the students. For once in her life, she didn't care. She stood her ground even as a slow burn started at her scalp and trickled to her toes.

Dom was in the process of pulling on his jeans. He gave Trotterman a pleading look.

The curator clapped his hands. "All right, class, we'll stop a few minutes early today. Remember, two still-life sketches are required for next period." As he spoke, he drew even with Honor.

The two historians shared a long look. Honor inhaled deeply, and exhaled equally deeply. The shuddery sigh released some of her pent-up tension. In that exchange of glances, for the first time in her career Honor felt total empathy from a colleague. Only another art historian could understand the wonder, the shattering joy, and then the terrible fear of loss that came with seeing a miracle come to life.

For a brief time . . .

As the students filed past, the last shutting the door, Trotterman led Honor to a seat. He sat down next to her and gravely offered his hand, proving his own thoughts were on a similar plane. "Pygmalion, I presume?"

A little laugh caught in Honor's throat. "I wish I'd created him. No, I only found him. And I'll have to give him back in a few months."

Wonder still darkening his eyes, Trotterman looked back at Dom. "No wonder you couldn't tell the police the truth. And no wonder he looked so familiar to me the first time I saw him. But who is he, really?"

Succinctly, she filled in the details.

Dom was drawing on his boots now, but when he was finished, he sat, legs spraddled, hands on knees, as he watched them talk.

Drawing another deep breath as she finished, Honor turned away from the hopeful gleam in Dom's eye. Why did he care about her approval or disapproval? He spent all his time avoiding her anyway. Really, his behavior, even for a man accustomed to the morals of a different era, was peculiar.

"But," Trotterman burst out, "this is the most wonderful opportunity an art historian has ever had! Michelangelo's assistant! What we can *learn* from him. And Leonardo—did he know him, too?"

"He says he did, but not well, apparently. As a matter of fact, he was rather . . . cavalier about their characters. Both are—ah, were—difficult to deal with, particularly Michelangelo."

Trotterman leaped up.

Honor had trodden his path, so sympathy softened her tone when she stood to catch his arm and stop his descent on Dom. "Wait. You can ask as many questions as you like, but—where will they lead? What will we claim as our source material?"

When he peered at her uncomprehendingly, she persisted. "As you so accurately pointed out to me, how could we document the information? Other historians would accuse us of rank speculation."

She didn't add that Dom had been quite close-mouthed about his own life back in Italy. He seemed to find the subject distasteful, or at least inappropriate. She could understand that it must be painful for him to think of the life he'd lost and might never return to.

Trotterman's Adam's apple bobbed again as he swallowed his disappointment. "You're right, of course." Still, he stared, fascinated, at Dom.

Unable to avoid it any longer, Honor also looked at Dom. He clasped his knees with his hands and stood to his full, imposing height. He walked down the aisle, searching her face intently.

When he drew even, Honor shielded her chaotic emotions behind a cool smile. "So does this mean you're not working as a stonecutter anymore?"

Dom shook his head. "No, Honoria Psyche. This was the first and only time I shall do this. But I had no choice."

So they were back to Honoria again. It hurt Honor almost past bearing that he wouldn't allow her even such a meaningless intimacy. Curtly, she replied, "I see. Well, I'm tired. I guess I'll head back."

"Wait. I shall walk with you."

Honor pretended not to hear, walking steadily toward the door. She heard Trotterman stop Dom, and then the rustle of crisp, clean bills. The door closed behind her as the curator said something she couldn't hear. A question, the first among many, no doubt. She hoped Dom was more forthcoming with Trotterman than he'd been with her.

Her tears tasted sour when they came, as if the bitterness in her heart ate at her, body and soul.

Honor tried to tell herself he must have a very good reason for needing money so badly. Maybe something to do with Castigi? But as the bustling city streets passed in a blurry haze, Honor knew that, deep down, she could never forgive him for this. To sell himself so cheaply to others, when she'd give her soul for one night . . .

At a stoplight, a handsome man in a thousand-dollar suit stopped next to her, turning his head. She sniffed, bowing her head in embarrassment, but not before she saw his eyes darken with sympathy. He offered her a clean, expensive handkerchief. He gave her a tentative smile, his gaze traveling over the long, thick blond hair she'd loosened from its tie. As the light changed, he helped her off the curb, and then he was gone in the crowd.

On the other side of the street, Honor took deep breaths and wiped her eyes. Enough. The kindness of a stranger brought home to her as nothing else could that the world wouldn't end with the year 2000. This obviously well-off businessman had found a girl from the coal fields of West Virginia attractive, and she was hardly at her best at the moment.

It was time she faced facts. She was obsessed with having sex with a five-hundred-year-old man, but losing her virginity in Dom's bed wouldn't change fate, or the same boring reality she'd have to endure when he left. He wasn't the only handsome man available. This was a very large city, a virtual playground for adults. If Dom didn't want to play, she'd find someone who did.

A small dress shop caught her eye. She paused

to look in the window at a slinky black silk number. Normally she'd never wear something like
that. But an image egged her on: Dom standing
there, unadorned, flaunting all the things he'd not
let her see, much less touch, while the women
students drooled over him so much she expected
their charcoal must have smeared.

Decisively, Honor turned the store's heavy, old-
fashioned knob and went in. She might not be
gorgeous like him, but when she tried, she could
attract men. She was tired of feeling like a reject.
She'd lost her career, her very way of life because
of Dom, and if he couldn't show her a little appre-
ciation, she'd find someone who could.

If the thought niggled at her that she was playing the same games she'd scorned in college, she
told herself that this time it was justified.

Once and for all, she had to know how Dom felt
about her.

As she knew firsthand, jealousy had a way of
stripping all subterfuge away. Especially from a
primitive alpha male. Honor shivered deliciously
and smiled at the sales clerk. "May I try on that
dress in the window?"

The next morning, Dom tried to talk to her, but
she cut off his halting explanation with a
brusque, "Doesn't matter. I don't own you. And
you don't own me." She smiled brightly at Ernie,
who'd watched with covert amusement as she
and Dom did their delicate dance of denial.

While Dom brooded over toast at her reply, she
asked Ernie, "What are you up to today?"

"I've been volunteering down at the museum in

197

between my days helping Nick. Hey, Honnie, I think Bruno Trotterman's about to offer me a job as his assistant. He's not such a bad guy, after all."

Honor didn't have the heart to tell Ernie that Trotterman's timing was suspicious. If he'd found out Dom was staying in Ernie's brownstone, he'd be on Ernie like a tick on a dog, as her father used to say. She smiled warmly at her friend. "He'll be lucky to have you."

Sourly, Dom eyed her glowing expression. She was glad that he didn't know about the facial mask and steam treatment she'd given herself to achieve that glow.

His gaze dropped to her tight sweater and jeans. "You are leaving dressed like *that?*"

She lifted an eyebrow at him. "So? I believe you've been seen in public in less."

Ernie choked on a sip of tea, pretending interest in his plate while he listened intently.

The small table needed only fluttering flags to make the perfect battleground. It harbored mine-fields of hidden resentment.

And Honor was in no mood to call a truce. Tapping her newly manicured nails against the table like a battle drum, she gave as good as she got. "I don't believe you have the right to object to anything I do—Dominico." *Dom, Dom, don't make me do this. Love me as we both know in our hearts is right.*

A cloud passed over his sunny blue eyes. He shoved his plate back and stood. "As you say. *Ciao.*" He was out the door almost before the words were out of his mouth.

Despite her determination, Honor sagged a bit as he left. She couldn't evade Ernie's sympathetic gaze.

"He's a stubborn bastard, isn't he?"

Honor shielded her eyes behind one hand, struggling with tears yet again.

"What's his deal? Why's he handle you with kid gloves?"

"Like I have the plague, you mean." Honor's hand dropped as she stared unseeingly into a bright day that offered her nothing. Nothing she wanted, anyway. Plague. Could that be it? Dom had lost his beloved Marta to the plague. Maybe he was so determined to hold himself aloof because, even if he won his quest and was allowed to return home, he feared subjecting her, a modern woman, to the dirt and danger of the Renaissance.

No. That was ridiculous. The modern age certainly had dangers aplenty, many even the geniuses of the Renaissance couldn't imagine. Chemical warfare. Atom bombs. Car crashes. Tired of the endless questions and the equally futile answers, Honor stood. "I'm off today, Ernie. Will you be back for dinner?"

He shrugged. "Don't know yet." When she turned to leave, he shoved away from the table. "Honnie."

She stopped.

"Yes?"

"This isn't any of my beeswax, but I do think Dom really cares for you. I'm not sure what he's waiting for, but when the time comes—"

Honor laughed harshly. "Didn't you know, dear friend? The end of the world is nigh."

Ernie watched her with such loving, troubled dark eyes that Honor choked back her bitterness and said lightly, "Thanks for your concern. But just between you and me, I don't know if Dom is waiting for a sign from heaven or an apocalypse, and frankly, I'm not sure I care anymore. I'm through pining for a man who doesn't want me. Do you blame me?"

Ernie shook his head. "I understand how you feel. But I'm not sure Dom does. He's a pretty old-fashioned guy, and if you try to make him jealous, well, you may get more feeling than you bargained for."

Stuffing her hands in her pockets, Honor managed, "I wish Dom understood me as well as you do."

Ernie's smile was melancholy. "No, you don't. Where's the fascination in that? And the only reason I understand you so well is because, well . . . " He trailed off, kicking one toe at a corner of the rug. "Let's face it, I'm not your typical guy."

She caught his shoulders in her hands and said fiercely, "Thank the Lord for that. Dom hasn't said anything to you, has he?"

"No. Not really. Mostly he just avoids me like the—"

"—plague," they both said in unison.

They burst out laughing. Honor hugged her friend. "I always knew we had a lot in common. What do you say you spend the day with me, show me around the city?"

"That sounds fun, but I promised Nicky . . . " Ernie trailed off, then added enthusiastically,

"Let's go together! I've been wanting the two of you to get to know each other better, anyway."

"Well, I don't know. Maybe Nick wouldn't want me there."

"He'll get over it."

Sure enough, Nick hid his quick scowl with a tact that surprised her. He nodded at her with forced cheerfulness and said heartily, "Sure! Come along. But you may be bored. We're just going to throw some balls in the park and then do some ice-skating. You play football before?"

Feeling like an intruder, Honor glanced at Ernie. He smiled with such warm anticipation that she bit back the demurral and said instead, "Sure. I have four brothers. And I love to skate."

"Good, good." Nick held the front door open for her to precede them. As they walked up the street to the garage, they passed the stop where Dom awaited his bus.

Pretending not to see him, Honor tucked her hand in Nick's arm and peeped flirtatiously up at her landlord. "It's awfully nice of you to let me come."

Awkwardly, Nick patted her hand and eased his arm away. "Sure, sure." He walked a little ahead, making Honor aware of his need for space, but they'd entered the garage now, so she didn't care.

Ernie lagged behind, looking over his shoulder. Shaking his head, he caught up with her. "Dom didn't look too happy to see you playing paddy fingers with my brother."

Honor did something then she'd always wanted to do, something she'd envied all the popular girls for pulling off with such grace. She tossed her head, her loose hair bouncing on her shoulders. The defiant femininity felt great. "So? I'm tired of caring what he thinks."

Deliberately, she waited for Ernie to climb in the back so she could sit in the front with Nick. In fact, for the rest of that day, Honor behaved in an atypical manner. Instead of staying quiet, listening to the two brothers discuss their favorite pro football teams, she got into a heated discussion with Nick about which team was better, the Broncos or the Jets.

At lunchtime, instead of hanging back, waiting to be asked what she wanted on her hot dog, she smiled prettily at the street vendor and requested her usual chili, onions and mustard.

After lunch, instead of skating off alone to give the two brothers privacy, Honor let Ernie catch her arm so they could skate in tandem at the wonderful outdoor rink. Nick caught her other arm, and soon many of the skaters at Rockefeller Center had formed a chain with them, half skating forward, half back as they circled to the music. Every time she passed the gilded Prometheus, Honor smiled, feeling as if he'd shared his strength with her.

When they reached the park, she didn't stay on the sidelines, watching. They recruited a young college kid to balance their numbers, and Honor allied with the burly young man against Nick and Ernie. She was small, but she'd always been swift, and to her delight, she was able to outrun Nick on several occasions. They'd decided to play touch ball, and Honor was so limber and slim that she could dance sideways out of Nick's reach, sprinting down the lush green grass to the tree that was her goalpost.

Leaning against the tree, she tauntingly tossed the football from one hand to another. "Fourteen to seven. Guess you're losing it, Nick, if you let a girl and a kid beat you."

Nick only smiled, but Ernie stuck his tongue out at her and tried to zip past with the ball. Honor ran as fast as she could, just able to touch his spine before he reached his own goalpost. "My ball!"

Pouting, Ernie handed her the ball. Around them, children toddled next to their parents, wrapped up like the precious bundles they were. Joggers ran past on the jogging path, and in-line skaters zoomed around the paved minifreeway in the distance.

For the first time since reaching the city, Honor felt like a participant instead of a spectator. A couple walking their poodle stopped to watch their game, smiling at the girl with long blond hair leaning against a tree while three males demanded the ball. The hardwoods in the park sported their fall party clothes. A blaze of gold and red backed Honor as her laughter rang in the sunny afternoon. More than one male head turned to look at her, but Honor didn't notice.

On her next turn, she pretended to pull back her arm for a long pass, but then tucked the ball against her side and scampered under Nick's reaching arms. This time he recovered quickly, faked one direction to put her off balance, and then blocked the other way. Their hips bumped together as he bent to retrieve the loose ball and toss it to his brother. Ernie dashed past her to the makeshift goalpost, spiking the football.

Nick stayed still, staring at her. "Tie game."

His brown eyes were softer than she'd ever seen them. He wasn't so bad, after all. Nick Escavido was finally starting to see her as a woman instead of as Ernie's irritating charity case. On some dim level, Honor knew she should be glad, maybe even tempted, but handsome as Nick was, his hair was too dark, his eyes too hard.

Her thoughts were leading where she didn't want to go, so she aborted them with a smile at this man who had, despite his obvious reservations, been kind to them in his own way. She didn't know her smile lit up her quiet, contemplative face like fireworks, all the prettier for its rarity. She didn't realize that her thick hair was dotted with leaves, blowing in lissome golden disarray around her face and shoulders. She didn't realize a smudge on her sweater was strategically tempting to any male.

And she didn't see Ernie glance sharply between his brother and his friend, mouthing an atypical curse to himself.

She knew only that she felt more alive than she had in years. She smiled, swept past Nick and Ernie, grabbed the ball and lobbed it to her teammate.

The chase was on. . . .

Late that night, Dom quietly let himself into the apartment. He hoped Honor was asleep. He was covered in marble dust, and his arms ached from using the air hammer, but in the one day since he'd raised the rest of the payment, he'd already had good success. If Michelangelo had had access to the tools of this age, he would not have had to leave so many unfinished works behind.

Still, the glow of accomplishment was muted by his concern for Rafe. On Dom's recommendation, the foreman had given Castigi a chance. For the first few days he'd shown up on time, apparently sober, but yesterday he'd been an hour late, and the next day he'd come in bleary-eyed after lunch. Today he hadn't shown up at all.

As soon as he cleaned up, Dom intended to go back out and look for his exasperating nephew. He knew Rafe had lost his tiny apartment and had been staying at cheap hotels, but he refused to tell him where. However, Dom had a shrewd suspicion exactly where to find him. Yet again, he'd try to explain to Rafe the importance of being on time for work.

"*Per Dio*, the people of this time have too much time, and too much freedom," Dom muttered to himself as he went into the small bathroom to clean up. In his time, if one didn't work, one didn't eat. Even then, working dawn to dusk on someone else's land, many vassals barely survived, having to poach and grow their own foodstuffs.

Dom was stepping out of the shower, naked and dripping, when he heard a noise. From the quietness of the apartment, he'd assumed Honor was asleep, though it was only ten of the clock. Tying a towel about his lean hips, he peeked outside the bathroom. Breath left his lungs in a whoosh.

She stood at the kitchen table taking things out of her sensible . . . now, what did she call that little valise? Ah, yes, a purse. She was packing nonsensical female items in a small black beaded bag to match her small black beaded dress. Two little wisps of fabric covered her body, sewn together by beads, hope and, in Dom's case, a prayer.

Silently mouthing one of the catechisms he'd learned at his mother's knee, Dom drank her in with his eyes. He'd always known she was lovely, but her slim hips, long, shapely legs and small but well-rounded bosom had never tempted him more than now. She literally made his mouth water.

Almost as hungry for the sight of her as he was for the touch of her, Dom propped both hands against opposite sides of the bathroom door frame and clasped it tightly to symbolically hold on to his baser urges. She dropped a comb and bent to retrieve it.

The bodice, what little there was of it, gaped open enough for him to see that she was not wearing that undergarment she called a bra. He'd recalled the image of her lovely breasts so often and so well that he could have sculpted them from memory. His hands clasped the door frame tight enough to whiten his knuckles, but the aching beneath the towel only grew harder.

When she straightened, she dropped the comb in and snapped the tiny valise closed. Glancing up, she started. "Why, Dom, I didn't see you standing there."

Little liar. One of the things he loved most about her was her total ineptitude at subterfuge.

She'd heard him come out and had put on that artful display for him. "*Bene, bellissima,* as they say in your time, I'll bite. Where are you going dressed like that? Or should I say, *un*dressed like that?"

Honor gave that little rippling, female laugh that he longed to snatch from her lips with his tongue and teeth. "Oh, just a date. Nothing for you to worry about."

With an effort that made the veins in his neck stand out, Dom managed not to sweep her up into his arms, carry her to that big bed and prove to her once and for all that only he had the right to look at her thus.

Once and for all . . . Dom swallowed harshly. In reality, the only time they had was rapidly fleeing. Less than three months now, and counting. He hitched up the towel, wondering why he always felt like a boy in the presence of this virgin.

When he didn't answer, Honor bit her lip and turned away. "Well, anyway, I'll see you later." She was reaching for the knob when a knock sounded. She opened the door.

Despite himself, Dom craned his neck to see who stood there. The primitive feelings stirring in his heart moved lower, to his gut, which began to burn with an urge to do more than stand there like an idiot in a scrap of fabric.

Why, of all the men in this cursed city, did Honor have to choose that insufferable fellow?

When Nick gave him a short nod, arching an eyebrow at Dom's sagging towel, Dom hitched the towel up. All the more imposing in his nakedness, he took one long stride forward as Nick ushered Honor out the door. Over her head, brown eyes met blue in that primeval, aggressive way that was the same in 1499 and 1999.

In one brief look, Dom warned, *Touch her at your peril. She's mine.*

With a cynical tilt to his long, sensuous mouth, Nick silently responded, *Funny, she doesn't seem to think so. Butt out, buddy.*

The door closed. The murmur of their voices faded with their footsteps.

The apartment was very quiet, very lonely and very cold.

Flinging the towel off, his face so tight with rage that he wondered it didn't split open, Dom grabbed clean clothes and began to dress.

He had no right to protest, or even to care about Honor's choice of date. But he did care. Far more than was good for either of them. The fury eating at him had only one remedy.

A flashing image of Honor writhing beneath him made him smile grimly. Make that two. But the second meant breaking the honor he'd almost lost.

And a very important, intimate part of the Honor he longed to deserve.

Buttoning his shirt so hastily he got two fasteners off-kilter, Dom hurried out of the apartment.

The first remedy would have to do. And when he returned, he'd be so drunk that he wouldn't care that the only woman he'd ever truly loved had dressed like a harlot to taunt him and make him jealous. Most irritating of all, her plan was succeeding beautifully.

As Dom caught the bus, he smiled so grimly

that a tough-looking teen next to him moved to a vacant seat. Maybe there was a third remedy, after all.

His hands began to itch to paddle Honor's pert little butt.

Chapter Nine

To Honor's relief, Nick didn't comment on her sexy dress, though his expression was compliment enough. She avoided the urge to pull the bodice up, wondering why she felt so right when Dom looked at her intimately, and so wrong when other men did.

Dom's desire had been strong enough to raise the towel at his groin—but his willpower was stronger. He wanted her for himself, yet he had not only let her leave dressed so suggestively; he had stood by while a man he detested escorted her out. Sometimes, she thought despairingly, it seemed he was still made of stone.

Her plan so far was a total zero. Why couldn't she forget this impossible obsession and enjoy the company of a very different, but equally handsome man? Yet, even as she answered Nick's question about which club she wanted to try, Honor brooded.

In an earlier lifetime, perhaps Dom really had been the David he so strongly resembled, proud enough and willful enough to establish an empire out of dust. He was stronger in some ways than that David, for the biblical king had finally been mastered by physical desire.

And almost led his kingdom to ruin because of it, Honor's conscience reminded her.

" . . . starts next week."

Honor dragged her attention back to Nick. "I'm sorry. What did you say?"

"Ernie starts work at the Metropolis Museum on Monday."

"That's great! I heard Trotterman had offered him a job. Ernie's a wonderful assistant, so he'll do well . . . He wasn't home when I got there. Do you know where he went?"

"Yeah, out to the country with friends. He won't be back until late Sunday night."

A delicious chill ran up Honor's spine as she realized she and Dom would finally be alone for a couple of days. For all the good that would do her.

Abruptly Nick pulled to the curb and killed the engine. "Look, I can take you back if you want. I'm not accustomed to dating women who can't stop thinking about other men."

Her head bowed, Honor toyed with the beaded fringe on her hem. "I'm sorry. It's just that you've been so nice that I—"

"*Nice?* That's something no woman's ever

211

accused me of." Nick grunted his displeasure, but then his expressive mouth began to twitch. "Nice, huh?" He laughed, the sound so rich and deep and mellow that Honor had to join in.

"It may not be a compliment to you, but it's meant as one," she said when she caught her breath. "To be honest, it's not a term I'd use for most of the men I know."

"So, you want to go on to the club or not?"

Vowing to put Dom exactly where he kept her—out of sight, out of mind—Honor replied, "Yes, please. That is, if you still want to. I promise not to moon over Dom—another man while we dance. I haven't been dancing since my college days."

Somehow Honor managed to keep her promise. The more she smiled, the more she found to smile at. The more she talked, the more she found to say. Only later did she realize that Nick was a master at listening, but confided little in return. By the time they entered the parking garage in the wee hours, her feet ached, her head spun with the alcohol she'd consumed, but her mouth moved nonstop. Nick even inserted a comment now and then instead of sitting there like . . . like a statue.

Dammit, here she was doing it again. For almost four hours she'd managed not to think of Dom. Furiously, Honor blinked away tears. Why did women feel an instinctive need for emotional intimacy, while men wanted only sex?

At least, most men.

Most *normal* men.

She forced a bright smile, dreading going back

into the apartment. She had a feeling Dom wouldn't be home, and she didn't want to spend the rest of the night wondering where he was. "Enough about me. It's none of my business, I know, but . . . do you want to talk about why you left the force?"

Nick turned off the car and turned to face her, one long arm on the back of the seat. "It's no big deal, believe me. You'd be bored, and I'd rather talk about you. Besides, you've never really told me why you came to New York."

Even tipsy, Honor was well aware of the deft way he turned the subject. God pity the woman who ever loved this tough, closed-off man. Honor searched his face. Those hard, dark eyes were as direct and unflinching as usual, but she saw no condemnation, suspicion or dislike. Only honest interest. She could hardly expect him to trust her with painful information if she didn't reciprocate. Her intuitive understanding of human nature assured her that even when he knew the truth, he wouldn't run straight to his old buddies downtown. It didn't look as though he had too many friends left there, anyway.

Feeling a weight shift from her shoulders, she confessed, "My former employer thinks I'm a thief. No doubt they've pressed charges against me by now."

He didn't even frown. "Of what?"

"Stealing a statue that I was trying to verify as one of Michelangelo's lost works."

"I see. Well, we both know that's not true."

"We do?"

"Sure. If you'd fenced this precious artwork or

213

something, you wouldn't be standing on your feet all day as a waitress. You'd be working on a tan in Tahiti."

Before tonight, his matter-of-fact reasoning might have made her angry. No assurance that he knew she wasn't that kind of girl, or that he believed she was honest. Just straight deduction. Typical. She tilted her head provocatively. "It's always better to hide in plain sight. Maybe I prefer to case your joint for some new loot."

He burst out laughing. "The only thing you'll find in my place that I value is Ernie." He snapped his mouth closed and turned away, as if wishing she hadn't surprised the admission out of him.

Finally they had found some common ground. "Ernie's important to me, too. He's the best friend I've ever had." She eyed his averted face. His features were very different from Dom's, less perfect, but equally strong and unbending. Something bedeviled her to make him admit how much he loved his brother. "So Ernie tells me you more or less raised him? That your parents died in a car crash when you were only seventeen? You dropped out of school so you could take three jobs, and only got your GED and went to college at night when you decided to be a cop. Right?"

He shrugged. "Ernie exaggerates." He turned back to face her. "Quit changing the subject. So what's happened to this statue?"

Honor's head began to ache. Rubbing her temples, she replied truthfully, if obliquely, "We won't know for certain for a few more months."

"I have a feeling there's a lot you're not telling me."

It was Honor's turn to shrug.

"So where does Dom figure in all this? And Castigi?"

She appraised a spot on the windshield.

He sighed. "I guess I can't blame you for not leveling with me. Though I promise not to rat on you." He smiled, teeth savage in the gloom. "I've done enough of that for one lifetime."

Arrested, Honor turned in her seat to stare at him. So that was why he'd quit.

Nick said slowly, "I don't know how Dom's involved in all this, but whatever's going on, he's right at the center. And you're there because of him."

Honor studiously found that spot again.

"And whatever's going on is keeping the two of you apart. Right?"

She heaved a deep sigh, her mouth turning down as she thought of facing Dom. If she couldn't even succeed at making him jealous, she might as well move out and get her own place, leave him to the fate he seemed determined to experience on his own. Try to put the shattered pieces of her life back together.

But she knew she wouldn't.

"Hey, don't look so sad." Gently Nick traced the outline of her solemn mouth. "Men are much denser than women realize. You tried telling him how you feel?"

Honor's mouth quivered under his finger. He drew away as if burned, a flush coloring his high,

215

aristocratic cheekbones, but she didn't notice. She was staring at her fingers, twisting the beaded fringe on the hem of her skirt. "Oh, yes. He knows."

Nick said something foul in Spanish under his breath. "So, as a last resort, you used me to make him jealous. Right?"

Honor peeped at him through downcast lashes, but he'd been too kind, and she was too tired to prevaricate. "Right. Didn't work, though."

"Chemistry can be pretty volatile unless you know exactly what you're doing. You prepared for the . . . reaction you may get?"

That delicious chill slithered down Honor's spine again. "Oh, yes."

Shaking his head, Nick patted her restive hands and walked around to open the car door. "OK, ma'am. Nutty Professor Escavido at your service, ma'am." Miming buckteeth, he crossed his eyes. He held out his hand.

Giggling, Honor let him help her out of the car. For the first time, she realized Nick was more like Ernie than he let on. He had the same inherent honor and a wicked sense of humor, even if he was a tad too arrogant.

I might as well face it, she thought as Nick escorted her up the brownstone steps. *I like arrogant men.*

Which was a good thing, Honor dryly decided as they started up to the second level.

She was surrounded by them.

Decidedly arrrogant male voices hollered more than sang in an odd, measured cadence. At first she couldn't make out the words. Nick pulled out his own key, realized the door was ajar, and shoved it fully open.

The scents of aged bourbon and cheap perfume hit Honor like a brick wall. She reeled back. Nick caught her arms reassuringly, his chest bracing her shoulder blades.

Dreading what she'd find, Honor looked around for the two men. The obscene singsong drill Castigi must have learned in the navy was all too plain now.

"I wish all the ladies were pies on a shelf, and I was a baker. I'd eat 'em all myself. Come on, you lazy Italian. . . . Sound off!"

Honor and Nick exchanged a glance. Where was Dom?

Castigi roared, "I wish all the ladies were holes in the road. And I was a dump truck, I'd fill 'em with my—"

Nick clamped his hands over Honor's ears just as Castigi looked up and saw them, biting back the last word. He waved at them merrily. "How's it hangin'?"

Letting his hands drop, Nick smiled sardonically. "Rather loose at the moment, apparently."

Sprawled on the sofa, Castigi had a woman's garter wrapped like a tight sweatband around his forehead, but the only warrior paint on his face was red. Carmine lipstick smeared his mouth and cheeks. His shirt was open to the waist, but even his washboard belly and huge, muscled chest only made him look like a caricature of a SEAL on a bender.

Still, his scruffy beard, tousled hair and bloodshot eyes couldn't hide his true self from Honor's

217

Colleen Shannon

kind heart. In that moment she recognized him
for what he was: a former idealist who'd had one
too many dreams shattered. He stopped chanting
as he blinked at them.

Hinting at the charisma he'd once obviously
possessed in abundance, a crooked smile played
about his lips as he raised the bottle to them.
"Salud!" He drank deeply.

Her heart in her throat, Honor looked around
for Dom. At first she couldn't see him. Not sitting
at the table, not in any of the chairs. The bedroom? She took a few steps until she could see
the bed through the open door. It was neatly
made.

And then an off-key humming drew her attention. Hesitantly she inched forward until she
could see inside her bedroom. Slouched at the
foot of her bed, Dom had her lingerie drawer
open and was happily flinging her underwear,
bras and nightgowns all over the room. Honor
was so hurt at the sight of the two garters on his
shirtsleeves, and the thought of another woman
with him, that it took her a moment to realize
what he was doing.

He seemed to be seeking something. When he
reached the bottom of the drawer, he froze, cursing in explicit Italian. He pulled out a black chiffon nightgown and slurred happily, "There. Good
secret."

Stunned, Honor realized he held a bit of nonsense she'd been foolish enough to order out of a
Victoria's Secret catalog with her second pay-
check. Back when she hoped Dom would come to
his senses. Or better yet, surrender to them.

218

She'd forgotten about it until now. Unfortunately, Dom had arrived home in time to glimpse her shaking it out. She'd blushed, hurried into her room and stuffed the nightgown in the bottom of her drawer, not bothering to remove the tags. When she came back out, Dom was reading the label on the package.

"Secret? Now this kind of secret I like." He'd smiled lazily.

Still stinging from his rejection of a few nights before, Honor had snatched the package away from him and crumpled it up. "You have a funny way of showing it."

The smile disappeared. A few seconds later, his footsteps did likewise, climbing quietly to the studio.

Honor blinked back to the present as Dom drew the chiffon to his face and inhaled. "Bah!" Tossing the frippery aside, he grabbed up a bra and a slip, sniffing them, too, growing increasingly frustrated as he discarded each scrap of fabric.

What on earth was wrong with him? Honor wondered. Even roaring drunk, even from a five-hundred-year-old perspective, he acted mighty strange.

Mystified, she looked at Nick.

Nick's mouth had a funny, twisted look she'd never seen before. He shook his head slightly, muttering something she had a feeling she wasn't supposed to hear. "Poor bastard. He's got it *bad*."

Realization hit her.

That strange twist of Nick's mouth was sympathy.

And Dom wasn't looking for something in her lingerie, at least not anything tangible. He wanted her scent, and all her clothes were clean, so he couldn't find it.

Honor went weak at the knees, feeling hot and cold, happy and sad, all at once. Her spike heel caught on the corner of the rug. Unaccustomed to the high heels, she stumbled and would have fallen if Nick hadn't grabbed her.

Dom looked up.

He blinked rapidly, obviously having trouble focusing. A blaze of joy lit his beautiful face. No frown, no anger, not even sadness or regret. Just sheer, unbridled jubilation at seeing her. "Honor!"

The sound of her own name had never moved her as it did now. He spoke her name as she thought of his: Dom equals hope equals happiness. Their own private formula defined in a few insignificant letters. She took a tiny step toward him. Perhaps he really cared for her, after all?

But then he blinked again and looked behind her. She felt Nick stiffen.

Like a shadow blocking the sun, darkness shrouded Dom's expression. He scrambled to his feet. "Get away from her!" He teetered slightly, one hand to his head, but he caught himself quickly, clutching the edge of the dresser.

The tone of Nick's voice increased the dread clutching at Honor's roiling stomach.

"Why? Grow up, Dominico. You're like a boy with a shiny new toy. She's too precious to play with, but by God no one else can have her either." Gently Nick moved her aside.

Honor rubbed her elbows, whispering, "No, Nick, don't."

He arched that sardonic eyebrow at her, his face saturnine. *You asked for this, babe,* his expression said. *I warned you.*

Lowering his head on his shoulders, Dom charged. At the last minute Nick ducked behind the doorway. Dom reeled through it, momentum carrying him into the living room before he caught himself against a table, but not before he bumped a shin.

The table scraped against the polished wood floor, leaving a long scratch.

Honor didn't know whether to laugh or cry when Dom's inherent courtesy made him gently move the table back to cover the spot. *"Scusi,"* he slurred. "I fix later. After I fix you." Squinting, as if his own arms were far away, he began to roll up his shirtsleeves.

The scraping noise had caught Castigi's attention. He slurped the last few drops of whiskey and tossed the bottle against the wall. Nick and Honor both winced at the sound of shattering glass. "Hey, Dom. You want I should beat him up for you?" He lurched to his feet, swaying like a mountain undergoing an earthquake.

Glaring at glass shards sprinkled over the floor and the mark on the clean white wall, Nick said, "All right, that's it. Time to bring this comedy of errors to an end." Nick caught Honor's wrist and hauled her into his arms. "You want I should show you how to treat a beautiful woman, you idiot?" Nick lowered his mouth over Honor's.

The instinct to struggle died swiftly, for Nick's

mouth was efficient, perfunctory and very gentlemanly. He set her aside as quickly as he'd grabbed her and smiled tauntingly at Dom, who was in the process of rounding the table, fists clenched.

"Get out of the way, Honor," Nick said coolly.

Nibbling her lips, which still tingled from Nick's kiss, Honor stayed put. "Nick, I don't think—"

He barely had time to give her an exasperated glare before Dom was on him.

Dom didn't resemble David now. His teeth clenched in a grimace, the tendons in his neck standing out, eyes shooting fire, Dom was all machismo. An alpha male defending his territory.

But Nick was Latin, too.

When Dom reached for his throat with both hands, Nick brought his wrists up and slashed outward, butting his head into Dom's chin at the same time.

Castigi frowned as his one and only friend went sprawling. He lumbered over to help.

Cursing herself for an idiot, Honor stepped in front of Castigi, set both hands flat on his chest and pushed. "Sit."

Castigi sat. He missed the couch edge and slumped to the floor hard enough to make it shake. He peered around her, tried to rise, but Honor stood over him, hands on her hips, legs long and imperious in black stockings, and shook her head fiercely.

Since he didn't want to hurt her, Castigi sighed, clasped his hands on his upraised knees and watched.

Dom got to his hands and knees, shaking his

obviously aching head, but he managed to stand. He glared at Nick for a long minute, glanced between Honor and his adversary, and apparently decided to fall back and defend his own instead of attack.

Honor was still standing guard over Castigi, so she didn't expect it when Dom reached out a long arm and hauled her to his side, pulling her off balance. She stumbled, but he caught her about the waist, clutching her so tightly that she could barely breathe.

He spread his legs in an aggressive stance and said with surprising steadiness, "You don't deserve her. No one deserves her. And no one will have her."

Nick propped one lean hip on a plush armchair. "Don't you think that's her choice?"

Honor's experiment had long since passed the volatile stage. She felt Dom trembling against her, and she could no longer doubt the force of his feelings. A reciprocal tremble quivered through her. She looked up at Dom, willing him to understand the depth of her need for him.

Dom turned his tousled head to look down at her. Honor gasped as those Adriatic eyes darkened to fathomless blue, pulling her in to a quiet, secret place that had no beginning and no end. It was if space itself beckoned her to an adventure she couldn't imagine.

But she could dream. . . .

Dreams had brought him to her. Maybe dreams could make him hers.

"Dom," she whispered, one hand rising to cradle his beautiful face.

Colleen Shannon

She felt the moisture on his lashes as he blinked and kissed her palm. "Ah, *bellissima*, do not tell me that you give another what I do not dare to take. I cannot bear it."

A soft sigh might have shaken Nick's shoulders slightly as he watched expressions play across their faces, but only Castigi saw it. The two men exchanged a long look that tacitly admitted to an envy both would later deny.

Nick stood and jerked his head at the door. "That's our cue. How 'bout some coffee, Rafe?"

Abruptly somber, Rafe levered himself to his feet. "I know when I'm a third wheel. See ya, pal." He was still shaky, and stumbled as he headed for the door.

Nick slipped his arm under Castigi's to steady him. The two big men paused in the doorway.

Totally unaware of their imminent departure, Dom and Honor stared at one another, trembling.

For the first time, Nick's large, dark eyes resembled Ernie's, betraying that same soft spark of humanity. "You learn fast, Dom. You need me, Honor, just give a good yell." Nick yanked Castigi's arm. The door closed gently behind them.

Vaguely, Honor sensed the quietness of the apartment. Rubbing her tears with the heel of her hand, she looked around. Where was Nick? Had he taken Rafe with him?

Dom, too, looked and realized they were alone. He took two big steps away from her, seeming to want to put a safe distance between them. The aggression, even the longing, had faded from his face, leaving a rigid, cold quietness that hurt Honor more than the garters he still wore.

"Why did you go with him?" The sentence was like the first arrow in an onslaught.

The rapid transition in Honor's emotions set her head spinning until she hardly knew up from down. But one emotion stood stark in her confused brain: outrage. What right had he to repeatedly reject her and then treat her to this little-boy fit of sullens because she went elsewhere for the closeness he denied her? A thousand defenses came to her lips, but fury was strongest. It was far easier to shoot back, to try to wound him as he'd wounded her. "Maybe because he makes me feel like a woman instead of a child."

Dom's fists clenched. "What did you do with him?"

Honor plopped down on the same chair arm Nick had appropriated, crossing one long, silken leg over the other. She waited until Dom's eyes compulsively traced the movement before she said blithely, "Not much. We just got down, dirty and sweaty together."

The slang was obviously no language barrier. He jerked as if she'd slapped him, taking another step back.

She tilted her head, pretending her conscience didn't chastise her for a liar. It was true, as far as it went. Let him imagine the worst. "The man can move, let me tell you."

Dom's teeth grated together. "*Zitto!*"

No, I won't shut up, Honor vowed. "You know, Nick's a perceptive guy. He was right about you." Honor waited for him to look at her before she concluded, "You don't want me, but you don't want anyone else to have me either."

Colleen Shannon

Dom took a long stride toward her, but he checked himself. He muttered something. " . . . *ut fideles, Spiritui, quem accepimus, maneamus.*"

She cocked her head, listening. Incredibly, she realized he spoke Latin. He was using one of the catechisms of his birth, trying to put her beyond limits. On a pedestal.

But Honor didn't feel like a madonna. Or even a virgin. At that moment she felt like a woman scorned. A woman who, in a few months, would lose the only man she'd ever love and wouldn't even have the memory of his lovemaking to sustain her.

Quietly Honor said, "Why don't you try a few Hail Marys and Our Fathers?"

Midword, Dom froze. Slowly, like a blind man, he looked at her blankly. And then, with a visible shudder, something in him seemed to snap. His face reddening with suppressed passion, he barreled toward her.

Honor stayed put, bracing herself as she watched the results of her explosive experiment. That chill, when it slithered down her spine this time, wasn't as delicious as she'd expected. He looked like he wanted to beat her and then take her to bed. In that order. . . .

Downstairs, Nick tried not to look at the ceiling and wonder. It was quiet up there, so at least Dom wasn't beating her. Not that he seemed the type, anyway. Nick poured Castigi another cup of coffee.

He slurped that one down equally quickly. "Man, that's good. A lot better than Mickey D's."

"I should hope so. I get it from a mail-order company to the tune of twenty bucks a pound."

Castigi froze in the act of putting the cup down. A shuttered look came down over his face. He was the inscrutable warrior again, still tipsy, but sobering. "Well, ain't that fine? Thanks for the joe, man. Gotta go." He stood.

Nick stood with him. "What's your rush? You can crash in my spare bedroom if you want." Nick wasn't certain why he made the offer. Perhaps it was because he sensed a kindred soul in this wounded warrior. Perhaps it was because Castigi was Ernie's project, and Ernie's interests tended to become Nick's interests. Or perhaps it was because, for the first time in a long time, Nick sensed he'd found a man who could be a friend.

And God knows, he thought dispassionately, *we both need more of those.*

Castigi shifted uncomfortably.

Nick saw refusal trembling on his lips and added, "Besides, I need to give you the name of a friend of mine. He's agreed to take your disturbing the peace case pro bono. When's the hearing set?"

"A month or so," Castigi admitted begrudgingly. But he sat back down. "What's his name?"

Nick scribbled the name and number on a pad and ripped off the top sheet, offering it.

Castigi glanced at the information and stuffed the sheet in his pocket. "Thanks." He obviously wanted to leave, but he stayed put.

Amused that the SEAL still remembered the rudiments, at least, of polite behavior, Nick

227

watched Castigi struggle for a topic of conversation that would segue to a graceful exit. But he had one of his own to bring up. "So how are you related to Dom?"

Castigi frowned. "I'm not."

"But Ernie said—" Nick broke off.

Ernie obviously hadn't said, at least not to Castigi.

Odd. Nick couldn't figure out why Dom was so interested in this man.

"Dom tell you he's related to me?"

"No. Not exactly."

Castigi shoved the coffee cup aside so he could lean forward with his elbows on the table. "Well, what, exactly?"

For the first time Nick realized that Castigi's eyes were the same unusual blue as Dom's. "I guess you'll have to ask Dom. All I know is that he told Ernie that the two of you are related."

Staring down into the dregs in the coffee cup, Castigi said slowly, his words becoming less slurred all the time, "So what do you know about Dom?"

"Not much. Except that he's from Italy, and he and Honor are accused in the theft of a statue. Though I don't think they actually took it."

Castigi's shaggy head lifted. "Statue?"

"Yeah. Some piece of work Honor believes Michelangelo might have sculpted." Nick's eyes narrowed as Castigi looked away again. Too quickly. "Come on, Rafe. Fess up. What's going on here? I assure you I have no intention of going to the police, even if malfeasance is involved, but

228

since my brother's helping them, surely I have a right to know what they've done."

Rafe rubbed his temples. "Couldn't tell you. But I'm working with Dom at the stonecutting plant out in Flushing, and he just brought in a big chunk of change to put down on a big chunk of marble. Spends every spare minute hammering away at it. Looks like he's sculpting a statue."

"Oh, shit." Nick leaned back weakly in his chair.

Could Dom and Honor be involved in some kind of forgery ring after all?

Dom's huge hands came out and caught Honor's shoulders. His breathing quickened at the feel of her soft skin, which he stroked as if he couldn't help himself. The contrast of his body language and his words was striking. He said coolly, "I am like the marble I love to work with, *bambina*. I don't bend. But I break. Press me further at your peril."

If he'd used any other endearment, she might have heeded the soft, dangerous warning. But for him to call her a child again . . . Honor slapped his hands away. "You're right about one thing," she whispered bitterly. She didn't notice that her spaghetti straps had slipped off her shoulders.

But Dom did. His jaw flexed as he stared at the long, pure line of neck meeting shoulder. And lower.

Honor finished, "You are like the marble you once were. Inflexible. Cold. And rigidly uncar—"

"Rigid?" Dom brought her hand to the front of his pants.

Flinching at the hard masculinity he thrust into her palm, Honor tried to pull away. Her hand burned. She burned. *Oh, heaven, why did you send him to me only to torment us both?*

He pressed her hand harder, saying with a snarl, "What do you know of rigid? I awake hard for you in the morning, I go to sleep hard for you at night. Even at work sometimes, I . . . " He flung her hand away and turned aside.

Driven beyond mercy, beyond even any sense of self-preservation, Honor surged to her feet and blocked him. Insolently she caught the garters at his sleeves and popped them. "I see how obsessed you are with me. Words. Words mean nothing. Especially when they're spoken by a rogue with no sense of hon—" She bit back the word too late. Even now, in the heat of passion, she knew she was being unfair to him.

And, from the look on his face, she'd also achieved the result she had sought in her little experiment.

She'd pushed him beyond his limits. Fascinated, she watched the explosion.

With a guttural, primitive snarl, he caught the front of her bodice in his fist. The delicate straps tore loose. Beads went flying. She felt the coolness at her bosom and knew the minute he let go, her bodice would drop to her waist.

Embarrassed? Afraid? No, she was fiercely, joyously glad. On some dim level she was aware that a sea change had taken place within her. She didn't cringe under his passionate gaze. She welcomed it, wanted it, reveled in it.

But only one thing would complete the transition.

Only one act would make her feel beautiful.

And only Dom could perform it with her.

Those fierce blue eyes were bright enough to shame the sun. This time the shiver that went through her as he stared at her mouth was both pleasurable—and humbling. Her pride had slipped along with her dress.

He said, fierce and low, his breath stirring the hair at her temples, "I have touched no other woman, not intimately, since I came into your life. I want you, Honor. Only you. But if I . . . lie with you, what morrow will we see with the sunrise? God sent me here to redeem my name, not commit further sin. I cannot sully the virgin who gave me life—"

Honor put her fingers over his mouth, the soft warmth making her tremors more delicious as they started a soft pulse in her lower body. "No, Dom. But you can honor her."

He stared at her.

For the first time since his rebirth, Honor felt that still, quiet fluttering over them. As if an angel watched unseen with steady faith in a fate only she saw. In a room with no wind, and silence with no music, a whispering hope of a breeze and a paean of angel chords blessed the man, the girl and the dream.

Consciously, Honor only knew that confusion, fear and pain were replaced by a great serenity. Certain she said the right thing, Honor finished simply, "Honor us both. Surely it would be a greater sin to cheapen the gift God gave us. I want to celebrate life with you before I lose you to the mists of time."

Honor gently slipped away from his easy clasp and shimmied out of the sagging dress.

Part Three

"Some feelings are to mortals given,
With less of earth in them than Heaven."
—Sir Walter Scott, *The Lady of the Lake*

Chapter Ten

He'd tried so hard to be strong. As Dom watched
Honor's lovely body reveal itself, he told himself
he must turn away, do the right thing. *Leave her.*
She is too good for you.

But he was weak. It was the drink, still running
warm and heady in his veins, that kept him from
penitence. *Liar.* Cretino! Honor herself was the
only stimulant he needed. Or wanted. . . .

Compulsively, his fingers clenching with the
yearning to touch, he watched her small, pert
breasts tremble. She took a deep breath and
stood tall, proud, letting him look. She seemed to
find joy in his fascination, for she stepped out of
her slip and posed bare before him in stockings,
garters and black silk unmentionables.

A smile trembled on her lips, one so lovely that he had to close his eyes to shield himself from pleasure-pain. The savage, instinctive need to conquer almost overcame him. To stamp his possession on this woman who'd dared him, tempted him, tormented him. She wanted it almost as badly as he did.

Everywhere, he ached—manhood, head, but heart most of all. . . .

He would give ten years of his life to know he had the right to offer Honor more than a few nights of stolen passion. But he didn't even know if he had a future, much less one that would include her. The best that could happen would be that he was allowed to return home. How could he ask her to come? A different image grew behind his lids. One far less lovely, but the only one that could grant him a last measure of sanity in the face of a temptation surely Adam himself had not endured.

While he struggled with himself, he felt her approach. She caught his hands, kissed his palms, and brought them to her breasts.

Groaning, he relearned their satiny texture and plump fullness with his sensitive sculptor's hands. Her heart leaped to his touch, and his own lurched in response.

"Reject me again and I'll never forgive you," she told him softly, nibbling at his lip.

Porca miseria! He was tired of hurting her. Tired of this interminable ache in his gut, and lower. He was probably damned anyway. And surely she could hate him no more afterward than she would when he was gone.

Besides, he could not bear to drive her into another man's arms.

Better his own soul face eternal hellfire than that.

The dam upon his feelings had cracked long ago, but when it broke, it swept all before it. Restraint. Fear.

And Honor . . .

Lifting her into his arms, he carried her into the bedroom.

Light upon darkness. Hard upon soft. Pain upon joy.

In the uncharted territory of a man's arms, Honor was like a babe who had to learn all the lessons of life again. She sinned with full knowledge of the price she might pay, and she loved with the full measure of a woman who knew what she risked.

In the process, she relearned the most basic lessons of maturity that so many spent their lives fleeing.

There is no light without darkness . . .

In the big bed in the small room, moonlight from the open window smiled down upon the couple learning one another by touch as much as by sight. As Dom kissed a slow, sweet path down her neck to her collarbones, pausing to nip and suck as if he'd memorized every sensitive point in her body to guide him in her initiation, Honor lay boneless. Eyes wide open, she saw the trees outside shifting restlessly in the wind, pointing accusing fingers at the moon as if to chastise it for a peeping Tom.

Even as she shivered at the unutterable pleasure, Honor watched the light against the darkness. A beacon to mark the way home in the vast
universe, smiling so brightly as if to bless them.

Dom bypassed her breasts, kissing his way
down one side of her body to her hip. He
removed her garter with his teeth, pulling it down
her leg, using both hands to unsheathe the long
leg from the nylon stocking as he went. He did
the same with her other leg, pausing at her feet to
nibble at her ankles. His bent head caught the
moonlight streaming across the end of the bed,
revealing muted shades of brown, red and gold.
Somehow he'd removed his shirt. The purity of
his perfect, flexing muscles had never been more
lovely than in this ethereal glow.

Patches of light upon darkness played on
Honor's open eyes as he moved into and out of
the shadows. There and gone. Real and a dream.
Even as she luxuriated in his patient seduction,
turning her leg about as he wished so he could
explore it with tongue and teeth, her sadness
made the moment all the more poignant.

Dom had brought her illumination. Eyes that
warmed her soul, a smile bright enough to chase
away Stygian gloom, and a heart so warm and true
that he seemed to carry a glow around with him.

When he left, light would leave with him, leaving her to face the same dull, gray world again.

But even knowing the price she paid for this
stolen night, Honor would change nothing of this
lesson of light upon darkness.

Tired of being patient, Honor caught his tough
sculptor's hands and brought him to the ache

he'd incited. She rotated his palms on her excited, needful nipples.

He caught his breath, staring at her in the shadows. He removed his hands, ignoring her little mew of protest, scooted on his knees to the head of the bed and flung the curtains open the rest of the way. Full moonglow touched them both. Honor saw her own radiance reflected in his eyes.

Holding her gaze, he backed off the bed, stood, unbuttoned his pants and shimmied out of them. He drew down the briefs and kicked them away. He took one step toward her, but this time he wore no intense frown. He smiled, one hand extended as if inviting her to follow him. He inhaled her essence through flared nostrils, absorbed her through darkened eyes.

For the first time in her life, she felt beautiful as she stared at this magical male. His manhood rose tall and proud from the curly nest of hair, a fitting tribute to her own femininity.

The time for a virgin's shyness was long past. From where her sudden confidence came, she knew not. But she knew who granted it to her. . . .

She sat up, caught his hand and kissed the callused fingertips, her head bowed in homage. She nibbled his forefinger and drew it into her mouth, suckling him like a babe seeking sustenance. He both took it and offered it in abundance.

Still standing, drawing her to her knees on the bed, he caught her waist, arched her over his arm and kissed her breast. He moved around the delicate globe, pausing to jab his tongue once at the nipple, just enough to bring it to a point. His erection pressed hard and urgent into her hip. He had to spread his legs for balance as he brought her closer, higher. He pressed more intimately into her.

Honor realized he was swaying on his feet, and she could not doubt that he was as swept away by sheer rapture as she was. Her senses seemed peculiarly linked with his. She knew when he was ready to sup at her other breast and offered it for his delectation. When he gently touched the vee between her legs, she groaned but spread her knees, then straightened her legs and let him shimmy the scrap of black silk down her legs and cast it aside. Half lying atop her on the bed, he pressed the heel of his hand exactly where she needed it most. Her neck bowed, her tendons tight with joyful agony, she let tremors take her. They arced from him to her and back, like the lightning that might have stirred the primordial pool into life long ago. Totally natural and totally right.

Honor ran her fingers through his luxurious hair, trying to draw his mouth to hers, but he made a little grunt of denial and latched harder onto her nipple. "Be still," he whispered into her flushed skin, running his tongue over the throbbing button while his teeth delicately nibbled. His free hand played upon her lower bud, coaxing it to a similar throbbing.

The current sizzled hotter through Honor, making every tiny hair on her skin stand on end. She was burning, dying, but she had to take him with her. . . . Instinct guided her to life's next lesson. Honor groped and found him with one hand.

There is no hardness without softness. . . .

Dom groaned into her breast and shuddered. Lifting his head, he brought his hand down to move her away. "Too fast."

"Too slow." Honor resisted, clasped her fingers around him and moved slightly back on her weak knees so she could see what she held.

She looked.

Dom looked.

And the sight of her small, soft hand upon his flaring manhood brought the march of time to a standstill. He leaped to her touch, his pulsing blood answering the primitive rush of her own. The room was quiet now in the beatific light, the only sound their soft pants and pleasured groans.

At the sheer wonder of what she held, Honor sagged down, sitting on her heels, feeling her own wetness. She brought up her other hand, delicately learning the heft and texture of his sac while she caressed his erection at the same time.

Despite his size, fear was beyond her. This sense of rightness, of belonging, left room for nothing but joy. She was built for this. She hadn't known it then, but she'd saved herself for this Renaissance rogue. Here was the essence of man, the power that drove him to mate, to expend himself and see his issue conquer new worlds.

Even when he was gone, she might still have a portion of him.

His hands clenched on her shoulders, Dom withstood her soft caresses as long as he could bear. Soon the tremors shook them both so hard that time began its relentless march again. To one end . . .

And one fate.

His teeth gleaming in a savage grimace, Dom managed to say between them, "Woman, stop! I do not want to hurt you. . . . " He ended on a long groan as Honor took his erection between both hands and kissed the tip.

She murmured softly against his excitement, "Hurt me? I've waited a lifetime for this. Please."

Leaning back, she opened her legs and tried to guide him home. She stared up at him, her eyes new-minted silver in the moonlight, her tousled blond hair flowing over the pillows like gold.

And with the greed of a man who'd been poor too long, he took what was offered. Pulling her hips to the edge of the low mattress, he knelt next to the bed, resting her slim hips easily upon the power of his own. The hard tip touched her in the most intimate caress she'd ever known, sliding, slipping upon her to prepare her for the length and power she so desperately wanted to sheathe.

Lying back, she closed her eyes, her hands pulling at his hips. "Hurry."

She felt him pause, resisting her frantic little tugs. He groped beside them on the floor. Something crackled in his hands.

She opened her eyes.

He fumbled with the unfamiliar tiny wrapping of a condom, clumsy with desire. Instinct had led her this far, so she let it guide her still. She snatched the condom out of his hands and tossed it away. Practicality be damned! If she were being practical, she wouldn't be here.

"No. I want to feel everything." She latched on to him.

For the barest instant, Dom resisted. "But Honor. If—"

She shook her head violently, but her grip upon him was soft and needful. "Don't deny me this. I deny you nothing." She squeezed gently.

His head arched back as a harsh groan shook him. "*Per Dio,* forgive me," he muttered, whether to her or to heaven, she couldn't say. To her, it didn't matter.

A little sin sometimes led to a great blessing. Honor didn't know how she knew, but somehow she did.

Mesmerized by her glowing face, Dom brushed her hands away, scooted forward and lowered her hips upon him again. Gladly, she opened her legs to complete her transition from girlhood to womanhood.

She was slick with her need of him, so the melding was quick, sharp and irrevocable. With one strong, imperious thrust, he pulled her hard into the cradle of his hips and sundered the maiden's veil.

Her scream and his groan mingled as one.

Even as pain lanced through her, she arched her neck in exaltation, learning the last, most powerful lesson of all.

There is no joy without pain. . . .

Deep within her, Dom stopped. "I'm sorry, *cara mia,* forgive me," he whispered. He trembled like a man with a fever, but somehow he managed to stay still and let her stretch to accomodate him. "But quick is better. It will hurt less in a minute."

On some faraway level, a spark of jealousy ignited in her mind. He spoke like a man who'd initiated more than his share of virgins. But she'd allow nothing to spoil the moment.

The pain faded slowly, aided by a more powerful stimulus. That essence of maleness she'd admired time and again and lusted over days without end was finally hers. He was joined with her in the most intimate way possible. At last their bodies were linked as their fates had always been.

Dom stayed still, cradling her face in his hands as she supported her weight on her elbows to look down at their coupling. The movement made her clench about him. He rose slightly on his knees in a reaction he obviously couldn't control, pressing still deeper into her womb.

The pain didn't hurt as much this time, perhaps because Honor's senses were so inflamed. Touch, smell, feel, but sight . . . oh, sight. The image of that hard male shaft within her until brown hair mingled with blond was the only aphrodisiac Honor needed. Fascinated, she sat up, inched her hips forward slightly, rocking upon him, her gaze lifting to his flushed face. She was so pleased at his grimace that she did it again. How delicious that he, too, felt the pleasure-pain of this merging.

He caught her hips hard enough to hurt, holding rock steady on his knees, forcing her to be still. His voice was so hoarse she scarcely recognized it. "Not yet. Oh, *Dio mio, Santa Maria*, don't move!"

Panting, she went limp. A fine mist of sweat sheened her skin in the coolness of the room, but she empathized with the agony in his voice.

Somehow she could wait, though she longed with every fiber of her being to launch herself upon him and ride furiously into the dawn.

Only when she relaxed did she feel the great rhythm beating between them. A strange pulsing built in the flesh that sheathed him. And he throbbed within her, as if his insistent maleness were a wild thing with a life—and will—of its own.

He shook his head slightly, sweat trickling down his face. "You are tight, my Honor. So soft and warm . . . " He gritted his teeth, closed his eyes and muttered something in Latin to himself, staying very still. Slowly she felt the tension leave him as he got control.

He pressed his strong chest to her aching breasts and rubbed his own erect nipples against hers. At the same time, he nudged her mouth open with his own, kissing her for the first time. Gently, so sweetly, holding her hips still so he could set the pace, he communicated with his lips all the longing throbbing deep inside her body.

And the tenderness he expressed, mouth softly rubbing side to side, then suckling, brought tears to her eyes. This man loved her. No man could pretend this near worship. The rogue he claimed to be would have taken her lustily, as she begged, not cherished her with mouth and manhood.

Pain pierced her, but it had nothing to do with what she'd won this night, and everything to do with what she stood to lose.

"Oh, Dom." She sobbed into his mouth. "I can't bear it if you leave me."

He caught the sadness from her lips and gave it

back to her in joy. "Shhh. Think not of tomorrow. Tonight is ours. Remember . . . "

With an impassioned groan, he deepened the kiss. The gentleness was no more. He drew her bottom lip into his mouth and suckled hungrily. When she gasped, he took full advantage and gave her what she wanted.

Simultaneously, he took her with tongue and manhood, thrusting deep above and below. Honor was helpless before the storm she'd aroused, so shocked at the twin intrusions that for a moment she felt invaded. But the pulsing in her secret place grew as he withdrew and pressed deep again, arching high, rubbing against the seat of her pleasure. Again he maneuvered her with his hands on her hips, pulling her forward on the upthrust, easing her back on the with- drawal, all the while probing her mouth with the intimate thrust of his tongue.

Honor had never known such a primitive dance, but that strange rhythm she'd felt earlier quickened. Her heart leaped to the exquisite, frantic pace, sending pleasure sparking to every nerve ending in her body. Slowly she learned the dance, and the lubricious pleasure of advance and retreat. Blindly she followed his lead, trust- ing him as she'd never trusted any man.

When he leaned back on his thighs and pulled her forward until she was astride him, she went gladly. Only her back and shoulders were upon the bed as he steadily lifted and lowered her with the power of his arms and hips. She caught his arms to steady herself, feeling the hard muscles bunch and flex everywhere they touched. High, and higher, where the glow was building, as if she did indeed ride him into the dawn.

She felt him hardening within her, and then the pleasure burst as the last frantic step took them to the sun. Honor bit his shoulder to stifle her scream as warmth exploded through her, centering on the flesh that pressed deep a final time. Pleasure spread outward to every pore in a starburst that destroyed Honoria Psyche, melancholy maiden, and created Honor, woman grown . . . and loved.

Tears in her eyes at the incredible rebirth, Honor clutched him tight about the neck, her legs wrapped as close about him as she could get. With a fractured groan he burst as well, the stream of life completing the cycle. In that climactic moment he was vulnerable, and more precious to her than anything heaven or earth could create. Tears streamed down her face as she licked his shoulder. She thought surely her heart would burst with the joy he spent into her womb.

Limp, he fell sideways onto the bed, still holding her to him, still nestled securely inside her, one powerful thigh trapping her beneath him. Honor realized he didn't want to break this bond any more than she did. She rested her cheek on his chest, feeling the thrum of his heartbeat. She didn't speak; no words, no matter how eloquent, could define this moment. Feelings were all she needed, or wanted.

It might have been minutes or hours, Honor neither knew nor cared, before he stirred. She held her breath, wondering if he'd be angry with her, but there was a lilt of laughter in his voice.

"Ah, if all virgins in your time are so responsive, perhaps I was born too early after all."

Honor whacked him, swiveling her hips to disengage. "And if all Renaissance rogues are so skillful, perhaps I was born too late."

He sat up, the smile fading from his face. Honor bit her lip, wondering what she'd said, but he merely stood and gently pulled her to her feet. He swept her into his arms and carried her into the shower.

They spent an hour bathing one another. There, in the warm water, his back against the tile wall, he took her again. And again, in bed, as dawn filtered through the trees. Finally, exhausted, they closed the curtains and slept. Even in sleep he kept an arm around her, as if he couldn't bear to be separated for an instant.

Hours later, she was awakened by his fidgeting. First his legs, then his arms flailed against her. He rolled over on his back and moaned, "No! Marta, come, *bellissima*, I find the physician." He screamed, his arms held out before him as if he shook someone.

So she was *bellissima* to him, too. Misery that he still apparently loved his Marta despite what had passed between them battled with compassion in Honor's troubled heart. Should she wake him? That would be a certain way for him to remember the terrible dream. She hesitated, fearfully watching horrific memories flicker across his expressive face.

"Mama, Papa, where are you?" He shifted his legs as if running. "Roberto, come, little brother, we leave this terrible place." Then, with outrage, he roared, "But it was a fair fight! He insulted me. . . . " And finally, with agonized fury, "*Dio,* why do you take everything from me? I hate you, I hate you, I curse you and all who serve you!"

Honor couldn't bear to hear any more. She was reaching out to shake his arm when he bolted to a sitting position and opened his eyes. They were wild, uncomprehending, as he stared at his strange surroundings, but then he saw her face. By slow degrees the panic faded. For an instant she saw her own misery in his dark blue eyes, but then his expression shuttered.

"Did I wake you?" He kissed her lightly and eased out of the covers to pull on his clothes.

The wonder of the night past seemed long ago and far away. But for the soreness between her legs Honor might have doubted it had happened. She waited, but he said nothing, dressing so fast that she couldn't doubt his urgency to be gone. Wasn't he going to tell her about the dream? How could they be as intimate emotionally as they were physically if he didn't share his feelings?

The old Honoria would have closed off her own hurt, but the new Honor probed gently. "Dom, you were dreaming. A nightmare, actually. Don't you want to tell me about it?"

He pulled his shirt over his head, muffling his voice. "No time. I'm late for work."

Honor glanced at the clock. It was after ten, but surely it wouldn't hurt for him to take one day off. It was Saturday, anyway. "But I thought perhaps we could see something of the city. New York is a wonderful place." *For lovers.* But the words wouldn't come.

He tucked his T-shirt in his jeans and gave her a quick smile that didn't warm his eyes. "No, I cannot afford even a day off." He bussed her on the cheek and turned to leave.

Honor bit her lip as the old Honoria surfaced. He wouldn't see her cry, no matter what. She'd thought, hoped, that the merging of their bodies would lead to the final merging of their hearts and lives. How, she did not know. Whether he stayed or she tried to go with him, she'd reasoned that somehow they'd find a way if they wanted it badly enough.

In the cold light of day, there was no magical, approving moonlight. Only harsh reality. And from the closed look on his face and his urgency to be gone, Honor could only conclude that he didn't want her badly enough.

In the doorway he paused. "I do not know if now is the proper time or place, but I would leave you with this thought, my Honor."

The knot of misery in her stomach loosened. *My Honor.* At least he didn't call her Honoria. Honor held her breath.

"I love you. Too much to risk taking you with me. Remember that, and do not hate me." He was gone.

She was left gasping on the bed, one hand reaching toward him. She slumped back on the pillows, her head spinning. How could he so casually tell her exactly what she wanted to hear, and then leave her? And if it were true, and he did love her, why did he fear taking her back with him?

* * *

250

Dom paused on the steps of Saint Patrick's Cathedral. He felt the curious stares of those who entered, but he was helpless to move. He couldn't shake the dread that God would smite him the second he set foot in His house. After work, he'd often attended evening Mass, finding there his only relief from his gnawing desire for Honor. For a while, penitence was a mighty shield, but in the end it had been too weak.

This magnificent building was one of the few places in the huge city where he felt at home. The tall spires, the lovely stained-glass windows, the liturgies he'd often heard inside and the magnificent tall altar, these seemed to be all that remained of his world, the world he and his fellow Italians had believed would dominate history ever after.

Dom smiled harshly. What hubris. Yes, Michelangelo, Leonardo and others of his time were remembered with awe, but only for their art and genius. The civilization that had seemed preeminent upon the globe and destined to live forever was dust under his feet. Now that he'd experienced the wonders of a new age, like toilets that flushed, those strange boxes called computers, the moving-picture televisions, the flying machines, the wonders of medicine that had conquered so many of the ills he and his kind had taken for granted, only now did he realize that the Renaissance was a savage time barely out of the Dark Ages.

That horrific image almost knocked him from his feet again. The thought of endangering Honor was abhorrent to him. Far better that he think of her as healthy and unhappy than to have her by his side, happy for the brief time she'd have before a sword, a sickness or a savage took her. If he loved her less, perhaps he could risk it.

He made an impatient sound in his throat, forcing himself to walk forward under the shadow of God's eminence. At least these strange, harsh descendants still worshiped God, though commerce seemed of equal importance here.

No burst of lightning smote him; no inferno swept him below.

He walked with more confidence to the confessional, but he'd have to wait his turn. Kneeling before the altar to pray, he clasped his hands and bowed his head. Even as he asked God's forgiveness, he could not regret the joys of the flesh he'd known last night with Honor. Somehow he felt the sin of his pride and broken vow more keenly. Even here, he couldn't regret that he'd known Honor so thoroughly, body and soul. In some ways, surely it would have been a worse sin to leave her untouched and make her hate him.

While he muttered his soundless prayer, a strange sense of peace overcame him. When it was his turn in the confessional, he stepped inside, drew the partition shut and said the ancient words, "Forgive me, Father, for I have sinned." And the words poured out of him, leaving him purified for the first time since his arrival.

Perhaps a little sin could lead to a great blessing. . . .

Honor ached all over. When she looked at her naked body in the mirror, she was fiercely glad of the bruises and love bites. She remembered giving him his fair share, as well. She stared at her slim form. The ribs were as prominent as ever, but for the first time she noticed the tiny curve of her waist, her flawless skin and pretty legs. She hefted her breasts, blushing as she recalled how many times Dom had kissed and suckled them. He certainly didn't seem to mind their smallness.

Honor waited for the usual sense of distaste and embarrassment at her skinniness. It didn't come. Instead she visualized her belly swollen, pregnant with his child. And she had to catch the bureau to steady herself, stricken with joy-sadness at the thought. Perhaps it had already happened. But somehow she knew it was not meant to be. She wasn't certain Dom would want to lie with her again, despite his claim to love her.

Before the gloom could totally shroud her, she made herself turn away and begin to dress. Her shift was the late one tonight, so she still had plenty of time. And she had an errand at the museum first.

An hour later she knocked on Trotterman's door. "Come in," came the muffled response.

She wasn't surprised to find him working on the weekend. He was as much a workaholic as she used to be.

He didn't look surprised to see her either. "Hello, my dear." He appraised her closely. "You look . . . different. Have you changed your makeup?"

Actually she was wearing a bit more than usual, partly to disguise the love marks on her neck. She nodded.

"Odd. I've never seen makeup give such a glow. You are quite a lovely girl, you know."

She blushed, looking down at her feet. She knew where the glow came from. Normally, when given a compliment, she'd make a self-deprecating response. This time she said nothing, though desolation took her at the realization that the man who'd gifted her with this budding self-worth was about to leave her with a barren legacy. She'd given her body, her heart, a measure of the secret soul she'd kept to herself since childhood, but it still wasn't enough.

What manner of man was he that he could profess to love her yet intend to leave her mourning him the rest of her days? Cherish her, honor . . . She gritted her teeth at the hideous pun, wishing her parents had named her something else. She swayed on her feet under the force of feelings she could hardly bear, much less admit aloud.

Looking concerned, Trotterman rounded the desk and gently pushed her into the chair before it. "What's amiss, my child?"

Briskly, Honor rubbed her cheeks until they tingled. She let her hands drop and folded them in her lap. "I'll get over it." And she would, she told herself fiercely.

Trotterman took his desk chair again. "I wondered when you'd come see me again."

Honor's fingers tightened in her lap even as she said lightly, "How did you know I would?"

His little mouth pursed in a perfect bow. "Why, curiosity, of course. To see what I had learned about your friend."

He was smart; she had to give him that, even if

he could be a bit insufferable at times. "So what did you discover?"

"So far, only that a Dominico Paolo Constantine Castiglione became captain of the pope's guards."

Clutching the chair arms, Honor managed to keep her voice even. "What year?"

He shifted through the papers on his desk to pick up a printout. He had to fumble with the half-glass bifocals in his pocket, adjusting them at the proper angle on his pudgy nose. He picked up the paper, perusing it slowly.

Honor gritted her teeth to master her impatience.

Finally, he looked at her over the bifocals. "Fifteen hundred."

The tiny lingering glow was snuffed, leaving her ashen. Honor jumped to her feet and ran out of the office. She bit savagely at her swollen mouth, but even the pain couldn't stop her tears. So it was true. He would leave her and return to his own time. She paused around a corner to wipe her eyes. She took deep, shuddering breaths, telling herself savagely that she was an idiot. She'd known while she was having sex with him that he'd leave her if he could.

She'd thought that maybe, just maybe, the bond of sexual intimacy would make him decide to stay with her. Or, at a minimum, make the leaving less painful.

Wrong on both counts.

It was very late when Honor returned home. She was opening the door to the dark apartment, telling herself fiercely that she didn't care that Dom wasn't home, when a door opened in Nick's quarters below.

Firm footsteps ascended, and Nick's voice said, "Honor, thank heavens you're home. I've been trying to reach you all day."

Pinning a smile to her face, she turned to meet him. "Evening, Nick. About what?"

He hesitated. "You got a cup of coffee to spare?"

The last thing Honor wanted was a heart-to-heart with Nick, especially now, when it felt as if her heart had nothing left to give. But politeness and the knowledge of how much she owed this man and his brother made her open the door and wave him in.

While she brewed the coffee, he stood at the large window in the living room, watching the city below. She saw tension in the outline of his tall, powerful body, and wondered what was eating him and how it concerned her.

Thinking she might take up drinking herself, she poured two cups of strong fortitude, shoved one before Nick and said baldly, "What is it?"

He took a sip, hesitating, but finally he answered equally bluntly. "I think you should know that your roommate is sculpting a statue. Of whom, I don't know. For what, I can only speculate. But the possibilities are somewhat troubling."

Setting her cup down so hastily that coffee sloshed over the sides, Honor caught the table edge to brace herself against the pain. She knew exactly of whom, and for what. Here was final, definitive proof. He had no reason to spend every spare moment sculpting his replacement unless he intended to leave her behind. In his own peculiar way, he was even being honorable. He'd ripped her away from her old life, and he was trying to restore it to her in the only way he knew.

Damn him and his cursed honor. Why could he not just let his feelings sweep him away, as they had so briefly for one stolen night?

Nick watched the expressions play across her face. "So is he part of a forgery ring, or not?"

Honor shook her head, still holding the table. "It's a gift. For me."

Nick arched a cynical brow. "A life-size statue in Carrara marble is a mighty costly gift."

Honor closed her eyes. If Nick only knew how costly it really was. The incredible joy that had begun her day had been followed by such incredible depression that Honor's head was spinning. She stood. The room reeled about her. She swayed and would have fallen if Nick hadn't rounded the table to catch her arms.

"Honor? Are you sick?"

She tried to shake her head, but her heart thumped so loudly she was growing nauseous. The lack of sleep and food was catching up to her, and her stomach was taking its revenge. She clutched her abdomen. He led her to the bathroom and supported her head while she threw up. She had only phlegm to lose, but she was still embarrassed.

When she was through Nick handed her a wet washrag. He watched her bathe her face and rinse her mouth with mouthwash. When she peeped at him over the cloth, he narrowed his imperious gaze at her and barked, "Have you eaten supper?"

She shook her head.

He muttered something that might have been "Silly twit," and marched her back to the table. He cooked her an omelette, keeping up a running commentary as he did so on the secret ingredients no one knew but the Escavido men.

He set the eggs before her. They were fragrant with herbs and cheese. Honor's stomach rumbled, and suddenly she was famished.

Nick turned his chair around, straddled it and rested his arms on the back. With what could only be termed arrogant satisfaction, he watched her eat. "Good, isn't it?"

Her mouth full of food, Honor nodded. When she'd swallowed, she gave him a smile and teased, "Like the man who made it."

He stared at her, the cynical twist at his mouth soft and warm. "That's a secret. Don't tell anyone."

They laughed, mirth muffling the sound of the opening door.

Dom stood on the threshold. Sweaty, covered in marble dust, his face drawn and haggard with the same hunger and tiredness Honor felt, he stared at them. His huge hands clenched into fists.

He slammed the door.

Starting, they both looked around.

"Miss me, Honoria Psyche?" a deep, dangerous voice drawled.

The long version of her name told her what

answer he expected. And she was in no mood to deny it. Let him think the worst.

Cutting a careful bite of her omelette, she said succinctly, "Yes, but I'm working on it."

Only the faint honking of the cars outside disturbed the brooding silence.

Chapter Eleven

Nick glanced between Honor's studiedly indifferent expression and Dom's aggressive one. Gulping the last of his coffee, he set the mug down and scraped his chair back. "Well, it's late. I guess I'll hit the sack."

Dom's eyes tracked him down to the door. His fists opened and closed repeatedly.

As soon as the door had shut behind Nick, Honor tossed her fork on her plate; suddenly the mere sight of the congealing omelette made her sick.

The rattling sound made Dom start. Honor was savagely glad he wasn't as calm as he seemed either. She shoved her chair back from the table, crossed her legs and bounced one of her low-heeled pumps, saying casually, "So will you finish your replacement in time?"

Dom dragged his attention from her long, slim legs back to her face. "What?"

"The new *David*. Or maybe we should call him Judas instead."

He ran his hands through his curly hair in obvious frustration. "I am not betraying you. I am using every last vestige of my strength to do the right thing by you."

"Like last night?"

As if she'd kicked him, he backed away a swift step. "Last night will not happen again. And I have already been to confession to ask forgiveness."

Honor leaped up so fast her chair scraped the floor. "How dare you cheapen my only happy memory of you!" She flew across the floor to beat his chest with her fists. "I hate you, I hate you, I—"
He dragged up her chin and kissed her. She went limp against him, her face upturned like a flower thirsting for rain.

Even as grief almost overcame her, she wondered how her weary body and soul could take sustenance from the source of their pain. How could he be so sweet, so tender, yet so obdurate? Feeling torn in two, Honor tore her mouth away and tried to sidestep, but he wouldn't let her.

Sweeping her into his arms, he sat down with her on the couch, holding her on his lap. When she tried to pull away, he pinched her side. "Be still. Listen to me, you stubborn woman."

"*Me?* You might as well still be made of stone!"

Breathing heavily, they stared at each other. Dom traced the outline of her pursed mouth until it relaxed and began to tremble. His hand dropped quickly. "*Bellissima,* why do you not believe that I love you, and want you to be happy and safe?"

She sat up straight on his lap to look him in the eye. "It's a strange sort of love if you can lose it so easily. Why haven't you offered to take me back with you?"

There, it was out. Now he couldn't wriggle out of it. Mentally, she braced herself. An odd look appeared on his face before he shuttered his expression. Dread? Fear?

"Because I cannot." He tried to move her off his lap, but Honor caught his shoulders.

"Why not?"

That dark look returned, black as hell and twice as mean.

Unintimidated, for she fought for happiness, Honor shook him slightly. "Tell me what's eating you, dammit, before you drive me mad!"

He slapped her hands away. "You have no comprehension of the vast differences between our worlds. Many are good differences, but some are . . . " When she stared at him with her own version of darkness, he burst out, "We have no toilets."

"We can make one," Honor said with a silent word of apology to Thomas Crapper. Many things she could give up, but not that. There had actually been some signs of a sanitation system as far back as ancient Crete, she reassured herself.

"Our doctors believe bleeding is the only cure for most ailments. I have seen many healthy men die after they've been treated."

"I'm healthy as a horse. Besides, I have to die sometime. Next."

"I . . . have nothing to offer you. No home, no money. A very powerful family wants me dead. I'll be a hunted man the second I set foot in Italy. If I even make it home."

"I know you will make it back."

He frowned. "Impossible. You are the most intelligent woman I've ever known, Honoria Psyche, but you are not a soothsayer."

Honor hesitated, wondering whether to tell him that a year after his transition, assuming he returned the same time he'd left, he would be given a very honorable position. In the end she only shrugged. "I've been poor all my life. Besides, with my knowledge of history I'll know what succeeds and what fails. We can save our money and invest in the right areas, and soon . . . " She trailed off at the look on his face.

He closed his eyes, as if he could not bear to say what he had to say next. Even sitting on his lap, she had to strain to hear. "Do you have any idea of the stench, the look of a village stricken by plague?"

Honor swallowed. She had a very good idea, as she'd researched the subject more than once. This fear was not so easy to answer.

"The rats and dogs feast on the dead," he droned on. "Some are so bloated they can hardly move. And then the rats die first, like evil harbingers."

Honor's stomach churned. "Rats spread the disease. Their fleas are the carriers. Keep the rats out and you keep the disease out. Simple sanitation—"

"Marta was the last one alive in her house. She buried her father, mother and twin sisters, sending courier after courier for me, but I was too busy carousing with my friends, going from town to town, tavern to tavern. Enjoy my last days of freedom, they told me. Freedom . . . " He shuddered.

Honor tried to calm him by laying her hands on his chest, but his heart pounded so hard she wondered that it didn't shatter. His eyes were so bleak that she wanted to weep. She was sorry she'd started this. But at least she was finally hearing his greatest dread, the real reason he refused to try to take her with him.

"By the time I got there, she was dying. All her servants had run off. I . . . hardly recognized her. Her tongue was black. She had terrible welts under her arms, and was in so much pain she cried continually—"

"Buboes," Honor said dully. "They're called buboes."

"Mercifully, she died in a few hours . . . " His voice broke. Tears seeped down his cheeks.

Honor's throat tightened at the pain in his strong face. Pain she could not ease, and fears she could not calm. She slipped off his lap, feeling like an intruder, and leaned wearily against the couch.

He rubbed his tears with the heels of his hands, drawing a harsh breath. When he looked at her again, his gaze was as steady as his voice. "The day I buried her, I vowed then and there that if I ever loved again, I would keep my woman safe.

My children safe. No matter the cost to me. No matter the cost, do you understand?"

What could she say? That there was a vaccine now? But it was only effective for about a year. That swift treatment with antibiotics was usually successful? How could she take enough pills to last a lifetime? They could get vaccines against smallpox and some of the other common ailments, but they couldn't protect themselves against all the dangers of the Renaissance. She searched for words to reassure him, but in the end there were none. She could only say simply, "I'm willing to risk it."

His hands latched on to her shoulders. "So many other things. I lost two aunts to childbirth. Our society is in a constant state of war. When the crops are bad, famine." When she opened her mouth again, he shook his head fiercely. "Far better that I remember you as you were in my arms. Whole. Healthy. Lovely. And safe. Do you understand, Honor?" He tightened his grip until her upper arms ached, but her heart hurt so much more that she scarcely noticed the pain.

"And miserable," she whispered. "How do you think I feel, knowing that the minute you leave me, you become dust? That I am forever lost to you because I won't be born for almost five hundred years? How do you even know you'll remember me?"

Shocked, he let her go. He said, soft and low, "I will remember you with every beat of my heart and breath in my body. This I know. Please, Honor. Do not ask me again. I have already taken too much from you. I cannot be selfish any longer." For an instant they stared at each other.

Impasse. They both knew it; they both grieved over it; but neither saw a way past the towering obstacles keeping them apart. Cursing, Dom stood and almost ran from the room.

Instinctively, Honor reached out toward him, but her hand dropped. Footsteps climbed quickly up to the studio. A door closed, and then all was quiet. She stayed put, too exhausted to move.

Her despair was so deep that she couldn't even cry. She felt drained, empty. A void. She tried to tell herself that she should be used to this. Even in the middle of a boisterous family, she'd always felt alone. Only her mother had understood her. Honor seldom heard from her brothers, and she seldom called them. They were all married now, with families, their lives a world apart from her own. She had nothing to lose in going with Dom, not even a career. She didn't really believe that the statue, in the unlikely event Dom was able to duplicate it, would save her name.

Yet despite all that, there was nothing she could say to reassure him, nothing strong enough to convince him that she'd rather risk dying in the past than spend a lifetime dying a little more every day. For without him, that would be her fate.

Honor lay back against the couch, holding a pillow to her bosom, and stared dry-eyed into the darkness. Her solitude was relieved only by the sound of the ticking mantel clock. Honor buried her head in the cushions, but she felt time trickling through her fingers, and nothing in the world could stop it.

In the world . . . Honor's head lifted. She could not shake the intuitive belief that heaven had some grand design she and Dom didn't understand. She hadn't prayed in a long time. Too long. Honor hesitated. Her mother had been a devout Catholic, but when she died they'd quit going to Mass. Honor had occasionally gone to church while in college, but when the curiosity of her restless mind was finally satisfied, her soul seemed less important.

The words were hesitant at first, but then they began to pour from her. A prayer for strength, a prayer for guidance. In the rush of whispered conversation with a power beyond herself, peace finally overcame her. She slept dreamlessly, deeply, feeling serene for the first time in weeks.

And somewhere an angel smiled. . . .

November blew in, colder than normal, grayer than normal—and gayer than normal. Everywhere, people partied. Restaurants had long waiting lists as tourists began to pour into the city the world watched every New Year, none more than this year. Technocrats fought on the airwaves about whether planes would fall from the sky on that apocalyptic date of January 1. Futurists debated what the world would be like during humanity's next millenium, or, indeed, if humankind would survive its own killing instincts.

Honor listened to the debates with half an ear,

unable to muster much interest in her future when her present was so problematic. Their own date with destiny drew uncomfortably near, and she seldom saw Castigi. When she did, he always seemed to have a hangover. Dom refused to talk about his errant relative, but she saw the concern in his face, and knew he brooded about Castigi as much as his own fate.

Honor didn't try to confront Dom, follow him or even slip into his bed as she wanted to. Now that she understood his reasons for leaving her behind, her raw fury and resentment were gone. But the dull ache of regret was constant. She took some comfort in her nightly prayers, though even spiritual guidance couldn't assuage the pain of love and longing.

As Thanksgiving drew near, questions were her constant companions.

Would Dom be able to complete his quest in time?

What would happen to her life once he left?

Could she even be a curator anymore, theorize now that she'd met history firsthand?

Most troubling of all—why had God given her this miracle only to leave her bereft and barren?

The morning before Thanksgiving, Honor stood naked before her mirror. She clasped her hands over her concave stomach, wishing fiercely that her period hadn't started some time ago. She'd hoped, prayed, that she might be pregnant, but that, too, had not come to pass. She wouldn't use a baby against Dom, try to blackmail him in any way, but oh, how she needed a tangible remnant of him.

Something more than memories, poignant as they would be.

Sighing, she turned away to dress. With the constant stream of visitors to the museum, Honor had managed to save quite a nest egg. She suspected that, now that Dom had earned enough to pay for the marble, he, too, was saving his money.

But for what?

This morning she'd risen early so she could catch him before he left for work. They needed to talk—about several things. Honor tried to ignore the calendars and huge millennium clocks on display all over the city, but one date was red-letter in her mind.

Thanksgiving. Despite everything, partly because of her recent discussions with heaven, she felt a deep need to be thankful. After all, few women were privileged to meet their dream man in the flesh, however briefly. Dom and Ernie and, to a growing degree, Nick, were the only family she had. She wanted to celebrate that bond with them, pull out all the stops and give them each a happy memory that would last the rest of their lives.

Especially Dom. The mere idea that he might forget her with that first step back to his own time caused her such pain that she had to grasp the bureau edge to steady herself. And if, in the back of her mind, she hoped to show him that the modern world had some of the traditions and old-fashioned values he seemed to miss, well, that was between her and her conscience.

Besides, she reassured herself, she wanted to

do her part in helping transform Castigi. Only six weeks remained until the deadline. Brushing her hair before the mirror, Honor shuddered as she considered the consequences if Castigi wouldn't give up his homeless wandering.

The brush stopped. But Trotterman had verified that Dom made it home, so they must succeed in redeeming Rafe. The brush started stroking slowly again. Maybe that was a different Dominico. Maybe heaven had the power to change the course of history itself.

Or maybe, Honor decided grimly as she tossed the brush aside, she was dreaming all of this and she'd awaken January 1, cold and lonely in her Portland bed. Her head spinning with mixed foreboding and anticipation, Honor left her room to confront the source of her pain and happiness.

To her relief, Ernie hadn't risen yet. She found Dom popping toast in the toaster and then standing guard. He tended to either overbrown it or leave it too soft. He glared down at the appliance, as if daring it to misbehave.

Honor smiled, glad her Renaissance man was all thumbs at a few things. Cooking was one of them.

He stood there, his profile so pure against the white cabinets that she wanted to cry, to throw herself at him and beg him to stay.

Instead she glued a smile to her face and tried to still her heart rate. "Morning, Dom. Got any extra bread?"

Whirling, he smiled at her, taking an automatic step toward her as if he longed to touch her as much as she longed to touch him. But he caught himself as he always did of late and said prosaically, "Always, for you." He dropped in another slice.

While they buttered the bread and slathered on jam, Honor asked, "Is Castigi still working with you?"

He sighed and shook his head, his cheeks taking on a drawn look. She'd noted he hadn't been eating any more than she had, but she could hardly berate him for her own failing. He didn't seem to like the food here, but she'd see what she could do about that, too.

"Do you still see him?"

"Sometimes he meets me after work and we go to taverns together, but he will not tell me where he lives."

"So you've had no luck in weaning him from the bottle."

"None, I fear. He would not take my advice, even if I offered it. And I know better. He is fiercely independent."

"A family trait, I guess." When he studied the crumbs on his plate, she sighed and said, "Would you give him a message for me?"

"Certainly."

"Tell him I'd consider it a favor, that I'll come track him down if I have to, but I want him here for Thanksgiving. I intend to put on a good spread, just like my mother used to."

Dom played with the knife on the table. "We will have plenty of jam and butter? That doesn't sound like—"

Honor giggled and covered his hand with her own. "No, silly. I mean I'll cook a lot. I'm off, and so are you, so . . . " Her voice trailed away. Their eyes met. Even the simple touch of hand to hand caused a jolt between them.

But this time she knew the power of it, and the majesty of two opposites attracting. Her eyes misted. "Oh, Dom . . . "

Wrenching his hand away, Dom surged to his feet. "I will tell him, but I do not know if he will come." He was at the door.

She rose and called, "Wait, Dom!"

He paused, his back still turned. "Yes?"

"Please, don't finish the statue on my account. I'm not sure I even want to be a curator any-more." *And I'd far rather spend these last few weeks with you, come what may.*

Frowning, Dom turned to face her. "Why?"

Honor wasn't certain why herself. She couldn't explain that now that she'd felt all the pains and joys life had to offer, she couldn't go back to spending her life exploring her mind.

Life was far more than that. That peculiar seren-ity descended over her again. "I just know, that's all. Maybe I'll become a social worker when . . . " She stopped, unable to say the words.

Dom stared at her, transfixed. Relieved of her insecurities, she glowed with a loveliness far more striking than model perfection. There was character in her face now, a certainty of who she was and what she had to offer. Perhaps he could-n't take it, but others would know the abundance of her generosity and kindness after he was gone.

Pain twisting his face, Dom hurried out with-out responding to her request.

* * *

The next morning Honor rose early to carry on her mother's tradition. There was something comforting in using the same recipes her family had enjoyed for generations. She was eager to see these hardened male New Yorkers react to cornbread stuffing, turkey, homemade cranberry sauce, mashed potatoes and pumpkin and pecan pie. She'd accumulated her supplies yesterday after work, so she had everything.

With the dawn she'd made two vows. One, just for today, she would not worry about tomorrow. And two, no matter what, she'd try to keep peace among three—and, she hoped, four—obstreperous males so they could all take away a happy memory.

When Dom entered the kitchen, she was wearing an apron and humming, elbow-deep in flour as she made the biscuits, and cornbread for the stuffing. Honor hadn't seen him before she went to bed last night, so she asked eagerly, "Is Rafe coming?"

He shrugged. "I invited him, but he would not say."

Stubborn Italian. Just like his uncle. Honor slapped the biscuit dough around and began to cut it with a round cutter. "Where is he? I'm going to go find him myself and drag him here, if necessary."

A melancholy little smile tugged at Dom's lips as he watched her, but he only said, "He could be at any of about five inns, and none of them are places I'd allow you to go."

273

Honor froze in the act of putting the biscuits in the pan. "Allow me? I'll remind you that you have no rights over me, by your own choice."

"Choice? Do you think it is my deci—"

Honor slammed the oven door open. "Enough! I promised myself, no fights today." She stuck the pan inside the hot oven and turned back to him, wiping her hands on a dishcloth. "Please, just find him for me and tell him I'll be very disappointed if he doesn't come." She blew a strand of hair out of her face, but it fell back, tickling her nose.

As if he couldn't help himself, Dom gently tucked the strand behind her ear. "I will try once more."

"Thank you," Honor whispered, her heart in her eyes.

For an instant his own longing was bare for her to see, but then he turned away.

An hour later he returned, still noncommittal. He admitted only that he'd found Rafe and tried again to convince him to come. But he seemed restless, stalking from the kitchen to the living area and back. Finally he hovered over her. "Can I help?"

Honor gave him a teasing look. "I thought cooking was women's work."

He shrugged. "I am good with a knife."

"I just bet you are." Honor assigned him the task of peeling the potatoes. She wasn't surprised to find him as expert as he claimed. She tried not to think about what practice he'd had with it, but she suspected that much of that dexterity had not been learned in a kitchen.

"What sort of vegetable is this?" Curiously he watched the white skin appear.

"Do you remember those long fried tubers we ate with the hamburgers?"

"Ah, yes. Those are quite tasty."

A sense of unreality descended over Honor. It was so easy to forget that he was from another world, another time she could only dream of. A time when potatoes had not yet been imported to Europe, women were decorations, and those bold enough to refute the mores of the church were often banished or burned at the stake.

Perhaps he was right. Perhaps she could never survive in his world. Why, then, could he not remain in hers? That was the one possibility they had not discussed. Honor opened her mouth, but Ernie, yawning, entered the kitchen.

He sniffed appreciatively. "What smells so good?"

"The turkey." Honor gasped and hurried to the oven to baste the majestic bird.

She soon put Ernie to work, too. When, around noon, a knock came, Honor's eyes met Dom's. Hopefully, he went to the door.

It was Trotterman. The curator stared at Dom as if he were a living, breathing work of art.

Which he was.

But Dom apparently didn't appreciate the compliment, for he was about to close the door in Trotterman's face. "We have no time for you today."

Ernie tugged his apron over his head and hurried to the door, opening it again. Trotterman still stood there. Ernie glared at Dom, who looked tempted to close the door again. "Move it, big guy. Last time I looked, this was still my apartment, and I invited him."

Shrugging, Dom retook his seat at the table to chop onions and celery.

Honor smiled sympathetically at Trotterman and shook her head slightly. *Later,* she mouthed.

Maybe Dom would open up a bit after the big meal. She knew Trotterman had tried to call Dom several times, but Dom refused to use the telephone. He looked at the modern convenience as if it were a snake, though he had learned to tolerate, and even enjoy, television.

A knock sounded again as Honor took the pies out of the oven. This time Honor hurried to the door. It was Nick.

Honor's face fell, but she quickly recovered, shoving the door wide in invitation. "I'm so glad you could come. Ernie said you had other plans."

Nick smiled at her sheepishly, glancing at Dom's tense face. "They fell through at the last minute, and the smell is permeating the whole building. What are you making in here? Ambrosia?"

Honor laughed. "No, just old-fashioned Southern cooking. Would you care for something to drink?" At his assent, she poured him a glass of wine.

At the sound of Honor's laugh, and the ease of her manner around Nick, Dom suddenly began chopping harder, the knife falling with vicious precision. Nick arched a sardonic eyebrow at Honor and leaned close enough for his breath to stir her hair. "You think I should sit across the room from him? Just in case he, ah, gets a bit reckless?" He glanced down at the front of his pants.

Giggling, Honor handed him the wineglass and whispered back, "He's almost finished, anyway. He's not nearly as fierce as he seems." She returned to her stove, not noticing Nick's doubtful look.

Nick sat down at the table—across from Dom. The three New Yorkers all watched Dom dice and slice the onions and celery so fine they became a puree. Dom steadily watched Nick all the while.

Finally Ernie reached across the table and caught Dom's wrist. "I think we get the point, Dom."

Dom stuck the knife, point first, in the cutting board. *"Bene."*

Honor had listened to the byplay while she cooked, and she gave Dom a cutting look of her own over Ernie's head that plainly said, *You have no right to this jealousy, since you don't want to keep me for yourself.*

Unabashed, Dom stared back with a look that answered, *He is not good enough for you.*

Gritting her teeth in frustration, Honor gave Ernie a bright smile. "So, Ernie, how's it going at work?"

"Great." He launched into a description of the upcoming Renaissance art exhibit he and Trotterman were planning.

Avidly, Trotterman watched Dom's expressionless face as Ernie concluded, "And we're not sure yet, but we may get some of Michelangelo's drawings on loan from a museum in Florence."

Despite herself, Honor glanced at Dom. He stared fixedly into space, but she saw longing flicker in his face at the mention of Florence.

As she arranged condiments in a relish tray, Honor watched Dom through her downcast lashes. "Bruno, did you get a chance to find out what happened to the other artifacts I found in the cistern? The clothes, the mirror, and so on?"

Dom's gaze snapped to her face. He was acutely interested in the response, obviously.

Honor had tried, shortly after she reached the city, to find out if Dom's possessions were still at the Portland museum, but since she couldn't identify herself, the museum personnel had refused to tell her anything. Once she and Trotterman were on better terms, she'd asked him to see what he could find out.

If the items had been shipped back to Italy, as she feared, Dom's resolve to go home might be pointless anyway. She didn't know how she knew, but she was certain the clothes or the mirror or the personal items were needed to take him home.

By the look on his face, Dom knew it, too. He'd asked her once what had happened to his things, and she'd had to tell him, honestly, that she didn't know.

Trotterman sipped his wine. "Strangely enough, they were brought here for examination by one of my competitors at a different museum. He, too, concluded that they were genuine. I believe they're slated to be packed up for shipment back to Italy."

"When?" Honor and Dom both said at the same time.

"That I haven't learned. Or where they are now." Trotterman twirled his wineglass to appraise the dry white wine as he added casually, "My colleague seems to think the Portland museum has a lead on the theft of the fake Michelangelo. Perhaps they're waiting so they can ship them back together."

Honor turned away to pull plates and napkins from the cabinets. Dom became occupied with washing his hands—for the second time.

Nick and Ernie, however, seemed very interested, leaning forward on the table with their elbows.

"What have they found out?" Ernie demanded. "Anything that clears Honor?"

Trotterman shrugged. "My colleague is just speculating. You know the police don't talk much about ongoing investigations. But apparently they have reason to believe the perpetrators are in the city."

China shattered as Honor dropped a plate. Keeping her face bent so they couldn't see how flushed it was, Honor began picking up the pieces. Dom knelt to help, muttering, "Still think I don't need to finish the statue?"

Biting her lip, she glanced up at Nick.

He watched them a bit too closely as he said casually, "I'll see what I can find out. If you want me to, Honor."

"Yes, please." She rose so fast that blood rushed from her head. She swayed, pieces of broken china in her hands, and pricked one finger. Dom hurried to toss his fragments in the trash so he'd be free to help her, but Nick was up and escorting her to a chair before he could return.

Nick held a small trash can before her. She dropped the pieces in. Nick stepped past Dom, set the can down, wet a paper towel and came back to kneel and dab at the cut on her finger. "It's not serious. Want a bandage?"

Honor shook her head. She stared at Dom, who stood aside while Nick tended to her. From the way his hands opened and closed, she knew the restraint was hard on him. But he managed nonetheless.

"I'll be fine as soon as it stops hurting." The words were out before she could stop them. She wanted to kick herself when the harsh blankness returned to Dom's expression. He certainly understood her double meaning. He walked across the room, distancing himself literally and figuratively.

Bleakly, Honor stared down at the welling cut on her finger. Dear Lord, let him try to become a saint, but she was all too human. Was she supposed to blithely wave him good-bye and wish him well? Her good intentions seemed to be falling in tatters about her feet, but so be it. Suddenly truth seemed more important than peace.

A knock disturbed the uneasy silence. Since Ernie and Trotterman were too busy frowning, trying to understand what the hell was going on, Honor was wrapping the paper towel around her finger and Dom was ignoring everyone, it was left to Nick to answer the door. Honor's head lifted as a familiar voice rumbled a husky hello.

Rafe Castigi stood there, shifting uneasily from one worn loafer to the other. For once he looked clean, his long, chocolate brown hair shining, slicked back from his forehead and falling over his shoulders in curly waves. His blue eyes were bloodshot but sober. He wore stained khakis and a white button-down shirt fraying around the edges, but at least he'd made an effort.

"Come on in, Rafe." Nick shoved the door wide.

Honor leaped to her feet, her expression lightening. She hurried over to Rafe, tossing the paper towel in the trash as she passed. "I'm so glad you could come." She offered her hand as Rafe moved inside and Nick closed the door.

He hesitated, pulled something from behind his back and set it in her hand. "Wanted to bring a little something. Don't let the guys hog 'em."

It was a gold box of Godiva chocolates. Even such a small box was costly, but it was his thoughtfulness that really touched Honor, and his fierce resolve not to be a burden on anyone. Honor bit her lip, trying to force her voice to neutrality as she took the gift. "Thank you. That was thoughtful. Would you care for some wine . . . ?" She trailed off in dismay, wondering what had possessed her to offer a glass of wine to an alcoholic.

But Rafe replied, "Yeah, I guess," with a notable lack of enthusiasm.

She poured a little in a wineglass, listening as the others greeted him and as Trotterman was introduced. Even to her ears, the cordiality sounded forced, and not just on Rafe's side. Honor handed Rafe his glass.

He took a tiny sip. Such a look of distaste passed over his face that Honor had to hide a smile. She had a feeling that if it didn't have a turkey or a crown on the front of the bottle, he wasn't tempted.

He didn't bother pretending that he liked the wine. After the one sip he shoved it aside. "Something smells great," he said a bit too heartily. "Can I help?"

"Uh, sure." Honor said on impulse, "Would you care to carve the turkey?" She'd debated whom to invite to perform the task, and this seemed the perfect compromise. She wouldn't have to insult the Escavido brothers, or infuriate Dom.

Indeed, Dom glared as Rafe looked at the golden brown bird steaming on a platter. Rafe smiled widely at Dom. "Glad to, babe."

Honor reached for a butcher knife, but Rafe leaned down, lifted his pants and pulled out of an ankle sheath the wickedest-looking knife Honor had ever seen. It was huge, with a serrated blade on one side and a straight cutting edge on the other.

"Wow, that's awesome," Ernie exclaimed. Even Nick looked impressed. Dom came closer to appraise the strange blade.

Am I the only one worried about germs? Honor wondered, glancing at her defenseless turkey. "Uh, Rafe, is it clean?" Honor asked as he poised the knife over a plump leg.

He scowled. "I was a SEAL. What do you

think? But if it makes you feel better . . . " He turned on the tap and ran his hands and the knife under hot water.

Honor breathed a sigh of relief. Nick smiled at her indulgently. Dom looked impatient. Again Honor realized that they came from different worlds. Hers was paranoid about germs; his had never heard of them.

With an even greater dexterity than Dom had shown, Rafe carved the turkey. Honor turned away, not liking the visions that came to her as she watched those expert cuts. Her sympathy for Rafe increased. What job could a former trained killer get in a civilized world? Honor smiled sadly. Maybe it was Rafe who should go back with Dom, not her. He'd probably fit much better in the Renaissance than she would.

As they sat down to eat, Ernie insisted that she sit at one end, Dom at the other. Honor swallowed hard as she tried not to think that this might be the last time she and Dom ever hosted a meal together. She tried to forget the symbolism of facing one another across a table, master and mistress of a time that would never come.

Nick poured wine for everyone and then stood to lift his glass in a toast. "To a new dawn and a new millennium. May we each try to make it a better one than the last." He drank deeply.

Trotterman and Ernie followed suit, but Honor's throat was so tight with emotion that she toyed with her glass instead of lifting it.

The two Italians sipped, their faces closed, remote.

Fleetingly, Honor saw a resemblance between

them. Not in bone structure or looks, but in their expressions and outlook on life. They were both tough realists, too busy getting through today to pine over tomorrow. Vaguely she wondered whether, if Dom had thought of the consequences of his actions, she would be sitting here today, trying to make peace between five very dissimilar men and make herself learn to lose love gracefully.

She felt Rafe staring between her and Dom, as if he sensed something was wrong. Finally she was able to struggle her emotions under control and touch the wine to her lips. But she could never drink to that toast, well intentioned as it was, for the new year brought her desolation instead of illumination.

While she picked at her food, she listened with half her attention as Nick, Trotterman and Ernie discussed art. Rafe and Dom were silent, wolfing down their meal. Honor was both glad and sad at their enjoyment, for she couldn't help wondering how often they ate anything hot, much less something prepared by a woman who cared about them. Honor shoved her turkey around her plate, trying to tell herself to stop these damnable comparisons, but her sense of hopelessness grew. Little earth mother, for one day at least, she'd wanted to make a home for five confirmed bachelors, give them each a sense of family and hope for the future. Or so she'd told herself.

In reality, she'd been perpetrating a lie upon herself, too. It was she who wanted a home and a family. And none of these men could supply it. Not even Dom.

Least of all Dom. Even if he wanted to. She tried to imagine Dom and herself sitting at a table in a simple hut in Italy, supping by candlelight as they tried to control a quarrelsome brood. The image would not jell. She'd wanted truth? Well, the truth was, Dom and Rafe were a lot alike. The truth was, they were both born warriors trying to be civilized to please her.

Honor took a deep breath. She covered her face with her napkin under the pretense of wiping her mouth, but this time she couldn't get control. Making a garbled excuse, she fled to the bathroom.

Dom half rose. "Honoria Psyche, please, everything is delicious, what is—"

At the bathroom door she whirled. Through her teeth she said, "If you ever call me Honoria Psyche again, I'll never forgive you." She slammed the door. The silence outside was total, making Honor even more miserable.

Great hostess she made! After all the trouble she'd gone to, she'd spoiled everything.

But seeing Rafe trying so hard to be polite, and then pulling a killer's knife out to cut her turkey, had brought home to Honor with brutal clarity that he and Dom were related not only by blood. Trying to domesticate them was like trying to tame a wolf. You might think you'd bonded with the animal, taught it to sit at your table and wait to be fed on command, but when it was hungry enough, or desperate enough, it would tear out your heart.

Or leave you and go back to its wandering ways.

Honor ran water into the basin to wash her face. She scrubbed fiercely with a washrag, determined to wash off the makeup and leave herself stripped bare. No more pretense. No more wishing or dreaming. She was tired of being a hopeful romantic and having her feelings lacerated.

Far better for her and for Dom if she learned to be a hopeless realist. She wouldn't scheme to get him to take her with him, or even beg him to stay. She could only spend the next six weeks trying to help him accomplish his quest.

When the makeup was gone, she stared at herself in the mirror. She saw the fine skin, the beginnings of crow's-feet at the corners of her eyes, the solemn mouth. There had been a time when she'd considered herself plain, even with makeup. Now she saw the maturity in her face, the steady gaze of a woman strong enough to survive broken dreams and come out a better person. The passionate curve of a mouth that knew, now, the glory of sex.

Somehow she'd get through this.

Somehow she'd help Dom go back to the life he wanted, and pick up the pieces after he was gone. Taking a deep breath, Honor hung up the washcloth and left the bathroom, aware that voices were rising in the next room.

In the kitchen she found Rafe looking ridiculous in her apron. It wouldn't even tie around him, but he washed dishes well enough that she had to wonder how often he'd been punished with KP duty while in the service. Meanwhile, Ernie and Nick cleared the table while Trotterman put the food in smaller containers, whispering to Dom all the while.

Dom slammed the plates together as he stuck them in the cabinet and turned on Trotterman. "I will not answer your questions, you nosy little man, so go away! I do not even know the answers to most of what you want to know."

"You some kind of art expert, pal?" drawled Rafe. "You don't seem like the type."

"I am nothing of the kind."

"Funny. Bruno seems to think you are," Nick contradicted softly. "Wonder why?"

Pulling the towel repeatedly through his hands, Dom replied, "Funny? I am equally tired of your poor attempts at humor, Escavido. You know nothing of me, so be quiet."

Waiting quietly by the bathroom, Honor debated saying something, but it was time Nick and Dom had it out. She'd already proved she was a poor peacemaker anyway.

"Maybe not, but I know a little something of Honor. Like, she deserves better."

The towel stretched taut in Dom's hands. "Than me? Or you?"

As Nick opened his mouth to answer, Dom flicked him in the cheek with the towel. "Maybe both of us," Dom answered his own question.

Honor saw a splotch appear on Nick's cheek, but it soon disappeared under a red tide of anger. Nick took a step toward Dom, but Trotterman got between the two larger men, holding out a chubby arm in each direction.

"Now see here, this is no way to repay Honor's hard work. Back off, both of you."

287

"Come on, bro," Ernie added with an uneasy glance at Dom's tense expression, "help me fold up this tablecloth."

Nick glared at Dom a moment longer, but he jerkily complied.

Honor sent Trotterman a grateful look and walked forward. All five men turned to look at her, but Honor only picked up a stack of clean dishes to put them away. Dom tried to catch her eye, but she ignored him.

It seemed the meal would end peacefully, at least. Everything was tidy—except human emotions.

Trotterman left first, nodding coolly at Dom even as he pumped Honor's hand. "Everything was delicious. I'll . . . continue checking on what we discussed. See if I can't get better dates for you."

"Thanks. I'm sure I'll see you at work."

Next Ernie left, saying he was supposed to meet friends. Honor was uncomfortable at the way Nick hovered over her protectively. Surely he wasn't afraid to leave her alone with Rafe and Dom? It seemed so, for, as Dom walked Rafe to the door, Nick sat half on, half off a couch arm. Ready for anything.

Rafe's tough face was unreadable as he glanced from Honor to Nick to Dom. After he thanked Honor for the great meal, he shook his head ruefully. "Better you than me, pal."

Honor stiffened. He glanced at her as if she might as well have *trouble* tattooed on her forehead.

Dom clapped Rafe on the shoulder. "Will I see you at work, *amico?*"

His hand on the doorknob, Rafe slowly turned back to face Dom. "Been meaning to tell you— I'm not cut out for a steady job. Don't think I'll be in anymore. But thanks for talking to your foreman. Good-bye, and good luck."

There was such an air of finality in the way he talked that Honor panicked. She caught Rafe's arm. He stiffened at her touch. She noted that he'd begun to tremble, though he was successful at hiding his need for a drink.

Flinching, she let go. "But . . . won't you leave us your phone number?"

"Don't have one. See ya."

Helplessly, she glanced at Dom. But he seemed frozen, staring into the distance at a foe that had defeated him. Honor only had to blink to picture him as he used to be, and the image of all his vitality stillborn in stone spurred her forward as nothing else could.

"But Rafe, we care about you."

Rafe looked down at his feet. "That's nice, but, well . . . " He shrugged. *So? I don't give a shit about myself.*

The message came through loud and clear. From the look on his face, Dom heard it, too.

Picking up on her urgency, Nick rose and came forward. He cleared his throat. "Rafe, I've been looking for a good covert ops man, someone to help me assess building security. Someone light on his feet, who knows how to get in and out of a situation without being seen—"

Incredulously, Rafe stared at Nick. "You offering me a job, rich man?" The hostility of the question didn't need Rafe's bitter laugh for emphasis.

"Well, yes. But I really think you'd be good at it."

"I tell ya, I've made lots of mistakes in my time, burned lots of bridges." He leaned forward to poke one finger in Nick's chest. "But I've never taken a dime in charity, and I won't start now. Just consider me a lost cause. Guess I won't be seeing you after all, Dom." He flung open the door, but paused, saying very softly, "Thanks anyway." And the door slammed behind him as he hurried down the steps.

Honor took one look at Dom's ashen face, saw his terrible resignation and bolted after Rafe.

"Honor, dammit, come back," Nick roared.

Honor ignored him. She didn't even have her coat, but Rafe's steps were rapidly fading, so she had to run to keep up. She hoped Nick and Dom didn't beat each other senseless, but she had something more important than Dom's body to worry about at the moment.

Like his soul.

Chapter Twelve

"Rafe, wait!"

Rafe tried to pretend he didn't hear the familiar voice. He walked faster.

The steps behind him only ran harder. Sprinting, swift as a swallow chasing a hawk—and maybe equally foolish—Honor finally caught up to him. She grabbed the back of his old leather bomber jacket and hauled him to a stop.

Turning on her, his expression murderous, Rafe said with a snarl, "You deaf or stupid, lady? I told you I just want to be left a—"

"Neither," Honor answered quietly. "Just desperate."

Under the streetlights, they stared at each other. The hostility faded from Rafe's expression as he drank in her upturned face. Honor didn't know that she'd never been more lovely than now, bare of makeup, bare of pretense, determined to help the man she loved. And she couldn't know that, in that instant, she was, for Dom, exactly what Rafe had always yearned for and never had.

Someone to love him. Someone to believe in him. Someone to be his champion.

Afraid she'd read his pain, Rafe shuttered his expression quickly.

She shivered. "Can you buy me a cup of coffee? Give me a chance to explain?"

Sighing, he glanced up the street at a deli with light on. Some other poor bastard who didn't have anyone to spend the holidays with. He hesitated.

"I didn't get a chance to have coffee after dinner," she said, teeth chattering.

Rafe almost wanted to smile. *Good one.* Appeal to his guilt. Blond, beautiful—and smart. He always had been partial to blondes. Resigned, Rafe fished in his pockets. He squinted down, counting. He stuck the change back. "OK."

He pulled his coat off and wrapped it about her shoulders, trying to ignore the soft sympathy in those strange silvery eyes, wishing he hadn't revealed that he was down to pocket change. When did those damn Godiva chocolates get so expensive? Sometimes, even though he'd grown up in Queens, he felt like an alien.

He'd gone into the navy fresh out of college, and then spent ten years in the SEALS. The military life was a good one—as long as you followed the rules. But it did tend to insulate a man. The next op became much more important than who was president, and how much a cup of coffee cost.

He smiled bitterly. The last two years had passed quickly. Too quickly. Occasionally, when he took time to surface and look around, he realized he was frittering his life away, but the hell with it; he had nothing better to do.

As they entered the deli, Rafe fought off his depression. Dammit, he just needed a drink, and then he'd be fine.

The Italian owner of the little deli rushed over to them, delighted to have customers. "I help you, yes?"

Automatically, Rafe pulled out a chair for Honor at a tiny table, helping her drape the coat over the back, before he nodded. "Yeah. Two coffees."

The little man's face fell, but he brightened quickly. "I make fresh."

Rafe watched Honor. "So? What's the big news?"

She twiddled with the salt shaker, set it aside and began moving the pepper. "Well, uh, didn't Dom ever tell you that you're . . . related?"

Rafe frowned. "No." He'd heard this song and dance from Escavido, too. Even if it was true, and he didn't see how it could be, why was it such a big deal? He began to get an uncomfortable feeling in his chest, the same one he used to get when the CO called them into the situation room to report their next assignment. A sense of inevitability—he might not like what was coming, but he had to hear it.

"Well, you are."

"How? And how do you know?"

"Well . . . he was related, uh, closely, to your great-great—well, many greats—grandfather back in Italy."

Rocking back in his chair so hard that it creaked, Rafe stared at her. This butter-wouldn't-melt-in-her-mouth little blonde was just as bold and brassy as her boyfriend. But he hadn't taken either of them for liars. "I see. He's a helluva prophet, then. 'Cause I don't know much about my family history myself."

She swallowed hard. He saw the wheels turning in her head. His life had once depended on his ability to read truth and lies; he could see every feeling in that expressive face. She was trying not to lie, but thinking about it.

Before she could speak, the deli owner returned with two fragrant, steaming cups of coffee and then wandered off again. Rafe drank his the way he liked life—bold, unadorned and hot enough to hurt as it went down.

Feeling fortified as he saw the bottom, he finally put the cup down and cut to the chase. "OK, babe. What's the angle? Why's Dom been trying to be my friend? Why'd you invite me, a stranger, to your little party?"

She'd barely sipped her coffee, but she took a big gulp, set her cup down with that prissy pre-ciseness in women that always irritated him and said equally frankly, "Because we need your help."

Aha! Rafe might have felt vindicated for his suspicions if his head hadn't ached like hell. He stuck his hands in his pants pockets to hide their growing tremor. He didn't even have enough money left for a beer. "Well?" he barked. "Spit it out. What can I do for the two of you?"

It must be a helluva favor, Rafe decided, based on the way she squirmed, searching for words. And she had the best damn vocabulary he'd ever heard. Dom sure must have a lot of fun shutting her up, he speculated. But thoughts like that only made his head ache even harder. He reached for his forehead, blushed as she stared at him curiously, and dropped his hand. He was about to get up and leave when she finally spoke.

"Well, we need you to take a job. Uh, you know, put down roots. Learn to be happy out of the service."

Rafe stiffened. What she really meant was that they wanted him to quit drinking. *That's it. Time to go.* Rafe slapped all his money down on the table, not caring if it was too much, and started to rise.

She caught his hand and tugged him back down. "Look, I can't explain fully right now. You wouldn't believe me anyway. But this is true, as God is my witness: Dom really is related to you, really cares about you, and . . . well, let's just say that whatever happens to you, happens to him. The two of you are kind of linked somehow."

A chill ran up Rafe's spine, lodging like an ice pick in his aching skull. Now she was being truthful, if mysterious. He detested BS, one reason why he didn't make it in the service. With a great effort of will, he managed to quit trembling long enough to say, very quietly, "That's too bad. Because I can't amount to much. Not anymore."

Again he made to rise. Again she pulled him back down. More vehemently this time.

"Can't? Or won't?"

Rafe's eyes narrowed. Bold and brassy didn't begin to cover it. He'd hit men for less. "I'll try to forget you said that."

"Why? Does the truth hurt?"

Hell, yes. More than she knew. But he stared at her in that cold, contemplative way that made the kids in his neighborhood run like rabbits. As if he were debating which body part to carve up first.

He saw her breathing quicken, saw fear darken her eyes, but she stayed put and said quietly, "I'm not just being nosy. I've been where you're sitting. After you've been hurt enough, it's easier, and safer, not to care. I found my escape in museums, not a bottle, but the result is the same. Recently— and Dom is, by the way, the one who helped me realize this—I've come to understand that protecting myself is like building a very high wall without a gate. It might keep everyone out. But it kept me in, too. Alone."

Rafe wanted to lurch to his feet and run. Instead he sat where he was, his expression frozen, hating her with his eyes. She had no right to talk to him like this. She didn't even know him, not really.

Apparently she read his rejection, for she drew a shuddery sigh. For an instant, such pain contorted her face that he almost forgave her. Almost.

She stood. "Thanks for the coffee. You know where to find us if you decide you want a friend." She walked out into the cold, her head high.

The ringing of the bell on the door sounded like his own death knell. He covered his ears with his hands, but the ringing echoed endlessly in his head. Shrugging into his coat, he staggered out into the cold, the tremors hitting his knees now.

The street was deserted. Lights glowed from all the apartments and brownstones around him, and he could hear music playing from several quarters. Double-parked cars crowded the curbs. Everyone in this neighborhood, it seemed, had people to party with.

Against his instincts, he'd tried to be part of something today. Something he hadn't had in so long that he'd almost forgotten what it was like. Companionship, good food, laughter.

And he didn't remember the last time he'd felt so miserable.

Alone. Alone. Her voice rang in his head.

I want it this way, he told himself savagely.

Rafe looked left, saw people coming from that direction, so he turned right. He didn't care where he went. Away. But even as he walked faster and then broke into a lope, the uncomfortable truth he'd denied too long jogged right beside him.

He couldn't outrun himself.

Fiercely, Honor dashed her tears away on her sleeve. She had to calm down before she could face Dom. It was hopeless. Rafe was so lost and afraid that he'd never let them in, much less quit drinking.

As Rafe said, another lost cause for another hopeless romantic. She hovered at the bottom of the brownstone's joint stairs, rubbing the goose-flesh on her arms. When her mother died, she'd thought she'd never have to face anything so devastating again. In part, she'd studied so hard and chosen museum work precisely so she could surround herself with beautiful things.

Artworks that were pleasant on the eyes, undemanding of the heart.

God must have an exquisite sense of irony. She smiled bitterly. Dom wasn't the only one paying penance. How would she bear it if he turned back to stone? In the cold clarity of that moment, she realized how selfish she'd been. She'd tempted Dom to break his vow, tried to talk him into taking her back with him when he was concerned for her own safety, and, today, tried to show him what a good little wifey she could be if only he'd stay.

She sagged down on the stairs, burying her face in her hands. Now that Dom's quest seemed in such grave peril, she was able to put her grief in perspective.

It was time she stopped mourning what she was about to lose and became thankful for what she'd won.

After all, the man she'd fallen in love with when she was an adolescent had taken form. Even as she learned he was not quite as perfect as his image, he gave her what she needed most.

Dom turned a sparrow into a bluebird. Gave her the confidence to chase after the most dangerous loner she'd ever met in an attempt to help him. The confidence to laugh, and flirt . . . and love. Honor lifted her head and took a deep, calming breath. Here was the greatest truth of all. For love, the love God had wanted for men and women, was strongest when it let go.

Truth? The truth was, she could only help Dom by losing him back to his own time.

Taking another deep breath, Honor stood. Somehow she'd find a way to reach Rafe. The alternative was simply unbearable.

She was climbing up to the second level when Nick's door opened. He beckoned to her. "I've been listening for your steps. Can I talk to you a minute?"

Honor clasped the baluster, glad to see that he didn't appear to have any black eyes or bruises. He and Dom must have parted quietly, if not amicably. "Can it wait, Nick?"

He shook his head. "I'm afraid not."

She climbed back down and entered his apartment. She barely took note of the leather seating and spare appointments. It looked much like Nick himself: enduring, elegant and repressed. Everything neatly compartmentalized. Honor sat down, too tired to spar with him. "What do you want?"

Nick perched on a sofa arm, restlessly bouncing one long leg. Whatever his subject, it wasn't easy for him to broach. "Why'd you run after Rafe?"

"That's complicated. Basically to help Dom."

"And what does Dom do to help you?"

Honor blinked. "Excuse me?"

"When you first moved in, I didn't give a rat's ass what kind of trouble you were in as long as you didn't drag Ernie into it. But . . . well, you seem like a nice girl. I can't believe you're involved in whatever scam Dom's—"

"Dom's not involved in anything except trying to save his own hide."

"How do you know? It's damn peculiar that he's working on a statue apparently exactly like the missing one."

Not if you know the truth. But since she couldn't tell him that, Honor made do with, "You don't need to worry about him. He'll be gone by January first." Her voice broke, and she had to look away from his arresting gaze.

His tone softened. "Look, Honor, I'm bringing this up because I know the head of museum security, and I just spoke with him. The police plan to question Ernie at work next week about you. They're looking for you. Apparently the Portland museum suspects you're in the city. Someone reported Ernie's license number and a description of you and Dom after some kind of fight on the interstate. They're determined to recover the statue. Ernie says since the issue of the provenance hasn't been settled, their insurance won't pay anything, especially nothing like the value of a genuine Michelangelo."

Honor's heart lurched. *Great.* "If they're looking for me, why are you mad at Dom?"

"Because I sense that he's dragged you into something, that he's the one behind whatever's going on."

A wild giggle cut him off. "I always did think you were a sharp guy." Honor stood. "Thanks for the warning. If you want us to move, we will."

Nick stood, too. He scowled. "I didn't say that.

I'm just suggesting that whatever allegiance you owe Dom might need a second look. If you want to turn yourself in, I'll do all I can to help you."

"I appreciate it, but believe me, your concerns are all wrong. Neither of us has done anything illegal." *Yet.* She was thinking of taking a baseball bat to Rafe's head, just to get his attention.

"Then why the hell won't you tell me what's going on? Even Trotterman seems to know more than I do."

That was what really pissed him off, Honor realized. "Maybe because I have no interest in what Bellevue looks like from the inside."

His hands clenched into fists.

Honor swung away to the door. "Guess that's my cue to leave before you strangle me."

As she left, she heard Nick mutter, "God, women are a pain in the ass."

She stuck her head back inside long enough to retort, "Only because men are such great teachers." She slammed the door. She heard movement at the top of the stairs and looked up in time to see Dom shutting the upper-level apartment door.

When she entered the apartment, Dom was storming up to the studio. He must have seen her leaving Nick's apartment. She tried to remember how long she'd been in there. It couldn't have been long.

Besides, what right had he to be jealous? Did he expect her to spend the rest of her life mourning him? She stared up at his closed door, narrow-eyed, but finally turned away with a muffled curse. She'd resolved to be strong, not to plead with him, and she'd keep the promise if it killed her.

But he certainly didn't make it easy. Ernie was gone, so she spent the rest of Thanksgiving evening alone, fuming. She tried watching TV, but all the excitement about the approaching millennium celebrations around the world made her feel ill. She went to bed early and read a bloody horror novel suitable to her state of mind.

The next morning, she arose the minute she heard movement. Tying her robe about her waist with decisive movements, she marched into the kitchen.

"Good morning, Dom."

Dom looked at her with deep blue eyes smudged with tiredness. *"Ciao."*

"Now will you tell me why you're mad at me?"

Dom concentrated on washing the bowl that had held his oatmeal. Oatmeal was one of the few things he could make, and one of the few that seemed to have changed little during the centuries. He dried the plastic bowl now as if it were fine china.

For about five more seconds, Honor tolerated his indifference, but finally she went up to him, put her hands on his broad shoulders and turned him to face her. "Talk to me, dammit."

She got her wish.

A furious spate of Italian broke from him, so swift that she could make out only a few words. Like, "Why do you torment me? I do this for you." He flung the bowl in the sink.

Numb, Honor let his black fury wash over her. He caught her upper arms and shook her, twice, hard enough to make her teeth rattle, still railing, but this time in English. " . . . he will not make you happy—"

Honor jerked away. "Don't you dare pretend my happiness matters a hill of beans to you! You couldn't leave me be—" She broke off, the words sticking in her throat. Turning away, she knotted and reknotted her robe sash to compose herself.

Dom bent his head, staring at his feet. When he spoke again, his voice was cool. "As you say, I have no right to be jealous. But . . . I only want the best for you. And you should not have run after Rafe that way. He can be overly aggressive. Besides, it will do no good."

To distract herself, Honor popped bread in the toaster and said, her back still turned, "So I'm supposed to stand idly by and do nothing to help you?"

Dom propped his hips on the table edge. "How can I make you understand that you have already done too much? At least, when the time comes, if you are safe, and have your name cleared and your job back, I will have only one regret to take with me to eternity."

"And I will have only one happy memory!" She whirled on him, her resolve weakening. "If you really cared about me, you would at least make our remaining time together something I can cherish as I grow old." Her voice softened on the last. Before she stopped to think, she moved in front of him, opened her robe and brought his large hand to her bare breast.

Groaning, he stiffened in rejection, but his hand compulsively took and enjoyed her offering. "My Honor . . . " He sighed, tenderly cupping her breast.

Tears shimmered in her eyes. "No, Dom. Maybe God sent you here not for your honor, but for mine. Maybe I, too, have a purpose in history. Maybe He wanted us to get together all along."

Dom hauled her close and buried his face between her breasts. "Sweet life, if I could give my legs to make it so, I would. But it is too late for us. At least I do not have to agonize over taking you with me any longer."

Honor's throat tightened.

His voice still muffled against her soft skin, he added softly, "I did my best, but I cannot reach Rafe. Please, please, do not make me compound my sins by dishonoring you again." Even as he spoke, he turned his face into the curve of her bosom, nuzzling with a hunger obviously beyond his control. "I have tried to be strong."

Honor clenched her hands in his hair and hauled his head up. "Then be weak. Let me use the strength you gave me to help us both." She kissed him, her arms wrapped around his neck.

For a heady moment he responded, his tongue hot and earnest in her mouth, his manhood growing against her abdomen. But a moment later he set her aside, tying her robe, his expression fierce with determination. "We cannot risk it, Honor. There was no child the first time, but again is tempting fate." He smiled bleakly. "And I have done enough of that."

"But . . . protection."

"You will let me use it?"

Honor looked away. No, she could not bear it. She debated telling him she'd cherish any child of his, but he was too chivalrous to want to leave her

304

with a burden like that. He didn't understand that, in her time, unwed mothers were not so repudiated. Again, the chasm between them seemed an abyss nothing could bridge.

At the look on her face, he moved her aside and strode to the refrigerator, saying harshly, "It will not be such a bad thing, to be a statue again."

Honor gasped. Depression flamed into fury. He couldn't have said anything more calculated to hurt her. She jerked the glass of orange juice out of his hand and slammed it down on the counter, not caring that juice sloshed on both of them. "You selfish bastard! You say you think of me, but it is always your honor, your conscience, your penance."

He backed away a step at her raw fury, his face twisting with reciprocal pain. The flour canister on top of the refrigerator wobbled and then fell, its lid coming off. Flour drifted over both of them.

Midspate, Honor stopped as flour dusted her tongue. She held her hands out in front of her. They were white. A hysterical laugh bubbled out.

"Holy shit," said a familiar voice. Vaguely, Honor looked in that direction. Ernie? How long had he been standing there?

Ernie wavered in his open bedroom door, and judging from the look on his face, he'd been there long enough. He peered at Dom as if he couldn't believe his eyes.

Flour dusting his face and hair, Dom scowled, looking so like his former incarnation that it was hardly any wonder Ernie accepted the strange truth without question. Honor slapped her hand over a silly giggle. Ernie always had been a romantic fool. Like her.

Groping for a chair, still staring at Dom, Ernie sagged down on the sofa as if his legs wouldn't hold him. "So you're the real *David?* Can't understand why I didn't see it before. The way you talk, look, act—"

"You believe in miracles, Ernie?" Honor asked dryly.

Ernie glanced at her. "I'm Catholic, Honor. What do you think?" He turned back to his subject, watching, wide eyed, as Dom wet a rag and began to wipe the flour from his face and hands. "But why? How?"

"Does it really matter? Maybe you can dream up a miracle, too, help us find a way to make Rafe quit drinking." Honor went to the sink to wash her arms and hands, but before she could rinse her face, Dom eased her aside. He cleaned his rag and tenderly wiped the flour from her face, ignoring the sputtering Ernie.

Despite the desolate darkness in his eyes, a wistful smile tugged at his lips. "What a temper! I would like to see you when you're old, Honor. What an imposing grandmother you will make. . . ." He trailed off at her gasp. Tossing the rag in the sink, he turned away. "I am sorry. Even when I do not intend to, I hurt you. *Scusi.*" He hurried upstairs to the loft.

Honor raked her hands through her hair. More flour drifted down. She wheeled and stalked toward the bathroom.

"But Honnie, you can't leave me wondering—" Ernie complained.

"Ask Trotterman at work today. He knows everything. I just can't bear to talk about this anymore." Honor slammed the door, hoping a long, hot shower would wash away her yellow streak along with the flour.

Every time she tempted Dom, and every time he resisted, she felt worse. Yet something stronger than pride, or propriety, or even the knowledge that they had so little time left together, drove her. Destiny was in the air, and not just because of the turn of the millennium.

Somehow she and Dom were fated to be together. And somehow she would convince him.

But first she had to convince Rafe.

On the way to work, she plunked some of her hard-earned cash down on a private detective's desk. He promised to let her know when he found Rafe. She exited, breathing a bit easier. Maybe Dom had given up. But she hadn't.

If heaven could bring him back to life, then faith could keep him alive.

After that, time moved very fast. Aside from her concern for Dom, Honor had more immediate worries. Maybe she was just being paranoid, but it seemed to her that every cop she came across watched her with suspicion, even the security personnel in the museum. She began to regret that she hadn't used an alias before beginning work. All she needed was one brush with the law, and when they ran her ID . . . Honor tried not to wonder what would happen to her after Dom left. Even if the museum recovered the statue, they certainly wouldn't be happy with her, or likely to give her a good recommendation.

No, life as she'd known it was gone. And, in a peculiar way, she wasn't even sorry. She was too different now to be happy as a bystander.

Nick began watching her closely again. She could hardly blame him, considering her blithe response to his questioning the other night. She was sorry to spoil the fragile friendship that had been building between them, but maybe that was just as well, too. Nick was too much of a cynical realist ever to believe the truth, so any association between them could only end badly.

Ernie acted strange, but at least he'd stopped firing questions. Honor assumed Trotterman had told him everything, including more than Honor would have wanted him to hear. But he seemed preoccupied with some project of his own even when he wasn't at work.

Of Dom, she saw little. He was resolved to finish the statue, so he went in to work early and left late. When she did see him, he was quiet and despondent. He still looked for Rafe, but his errant nephew scorned all his old haunts. Even more hurtful, Dom went to great lengths not to touch her.

She tried to tell herself it was for the best, that loving him from afar was all that was left to her. She'd loved him from afar all her life, so what was different now? Except everything *was* different. Now he was flesh and bone, and as much temptation to a bluebird as he had been to the sparrow.

And then, two days before Christmas, when all seemed lost, the detective tracked down Rafe, and Dom finished the statue.

That day began on a note of hope for Honor. The phone rang early. It was the detective, informing Honor that he'd found Rafe as a some-time resident of a homeless hostel. He gave her the address, and ended with a curt warning: "He usually comes in on the coldest nights, and it's supposed to snow this evening. You want I should come with you? It's not a good part of town."

"No, you've done enough. I really appreciate the help. I'll be fine. It's not like he's dangerous or anything." At least she hoped not. As she hung up she thought back to her last meeting with Rafe. Somewhere, beneath the tough iconoclastic exterior, lurked a man who needed love and understanding like everyone else. On that Thanksgiving day, she'd seen the flicker of shock in his eyes before cold fury almost froze her to the chair. She'd struck a nerve. Somehow she could reach him.

Without telling him the truth? She doubted he was a devout Catholic like Ernie.

Honor had already quit the museum, deciding to spend these last days before January 1 doing all she could to help Dom. So, late that afternoon, just before dark, about the time she'd expect Rafe to show up for the evening meal, she dressed in her plainest clothes, pulling on a heavy, shapeless coat. She left her room to find Ernie frantically typing on his laptop, hooked to the Web. When she entered the room, he started, turned beet red and hastily shut off his computer.

"Uh, evening."

"Evening, Ernie," Honor replied coolly. "What are you doing?" *And why do you look so guilty doing it?*

"Oh, just some research."

"Must be fascinating, if it requires so much overtime," Honor said dryly.

"This is something I'm . . . interested in. I need to do it on my own time."

Honor sighed. She was tired of being surrounded by stubborn men, each with his own agenda. And frankly, at this moment she was too busy to worry about whether Ernie had gone off on another tear that would get him in trouble. He did tend to obsess about things.

Honor replied, "Well, good luck. See ya."

Ernie had relaxed when she didn't question him, but as she pulled on snow boots beside the door, he frowned and said, "Aren't you going to ask me what I'm doing?"

"Not today."

"But where are you going?"

"Uh . . . to see a friend." Honor collected her purse and made sure she had enough cash for a cab there and back.

"What friend?"

"Oh, for heaven's sake." She winced at her own exclamation and jerked her hood over her tied-back hair. "Can't a girl have a moment's privacy from all you proprietary males?"

"But what will I tell Dom?"

The door slammed on his sputtering. She didn't want Dom to be told anything until she brought Rafe home. He'd go ballistic if he knew she was going to a bad part of town alone to badger a man who hated to be badgered.

She found a cab quickly, which was good, because it was cold. The gray heaviness in the air did seem to indicate that snow would come any moment. As the cab drove off, Honor leaned back, trying to reassure herself that she'd be fine. She used to serve at a homeless shelter back in college, so she knew what to expect.

She was so preoccupied that she didn't see the curtain in the apartment above flick back, or Ernie silhouetted by the light, writing down the name of the cab company and the taxi number.

When he finally finished the statue right after dark, Dom was stone-cold weary. *Per Dio*, but his back ached. His hands were raw with the grit of marble dust, and he wondered if he'd ever breathe again without smelling the scent of freshly ground stone. But the statue was finished.

The other stonecutters gathered around him in awe, walking around the image, making teasing comments about the genitalia. Dom barely managed to avoid crossing his legs as they talked, wondering irritably how many men had to listen to themselves being rated this way.

One of them, an erudite fellow who'd quoted lovely homilies and attributed them to an English writer by the name of Shakespeare, even recognized the statue.

311

"It looks exactly like *David!*" When the other workers peered at him curiously, he added, "You know. Michelangelo. But this one's much smaller. What will you do with it, Dom?"

"It's a gift," Dom said softly, staring at himself. He felt no elation, and little pride. He had merely piggybacked on the shoulders of genius, copying every angle from the art pictures he'd found in books. Many times he'd regretted tearing up those posters, as they had offered an excellent frontal view. It had felt a bit strange when he did the face, but he'd ignored his discomfort and tried very hard to see himself as Honor apparently saw him.

Only she would be able to tell whether his effort would pass muster.

"So, buddy," said the foreman. "You want us to deliver it for you?"

"That would be most generous. And I must regretfully inform you that I can no longer—"

"Yeah, yeah, I been expecting this. Anyone who can sculpt like this has no business cutting stone. You been a good worker, Castiglione. Wish all my guys were so honest about putting in their time. Hell, I'll be surprised if your lady is still waiting for you, much as you been here."

Heaviness descended on Dom's shoulders. He didn't expect Honor to wait for him.

Quickly, he turned away from the statue to smile at the foreman. "I appreciate the use of your tools. I never could have finished it so quickly without them. I shall be happy to pay to have them sharpened—"

"Nah. Consider it a Christmas bonus."

And so Dom found himself riding home on a truck, with his alter ego wrapped and tied firmly in the back.

By the time they fought through the heavy holiday traffic to midtown, it was late. While his coworker went to the back to lower the statue down on the lift, Dom ran upstairs. "Honor! Honor, come see . . . " He trailed off when he found only Ernie staring at him. "Where's Honor?"

"I don't know." Ernie glanced at his watch. "But she's been gone for hours. She said she was going to see a friend."

Dom scowled. "Your brother?"

"No, she left in a taxi. I wrote the number down, just in case. If she doesn't come back soon, I guess we can try to track her down."

A sinking feeling tugged at the pit of Dom's stomach. This had something to do with Rafe. But at the moment . . . "Do you think you and your brother might help me for a minute? I have Honor's Christmas present outside and it's a bit heavy."

Ernie returned very shortly with Nick. He eyed Dom, eyed the bulky object under the tarp, and such a cynical look turned down the corners of his mouth that Dom wanted to punch him. He was well aware of Nick's opinion of him. All Dom did, however, was nod brusquely and lead the way to the street.

The motorized dolly had a special mechanism that allowed it to climb stairs, but the statue was so heavy that it still took all four of them to tilt it and maneuver it through the door into the vestibule.

Colleen Shannon

Swearing, Nick wiped his forehead off. "You don't really expect us to take it upstairs, do you?" He glared at Dom. "Frankly, I'd prefer that you store it somewhere else."

Dom glared back. "I assure you, I sculpted it."

His coworker nodded. "Took him forever, but he did it all by his lonesome."

"I don't doubt that," Nick said grimly.

Ernie obviously itched to take off the tarp, but Dom wanted Honor to unveil it, so he shook his head at Ernie's inquiring look.

Begrudgingly, Nick allowed, "I suppose we can leave it here for now. It's too heavy for anyone to take, anyway."

They all helped rock it, little by little, off the dolly. Wishing them a cheerful, "Merry Christmas and Happy New Year," the stonecutter left.

Ernie winced.

Dom closed his eyes wearily. Would he turn white at the stroke of midnight on December 31, or would the angel give him a chance to say goodbye? He tried to remember exactly how it had happened before, so very long ago, literally and emotionally, but he'd been drunk and miserable. One thing was growing increasingly obvious: very soon there could be a matched pair of life-size *Davids*.

Maybe he'd just stand in this vestibule and watch the centuries go by, spending eternity wishing for the sight of Honor. He smiled wistfully. There would be no virgin's tears this time.

Nick glared between Ernie and Dom. "Why do I always get the feeling I'm the last one to know what the hell's going on?"

314

"You don't want to know, bro, believe me," Ernie said, his mellow brown eyes soft with sympathy as he watched Dom.

Dom opened his eyes. "What time is it, Ernie?"

Ernie glanced at his watch. "Almost eight."

"She should have been back by now."

Nick peered upstairs at the open door and silent apartment. "Where *is* Honor?"

Ernie explained. "You still know that guy at Yellow Cab?"

"Yeah."

"If we give him the cab number, you think he'd tell us where he took her?"

"Not without some persuasion." Nick's smile was a slash of white in his dark face. "But I can be real persuasive when I want."

"No duh. Come on, Dom, we'll find her. I'm sure it's nothing. She probably just got caught up in Christmas shopping, what with everything open so late."

As the cab pulled up before an institutional gray brick building near the wharf, Honor gave the driver his fare plus a generous tip. She hesitated. She didn't want to be extravagant and ask him to wait, but at this time of year, she couldn't count on finding a cab easily, especially in this part of town. "Can you come back for me in a couple of hours?"

"If I don't get a long fare out of town, I can," the cabbie said. "You sure you want me to leave you here?"

Honor checked the address on the building again. It matched the one she'd written down.

She felt uneasy at the hard-looking characters entering and exiting the building, many of them giving her the eye, but at this point she had few options. A thin young woman holding two small children by the hand entered as she watched, and she relaxed a bit. At least she wouldn't be the only woman here. "I'll be fine. Thanks again, and Merry Christmas."

"Same to ya." He drove off, his tires screeching in his eagerness to be gone. Plump snowflakes had begun to fall.

As she navigated the crowded sidewalk, Honor pulled her hood tightly about her face. She saw enough old caps and tattered combat boots to realize that this particular shelter catered to homeless vets. A few of the men had brought steaming soup bowls outside to eat, lounging on the steps and against the wall. A couple of younger men whistled, and one made a coarse proposition, but she made it inside unmolested.

She blinked. After the chilly darkness outside, the shelter was bright, clean and warm. But even the strong institutional soap and fragrant odors of stew and baked bread couldn't totally eclipse the smell of unwashed bodies, and other scents she didn't want to name. Honor walked from table to table, looking for Rafe. Several interested stares turned up to her, but most of the men and the sprinkling of women concentrated on their food, ignoring her. There was little conversation, either.

"I help you, miss?" said one tired-looking woman wiping down a table.

"Hi. My name's Honor Fitzhugh. I'm . . . a friend of Rafe Castigi."

The volunteer shrugged. "Don't know the name, but we get lots of part-timers. Look around, if you want."

Honor circulated the large, crowded room. Once she saw a beat-up bomber jacket and a shaggy head of dark hair, but when the diner turned to look at her, he smiled through a scraggly gray beard. Honor smiled weakly in return and walked on. Darkness had fallen outside, and she wondered how much longer she should wait. Her unease kept pace with her urgency.

She was on her fourth tour of the room when a worker went outside and yelled, "Beds full! Dinner hour's over in fifteen minutes." The woman returned to the serving line.

Dammit, she couldn't come this close and not find him. She was about to go outside again when she saw a young man watching her with more than usual interest. Almost as if he recognized her. He wore a navy cap and a SEAL insignia on his sleeve.

Casually, she stopped at his table. He quickly turned his attention back to his food. "Ah, excuse me, do you know Rafe Castigi?"

He ignored her.

She sat down across from him and folded her forearms on the table. "Look, I . . . owe him some money. I mean him no harm. Please tell me where I might find him."

He glanced at her, his gaze zigzagging erratically from her shining blond hair down to her

317

slim neck and the breasts hidden under her coat. "Don't look like a cop."

"I'm not." Honor smiled ruefully. "Believe me, I'm not too popular with the police at the moment myself."

Tobacco-stained teeth grinned at her. "Me neither. Rafe'd kill me if I brought you to him."

"No, he won't. I won't let him."

"He said some beautiful blond or crazy Italian might be looking for him. I was to keep my yap shut."

"Please . . . "

"Don't know why he's so pissed at you, but he ain't as tough as he thinks. He's sick, which is why he didn't come in tonight. I think he needs to go to the hospital. You think you can convince him, if I take you to him?"

Alarmed to hear that Rafe was sick, Honor stuffed her clenched hands in her pockets. "I'll convince him, all right."

Her grim determination seemed to reassure the vet, for he scraped up the last of his stew with his bread, wiped his mouth on his sleeve, and stood. He exited quickly, limping, but he was tall and Honor had to hurry to keep up. She wished she had time to leave word with one of the volunteers in case the cabbie came back before she returned, but what would she say? She had no idea where she was going.

The vet had no such concerns. He veered into alleys, walked past rotting garbage bins, and then turned onto a long street lined with wharves. Honor was walking too fast to talk, but her unease was growing. When they turned down yet another alley, she almost balked, but the image of Dom's vitality forever frozen in stone kept her going.

At the end of an alley, Honor saw lights and heard laughter. As they drew nearer she realized the warehouses on each side were connected by a catwalk above, offering a three-sided shelter from the elements. Cardboard boxes, old sheets of plywood, siding—anything that could be tied together—were stacked against each side wall as makeshift homes. Honor almost tripped over several extended feet, and she heard loud snores as she picked her way deeper into the dead-end alley.

The shivers that traveled down her nape to her spine had little to do with the cold. She tried to ignore the hostile stares, the snide remarks and sexual asides that were flung at her from every quarter, telling herself these men wouldn't hurt her. They resented her not as a woman, but as an outsider. All she had to do was find Rafe and—

She tripped, almost sprawling to the pavement. Her purse flew off her shoulder.

The vet grabbed it just as someone else touched it. He wrapped it over her shoulder, saying in a hiss, "Stay close and be quiet."

Harsh laughter sounded from several quarters, and a huge man warming his hands over a fire pit chortled. "She don't look like your type, Josey. How's about I take her off your hands?"

Josey put his arm around her shoulder as the man lurched toward them. "Nah. She ain't mine. She's Rafe's."

The man froze and glanced under a fire escape

near the end of the alley. "He won't never know the difference." He started forward again.

Josey said, "He ain't drunk all the time."

Honor's heart beat so loudly that she barely heard the man's sullen, "Aw, she's too scrawny anyways." He returned to warming his hands.

"Over there. And make it fast." Josey jerked his head at the fire escape, crossed his arms and stood guard.

Honor knelt next to a long form beneath a ragged blanket. Shadows cast by the flickering flames danced on the walls, giving Honor an eerie sense of impending doom accented by the now driving snow. She squinted, and finally her eyes adjusted enough for her to make out the craggy face and thick head of chocolate brown hair resting on an old duffel bag for a pillow. She felt for what she thought was Rafe's shoulder and shook him. He didn't move, didn't make a sound.

For a terrible moment she wondered if he was dead. But then he groaned, his long legs shifting, and muttered, "Fuck orders! They're civilians, dammit. We don't have the right . . . " He moved restlessly, as if he were running.

Honor shook him harder. "Rafe, wake up." She groped and felt for his forehead. She flinched away. He was burning up with fever. Finally he opened his eyes.

For an eternal moment he stared at her blankly.

Had he lost his mind? Was it too late?

Recognition flickered to life. "Go 'way."

"No," she whispered equally fiercely. "Tell me

something, Castigi. Who's it hurt, what's it prove, if you die out here alone?"

He sat up, almost hitting his head on the platform above, and said in a growl, "I've had enough of your lip, little girl. Go away and play with your pretty Italian boy and leave me the hell alone."

He tried to turn away, but Honor caught his shoulder. She fumbled in her purse and held out her makeup mirror. "So, if I'm a little girl, what's that make you? A big man? Come on, Rafe, tell me what you see." She stuck the mirror under his nose.

Maybe heaven was watching, for the fire flared up as someone threw on more wood. Rafe lifted his hand to slap the mirror aside, but he caught his own gaze first. He gasped, staring at himself.

Grimly, Honor watched him look, wondering how long it had been since he'd seen a mirror. Quite a while, judging from the dark beard and smudges under his eyes. His face was thinner than the last time she'd seen him, and she heard his lungs rattle as he took several deep breaths. His eyes closing in disgust, he turned away. "What do you want?"

"To take you home and put you in a warm bed, give you some soup, call a doctor. That's all, for now. I promise."

"And then?"

"Then it's up to you. I'll tell you what Dom needs of you and you can believe me or call me crazy. Fair enough?"

"Guess so." Rafe shuffled around in the darkness, packed his duffel bag and inched out of his hiding place. He tried to stand, but his legs buckled. Josey took him under one arm, Honor under the other, but they still staggered under his weight as they turned toward the exit out of the alley, his legs half walking, half dragging as he tried to help.

The troublemaker grinned when he saw how weak Rafe was. "So, even SEALs're human, right, guys?" Several of his bunkies grinned and nodded.

The troublemaker pulled a switchblade out of his pocket. He flicked it open with a lethal hiss. "Let's see you shove your weight around now, Castigi. Don't think you should leave our five-star joint without paying your share . . . "

He kicked a can out of his path and rounded the fire. Blood red, the knife reflected the flames.

Chapter Thirteen

Dom scowled at the shelter director. "What do you mean, you do not know where she went?"

"Look, it's not my job to keep up with the women who come here looking for cheap thrills—"

Nick grabbed Dom before those large sculptor's hands could clench about the man's throat. "Thanks anyway." He shoved Dom toward the door. "You have a real talent for alienating people who might want to help you, you know that?"

Snarling, Dom turned on Nick. "That man does not care about Honor—mine or his."

"That's not his job. Look, he's not the best one to ask anyway. Why don't we ask around the dining room, see if anyone saw her leave."

His chest heaving as he tried to control his fear for Honor, Dom finally managed a nod. The taxi person they'd spoken with said he'd returned here at the appointed time, but Honor hadn't been waiting, so he left.

The snowfall outside was about to become a blizzard. If they didn't find her soon . . .

Most of the people sipping cocoa at the tables looked away whenever they approached. Nick took one side of the room, Dom the other, but their description won only curt shakes of the head. Ernie talked to the volunteers, but all of them had been too busy to notice where Honor went. One lady did remember seeing her, and that she'd asked about Rafe.

Finally, a weasely-looking little guy grinned at Nick. "Is there a reward?"

His side of the room completed, Dom turned back toward Nick in time to hear the question. He felt like the top of his head would blow off with anger, but Nick caught his arm with brutal fingers and hauled him to a stop.

Nick slapped a twenty before the guy. He grinned wider but didn't say anything. Nick added another one.

The weasel scratched his head, as if the cobwebs were lifting from his brain, but when Nick slapped a last bill down, he finally nodded. "Saw a pretty blond leave with Josey."

"Where?" Dom demanded hoarsely.

Greedily stacking his money, the little man shrugged.

Flinging off Nick's staying hand, Dom lifted the weasel by his coat lapels. "Perhaps I should pound your head with my fists, open it *solo un po'.*" For good measure, he lifted until the man's toes barely touched the floor.

Gasping, the weasel stuttered, "D-didn't see where, b-but Josey beds down with Castigi in an alley by the wharf!"

"What alley?" Slowly Dom let the weasel's feet reach terra firma again.

Tersely, Nick clarified the somewhat garbled directions. The little man had barely sat down before his questioners were out the door. He shot them the finger as they ran out, but they ignored him.

Dom hitched up his slingshot over his shoulder.

Nick checked the pistol in his shoulder holster.

And Ernie looked as if he were about to puke, but he followed gamely enough.

Desperately, Honor glanced behind them to gauge the distance out of the alley. They'd never make it, especially dragging Rafe. She felt Josey's abrupt stillness and knew that if he bolted, she and Rafe were cooked. "Let us leave, and I'll give you all my money."

"That's not all you'll give, blondie." The big man kept coming. His two bunkies shambled after him, each taking an opposite side of the alley.

Tactically, they were trying to close them off, Honor realized. Honor had always detested guns, but at the moment she'd give a king's ransom for one.

Josey wavered. "Hey, guys, Rafe has some rich friends."

Close enough now that she could smell his foul breath, the ugly man laughed. "Yeah, like blondie here? Let's see what you got." He reached out for Honor's purse with one hand and her breast with the other.

Rafe straightened with an effort that Honor could feel ripple through him and shoved her behind him. "Come through me first, dawg."

The knife turned on him, slashing at Rafe's belly.

Rafe sucked in and tried a chopping motion at the guy's wrist, but his reactions were slower than normal, and the troublemaker danced back out of the way.

"Get 'em!" he yelled to his bunkies. One grabbed for Honor, and the other slashed a broken bottle at Josey.

With a bleat of terror, Josey turned and ran.

Honor stomped her snow boot down on her assailant's toes. He yelped, dancing back, giving her enough leverage to whirl her purse as a weapon. She aimed for his head, but only hit his shoulder. However, her purse was heavy enough to make him grunt and fall back another step. She heard movement behind her and spun in time to try the same maneuver with the other man, but he was too close. He grabbed her purse and ripped it from her hands.

Vaguely, Honor sensed the other homeless men slipping away into the darkness. No one would come to help. They were on their own.

Meanwhile Rafe struggled with the ringleader, his hand wrapped about the assailant's wrist. Half rushing his opponent, half falling on him,

Rafe shoved him back against the wall and tried to beat his hand against the brick to make him drop the knife. But the troublemaker was as tall as Rafe, and heavier, and, at the moment at least, stronger. Tightening his grip on the knife, he began to turn it toward Rafe's face.

Honor heard Rafe groan, but she was busy fighting for her own life. The man behind her grabbed her shoulders to hold her still while the man in front drew back a fist.

For the first time, Honor was glad she was small and skinny. Her heavy coat was unzipped from the activity anyway, and she ripped it the rest of the way off, ducking down as she jerked her arms out of the sleeves. The fist above connected to an unshaven male throat instead of Honor's jaw. Both men yelped, giving Honor time to dive sideways.

One man coughed, holding his throat, and the other stared stupidly at the coat in his hands. He tossed it aside, looking for his prey.

Backing away, Honor looked around for a weapon. A desperate glance showed her Rafe's bloody face. Rafe was weakening, both hands wrapped about the stronger man's wrist. Now the SEAL was barely able to keep the knife away from his throat.

Honor's assailants began stalking her again, but this time they were more wary. She backed away, feeling heat singing her buttocks. She spared Rafe one last frantic glance, her heart pounding so loudly that only on a very dim level did she hear a car screeching to a stop at the alley entrance.

Rafe fell to his knees, his arms extended as he tried to push against the man's strength. Teeth bared in a feral grin, the troublemaker shoved back harder. Slowly the knife came closer, close enough to shave Rafe's throat, but Rafe still managed to hold it at the wrong angle. The big man paused to shift slightly and bring the point to bear.

Without stopping to think about what she did, or even about Dom and what was at stake, remembering only that she cared for Rafe and wanted to help him, Honor whirled, bent and grabbed the closest burning log from the fire. She waved it in a wide arc at the two other homeless men. They backed off.

Rage gave her strength. The heat singeing her gloved hands didn't seem so severe at first, not when she was freezing everywhere else. With a guttural cry, Honor leaped the short distance to Rafe. As the troublemaker shifted to strike the killing blow, Honor brought the burning timber down on his head with all her might.

Looking stunned, his cap smoking, the man fell against the wall and slid down to the ground. His head slumped against his shoulder as he toppled sideways.

Rafe crumpled to the ground. Tossing the log aside, pain finally penetrating the adrenaline rush, Honor stood guard over Rafe, her back to the wall.

What the hell did she do now? Outrage had brought her this far, but she was fresh out of options.

The last two assailants looked torn between

fear and aggression as they glared first at Honor and then at their unconscious leader. With a vicious curse, one started to lunge at Honor while the other bent to pick up his own burning log.

A whistling noise split the muffled silence. Honor blinked, but snow stung her eyelashes as she tried to peer at the source of the sound. Somewhere, at the head of the alley, where the car had stopped, she barely made out three silhouettes moving in.

Fast.

While she was still trying to figure out what was going on, there was a *thunk!* and the man lunging at Honor fell like a stone. He was out cold before he hit the ground.

Stones . . . Dumbly, Honor watched the rock hit the ground a split second before her assailant's fallen head.

The second man yelped and tried to dodge the approaching trio. In the light cast by the fires, Honor made out Nick, Ernie and Dom. They formed a triangle to cut the assailant off. He froze. Nick stuck a pistol in the man's ribs and grinned, his face satanic in the shadows.

"Lowlifes who attack women should crawl through life the way you belong." Nick brought the pistol butt down hard on the man's head. "On your knees!"

Honor barely had time to watch the man fall, half-dazed, before Dom leaped to her side, wrapping his slingshot over his shoulder as he came. As he drew closer to the fire, for an instant she saw a strange look in his eyes.

Part exhilaration, part shock, and all wonder.

But then he was cupping her face in his hands, lifting her chin so he could see if she had any bruises, running his palms down over her to check for broken bones. "You are all right, *bellissima*, they did not harm you?"

Reaction settling in, Honor could only nod. She was too busy shivering and biting back groans. "Ch-check on R-Rafe."

Dom paused long enough to wrap his coat about her shoulders and then bent to feel for Rafe's pulse. He frowned, and felt Rafe's forehead. "He is hot."

A siren wailed in the distance. Nick turned away from the homeless man sitting half-dazed on his haunches and bit out, "Come on, we need to book!"

For once Dom didn't bother to ask for clarification, as the situation was obvious enough. He knelt and heaved Rafe over his shoulders. He staggered under the considerable weight, but managed to get down the alley to Nick's Firebird.

Tossing her purse and coat on the floorboard as he opened the car door, Ernie mouthed, *You OK, Honor?*

She nodded, wondering if she should try to pull off her gloves now. They felt like they were sticking to her skin.

She followed Ernie into the back seat and cradled Rafe's head in her lap, using the very tips of her fingers to push his hair aside so she could see the gash on his temple. It oozed blood, but didn't look deep. He'd have another scar to add to his collection.

The other two took the front seat. Tires screeching, slipping and sliding in the snow, Nick turned them around and barreled off in the opposite direction from the cop car rounding a curb in the distance. Nick looked in his rearview mirror and mouthed a coarse Spanish oath.

Honor looked out the back. Several of the homeless apparitions had reappeared, and one of them was flagging down the police. If they got their license numbers . . .

Meeting Nick's eyes in the mirror, Honor read the same concern. But at least for now, the cruiser had stopped and was soon lost behind them in the driving snow.

Despite her own pain and shock, Honor groped in her purse for a moist towelette to clean Rafe's wound. She owed him, big-time. Even sick as a dog, furious with her, he'd mustered enough effort to try to protect her. Barehanded. Against a man with a knife. Her lingering doubts about his strength of character dissipated. She had to smile as she pictured his expression when they told him she, too, had risked her life to save him. Somehow she thought he'd been too delirious to notice.

Now he owed her, too.

And he wouldn't be happy about it.

In the darkness she sensed Dom watching her. Strong emotion emanated from him, but she was too exhausted to try to decode his cryptic signals. She realized the cavalry had arrived in time to see the infantry's last stand, but as to what her warrior lover thought of her now, she hadn't a clue.

They all breathed a bit easier as the familiar streets of midtown came into view. When he stopped at a streetlight, Nick glanced over the seat at her. "You think he's bad enough to need a hospital, Honor?"

"His cut's not serious, but he obviously has a virus or an infection."

"It's best if we treat him at my place. If the police are looking for him and hear about the fight, the hospital's the first place they'll look."

Honor frowned. "Why would the police be looking for him? All he did was defend me. I'm the one who hit the guy."

"I didn't want to tell you both, especially since he disappeared so fast, but Rafe didn't show up for his hearing the week after Thanksgiving. They've had a warrant out for him since."

Wearily, Dom rested his head against the seat back.

Her throat tight with fear, Honor brushed Rafe's hair back from his brow. She'd assumed he'd been hiding out to escape her and Dom, but it seemed he had more practical reasons. They could try to protect him from the police and get him well, but they couldn't protect him from himself.

When they got to the brownstone Ernie generously offered his bedroom, said he'd bunk with Nick until Rafe was well. While Ernie and Dom undressed Rafe and tried to clean the worst of the grime away, Nick went to the phone to call the old family doctor. The man had retired, but he'd delivered both Nick and Ernie, and Nick thought he'd probably come by if he begged hard enough.

During all the activity, Honor sneaked into the bathroom to try to remove the gloves. The pain was really bad now, and she knew she had to get them off so she could ice the lesions down. But the lining seemed to be stuck at the most acute burn spots, the middle of her fingers and her palms, where she'd gripped the log. She was biting her lip to keep from crying out as she tugged gently at the gloves when the bathroom door flew open and crashed against the wall.

"Bellissima, what are—" Dom took one look at her guilty start and the way she tried to hide her gloved hands behind her back and stormed into the room. A barrage of furious Italian went over her head. Dom pressed her down on the closed toilet lid.

"You foolish girl, why did you not tell us you burned yourself? With your gloves, and the fact that you didn't seem to be in pain, I thought you'd dropped the log before . . . " He trailed off with a gasp as he tried to ease one glove off and saw that it wouldn't move. "Nick!" he bellowed.

Footsteps came running. Nick eased the door open and peeked inside. "Yeah?" His eyes widened as he realized what was going on. "Ernie, bring me a big bowl!"

They dumped ice water in the bowl, poured in a bottle of hydrogen peroxide, and made Honor sit at the table to soak her hands. She couldn't avoid a groan, because the pain was excruciating as the concoction seemed to attack every burned nerve ending with icy-hot darts.

His brow dripping with sweat, Dom rested her wet hand on a towel in his lap and slowly, as gently as he could, eased the glove off, fiber by fiber, managing to leave most of her skin intact. He kept glancing at her face, grimacing in sympathetic pain every time she moved a muscle, so she kept her jaw still and let him work.

When both gloves had been removed, the three men clustered around. Nick held her wrists and turned her palms up to the light. He whistled softly as he saw the pus oozing from her blistered, reddened finger joints and palms. "Good thing the doctor's coming."

Dom, too, looked at her as if she'd suddenly grown two heads. As if he'd never seen a woman before. As if he not only had to reappraise his previously conceived notions, but had none left that made sense. "Women are not supposed to be heroic," he said softly. "But here, nothing is as it seems."

"Maybe it always was this way, if you had your eyes open wide enough to see it," Honor replied, watching him. "Lots of women changed the world by being heroic. Joan of Arc, Eleanor of Aquitaine . . . " He still stared at her in that strange way, but she saw the sunny glow, which had been missing for so long from his eyes, glimmer back to life.

Her heart skipped a beat. Was he beginning to realize that maybe she could handle herself better than he'd thought?

Nick looked confused at the strange conversation, but Ernie drew his brother out of hearing distance. Ernie was the only one who didn't seem shocked at the lengths Honor could go to when pressed hard enough.

Honor cleared her throat. "Rafe . . . how is he?"

The glow went out. "Still unconscious. I fear he is gravely ill. You may have risked your life for nothing."

The words were barely out of his mouth before the buzzer sounded below. Ernie hotfooted it down to escort the doctor up. The older gentleman carried a black bag and went into Rafe's room along with Ernie. When he exited some time later, he was grave.

"That young man has pneumonia. He needs to be in a hospital."

Since this pronouncement was greeted with a marked lack of enthusiasm, he sighed and admitted, "But I've given him a shot of antibiotics. I'll return tomorrow for another one, and if his fever breaks, he'll probably be all right. He seems quite strong." The doctor had been watching Honor as he spoke, and now he turned her hands up where he could see them. He glared at Nick.

"Is this the way you take care of houseguests, boy?" he demanded.

Nick smiled sardonically. "You should see the other guy."

Shaking his head, the doctor seated Honor at the table, put antibiotic salve on her hands and wrapped the burns in white gauze. "They look worse than they are. You need to change this dressing daily, and take this medication." He slapped a bottle down on the table. "In a few days you should be able to move without pain, though you may be scarred."

Honor stared at her palms. At least she'd have tangible proof that this hadn't all been a dream.

Nick walked the doctor to the door. "I'd appreciate it if you don't report this anywhere, Doc."

Glaring, the doctor retorted, "Nicco, I was the first man to spank your butt. You really think you need to tell me that? I'll be back tomorrow. If your friend isn't better, I'm afraid he'll have to go to the hospital, no matter what kind of trouble he's in." He departed.

An uncomfortable silence fell. Honor was abruptly exhausted. It was after midnight. All she wanted was a shower, a bed, and a week of sleep. Now that Rafe was safe, at least for the moment, maybe she could finally rest. She tried not to think about how heaven would interpret Dom's covenant if the man he was supposed to redeem died. They'd tried their best, but would that be enough?

Again she looked down at her hands. How on earth would she clean herself?

She felt an intense stare and looked up to meet the liquid warmth of Dom's eyes. He understood her dilemma and obviously looked forward to helping her overcome it.

Nick glanced between the pair, rolled his eyes, and stood. "Come on, Ernie, I have a feeling we're not welcome. 'Night, you guys."

Honor smiled weakly. Dom nodded, still staring hungrily at Honor.

Waving, Ernie preceded Nick out the door. Nick paused. The smile that played about his lips this time was a bit less cynical. "Honor, if I ever called you a girl, I'm sorry." He arched an eye-

brow at Dom. "You let her go, Dominico, or who-
ever the hell you are, and *you'll* be sorry."

The door closed. Smiling weakly, Honor stood.
"I need to get cleaned up." She waited for Dom to
offer to help, but he said nothing.

His eyes, however, quoted sonnets. Longing to
believe him, Honor went to her room to collect a
clean nightgown and robe out of her drawer. He
walked slowly to the front door. Honor heard the
lock click. She straightened, blood rushing to her
head, telling herself that he was only securing
them for the night. She was afraid to hope . . . and
afraid not to.

To distract herself, she turned on the bathwa-
ter. While it was running she went back out to
check on Rafe. Dom already stood over his
nephew. He moved the humidifier Nick had
hooked up closer to the bed.

Honor felt Rafe's forehead. It didn't seem quite
as hot as before, and, propped up on pillows with
the medicated moisture filling the room, he
seemed to breathe a bit easier.

They tiptoed out, leaving the door ajar so they
could hear him if he called out. In the quiet living
room, snow muffled the sounds of a bustling
world that seemed very far away. They stared at
one another.

The pain in Honor's hands had died to a dull
throbbing, but it made the risk all the more real
as she said, her voice catching, "Will you help me
bathe, Dom?" If he rejected her again, she'd crawl
off and die.

A smile had chased away the frown that was
beginning to seem permanently etched on his

brow. Honor's spine wilted as sensual heat began to radiate from him. Strong? No, before this man she was putty. And then it struck her.

He was the Pygmalion, not she. He was the sculptor, she the medium. He had changed her as surely, and as permanently, as if he had formed her out of the marble from which he came. Nothing in her life would ever be the same, no matter if she went back with him or stayed in this dull, gray world. Because she would never be the same.

Honor held her hands out to him. "Dom . . . "

And then he was there, lifting her in his arms to carry her to the bathroom. Gently, as if he unwrapped the best present a man could wish for, he undressed her. He helped her into the tub and soaped up the sponge. Placing her hands lightly on his shoulders, he stroked her all over. Ankles, calves, knees, thighs . . . When she was sighing, boneless and about to ooze down into the water, he bypassed the throbbing between her legs. Instead, he cleaned her flat stomach, her breasts most gently of all, and finally stroked around her neck, tickling under her ear.

She laughed, gooseflesh prickling her skin, and leaned back to kick water at him. He splashed her back, but since he was dressed, she had the advantage. When his soaked shirt clung to the purity of his muscles, she leaned back against the tub, sighing with sheer joy as she absorbed him through her eyes, her pores, her very atoms. To store up for all the long tomorrows . . . She blinked to hide the tears that came to her eyes.

But he noticed. He went very still. The sponge

dropped from his hands. He clenched his fingers on his thighs as if he, too, longed to grasp all that heaven allowed. His tone was very low, very fierce and very sincere. "I will never be a saint, Honor of my life. And if I am doomed as a rogue or a sinner, the result is the same. I will turn to stone with your name upon my lips for all eternity. I will feel only joy that I was privileged to know you in every way, the best way a man can. And if I am fortunate enough to survive the new year as blood and bone, I will cleave you to me and make you mine though heaven itself try to deny me. This I swear."

He bowed his head and crossed himself.

Honor's tears trickled down her face, mixing with the warm water. But now they were tears of joy. Suddenly it didn't matter anymore whether he stayed or she went. Finally she knew that her parents had named her well.

For she had never felt more honored in her life. Whatever happened, they'd always have this moment to cherish. Feeling like a phoenix rising out of the ashes, she got out of the tub. Forgetful of the throbbing in her hands, forgetful of her nakedness, aware only that she had to touch, to cement this bond and make the miracle come true, if only for tonight, she knelt next to him.

Shuddering, he lifted her chin to kiss her, as if he, too, felt a need to revel in intimacy. Eagerly Honor kissed him back, her mouth hot and open and giving.

His lips grew hard and needful, his tongue beginning to probe, but with an effort that made his neck muscles tense, he said, "Not yet. First, I made a promise to myself, too." He was out of the bathroom before she could more than open her mouth to ask him what was wrong. She dried off while he was gone, sprinkling herself with perfumed powder.

He returned, holding something behind his back, and gently turned her away from the mirror to face him. A black cloud settled over her shoulders. The nightgown she'd ordered so long ago. Through the wispy chiffon, he smiled at her.

A rogue's smile, lusty and brash and eager. His eyes tracked the shimmering fabric as it settled on her curves. He stroked her shoulders and fluffed up the fall of lace at the low neckline. "I promised myself, before I left here one way or the other, that I would dress you in this nonsense and then take it off, inch by inch."

Taking her wrist so he didn't have to touch her damp, bandaged hands, he led her, limp with expectation, to the bedroom.

But she didn't remain limp for long. . . .

She expected him to take her straight to the bed. Instead he moved her in front of the mirror. Holding her eyes in the glass, he slowly undid his buttons and shrugged out of his shirt. Equally slowly, he pulled off his pants and briefs.

The fabric over Honor's breast trembled with the force of her heartbeat, but he wouldn't let her turn to face him. Instead, when he was naked, a stalwart male contrast to her sweet femininity, he rubbed his erection sensuously against her hips, letting her feel his heat through the wispy barrier between them. All the while he lightly touched her waist, tightening his grip if she tried to turn. And then, still holding her eyes, he lowered his hands to her hips and began raising the fabric.

Inch by delicious inch. She felt a warmth touch her skin, but it had nothing to do with the heat blasting from the vents. Paradoxically, as the fabric moved higher, baring more of her skin, the warmth grew. But she couldn't look away from the predatory stare that had her pinioned.

She could only drown in those Adriatic eyes and think the world well lost.

The fabric had reached her waist now. He reached higher under the chiffon and cradled her breasts. She felt her heart leap to his touch, and knew he felt it, too. His teeth gleamed in a smile with a touch of savagery that allowed her a glimpse of his own driving desire.

And then that glorious autumn-shaded curly head bent to kiss and nip at her throat, down the valley between her breasts. Her nipples thrust up to meet him, but, breathing heavily, he left them pouting and hard.

"Look at me, Honor." She'd closed her eyes, but she opened them at his husky command.

While she watched, he pulled the nightgown over her head. Now she was bare, with no defenses, staring at the intimate picture they made. His arms were crossed possessively over her abdomen; his chest rubbed against her back; his loins throbbed for release as they butted against her.

"Do you finally see yourself as I see you, *bellissima*? You are lovely everywhere. Heart. Mind. And body."

Honor's dreamy gaze left his beautiful face to look at her own. She would never be gorgeous, but, in Dom's presence, she felt pretty. But more important, she felt loved. "Yes, Dom. But it is a tribute to you as much as it is to me." She hesitated, and some of the carnal urgency became quiescent as she said softly, "And if there's a child?" She crossed his hands tighter about her waist, fiercely wishing for him to give the right answer.

His smile faded, but he softly kissed her brow. "You are strong enough to do anything, my Honor. And here, well, Ernie has explained to me that people here do not ostracize a woman who bears a bastard."

Honor sighed. *Bless Ernie.* Literally, according to the beatitudes. Ernie had one of the purest hearts she'd ever known. Her last reservation settled, she covered Dom's strong hands with her own bandaged ones and smiled.

Arrested, he stared at her. That strange current had started again. It was so powerful that, in the blink of an eye, it transcended the centuries between them and brought them, ageless, to destiny. A destiny where rogues could learn humility and honor, and sparrows could learn to soar unafraid, lifted on the wings of faith. . . .

In the end, it was she who led him to the bed, and the rogue who lay humbled before her to know again the wonder of Honor.

Dom stared at her, trying not to cry as she kissed him, trying not to wonder if this last week would be all they'd have. Trying not to worry about whether he would make her pregnant, for that, too, was in the hands of fate. He knew she would not let him use one of those handy little sleeves, and, in truth, he didn't want anything between them either. They had a lifetime of loving to pack into one week. . . .

With her thick hair a golden nimbus about her head, she glowed so brightly that his fears and troubles evaporated in the warmth of her skin.

Starting at his neck, she kissed the throbbing hollow, working a delicious path down to his chest, where she paused to sip and suckle his nipples. Dom bowed against the bed, the primitive need to shove her under him and press deep almost overcoming him, but he sensed her need to give herself to him and offer her own brand of homage. She didn't seem troubled in the least that she couldn't use her hands very well. In fact, her injury seemed to inspire inventiveness with her lips, tongue and teeth.

So he gritted his teeth and stayed still even when she raked her teeth against his nipple. Even when she stabbed her tongue into his navel. And even when she draped his powerful thigh over her arm to nip the back of his knee. But when she rested her cheek against his stomach, her face so close to his rearing manhood that he could feel her teasing breath, he began to squirm. Finally, when she softly, gently, kissed the proud tip, he could bear no more.

Groaning, he flipped her on her back and straddled her hips. "You're a saucy wench all of a sudden."

"You made me so. It's only fitting that you reap the benefits." She had the audacity to wink.

Spreading her thighs wide, he nudged her first, assuring himself of her readiness, but she was more than eager. For a recent virgin, she was passionate—passionate enough to make him forget that he sinned, that his life might end in a week, or even that a world waited beyond this bed. He knew only the need to bury himself in her and experience again the wonder of the bonding the good Lord gave to men and women.

Holding himself in check with great effort, he dipped himself into her instead of plunging as he longed to do. But her eyes opened wide at that first stretching, and her harsh sigh shivered through him, too. Heedless of her own wounds, she pressed her hands on his hipbones to urge him on.

His heart as full as his manhood, in one thrust he drove deep. The tight sheath aroused him to his core, but he never lost his awareness of Honor. Cradled within the depths of her body, he drew her legs about his waist, manacled her wrists above her head with his hands and plundered her equally with his gaze. Now that the deed was done, he was content to be still and let her know that she belonged to him, and only to him.

"Who's reaping now, wench?" he demanded huskily.

Very slightly she lifted her hips, her inner muscles clasping harder about him. "Both of us, I should say—"

He smothered her sass with his tongue. He drew himself out, still keeping her hands above her head, and made her wait, squirming, while he sampled other parts of her body. He dallied, turning pleasure-pain to exquisite torture, taking a nip here and a nibble there, rubbing one hairy leg between her legs as he dined. He hid a smile at the fixed look on her face, for he well knew what that glazed concentration meant. He only switched from using teeth to using lips and tongue, feeding the fire roaring high between them.

The last time, he'd been a rogue initiating a virgin. A virgin he loved. This time he was a man cleaving to his woman. From the moment he saw her swinging that fiery log in the alley, a virago without protection or fear, he'd known that he was wrong about her. There was nothing she couldn't dare, nothing she couldn't handle. The Renaissance was little more dangerous to her than leaving her behind in the "civilized" world without his supervision. It was too late, anyway.

The choice had been taken from him.

For this night would mark him as well. He would not be able to be noble and leave her behind. She was his, golden hair to slim feet. After this intercourse, in the best, truest sense of the word, she'd know it ever after. And if his soul was forfeit for these stolen hours, so be it. He had lived more—and better—these few months with Honor than he ever had with all his roistering about.

Smiling savagely, he redoubled his efforts, inserting his hard tip just enough to tease her in exactly the right spot. She began pulling at her wrists to get free, tossing her head until her hair made a golden storm about them. "Damn you, do I have to show you how?" she finally burst out.

345

Virago indeed. And there was only one certain way to quiet a virago's tongue. . . .

She sighed in relief against his hard, demanding kiss as he gave her what they hungered for. In one impassioned lunge he made them whole, thoroughly exploring her mouth at the same time. And she kissed him back as she'd never kissed him back, without an iota of restraint or shyness or regret. As if she were staking her claim on him, too. He released her wrists and let her fly free. Immediately she brought her hands back to his hips, pulling at him frantically every time he shoved deep, as if she could never have enough of him.

He whispered her name, then husky, explicit Italian words mixed up with words of love and encouragement. Maybe she didn't understand their definition, but she understood their meaning. With every passionate lunge, she got better at the primitive thrust and retreat.

When he felt himself swelling, felt her tensing beneath him and around him, he knew only the need to get deeper, to fill her with all she'd helped him become. Lifting her legs over his shoulders, he caught her breasts in his hands and groaned. "Look at me, Honor."

Her eyes were so dark a gray they were almost black. That glazed, fierce look of need was the same one he wore, and he satisfied it in the only way possible. A final time he delved into her, tipping her hips up so she could feel the long, masterful slide. Deeper, deeper, until the feminine shudders took him and squeezed him with their delicate finality. She arched her neck and drew a harsh breath to scream, her nipples growing rock hard. He could bear her shattering fulfillment only an instant longer before she called forth his own. He kissed her and tasted the glory of her scream on his tongue even as his own groan of joy escaped their bonded lips.

Pressing high into her so she'd feel him to the fullest, he shook with the little death, splashing his essence into her. Sensations more powerful than any he'd ever felt almost tore him to shreds, so potent they bordered on pain. But even then, at the height of his sexual enjoyment, she was present to him. Not just a vessel, but the love of his life. Honor in every sense of the word.

Boneless in the aftermath, he slumped on her, with no identity apart from hers. She didn't seem to mind his weight, for she pulled at him, caressed him, as if needing to keep him within her as much as he wanted to stay there. Then she began to tremble, tears streaming from her eyes, but he understood that she cried in joy. "Shhh . . . I will not leave you. Ever again. There now, *bambina*, be still. Hold on to me."

Finally, with a watery, exquisitely beautiful smile, she managed, "Only a rogue like you could call me a baby at a time like this."

Baby . . . Their eyes met. Dom whirled them about, pulling her atop him, but still maintaining their link. Belatedly he realized that he'd not discussed the issue of taking her back with him. His heart lurched in fear. What if she didn't want to come?

He spread his large hands on her flat stomach. It was a wonder she could hold all of him. Her hips were narrow . . . how would she ever survive having a son of his? Especially back in Florence, without all the wonders of the medicine of her world.

She must have seen the fear in his face, for she lightly rested her wounded hands upon his shoulders as if she needed to brace herself. "You will take me with you?" she whispered, holding her breath. And again, strangely, he understood. It was as if this bonding had ripped blinkers from his eyes: after all the bitterness and the fear, she had to hear the words to be reassured.

"I will be honored to do so, if God gives me the chance. You will come?" He tried to hide his own fears as he kept his hands flat against the belly that could already be seeded by him. And despite everything, and the uncertainty of his future, he was exalted at the thought that this amazing young woman could carry on his name, whether he was there to see it or not.

But he owed her truth. "It will not be an easy life, my Honor." It was the hardest thing he'd ever had to say, but he managed. "If you cannot bear my time, I will try to be happy in yours."

Incredibly, he felt laughter trilling through her. She leaned down to kiss his cheek. "Somehow I can't see you kissing me good-bye every day as you take the bus to work, hard hat in hand."

He wrinkled his nose. "I detest those smelly things, I admit."

She sobered abruptly, as if she, too, knew what was at stake. "I'm a historian, Dom. I know something of what to expect. And I have nothing here.

Nothing I value." She looked at him, her eyes turning smoky again. She wriggled atop him.

Minx. He gripped her hips to hold her still. Rafe. They needed to check on Rafe. "Woman, you'll wear me out."

"So you're not made of stone any longer? So many times I wondered." She shifted again, half rising only to lower herself upon him exactly as he needed.

With a little grunt, he made it plain that he was all too human. "Ah, I do not deserve you." His manhood, full and glorious, gave its own version of homage as he said fiercely, "But I will be faithful, and I will honor you all the days of my life, whether I have a week or a century." He finished the promise in her mouth, then pulled her off him and slapped her lustily on the butt. "Come, woman, help me check on our invalid."

They put on robes and eased into Rafe's room. His breathing still rattled in his lungs, but it sounded better than it had before. Best of all, he was sweating.

Honor said in relief, "Thank God. His fever broke." She dipped a clean towel in the bowl of water beside the bed and bathed his face. "You think you can shave him?"

Doubtfully, Dom eyed him. "Of course, but I'm not sure he'd welcome that. Best we leave it until he wakes."

Honor draped the towel over a chair and followed Dom out. They made themselves a snack. Honor asked him about Florence. He talked so long and so poignantly that it was daylight before they even noticed the passing of time.

Honor yawned. Dom kissed her. "Back to bed, my Honor. Or you will be useless for the activity I have in mind for the next week."

Fear flickered in her eyes as he mentioned the passing of time, but she smiled through it. "And you?"

He hid a yawn of his own. It would not be the first time he'd gone two days without sleep. "I'll stay with Rafe until the doctor comes." He kissed her and tucked her into bed.

His vigil was lonely, but he wanted to be there when Rafe awoke. He had a shrewd suspicion that Rafe would be none too happy when he realized Honor had saved his life. Dom wanted to be there if he remembered, so he could see his reaction. If Rafe didn't turn away from his futile manner of living now, he never would.

And my quest is hopeless, this magical gift of love doomed. . . .

However, Christmas came and went before Rafe really came to his senses. The doctor gave him two more shots, and Dom and Ernie gave him sponge baths and helped him to the bathroom. They all tried to take some of Honor's homemade eggnog in to him—unspiked—but he shoved it away with a muttered, "Tired. Sleep." And he started snoring again. He drank a few liquids, but the doctor assured them that he could go without food for days, as strong as he was. Every day his breathing seemed to become easier.

Christmas had arrived quietly. Honor had searched high and low to find her gift for Dom, but she'd finally managed it—and spent half of

her savings to buy it. Dom gave her a new cashmere coat to replace her torn parka. While she
paraded around in it before the three men, she
caught the weird looks Ernie and Nick gave Dom,
as if they wondered why he'd changed his mind
about what present to give her. What did they
know that she didn't? Honor wondered.

But Dom only smiled and stroked the soft wool
on her shoulder, his eyes making it apparent that
he enjoyed what was under the coat even more.

Ernie happily ensconced himself in a chair to
read the expensive books Honor had purchased
for him on the Renaissance, and Nick went off to
play his jazz CDs. Honor was glad that no one
else was watching when Dom finally opened her
tiny box. He found a minuscule leather bag and
dumped the contents into his hand. Even in the
dim apartment, with snow falling outside, the
gold shone dimly.

Transfixed, he stared, at Honor, and then
looked back at his hand. "A florin! I have seen
precious few of these in my lifetime, but I recognize it. Where did you find it? I didn't know they
still made them."

"They don't. But at least you won't be penniless
when you return." And he will return, she begged
God as Dom took her in his arms and kissed her.

During those days that heralded the end of the
millennium and the greatest happiness Honor
had ever known, she avoided calendars and
clocks. Strangely, now that Dom shared her bed
nightly and any other time they could manage,
she'd begun to share some of his temperament. A
sense of fatalism descended over her. Weeping

and gnashing of her teeth would change nothing. The city bustled with joy, and she did her best to participate. When Ernie stayed with Rafe, she took Dom to the park—to Belvedere Castle and the Ramble and the carousel.

Dom seemed to love the carousel most. Around and around they went, sitting on their magnificent painted steeds, riding into the sunset to the tune of the calliope. And somewhere on that journey to nowhere, she found illumination. Her eyes fixed on Dom's face, she realized that, granted a week or a lifetime, she was the luckiest girl on earth.

She smiled at him joyfully. *Make that woman.*

On the way home from the park, he taught her a troubadour's song. They were singing it loudly as they entered the vestibule. The bright overhead light cast odd shadows, and she spied a tall object shoved far in the corner of the vestibule. It was covered with a cream-colored tarp and in all the excitement of the last few days she hadn't noticed it against the pale walls.

She stopped. "What's that?"

Dom's happy expression froze. "Ah, I did not want to show it to you until I had to. Not upset you."

"Upset me? Why?" Honor walked over to it. The minute she touched it she knew what it was. For an instant she felt as if heaven had smote her as well, so heavy and lifeless did her feet become, as if they couldn't bear her weight. But she had to know. She untied the tarp. It fell to the feet of Dom's image.

Exactly as he had looked the first time she saw him.

Exactly as he could look the last time, too.

A chill took Honor by the throat. The image was beautiful, a perfect specimen of manhood, exactly as she'd believed Dom to be on that strange, wonderful day when he stepped into her life. But now he was so much more to her that seeing what he could shortly become again was a taste of hell after being granted heaven.

Turning away, her teeth chattering, she said brightly, "It's . . . m-magnificent. Exactly l-like you. I had no idea you were s-so talented." But her eyes told a different story. *Get it away from me. I can't bear to look at it.*

Dom drew her face against his shoulder. "Hush, *bellissima*. It does not matter now. I wish I had not wasted all the time carving it. Come now. I make you chocolate."

Weakly, she smiled. Chocolate was one thing he'd grown to love. Honor had explained to him that he'd have to wait almost thirty years for Cortés to bring chocolate to Spain.

Four days before New Year's Eve, they were pouring hot chocolate into mugs when a loud crash from Rafe's room made Dom spill the precious liquid. Cursing, he set the pot down, tossed a rag over the spreading stain and bolted for the bedroom, with Honor hot on his heels.

Looking furious, Rafe was in the process of pulling himself up from the floor. Dressed only in briefs, he still looked imposing and powerful, but his ribs showed now and his face was yellow beneath the beard. Worst of all, he was trembling so much he could barely stand. "What the hell happened to me?" he demanded, glaring at them as if his condition were their fault.

Honor and Dom exchanged a look. Honor nodded at Rafe's uncle. *Your call. And good luck.*

"You have been quite ill, *amico*," Dom explained tactfully. "Something called pneumonia." Dom didn't pronounce the strange word quite right, but Rafe understood.

His eyes widened. He plopped down on the bed, sticking his trembling hands under his armpits. "Why can't I remember it?"

"I suspect there's a good deal you don't remember," Dom agreed. "Do you wish us to explain?"

At the "us," Rafe glanced at Honor. He stared at her as if he'd never seen her before. He blinked once, twice, and then such horror transformed his expression that it became obvious he remembered the last time he'd seen her. All too well.

He sagged back on the bed. Supine and shivering, he looked about as miserable as Honor had ever seen a human being look. "God, my head aches. Go away. I'm a mess. I need a drink."

Dom said grimly, "That is the last thing you need. Honor risked her life to save yours, Rafe. It's up to you what you do with it. I will be back in a moment with something for you to drink." He hurried out, closing the door.

Scowling at her so fiercely that Honor wanted to laugh and cry at the same time, Rafe jerked the covers over himself. "What're you staring at?"

"I'm not sure." That, at least, was true. Was he really so alienated from life that he'd rather die in the gutter? At least this time he was too weak to hit her if she really pissed him off.

Rafe struggled up on his elbows. "You've got a lip on you, babe, I'll give you that. Based on the screams I hear sometimes at night, Dom's doing a pretty damn good job of shutting you up, though." He smiled in satisfaction at the wave of red that consumed her face and neck.

"So you've been hiding out here, too?" she shot back. "If you want, I'll go back and see if your Hilton near the docks is still on reservation for you." Honor swallowed at the cruelty of her own remark, but she sensed that only fury, deep down where he lived, would awaken Rafe's slumbering sense of self-respect. She knew it was there, as much a part of him as the curly lock of hair that always fell over his forehead.

Shock was in his gaze as he looked at her. But then he turned away, so weary and so alone that tears misted her eyes. And she didn't want to hurt him anymore. For the second time, something instinctive in Honor made her fly to his rescue. He was too fine a man to waste himself like this. She sat next to him on the bed and put a tentative hand on his shoulder. He trembled as if his fever had returned, but she knew it was the DT's.

Softly she said, "Rafe, I don't know what happened to make you leave the service, or what civilians you tried to protect—"

Gasping in shock, he turned to face her. "How the hell do you know that?"

Honor responded, "You were delirious when I found you. But that doesn't matter. I swear to you that what you tell me will not leave this room if you don't want it to. Even to Dom. Don't you want to talk about it?"

Looking utterly defeated, Rafe slumped back against the pillow to fling his arm over his eyes. "I'm a screwup. Couldn't save them even when I disobeyed orders."

Dom poked his head in the door, but Honor shook her head fiercely, and he ducked back out. Honor held her breath, but Rafe was too caught up in memories to notice the interruption. Once he began, he talked rapidly, as if he couldn't help himself.

"I'd already been assigned some missions that turned my stomach. When you're in the SEALs, you're not supposed to ask questions. We're trained to do the stuff nobody else wants to do, put it all on the line. For honor and country." He sneered the last words. He dropped his arm, his eyes bleak with memories. "I had to shoot a woman once. She was a Palestinian about to fire a grenade launcher at my team's Hummer, and I was riding post. God, it made me sick, the way she—"

He gagged, taking several deep breaths, and finally managed, "But the next year, when we were sent in to the Gulf War, things got better. Easy justification. The Iraqis invaded Kuwait. Of course we had every reason to fight back. Those were the good times, with the country behind us. But then, in the last few years, when Iraq started causing problems again"—he closed his eyes, his ashen face twisted, and finished—"they told us the ship we were supposed to plant the mines on was a command post. Blow it out of the water and half the Iraqi officers in the navy wouldn't be a problem anymore. So we went in. I did my duty like a good little patriot. It wasn't until we were finished, taking our submersibles back out, that I heard the singing."

Honor held her breath. It was horrible just watching him remember this, so she could imagine how he felt.

"Birthday party. A whole passel of kids poured onto the deck carrying balloons and playing games. Moms, dads, some in uniform, all right. Even a few grandmas. I tried to turn around to warn them, disarm the mines, anything, but my CO had been watching me, knew I was losing my stomach for it. He whacked me over the head and pulled me out. I didn't even hear the explosion."

Horror made Honor's voice hoarse. "But surely the head honchos didn't know. . . . "

The doubt in Rafe's eyes made her catch her breath. She felt as though she was about to throw up, but she persisted. "Maybe the Iraqis knew, and were just trying to stop you doing your job."

"Yeah, despots sometimes use their people as shields, but this was before all the weapons inspectors were kicked out, in international waters. But I swear to you, those officers on board didn't know, or they never could have acted so happy. I don't think my CO knew either. . . . Maybe it was an accident. But when I came back and tried to report it so there could be an investigation, they slapped me down so hard that I had to believe someone in Washington knew. And didn't care. In war, even civilians are expendable. And that, in the end, is what I couldn't bear. I could never trust another one of their orders. And they knew that, so they smeared me."

Honor caught Rafe's hand, holding it when he tried to pull away. "But Rafe, it's not your fault. What could you have done? They'd have shot you on sight even if you'd tried to warn them."

"I don't know. But I'll go to my grave knowing that I didn't try hard enough and that I have the deaths of women and children on my hands."

"And how does killing yourself bring them back?"

Rafe froze. "Don't think that just because I told you a few things, you hold any power over me. Yeah, you saved my life, and I'm grateful—"

"Only after you barged in to save mine—"

"But that's as far as it goes. If I want to go to hell in a handbasket, it's no skin off your nose."

Teasingly, Honor stroked the bandage on his temple. "Not this time."

For the first time, apparently, he noticed the bandages on her hands. "How'd you get those?"

Honor hesitated.

The door opened and Dom's hard voice said, "Picking up a burning log to keep those dogs at bay while she stood over you to save your carcass."

Rafe tried to turn away, but he was faced with a mirror on one side of the bed and truth on the other. Honor had been around him enough now to read the abrupt, weary resignation that came over him. She saw the look on his face: he was low now, as low as he could be. He could either start climbing back up or pack it in and die.

She smiled at him as if she knew which choice he'd make. And suddenly, she did.

Grumpily, he sat up in bed, stuffing pillows behind him. "What the hell do you want from me?"

Honor looked at Dom, but he nodded gravely, as if realizing Rafe would accept the choice better from her.

Briskly, Honor whacked his pillow with the backs of her hands to fluff the edges, and then she stood and looked down at Rafe. She saw the flash of irritation in his eyes and knew he didn't like anyone to hover above him. Least of all a little slip of a blonde with dreams of glory.

The little slip of a blonde gave him a taunting smile. "You really grateful, Castigi? Prove it. Quit drinking. Civilian life can be pretty exciting, too, as we just proved a few days back. Come on. 'Be all you can be.' Or maybe, 'It's not just a job, it's an adventure.'"

"I get the idea, babe—"

As if he hadn't spoken, she finished coolly with, "But maybe the best slogan is, 'The few . . . the proud.' Which is it to be, Rafe?"

Part Four

"He who sows virtue reaps honor."
                        —Leonardo da Vinci

Chapter Fourteen

For a moment, Rafe looked as though he might explode, but then he laughed bitterly, folded his arms over his massive chest and looked at Dom with interest. "So what's the deal? What's this mysterious link between us and how the hell does my drinking hurt you?"

Dom left and soon returned with a loaded tray. While Rafe ate the meal of soft-boiled eggs, toast, fruit and juice, Dom talked, slowly at first, feeling his way, but when Rafe didn't react except to eat faster, Dom became more specific.

"So on December thirty-first, I go back to my own time if I am able to . . . convince you to stop drinking and become the man you can be. Or I am forever doomed if you go back to your wandering." Dom had not explained in what form he had arrived, or to which he could return.

Holding her breath, Honor watched Rafe.

He sopped up the last drizzle of egg with his toast, popped the morsel in his mouth and chewed slowly. "You finished?"

Dom nodded. Honor was troubled that Rafe hadn't reacted more strongly, and she had a sinking feeling he didn't believe them. Who could blame him?

"Tell me one thing—is it true we're related?" Rafe asked, setting the tray aside and wiping his mouth on the napkin Dom provided.

"Oh, yes. Surely you believe that, at least. The Castiglione eyes have remained true through all the centuries, even those earlier than mine. And I do not doubt that your own descendants in the years to come will have them, too."

"Dominant genes," Honor said. "It takes no leap of faith to believe in those."

Sighing, Rafe leaned back again, but some of the color had already returned to his pasty complexion. "Well, here's the deal. I'd like to believe you, Dom; I really would. And I've seen some strange things on the battlefield, things that would make even a nonbeliever like me trust in the power of faith. I was an altar boy more years ago than I care to remember, but this is a bit hard to swallow. Time travel, angels, penitence—give me a break. You're either a very talented actor or suffering from millennium fever big-time."

Dom sagged down in the chair next to the bed. He looked at Honor helplessly. *What now?*

"Does it really matter whether you believe us,

Rafe?" Honor sat down on the bed next to him again. "Forget us, or what we have to lose. You have a very important decision to make. Probably the most important one you've ever made. We're all our best ally and our own worst enemy, but you've carried it to extremes. You did what you could for those people, and drinking yourself into a grave, seeing the Castigi name die that way—"

Rafe winced, and Honor was glad that one of her points hit home, anyway.

"—won't accomplish anything but one more victory for the men who set you up. They'd be tickled pink if you died in an alley somewhere. You ever thought of that?" Honor cupped her hands around Rafe's face. He jerked restively at her tender touch, as if he knew it must have hurt her bandaged hands. But then he fixed his gaze on her as if he couldn't look away.

Deep inside him, a fire flickered to life, turning those unusual eyes to molten turquoise. For an instant she was startled at his resemblance to Dom.

Smiling at him with simple trust, because she liked him and truly wanted the best for him, she finished, "It's an easy choice Rafe. Love. Or hate. For yourself, and for life." Kissing his cheek, Honor stood, picked up the tray and walked out.

Dom followed her shortly, spreading his hands at her inquiring look.

But that night, when they went to bed together, he whispered against the hollow of her throat, "I've always wanted a champion who looks like you. But if you start wearing armor when we get home and march into battle, I'll lock you in your room. I don't want to have to remove chain mail to get to you." And he proceeded to show her exactly why.

They awoke the next day to a pristine, sparkling world. Three days now to New Year's, and counting. Three days to what some believed would be the end of the world.

And they awoke to a cold, quiet apartment. When they took a hearty breakfast in to Rafe, they found him gone. No note, no duffel bag, no remnant of his presence. Even the bed was neatly made.

"More for us," Honor said, marching the tray back to the breakfast table to eat with pretended appetite. She tried not to notice the gathering darkness in Dom's face. She said only, "Give him time, Dom. He'll be back."

She saw the truth in his eyes: time was the one thing they didn't have.

If love could hold back the dawn, they could have frozen time that day. It would forever remain a magical memory to Honor, filled with laughter and snowball fights and lovemaking.

Snow tended to dirty quickly in New York, but the elements themselves seemed to want to begin the new year on a pristine note, sending new flakes faster than the old could be removed. Slowly, partly because of nature, and partly because of the millennium celebration, the city's business districts began to grind to a halt.

Wall Street and Madison Avenue were almost deserted, but Broadway and Fifth Avenue were packed, as partygoers from around the globe continued to pour into the city. That crisp winter day, with the sun so bright upon the new-fallen snow that its sparkling hurt the eyes, she and Dom and the Escavidos tried to find a restaurant for lunch. But the lines were long—even the midtown delis were crowded—so they ended up buying hot dogs and eating them in the park.

Nick and Ernie watched indulgently as Dom tasted his hot dog with wary little nibbles.

Looking shocked, Dom exclaimed, "I would not have believed anything so disgustingly named could taste good. Me, I do not usually care for dog."

Ernie choked on his food. Nick slapped his brother on the back, frowning.

Hiding a smile in her napkin, Honor was well aware that Nick couldn't believe that anyone in this day and age had never tasted a hot dog. Well, he was right. Dom wasn't from this day and age. Honor wondered how Ernie would explain their disappearance to Nick. And she continued to tell herself, whenever her mind betrayed her by thinking of something so ephemeral as the passing of time, that somehow she and Dom would be walking a different, more primitive road three days from now.

After lunch, Honor ducked behind a tree. She was warm in her new cashmere coat, and Dom looked surprisingly contemporary in the leather jacket Nick had lent him. He'd look even better, she decided judiciously, decorated with a snowball. She splatted him square on the back, surprising him while he was searching for her.

Brushing the snow away, he turned, roaring, "Who dares—" When he saw Honor hefting another snowball, an evil smile on her face, he ducked behind his own tree and rolled a baseball-size wad of snow.

Honor dodged at the last minute and returned her own missile, this time hitting him in the throat. He yelped as snow trickled down his shirt. Nick shook his head at them, but his boredom didn't last long when Ernie tossed a strategic projectile at his brother's butt.

The battle was on. Ernie took Honor's side, and what the two of them lacked in strength, they made up in cunning.

Thirty minutes later, his black hair covered with snow, Nick held up his hands, laughing so hard he was wheezing. "Pax! Pax! You win."

Honor stood over Dom, bouncing a snowball from one gloved hand to the other. Her hands were healed enough to use them now, but she always wore gloves. "*Et tu*, Dominico?"

Dom held up his empty hands. "I am defeated by a superior strategist. Machiavelli could take lessons from you."

Laughing, Honor tossed her ammunition aside and complacently dusted off the snow.

Nick met Dom's eyes. Grinning, the two picked Honor up, one on each side, and rolled her in the snow.

"But I'm stronger," Dom added, tickling her for good measure. Standing over the vanquished, he tossed back his arrogant head and laughed at the vision of Honor's snow-dusted cheeks and eyelashes.

Honor sat up on the embankment, her laughter joining his, but suddenly she grew quiet, her face luminous beneath the fairy dusting of white crystals. "Do you know what I do when I fall down in the snow, Dom?"

Sensitive to her moods now as never before, he quit smiling. "What, Honor?"

"I make angels." And Honor moved her arms and legs from side to side.

He frowned, not understanding, until she stood up. She saw from the look on his face that he'd never heard of snow angels, and could only deduce that the people of his time viewed snow as something to get through, not play in. But he looked from the perfect snow angel to Honor. Without another word, he drew her fiercely under the curve of his arm and kissed the snow from her lips.

Turning aside from the intimate moment, Ernie peered across the park, tears misting his eyes.

Grumpily, Nick turned up his coat collar. "Come on, Ernie. I'm sick of feeling like an idiot. See you guys back home." He stalked off.

Slowly, arm in arm, Dom and Honor walked toward home as darkness approached, his longer stride adjusted to hers. They didn't talk. They could only wait, trying not to count every second.

They'd said all there was to say, done all there was to do, and tried all there was to try.

Except . . . Honor looked up at St. Patrick's, hearing the organ music, and realized why Dom had come this way. Climbing a step, he held his hand out to her. Against the backdrop of heaven's home, he'd never seemed more beautiful than now, with quiet acceptance on his perfect face.

She finally understood why Michelangelo had used him for the model of *David*.

Heaven's rogue. Dom embodied the best of man. He was beautiful not in spite of his flaws, but because of them: he was deeply, majestically human, as Michelangelo had somehow captured. Like David, he'd paid a terrible price for his own pride. And if, in a few days, God punished him for those sins, he'd accept the punishment, head high, and go to his doom with serenity.

When Dom loved, he loved fiercely. When he fought, he fought to win. And when he believed, he believed with all his heart and soul. Her throat tight with tears, Honor took his hand and walked into church with him.

A higher power watched over them now. And for the first time in her life, she trusted that power with her mind as well as her heart.

Darkness had fallen by the time they got home. Ernie paced in the vestibule, waiting for them. As soon as they came into sight, he said, "Hurry up! I've packed your things. You need to get the hell out of here!"

"What's wrong?" Honor asked, her wonderful serenity slightly shaken.

"One of Nick's buddies called, warned him Frankie and his pals are on the way to question you," Ernie explained, herding them upstairs.

"But why? How'd they track me down?" Honor began tossing toiletries into a carryall.

"I don't know. They got nothing out of me and Bruno—"

The buzzer sounded below. Dom glared at the door, his fists clenching.

Whitening, Ernie stared at Dom. "Nothing stupid, big guy. I'm sure they don't have enough to arrest her."

"They will not take Honor anywhere," Dom vowed.

Fatalism was a wonderful thing, Honor decided. It made your choices less important. She set the case aside and turned toward the door.

Dom stepped in front of her. "No. This is my fault, and I will not let you take the blame."

"How are you going to stop it? You really think they'll believe your story?"

"I will think of something."

"We have the statue, at least. We can tell them we came to the city to track it down, clear my name. It's sort of true, anyway. Ernie, call Bruno, ask him to come over. Maybe they'll believe him if they won't believe me."

Eagerly Ernie grabbed the phone, spoke briefly. He slammed it down, saying, "He's on his way."

He'd barely finished talking before Nick hurried up and poked his head inside. "Police have a warrant for your arrest, Honor. We'll get this cleared up quickly, I'm sure, but for now, you'll have to go with them. I told them I'd get you. Best you come downstairs so they don't see Rafe."

"Rafe's gone, Nick," Honor said.

Nick looked relieved, but he only held the door wider. "I hate this, but . . . "

Taking a deep breath, Honor stepped through,

brushing past Dom when he tried to stop her again. She said out of the corner of her mouth, "This isn't like in your time, Dom. They won't hold me forever. I can probably get out tomorrow on bail."

Cursing, he followed her downstairs, a large, imposing shadow.

The cop Honor had seen before, the one Nick called Frankie, plus two more Honor didn't recognize, stood in the vestibule. At Dom's aggressive posture, the two cops with Frankie backed up an automatic step.

But Frankie held his ground. "Well, well, well. One happy family again. Only one missing is Castigi. Nice little hideaway you got yourself here . . . Miss Fitzhugh, I believe the name is."

"OK, Frankie," Nick said. "Here she is. Cooperating, I might add. Now tell us what the hell's going on and why you think Honor—who's beautifully named, by the way—is a thief."

"Yeah, we all know what your notion of honor is, Nicky. Don't make me puke." He smiled at Honor, too many teeth showing. "Routine follow-ups can sometimes crack open other cases, ya know?"

"What follow-up?" Nick demanded.

"Seems some poor homeless guys were beat up down near the wharf," Frankie said, his scatter-shot gaze spread evenly between Nick, Honor and Dom. "Not our precinct until we got a hot tip about who might have been involved."

"Yeah? What tip's that?" Nick asked, sounding uninterested.

"A car seen leaving the crime looks a lot like

yours, Nicky. Same make, model and color. And would ya believe it? One of the guys leaving the scene was one Rafe Castigi, seen with a little blonde who looks just like Miss Priss here. You know the guy: bail jumper, drunk, all-around scumbag."

Honor was so outraged at the way he twisted the truth that she burst out, "But we were defending ourselves!"

Nick glared at her. She winced and stared at her feet. Big mouth.

Shoving his cap back with one fingertip, Frankie grinned. "Ya know, what with the millennium crap, enlightened age dawning and all that, commissioner's starting to get antsy. Wants us tough New York cops to start to show a little more compassion for the most unfortunate in our great city."

Frankie's voice dripped with sarcasm. It was obvious to Honor that he wouldn't know the definition of compassion if it reached up and bit him on the butt.

"And when the workers at the homeless shelter were questioned, one of the volunteers remembered your name, Miss Fitzhugh. Got real curious. It took me a while to make a match, since we don't share a database with the Portland, Oregon, police, but lo and behold a complaint was filed against Miss Goody Two-shoes for art theft. I transferred special just to follow up. Above and beyond, don't you agree, Nicky?"

Nick's famous cool was beginning to melt. A tic began beating in Nick's jaw, but he didn't have to say anything to egg Frankie on. Frankie knew he was getting to Nick. And he reveled in it, turning the screw a bit harder with every word.

"Don't know what the world's coming to. Except this. Let's just have the facts, ma'am," Frankie said nastily. "One, you and this big ass-hole here match descriptions given to the state police by a trucker who filed against the driver of one Ernie Escavido's car for assault." He jerked his head at Ernie. "No positive ID on that one . . . yet. This little pretty boy, the great Nick Escavido's brother, just happens to be an ex-employee of the same Portland museum that reported the theft. Even weirder, he's the ex-assistant of the same woman who recently hired on at the Metropolitan Museum posing as a waitress—"

"I posed as nothing," Honor shot back. "And I'm sure any number of employees at the café will verify that!"

As if she hadn't interrupted, he continued, "Who knows why she came here? Maybe to fence the statue. Maybe to join the rest of her ring, scope out the next target. But one thing's for sure. . . . " He trailed off until they all waited tensely. "I got a warrant for your arrest, and you're coming with me. We got you on two counts now. Assault and theft." He came forward, reaching for the hand-cuffs at his belt.

The other two cops backed him up, watching the three men warily, their hands hovering over their nightsticks.

"And Nicky lad here has been harboring a fugi-tive." Frankie glanced up the stairs. "Maybe two, if that Castigi jerk's here like I suspect."

Unimpressed, Nick leaned his hips against the

balustrade. "Guess we won't know the answer to that, not today anyway. You're so good with facts. Can you spell *S-E-A-R-C-H-W-A-R-R-A-N-T*, Frankie?" When Frankie glared at him, Nick smiled. "Didn't think so."

Frankie pulled the cuffs from his belt. "Come on, doll face. You'll be real popular down at the jail."

Dom stepped in front of Frankie, shoving Honor behind him. "Just a minute. She's stolen nothing, and I can prove it."

"Oh, yeah?" Frankie stopped, looking curious. "This will be good."

Dom went to the corner of the vestibule and grabbed the rope tying down the tarp. "Here's the statue. You were right about one thing. We did follow it to the city—to clear Honor's name. And we found it. We only recently were able to bring it here, and planned to call the police tomorrow."

Frankie laughed. "I may be no art expert, asshole, but even I know what the *David* looks like. . . . " He trailed off with a gasp as Dom whipped the tarp away.

Blinking, Frankie walked over to the statue and poked it, as if he couldn't believe it was marble.

Honor waited, but her heart sank when he shrugged and reached for the cuffs again.

"Not my decision. I can't identify the thing as genuine. Besides, we still got the assault charge. And we'll get Castigi, too. I just put out an APB."

When reason failed . . . Dom stepped in front of Frankie. "I presume it will not do any good to appeal to your sense of mercy?"

Frankie had to look up to meet Dom's eyes, but

he didn't seem intimidated. "Sure, go ahead. I won't beat you up too bad. You first, Escavido next. It's the best Christmas present I ever had."

Reaching for his stick, Frankie turned to meet Dom.

The other two cops tensed, going for their sticks, too.

Nick pushed away from the balustrade, no longer relaxed. Even Ernie balanced on his toes.

Under the circumstances, Honor took the only option left to her. It wasn't easy, but she managed to shove Dom aside enough to get past. Coolly, she held out her hands. "Guess you haven't been a good boy after all, Frankie."

And so it was that Honor found herself, the next day, two days before the turn of a new age, sitting in a smelly, crowded jail with two hookers, three drunks and one girl who looked even more scared than she was. She'd awakened grungy and depressed, expecting Nick and his lawyer to meet her before breakfast.

But no one had come. The day crawled by, and since there were no windows, she couldn't tell if night had fallen or not. Only the big institutional clock on the wall outside the cell, ticking relentlessly, gave her any sense of perspective—and growing urgency.

Would Dom have only one chance to go home? And if she was stuck here, would she be able to go with him? But maybe it was just as well. Rafe had totally deserted them, so maybe it would be better if she didn't have to watch Dom turn back to stone.

Turning her face toward the wall, she tried to stem the tears. One of the hookers patted her on the shoulder. "Go ahead, girl. Cry all you want. Maybe even scream a little." She popped some gum. "That really drives 'em nuts."

Fiercely, Honor blew her nose on a tissue. She was about to respond when a guard came to the bars and barked, "Fitzhugh! Time's up. Step aside, ladies." He opened the door and waved her out.

As they walked down the hall, Honor looked behind him into the waiting room, but she saw no familiar figures. After she collected her belongings and changed back into her own clothes, they made her sign some papers. Her eyes opened wide when she saw the release documents.

"But why?" she whispered to the hovering processor.

The bored-looking woman shrugged. "They didn't tell me. 'Cept that you're free to go and both charges have been dropped. But they want to question you some more. This way."

The woman led her down another warren of hallways to an interrogation room. Honor's hand covered her mouth when she saw who else sat there.

"Rafe," she whispered.

He'd shaved, taken a shower and cut his thick chocolate brown hair. He looked up at her with bloodshot—but sober—eyes. He was the most beautiful thing she'd ever seen, worn bomber jacket, tattered jeans and all.

He gave her a rakish smile and winced, as if his head hurt. "Hey, babe. I'm glad to see you, too."

One of the plainclothes officers in the room

identified himself as being with Internal Affairs and pulled out a chair at the table for her. "Miss, we're sorry you've been put through this. The officer responsible will be dealt with, we assure you. Forensics matched the prints on the weapon at the scene to one of the guys who filed the complaint, and since the blood type on the knife matched Mr. Castigi's, and he has a wound matching the blade imprint, well, it's obvious that the whole assault thing was a trumped-up charge by an overeager officer. We were told you were wounded as well?"

While he looked at her healing hands, Honor, big-eyed, stared at Rafe. "But how? You turned yourself in?"

Rafe shrugged, winced again and held on to the table edge. "Came back to apologize when I had a chance to think, found no one there but Ernie. He told me what happened. I knew it was time to face the music."

The officer released Honor's hands and eyed Rafe severely. "Yeah, well, you know we can't let you go now. Bail jumpers don't get second chances. Still, I'm sure the judge will be lenient now you've turned yourself in and agreed to enter an alcohol treatment program. Especially on a misdemeanor."

Honor closed her eyes on a prayer of gratitude, opened them and asked softly, "And the theft charges against me?"

"Yeah." The guy pulled a pad from his coat pocket and flipped it open. "A Mr. Bruno Trotterman, art expert at the Metropolis Museum, positively identified the statue you and Mr.

Dominico Castiglione came to the city to track down as being the lost artwork. The statue's already on its way back to Portland, and the museum there has agreed to drop all charges against you."

Rafe winked. "With a little encouragement from a bandy-legged little bow-tied guy."

Honor's throat was so tight with tears that she could barely manage huskily, "And you? How long will you have to stay in?"

Rafe shrugged, looking unconcerned.

The officer opened his pad to a clean page. "So we only need to ask a few questions, and then you're free to go."

To Honor's relief, the IA lieutenant seemed more interested in details about Frankie's behavior during both arrests than in info on how they'd tracked down the statue. He seemed satisfied at her answers, for he nodded and pulled back her chair. "Same story Escavido and Castigi gave us. If we need you to, will you testify in court to this officer's behavior?"

How could she answer that? Would she even be here? Honor looked around frantically for a clock. "What time is it?"

He seemed confused at her odd response, but he flicked back his cuff to glance at his watch.

"Ten. I think you got people waiting for you, but I need to be able to get in touch."

"As long as I'm in the city, I'll be at Nick's."

Stuffing the pad back in his pocket, the officer didn't seem too thrilled at her response, but he led her to the door.

Her steps dragged as she stared back at Rafe.

God, she hated leaving him. Wasn't there some way they could get him released? That same fatalistic serenity that had led her this far told her that Rafe needed to be present when she and Dom left.

He waved her out. "Don't worry about me, babe. You go on and join that crazy Italian. If I don't get the chance, tell him . . . tell him . . . " He looked down.

But Honor understood. She dashed back and cupped his strong face in her hands. "We'll do all we can to get you out. Thanks, Rafe. I knew you had it in you." She kissed him and hurried out.

Honor expected to find Nick's car waiting for her, but it was Ernie and Bruno who led her out to Ernie's old car. Honor barely managed to leash her impatience. "But where's Dom?"

"He and Nick have gone to the DA to try to get Rafe released," Ernie explained, helping her into his car. "You all right, Honnie?"

Sort of, Honor longed to reply. Instead she nodded, while her head swirled with confusion.

But she was coherent enough to lean forward from the backseat and clasp Bruno's arm. "What can I say to thank you, Bruno?"

Straightening his prissy bow tie in embarrassment, Bruno muttered, "Nothing's necessary. I didn't even have to lie, Honor. After all, that statue *is* a great work of art. Sculpted in the style of Michelangelo, by Michelangelo's own assistant. A work of art by a work of art, so to speak. I'm already talking to our museum board to try to convince them to buy it from Italy before they have a chance to conduct any more tests. Of course, since I can't tell them how I know it's so valuable, it will take some pretty fancy speeches. But I'll manage."

Honor smiled. Part of her was tickled that, even when he was gone, Dom's magnificent spirit would survive to the new millennium and beyond.

It was tangible proof of the power of dreams. Honor very much hoped that some other lucky young woman would be as inspired by it as she had been. "And Dom's things? Did you ever find them?"

Bruno sighed. "Yes. They're at the docks, crated and about to be shipped back to Italy. What with the time of year and everything, I haven't been able to get anyone to let me have access to them, but Nick's using some of his contacts—"

"And bitching royally about it, I might add," Ernie interrupted. "He can't understand why Dom's possessions are so important, but he spent part of the day calling some people he knew, and the other part trying to track down the DA. That's why he couldn't be here." He slammed on the brakes as a crowd of wildly dressed teens jaywalked in front of them.

The streets were so packed with revelers that their car moved at a virtual crawl. Many had already begun the countdown, Honor could see, a full day early. Several couples wearing silly cardboard caps staggered out of a bar.

How on earth would they even get to the docks? Honor slumped back against the seat, trying to go with the flow. She'd put herself in the hands of heaven some time ago, but still, the waiting and wondering were hard. Despite her best efforts to calm herself, her pulse kept time with the muffled heartbeat of a great city filled to bursting with people celebrating one goal.

A very different goal from Honor's. Millions of people, packed on the small island of Manhattan, reveled in the dawn of a new age. Honor, on the other hand, prayed for the chance to experience a previous one, a pivotal one that had helped shape her world and give her the knowledge she needed to survive in the past. It was strange to think of what she dared, and for a moment fear overshadowed her growing excitement.

Smiling, Ernie caught her eye in the mirror as he had to stop yet again for more pedestrians. She knew from his expression that he, too, wondered where she'd be this time tomorrow, but there was a twinkle in his brown eyes that hinted of a joyful surprise he'd not yet shared with her.

She wrinkled her nose at him. "Out with it, Ernie. You never could keep a secret."

Strangely, he and Bruno exchanged a complacent smile. Ernie only replied, "When the time comes, Honnie. But . . . I sure will miss you."

She clasped his shoulder in response.

Ernie dropped Bruno off at his apartment. Glancing surreptitiously at Honor, Bruno said, "I'll meet you tomorrow as we discussed, Ernie. It'll take me half the day to get to Columbia and back, if my friend meets me there like she promised. Don't you dare leave without me."

Honor yawned, blinking. "What are you talking about?"

"OK, Bruno," Ernie replied as if she hadn't spoken.

Honor wasn't too happy at the way they talked over her head, but that head was spinning with weariness, so she let it slide.

The apartment was dark when they got back. It was almost midnight. Honor began to worry about Dom. Surely he wouldn't try to leave without her? Had he changed his mind, let his fears take control again? *Please, no.*

But Dom didn't seem in the least fearful when he returned an hour later. In fact, his feelings were quite simple when he finally saw her. Unbridled joy lit his beautiful face as he and Nick tromped in from the cold, stamping snow from their feet. He hurried across the room to where she sat, comfortable in her robe, sipping chocolate with Ernie.

"Honor!" He pulled her up into his arms, thunking the mug down so hard that chocolate sloshed over the side. "Bruno said he and Rafe could get you out, but . . . " He kissed her, running his hands over her shape as if to assure himself of her reality.

Shaking his head, Nick cleaned up the mess. Even when the kiss ended, Dom sat down with her in his lap. Nick and Dom listened to her side of the story, and then Nick explained what he'd been doing.

"Took me a while to track the DA down—he's been attending so many official celebrations. He wasn't too pleased to see me, either, but I finally got him alone. He agreed to drop the charges against Rafe if I agreed to be Rafe's mentor, see he goes to his AA meetings, all that. He owes me, big-time, and he's so happy to finally have Frankie on the hook that Rafe's small-fry, especially since he can testify to Frankie's uh, over-eager arrest style."

Smiling ruefully, Dom admitted, "But of course, Rafe doesn't know yet that he's supposed to stay with Nick."

Honor's returning misty smile was spoiled by a yawn. "Rafe'll do what needs to be done. I think he's finally decided to turn his life around. But Dom . . . how do we get home?"

"Shhh, *bellissima*. Leave that to us. We need to get you to bed."

As Dom carried her from the room, Honor saw Nick's scowl and Ernie's condescending smile. For once Ernie knew more than Nick, and he wasn't above rubbing that in. Nick couldn't understand why they didn't just hop a plane. Honor tried to picture Nick's expression if an angel appeared to him, and her mind boggled. He was too hard and too practical to believe the evidence of his own eyes. Miracles, in Nick Escavido's mind, all had reasonable, scientific explanations.

Dom pulled the covers back, took off her robe and covered her snugly. "Why are you smiling?"

"I'm trying to picture Nick's face if he really knew the truth about you."

"Truth will come hard to Nick Escavido, and it will lay him flat when it does. But he shall be a better person for it."

"Prediction?"

"Sympathy. He is a strong man. Honor, are you sure you want to go back with me?" Dom sat next to her on the bed, serious now.

A deep sigh moved the covers over Honor's bosom. "I admit I'm a bit afraid. But I will risk anything to stay with you. If heaven allows."

Dom kissed her, a featherlight brush of tenderness that took her fear and turned it to goose down. "Heaven will allow. This I believe with all my heart. Sleep, now, *bellissima*. Tomorrow will be a busy day."

"Where are you going?"

Turning toward the door, he tossed over his shoulder, "To use that devilish invention you call the telephone. I promised that horrid little man that I would answer his cursed questions." He stomped out.

Honor's laughter rang in the quiet bedroom. Bruno wasn't a pug; he was a bulldog. But she was glad he'd finally gotten what he wanted, too. The smile still stretched her lips as she fell asleep.

Time, throughout the last four months, had been Honor's enemy, her goad, and her curse. Now, on the last day of Dr. Honoria Fitzhugh's present life, it became her friend. In one dreamlike span of a few hours, it seemed that she was to be rewarded for all the good deeds she'd ever practiced by having all the hopes she'd ever wished for come true. Somewhere in the mists of time lay the home, the family, the illumination she'd always wanted.

Normally she would have been irritated at the way the men in the household whispered their plans, expecting her to be a good little girl and do as she was told without question. But today was not a normal day. Today saw the rebirth not just of Dom, Renaissance man, but of Honor Castiglione. Today was the first day of the new life that had slowly formed for her the moment a statue came to life. She wanted to cherish it to the full.

It was late when Bruno finally arrived, breathless, carrying a heavy case. Dom quit his pacing and whirled to fetch the small bag that was all he intended to take with them. It contained medicines, the gold florin Honor had given him and, Honor was amused to find, chocolate.

"All the necessities, Dom?" she teased. "I'm glad there are a few things you'll miss."

Dom winked at her.

Nick stared at the tiny bag, and looked even more confused when Ernie walked them to the door without carrying anything for Honor. "But Honor . . . your things. Don't you want to take them back to Italy?"

"Uh . . . I'll try to send for them," she answered. She'd dressed in her longest skirt, plus a lacy blouse, but knew she didn't look anything like a respectable lady from Florence. She kissed Nick's cheek, smiling when he turned red. "I don't know how to thank you for everything. But I'll miss you, Nick."

Raising a challenging eyebrow at Dom, Nick hugged her back. "If I'm ever in Italy I'll look you up. Send us your address. I don't understand why you guys have to stop at the wharf first, but my acquaintance in security said he'd be there to let you in." He turned away to shake Dom's hand, not noting the smile she and Ernie exchanged. "You're lucky to have her, Dom. Take good care of her. Got your plane tickets?"

Ignoring the last question, Dom pumped his hand. "Do not fear for her, *amico*. I do not, any longer." He turned to the door, holding out his hand. "Come, *bellissima*. It is time."

And the words must have been prophetic, for the four of them managed to make it to the docks in record time. They took the subway as close as they could get and managed a taxi from there. Darkness was falling, and even this far from the heart of the city, they could hear a naked jungle throb of life: honking horns, blasting music, noisemakers and excited voices.

The taxi driver popped gum as he left them at the lading office. "You guys sure this is the right place? You don't want to miss the party. Not every day a new age comes."

Bruno gave the cabbie a generous tip. "Tell you what, you come back in a couple of hours, and I'll pay twice your usual fare." Since rates were already astronomical because of the high demand, that was a lot.

"Sure thing, bub." He drove off.

An impatient guy wearing street clothes let them into the office, comparing the picture Nick had given him to Bruno's face. He led them into a side storage area, and was kind enough to help them open the crates with a crowbar, complaining all the while, "Don't see what's so damn urgent, today of all days, but Nicco said you needed to reexamine the artifacts, Doc. Be quick.

387

I'll wait out here. They your help?" He nodded at Honor, Dom and Ernie.

"I couldn't do it without them," Bruno assured him. "And we'll hurry." As soon as the door closed, he said quietly, "I don't know what on earth I'll say to him when you don't come back and Dom's things go missing, but I'll think of something. Here, Honor." He thrust the suitcase at her. "A friend of mine in the Columbia drama department gave me a costume. The fabric's not real strong, but . . . " He pinkened when Honor kissed his cheek.

"Bruno, you're a prince." She lugged the case behind a tall stack of crates. When she came back out, she caught her breath.

Impatiently tapping one big foot, Dom stood waiting for her. Finally, gloriously, he was exactly as she'd always seen him in her mind's eye. He wore the clothes she'd found in the cistern: a scarlet doublet laced through with golden threads, and a ruffled linen undershirt that peeped at the neck and showed through slits in the doublet sleeves. His full black velvet breeches stopped at the knee, barely showing beneath the doublet skirt, and the bottom cuff of one was accented by a garter. His perfect legs were put on beautiful display in the tight flesh-colored wool stockings. A rakish black velvet cap perched on the side of his arrogant head, adorned by a seed pearl–and-jet brooch anchoring a short spray of pheasant feathers. He was a walking, breathing model for a Raphael painting. But he was much more than that to Honor. He was her past, her future and her hope of happiness: a Renaissance rogue. A very impatient rogue—until he turned and saw her. He froze.

Honor was so busy salivating over him that it took her a moment to realize all three men stared at her, mouths agape. Uncomfortably, she fidgeted with the gold mesh coif in which she'd wrapped her thick coil of hair. "Is it on straight?"

"Honor," Ernie managed at last. "You look . . . magnificent. Exactly—" He broke off. "Come see." He led her to the tall, ornate wall mirror they'd moved to the middle of the room and propped against a pile of crates.

Fluorescent lights above cast back cold practicality, but the ancient mirror, encased by a cracked and peeling gilt frame, had a peculiar glow in its surprisingly clear glass.

Honor stared at herself, shocked. Her slight form seemed made for the resplendent attire. The royal blue velvet square bodice pressed her small breasts together, hinting at cleavage beneath the filmy chemise that just peeped at the neck and at the cuffs of the long sleeves. Gold mesh ribbon to match the coif laced the bodice to an inverted vee shape at her tiny waist, where a pale blue taffeta underskirt fell in luxurious folds to her feet. Her slippers, like Dom's, were plain black leather. Dressed in velvet and gold, she looked as comfortable and natural as Dom, a fitting lady for a noble rogue. At this moment she knew she didn't just feel beautiful.

She *was* beautiful.

"I look . . . "

"Like a Botticelli portrait," Bruno whispered. "You were born for this moment, Honor. You're not leaving home; you're finding it." Bruno rummaged in the small bag Ernie had carried and handed her something.

Honor hefted it. It was a heavy round ball suspended from a gold chain. Bruno showed her how to wrap it and attach it at her waist. It added exactly the right touch to the elaborate costume. When the ball swung from side to side, making a clinking sound, Bruno stopped her from opening it.

Fussing with his tie again, he blurted, "Ernie and I combined part of our savings. Instead of the usual pomander in the ball, you have a few florins. Just to get you started."

Dom and Honor exchanged a dumb look. Dom pounded Bruno on the shoulder. "I will always remember you fondly, little man."

"And I you, big man. Be good." He smiled a smug smile when Dom gave him a mock *terribilita* frown.

Honor hugged him. "If I dared to send back answers, I would," she whispered.

"I know, Honor. You can't afford to change history. Just be happy."

Sighing, Ernie was watching the strange glow growing brighter in the mirror. "I envy you, Honor." He'd been about to remove a book from his case, but he stuck it back inside. "I guess this doesn't matter now."

Honor cocked her head at him, but then Dom stepped up behind her and put his hand on her shoulder. That strange current flickered to life between them. She looked back at him in the mirror. For an instant, the love on their faces was so pure and bright that Ernie and Bruno shut their eyes as if blinded.

On a vague level, Honor heard footsteps, and then an exclamation. She dragged her gaze away from Dom's luminous blue eyes long enough to see Rafe's shocked expression. She smiled a welcome at him, somehow not surprised that Nick had apparently told him where they were.

He, too, was fated to be here, for he was part of the past and would somehow be important to the future. She didn't question that any more than she tried to find a scientific explanation for the eerie light source in the mirror, or the fact that, curiously, the mirror seemed to be growing taller and wider before her very eyes. The time for logic was past; only a leap of faith could take them home.

Dom put both hands on her shoulders now. Again their gazes met. The mirror grew so brilliant that rays burst outward, sending shards of beatific light to every shadowed corner. Their reflections blurred in the glass, merging as if the properties of light and refraction no longer had any meaning. As if here, in each other, and in the arms of their mutual faith, they found the source of all light and life.

The strange fluttering wisp of air she'd sensed a few times before returned. A faraway music, so divine that Honor had never heard chords so sweet, sounded softly. A shadow fell on them. They all looked up. Dom and Honor whispered a prayer of thanks, kneeling as they looked at the angel hovering in midair. Their faces reflected back her glow.

Ernie fell to his knees, crossing himself. Bruno backed up several steps, staring upward. And Rafe stood stock-still, an unbeliever faced with irrefutable proof of the power of miracles.

The angel glowed as brightly as the mirror, and she was so beautiful she might have stepped down from the Sistine Chapel. She hovered there, wings barely beating, real yet incorporeal, fragile yet invincible.

"You wish to return home, Dominico? You repent your sin of pride, and vow never to curse your Lord again?"

Dom swallowed, "*Sì*. Never. But please, oh please, I may not deserve it, but allow me to take this woman, my wife-to-be, with me."

The bright countenance turned on Honor. "And you, my child, do you wish to leave your world for his?"

"With all my heart," Honor replied. And when the angel still waited, as if not satisfied, Honor added huskily, "And with all my soul."

The angel nodded, watching them both closely. "You will sin no more. You will wed and bear descendants." It was not a command; it was a statement of fact.

Dom burst out, "Forgive me. I tried to leave her honorable, but I was not strong enough. As to everything else"—he smiled his thanks at Rafe, who hadn't blinked once—"I think we succeeded."

The angel's smile widened as she glanced at Rafe's stunned expression. "So it was written. And much remains to be done according to God's plan. Go, my children. Be fruitful. And remember always that the love of God is in you. Share it, and your generosity will return to you tenfold."

Still smiling, the angel disappeared.

Immediately, the glow in the mirror muted, still lovely, still mesmerizing, but its source now earthly instead of heavenly. A different image formed: trees towered on all sides, and a stream, so pristine it could only have existed long ago, burbled in the distance. And far away, church bells rang. Shifting the small case to his opposite side, Dom moved beside Honor. With a last smile of love and gratitude over her shoulder at the three men, Honor caught his big hand and stepped through the mirror with him into destiny.

The image dissipated. The glow went out. The mirror dwindled into its former practical size. Leaving a very quiet, very profound silence as three Catholics, one devout, one part-time, and one lapsed, all stared at the blank glass.

Tears in his eyes, Ernie crossed himself again. "Good-bye, Honnie. Godspeed. Maybe, if it's meant to be, we'll meet again one day."

Bruno sagged against the wall, as if he couldn't support himself any longer. "I'm going to start attending Mass again."

And Rafe still stood exactly where he was, staring at the now dark mirror as if he were hallucinating. Finally, his voice rasping, he managed, "But . . . but . . . "

Smiling, Ernie stood, slipped his hand back into the bag and removed the book. "Don't credit the evidence of your eyes, Rafe? You miss the point, you heathen. This isn't about fact; it's about faith. But if you need help understanding, how about the evidence of cold, hard print?" Ernie opened the book, which looked very old, to an obviously well-thumbed page. "I looked for this for weeks, trying to comfort Honor. I've always believed, since I found out the truth, that she and Dom were meant to be together. Look." He took the book over to Rafe, who stood as if he'd grown roots.

His hands trembling, and this time not because he needed a drink, Rafe took the book and stared down at a beautiful Renaissance lady. She held a baby in her lap, a chubby cherub with autumn-hued hair, and a little golden-haired girl of about three clung to her skirts. Honor was even lovelier in the picture, as if she'd found her home far in the past. She looked a few years older, but happy and fulfilled, glowing as golden as the wedding ring on her left finger. An enormous pearl dipped between her fuller breasts, hinting at the prosperity she and Dom must have found. The title read, *Unidentified Renaissance lady and children, approximately 1504. In the style of Michelangelo, but artist unknown.*

Dumbfounded, Rafe looked up. His voice sounded rusty. "So everything they told me was true."

"What is truth?" Ernie asked, giving a philosophical shrug. "In the end, it's different for everyone. Truth is just another word for what we believe. As for you . . . well, what you do with this revelation is probably the biggest decision you'll ever make." Sympathetic to the fear and shock in Rafe's strong face, Ernie clasped his friend's shoulder. "You'll do the right thing, Rafe. Honor believed in you. And so do I."

Ernie turned away to peer yearningly into the mirror. "As for me, I'll never doubt the power of miracles again." He closed the book.

Outside, the world celebrated the dawn of a new age. And somewhere, long ago and far away, in an age built on the power of faith, a new dynasty began. . . .

The Steadfast Heart

Colleen Shannon

Though it has been nearly ten years since Vincent Anthony Kimball's first and only love, Chantal, disappeared from his life, memories of her sweet face still haunt him. Then he sees her at the ballet, and is engulfed by waves of need and longing. But is she really his long-lost Chantal, or the prima ballerina Papillone? Whatever the case, Vince knows that, like the brave tin soldier of the fairy tale, he will do anything to return his true love to him, give anything to unite their hearts as one.

___52271-3 $5.99 US/$6.99 CAN

Dorchester Publishing Co., Inc.
P.O. Box 6640
Wayne, PA 19087-8640

Please add $1.75 for shipping and handling for the first book and $.50 for each book thereafter. NY, NYC, and PA residents, please add appropriate sales tax. No cash, stamps, or C.O.D.s. All orders shipped within 6 weeks via postal service book rate. Canadian orders require $2.00 extra postage and must be paid in U.S. dollars through a U.S. banking facility.

Name_____
Address_____
City_____ State_____ Zip_____
I have enclosed $_____ in payment for the checked book(s).
Payment <u>must</u> accompany all orders. ❑ Please send a free catalog.
      CHECK OUT OUR WEBSITE! www.dorchesterpub.com

A Faerie Tale Romance

Prince of Kisses

COLLEEN SHANNON

Daughter of wealth and privilege, lovely Charlaine Kimball is known to Victorian society as the Ice Princess. But when a brash intruder dares to take a king's ransom in jewels from her private safe, indignation burns away her usual cool reserve. And when the handsome rogue presumes to steal a kiss from her untouched lips, forbidden longing sets her soul ablaze.

Illegitimate son of a penniless Frenchwoman, Devlin Rhodes is nothing but a lowly bounder to the British aristocrats who snub him. But his leapfrogging ambition engages him in a dangerous game. Now he will have to win Charlaine's hand in marriage–and have her begging for the kiss that will awaken his heart and transform him into the man he was always meant to be.

——52200-4 $5.99 US/$6.99 CAN

BELIEVE *Victoria Alexander*

Tessa thinks as little of love as she does of the Arthurian legend—it is just a myth. But when an enchanted tome falls into the lovely teacher's hands, she learns that the legend is nothing like she remembers. Galahad the Chaste is everything but—the powerful knight is an expert lover—and not only wizards can weave powerful spells. Still, even in Galahad's muscled embrace, she feels unsure of this man who seemed a myth. But soon the beautiful skeptic is on a quest as real as her heart, and the grail—and Galahad's love—is within reach. All she has to do is believe.

___52267-5 $5.99 US/$6.99 CAN

Dorchester Publishing Co., Inc.
P.O. Box 6640
Wayne, PA 19087-8640